The Short Strange Stories of Grant Allen

Charles Grant Blairfindie Allen was born on February 24th, 1848 at Alwington, near Kingston, Canada West (now part of Ontario).

Home schooled until 13 when his family moved to England, Grant was to become a highly regarded science writer who branched out to a fiction career and became enormously popular.

His work helped propel several genres of fiction and whilst his career was short it was enormously productive.

Grant's scientific background enabled him to root much of his work in a plausibility that was denied to others. He had little fear in challenging a society that treated women as second class citizens and creating best sellers from such works.

On October 25th 1899 Grant Allen died at his home in Hindhead, Haslemere, Surrey, England. He died just before finishing Hilda Wade. The novel's final episode, which he dictated to his friend, doctor and neighbour Sir Arthur Conan Doyle from his bed appeared under the appropriate title, The Episode of the Dead Man Who Spoke in 1900.

Index of Contents

PREFACE

It is with some little trepidation that I venture to submit to the critical world this small collection of short stories. I feel that in doing so I owe some apology both to my readers and to the regular story-tellers. Being by trade a psychologist and scientific journeyman, I have been bold enough at times to stray surreptitiously and tentatively from my proper sphere into the flowery fields of pure fiction. Some of these my divarications from the strict path of sterner science, however, having been already publicly performed under the incognito of "J. Arbuthnot Wilson," have been so far condoned by generous and kindly critics that I am emboldened to present them to the judgment of readers under a more permanent form, and even to dispense with the convenient cloak of a pseudonym, under which one can always so easily cover one's hasty retreat from an untenable position. I can only hope that my confession will be accepted in partial extenuation of this culpable departure from the good old rule, "Ne sutor ultra crepidam;" and that older hands at the craft of story-telling will pardon an amateur novice his defective workmanship on the general plea of his humble demeanour.

I may perhaps also venture to plead in self-defence that though these stories do not profess to be anything more than mere short sensational tales, I have yet endeavoured to give to most of them some slight tinge of scientific or psychological import and meaning. "The Reverend John Creedy," for example, is a study from within of a singular persistence of hereditary character, well known to all students of modern anthropological papers and reports. Members of barbarous or savage races, trained for a time in civilized habits, are liable at any moment to revert naturally to their primitive condition, especially under the contagious influence of companionship with persons of their own blood, and close subjection to the ancestral circumstances. The tale which I have based upon several such historical instances in real life endeavours briefly to hint at the modes of feeling likely to accompany such a relapse into barbarism in an essentially fine and sensitive savage nature. To most European readers, no doubt, such a sheer fall from the pinnacle of civilization to the nethermost abysses of savagery, would seem to call for the display of no other emotion than pure disgust and aversion; but those who know intimately the whole gamut of the intensely impressionable African mind will be able to treat its temptations and its tendencies far more sympathetically. In "The Curate of Churnside," again, I have tried to present a psychical analysis of a temperament not uncommon among the cultured class of the Italian Renaissance, and less rare than many people will be inclined to imagine among the colder type of our own emancipated and cultivated classes. The union of high intellectual and æsthetic culture with a total want of moral sensibility is a recognized fact in many periods of history, though our own age is singularly loth to admit of its possibility in its own contemporaries. In "Ram Das of Cawnpore," once more, I have attempted to depict a few circumstances of the Indian Mutiny as they must naturally have presented themselves to the mind and feelings of a humble native actor in that great and terrible drama. Accustomed ourselves to looking always at the massacres and reprisals of the Mutiny from a purely English point of view, we are liable to forget that every act of the mutineers and their aiders or abettors must have been fully justified in their own eyes, at the moment at least, as every act of every human being always is to his own inner personality. In his conscience of conscience, no man ever really believes that under given circumstances he could conceivably have acted otherwise than he actually did. If he persuades himself that he does really so believe, then he shows himself at once to be a very poor introspective psychologist. "The Child of the Phalanstery," to take another case, is a more ideal effort to realize the moral conceptions of a community brought up under a social and ethical environment utterly different from that by which we ourselves are now surrounded. In like manner, almost all the stories (except the lightest among them) have their germ or prime motive in some scientific or quasi-scientific idea; and this narrow link which thus connects them at bottom with my more habitual sphere of work must serve as my excuse to the regular story-tellers for an otherwise unwarrantable intrusion upon their private preserves. I trust they will forgive me on this plea for my trespass on their legitimate domains, and allow me to occupy in peace a little adjacent corner of unclaimed territory, which lies so temptingly close beside my own small original freehold.

I should add that "The Reverend John Creedy," "The Curate of Churnside," "Dr. Greatrex's Engagement," and "The Backslider," have already appeared in the Cornhill Magazine; while "The Foundering of the Fortuna" was first published in Longman's Magazine. The remainder of the tales comprised in this volume have seen the light originally in the pages of Belgravia. I have to thank the courtesy of the publishers and editors of those periodicals for kind permission to reprint them here.

G. A.   THE NOOK, DORKING,   October 12, 1884.

CONTENTS.

I

"On Sunday next, the 14th inst., the Reverend John Creedy, B.A., of Magdalen College, Oxford, will preach in Walton Magna Church, on behalf of the Gold Coast Mission." Not a very startling announcement that, and yet, simple as it looks, it stirred Ethel Berry's soul to its inmost depths. For Ethel had been brought up by her Aunt Emily to look upon foreign missions as the one thing on earth worth living for and thinking about, and the Reverend John Creedy, B.A., had a missionary history of his own, strange enough even in these strange days of queer juxtapositions between utter savagery and advanced civilization.

"Only think," she said to her aunt, as they read the placard on the schoolhouse-board, "he's a real African negro, the vicar says, taken from a slaver on the Gold Coast when he was a child, and brought to England to be educated. He's been to Oxford and got a degree; and now he's going out again to Africa to convert his own people. And he's coming down to the vicar's to stay on Wednesday."

"It's my belief," said old Uncle James, Aunt Emily's brother, the superannuated skipper, "that he'd much better stop in England forever. I've been a good bit on the Coast myself in my time, after palm oil and such, and my opinion is that a nigger's a nigger anywhere, but he's a sight less of a nigger in England than out yonder in Africa. Take him to England, and you make a gentleman of him: send him home again, and the nigger comes out at once in spite of you."

"Oh, James," Aunt Emily put in, "how can you talk such unchristianlike talk, setting yourself up against missions, when we know that all the nations of the earth are made of one blood?"

"I've always lived a Christian life myself, Emily," answered Uncle James, "though I have cruised a good bit on the Coast, too, which is against it, certainly; but I take it a nigger's a nigger whatever you do with him. The Ethiopian cannot change his skin, the Scripture says, nor the leopard his spots, and a nigger he'll be to the end of his days; you mark my words, Emily."

On Wednesday, in due course, the Reverend John Creedy arrived at the vicarage, and much curiosity there was throughout the village of Walton Magna that week to see this curious new thing, a coal-black parson. Next day, Thursday, an almost equally unusual event occurred to Ethel Berry, for, to her great surprise, she got a little note in the morning inviting her up to a tennis party at the vicarage the same afternoon. Now, though the vicar called on Aunt Emily often enough, and accepted her help readily for school feasts and other village festivities of the milder sort, the Berrys were hardly up to that level of society which is commonly invited to the parson's lawn tennis parties. And the reason why Ethel was asked on this particular Thursday must be traced to a certain pious conspiracy between the vicar and the secretary of the Gold Coast Evangelistic Society. When those two eminent missionary advocates had met a fortnight before at Exeter Hall, the secretary had represented to the vicar the desirability of young John Creedy's taking to himself an English wife before his departure. "It will steady him, and keep him right on the Coast," he said, "and it will give him importance in the eyes of the natives as well." Whereto the vicar responded that he knew exactly the right girl to suit the place in his own parish, and that by a providential conjunction she already took a deep interest in foreign missions. So these two good men conspired in all innocence of heart to sell poor Ethel into African slavery; and the vicar had asked John Creedy down to Walton Magna on purpose to meet her.

That afternoon Ethel put on her pretty sateen and her witching little white hat, with two natural dog-roses pinned on one side, and went pleased and proud up to the vicarage. The Reverend John Creedy was there, not in full clerical costume, but arrayed in tennis flannels, with only a loose white tie beneath his flap collar to mark his newly acquired spiritual dignity. He was a comely looking negro enough, full-blooded, but not too broad-faced nor painfully African in type; and when he was playing tennis his athletic quick limbs and his really handsome build took away greatly from the general impression of an inferior race. His voice was of the ordinary Oxford type, open, pleasant, and refined, with a certain easy-going air of natural gentility, hardly marred by just the faintest tinge of the thick negro blur in the broad vowels. When he talked to Ethel, and the vicar's wife took good care that they should talk together a great deal, his conversation was of a sort that she seldom heard at Walton Magna. It was full of London and Oxford, of boat-races at Iffley and cricket matches at Lord's; of people and books whose very names Ethel had never heard, one of them was a Mr. Mill, she thought, and another a Mr. Aristotle, but which she felt vaguely to be one step higher in the intellectual scale than her own level. Then his friends, to whom he alluded casually, not like one who airs his grand acquaintances, were such very distinguished people. There was a real live lord, apparently, at the same college with him, and he spoke of a young baronet whose estate lay close by, as plain "Harrington of Christchurch," without any "Sir Arthur"—a thing which even the vicar himself would hardly have ventured to do. She knew that he was learned, too; as a matter of fact he had taken a fair second class in Greats at Oxford; and he could talk delightfully of poetry and novels. To say the truth, John Creedy, in spite of his black face, dazzled poor Ethel, for he was more of a scholar and a gentleman than anybody with whom she had ever before had the chance of conversing on equal terms.

When Ethel turned the course of talk to Africa, the young parson was equally eloquent and fascinating. He didn't care about leaving England for many reasons, but he would be glad to do something for his poor brethren. He was enthusiastic about missions; that was a common interest; and he was so anxious to raise and improve the condition of his fellow-negroes that Ethel couldn't help feeling what a noble thing it was of him thus to sacrifice himself, cultivated gentleman as he was, in an African jungle, for his heathen countrymen. Altogether, she went home from the tennis-court that afternoon thoroughly overcome by John Creedy's personality. She didn't for a moment think of falling in love with him, a certain indescribable race-instinct set up an impassable barrier against that, but she admired him and was interested in him in a way that she had never yet felt with any other man.

As for John Creedy, he was naturally charmed with Ethel. In the first place, he would have been charmed with any English girl who took so much interest in himself and his plans, for, like all negroes, he was frankly egotistical, and delighted to find a white lady who seemed to treat him as a superior being. But in the second place, Ethel was really a charming, simple English village lassie, with sweet little manners and a delicious blush, who might have impressed a far less susceptible man than the young negro parson. So, whatever Ethel felt, John Creedy felt himself truly in love. And after all, John Creedy was in all essentials an educated English gentleman, with the same chivalrous feelings towards a pretty and attractive girl that every English gentleman ought to have.

On Sunday morning Aunt Emily and Ethel went to the parish church, and the Reverend John Creedy preached the expected sermon. It was almost his first, sounded like a trial trip, Uncle James muttered, but it was undoubtedly what connoisseurs describe as an admirable discourse. John Creedy was free from any tinge of nervousness, negroes never know what that word means, and he spoke fervently, eloquently, and with much power of manner about the necessity for a Gold Coast Mission. Perhaps there was really nothing very original or striking in what he said, but his way of saying it was impressive and vigorous. The negro, like many other lower races, has the faculty of speech largely developed, and John Creedy had been noted as one of the readiest and most fluent talkers at the Oxford Union debates. When he enlarged upon the need for workers, the need for help, the need for succour and sympathy in the great task of evangelization, Aunt Emily and Ethel forgot his black hands, stretched out open-palmed towards the people, and felt only their hearts stirred within them by the eloquence and enthusiasm of that appealing gesture.

The end of it all was, that instead of a week John Creedy stopped for two months at Walton Magna, and during all that time he saw a great deal of Ethel. Before the end of the first fortnight he walked out one afternoon along the river-bank with her, and talked earnestly of his expected mission.

"Miss Berry," he said, as they sat to rest awhile on the parapet of the little bridge by the weeping willows, "I don't mind going to Africa, but I can't bear going all alone. I am to have a station entirely by myself up the Ancobra river, where I shall see no other Christian face from year's end to year's end. I wish I could have had some one to accompany me."

"You will be very lonely," Ethel answered. "I wish indeed you could have some companionship."

"Do you really?" John Creedy went on. "It is not good for man to live alone; he wants a helpmate. Oh, Miss Ethel, may I venture to hope that perhaps, if I can try to deserve you, you will be mine?"

Ethel started in dismay. Mr. Creedy had been very attentive, very kind, and she had liked to hear him talk and had encouraged his coming, but she was hardly prepared for this. The nameless something in our blood recoiled at it. The proposal stunned her, and she said nothing but "Oh, Mr. Creedy, how can you say such a thing?"

John Creedy saw the shadow on her face, the unintentional dilatation of her delicate nostrils, the faint puckering at the corner of her lips, and knew with a negro's quick instinct of face-reading what it all meant. "Oh, Miss Ethel," he said, with a touch of genuine bitterness in his tone, "don't you, too, despise us. I won't ask you for any answer now; I don't want an answer. But I want you to think it over. Do think it over, and consider whether you can ever love me. I won't press the matter on you. I won't insult you by importunity, but I will tell you just this once, and once for all, what I feel. I love you, and I shall always love you, whatever you answer me now. I know it would cost you a wrench to take me, a greater wrench than to take the least and the unworthiest of your own people. But if you can only get over that first wrench, I can promise earnestly and faithfully to love you as well as ever woman yet was loved. Don't say anything now," he went on, as he saw she was going to open her mouth again: "wait and think it over; pray it over; and if you can't see your way straight before you when I ask you this day fortnight "yes or no," answer me "no," and I give you my word of honour as a gentleman I will never speak to you of the matter again. But I shall carry your picture written on my heart to my grave."

And Ethel knew that he was speaking from his very soul.

When she went home, she took Aunt Emily up into her little bedroom, over the porch where the dog-roses grew, and told her all about it. Aunt Emily cried and sobbed as if her heart would break, but she saw only one answer from the first. "It is a gate opened to you, my darling," she said: "I shall break my heart over it, Ethel, but it is a gate opened." And though she felt that all the light would be gone out of her life if Ethel went, she worked with her might from that moment forth to induce Ethel to marry John Creedy and go to Africa. Poor soul, she acted faithfully up to her lights.

As for Uncle James, he looked at the matter very differently. "Her instinct is against it," he said stoutly, "and our instincts wasn't put in our hearts for nothing. They're meant to be a guide and a light to us in these dark questions. No white girl ought to marry a black man, even if he is a parson. It ain't natural: our instinct is again it. A white man may marry a black woman if he likes: I don't say anything again him, though I don't say I'd do it myself, not for any money. But a white woman to marry a black man, why, it makes our blood rise, you know, 'specially if you've happened to have cruised worth speaking of along the Coast."

But the vicar and the vicar's wife were charmed with the prospect of success, and spoke seriously to Ethel about it. It was a call, they thought, and Ethel oughtn't to disregard it. They had argued themselves out of those wholesome race instincts that Uncle James so rightly valued, and they were eager to argue Ethel out of them too. What could the poor girl do? Her aunt and the vicar on the one hand, and John Creedy on the other, were too much between them for her native feelings. At the end of the fortnight John Creedy asked her his simple question "yes or no," and half against her will she answered "yes." John Creedy took her hand delicately in his and fervidly kissed the very tips of her fingers; something within him told him he must not kiss her lips. She started at the kiss, but she said nothing. John Creedy noticed the start, and said within himself, "I shall so love and cherish her that I will make her love me in spite of my black skin." For with all the faults of his negro nature, John Creedy was at heart an earnest and affectionate man, after his kind.

And Ethel really did, to some extent, love him already. It was such a strange mixture of feeling. From one point of view he was a gentleman by position, a clergyman, a man of learning and of piety; and from this point of view Ethel was not only satisfied, but even proud of him. For the rest, she took him as some good Catholics take the veil, from a sense of the call. And so, before the two months were out, Ethel Berry had married John Creedy, and both started together at once for Southampton, on their way to Axim. Aunt Emily cried, and hoped they might be blessed in their new work, but Uncle James never lost his misgivings about the effect of Africa upon a born African. "Instincts is a great thing," he said, with a shake of his head, as he saw the West Coast mail steam slowly down Southampton Water, "and when he gets among his own people his instincts will surely get the better of him, as safe as my name is James Berry."

II

The little mission bungalow at Butabué, a wooden shed neatly thatched with fan palms, had been built and garnished by the native catechist from Axim and his wife before the arrival of the missionaries, so that Ethel found a habitable dwelling ready for her at the end of her long boat journey up the rapid stream of the Ancobra. There the strangely matched pair settled down quietly enough to their work of teaching and catechizing, for the mission had already been started by the native evangelist, and many of the people were fairly ready to hear and accept the new religion. For the first ten or twelve months Ethel's letters home were full of praise and love for dear John. Now that she had come to know him well, she wondered she had ever feared to marry him. No husband was ever so tender, so gentle, so considerate. He nursed her in all her little ailments like a woman; she leaned on him as a wife leans on the strong arm of her husband. And then he was so clever, so wise, so learned. Her only grief was that she feared she was not and would never be good enough for him. Yet it was well for her that they were living so entirely away from all white society at Butabué, for there she had nobody with whom to contrast John but the half-clad savages around them. Judged by the light of that startling contrast, good John Creedy, with his cultivated ways and gentle manners, seemed like an Englishman indeed.

John Creedy, for his part, thought no less well of his Ethel. He was tenderly respectful to her; more distant, perhaps, than is usual between husband and wife, even in the first months of marriage, but that was due to his innate delicacy of feeling, which made him half unconsciously recognize the depth of the gulf that still divided them. He cherished her like some saintly thing, too sacred for the common world. Yet Ethel was his helper in all his work, so cheerful under the necessary privations of their life, so ready to put up with bananas and cassava balls, so apt at kneading plantain paste, so willing to learn from the negro women all the mysteries of mixing agadey, cankey, and koko pudding. No tropical heat seemed to put her out of temper; even the horrible country fever itself she bore with such gentle resignation. John Creedy felt in his heart of hearts that he would willingly give up his life for her, and that it would be but a small sacrifice for so sweet a creature.

One day, shortly after their arrival at Butabué, John Creedy began talking in English to the catechist about the best way of setting to work to learn the native language. He had left the country when he was nine years old, he said, and had forgotten all about it. The catechist answered him quickly in a Fantee phrase. John Creedy looked amazed and started.

"What does he say?" asked Ethel.

"He says that I shall soon learn if only I listen; but the curious thing is, Ethie, that I understand him."

"It has come back to you, John, that's all. You are so quick at languages, and now you hear it again you remember it."

"Perhaps so," said the missionary, slowly, "but I have never recalled a word of it for all these years. I wonder if it will all come back to me."

"Of course it will, dear," said Ethel; "you know, things come to you so easily in that way. You almost learned Portuguese while we were coming out from hearing those Benguela people."

And so it did come back, sure enough. Before John Creedy had been six weeks at Butabué, he could talk Fantee as fluently as any of the natives around him. After all, he was nine years old when he was taken to England, and it was no great wonder that he should recollect the language he had heard in his childhood till that age. Still, he himself noticed rather uneasily that every phrase and word, down to the very heathen charms and prayers of his infancy, came back to him now with startling vividness and without an effort.

Four months after their arrival John saw one day a tall and ugly negro woman, in the scanty native dress, standing near the rude market-place where the Butabué butchers killed and sold their reeking goat-meat. Ethel saw him start again, and with a terrible foreboding in her heart, she could not help asking him why he started. "I can't tell you, Ethie," he said, piteously; "for heaven's sake don't press me. I want to spare you." But Ethel would hear. "Is it your mother, John?" she asked hoarsely.

"No, thank heaven, not my mother, Ethie," he answered her, with something like pallor on his dark cheek, "not my mother; but I remember the woman."

"A relative?"

"Oh, Ethie, don't press me. Yes, my mother's sister. I remember her years ago. Let us say no more about it." And Ethel, looking at that gaunt and squalid savage woman, shuddered in her heart and said no more.

Slowly, as time went on, however, Ethel began to notice a strange shade of change coming over John's ideas and remarks about the negroes. At first he had been shocked and distressed at their heathendom and savagery, but the more he saw of it the more he seemed to find it natural enough in their position, and even in a sort of way to sympathize with it or apologize for it. One morning, a month or two later, he spoke to her voluntarily of his father. He had never done so in England. "I can remember," he said, "was a chief, a great chief. He had many wives, and my mother was one. He was beaten in War by Kola, and I was taken prisoner. But he had a fine palace at Kwantah, and many fan-bearers." Ethel observed with a faint terror that he seemed to speak with pride and complacency of his father's chieftaincy. She shuddered again and wondered. Was the West African instinct getting the upper hand in him over the Christian gentleman?

When the dries were over, and the koko-harvest gathered, the negroes held a grand feast. John had preached in the open air to some of the market people in the morning, and in the evening he was sitting in the hut with Ethel, waiting till the catechist and his wife should come in to prayers, for they carried out their accustomed ceremony decorously, even there, every night and morning. Suddenly they heard the din of savage music out of doors, and the noise of a great crowd laughing and shouting down the street. John listened, and listened with deepening attention. "Don't you hear it, Ethie?" he cried. "It's the tom-toms. I know what it means. It's the harvest battle-feast!"

"How hideous!" said Ethel, shrinking back.

"Don't be afraid, dearest," John said, smiling at her. "It means no harm. It's only the people amusing themselves." And he began to keep time to the tom-toms rapidly with the palms of his hands.

The din drew nearer, and John grew more evidently excited at every step. "Don't you hear, Ethie?" he said again. "It's the Salonga. What inspiriting music! It's like a drum and fife band; it's like the bagpipes; it's like a military march. By Jove, it compels one to dance!" And he got up as he spoke, in English clerical dress (for he wore clerical dress even at Butabué), and began capering in a sort of hornpipe round the tiny room.

"Oh, John, don't," cried Ethel. "Suppose the catechist were to come in!"

But John's blood was up. "Look here," he said excitedly, "it goes like this. Here you hold your matchlock out; here you fire; here you charge with cutlasses; here you hack them down before you; here you hold up your enemy's head in your hands, and here you kick it off among the women. Oh, it's grand!" There was a terrible light in his black eyes as he spoke, and a terrible trembling in his clenched black hands.

"John," cried Ethel, in an agony of horror, "it isn't Christian, it isn't human, it isn't worthy of you. I can never, never love you if you do such a thing again."

In a moment John's face changed and his hand fell as if she had stabbed him. "Ethie," he said in a low voice, creeping back to her like a whipped spaniel, "Ethie, my darling, my own soul, my beloved; what have I done! Oh, heavens, I will never listen to the accursed thing again. Oh, Ethie, for heaven's sake, for mercy's sake, forgive me!"

Ethel laid her hand, trembling, on his head. John sank upon his knees before her, and bowed himself down with his head between his arms, like one staggered and penitent. Ethel lifted him gently, and at that moment the catechist and his wife came in. John stood up firmly, took down his Bible and Prayer-book, and read through evening prayer at once in his usual impressive tone. In one moment he had changed back again from the Fantee savage to the decorous Oxford clergyman.

It was only a week later that Ethel, hunting about in the little storeroom, happened to notice a stout wooden box carefully covered up. She opened the lid with some difficulty, for it was fastened down with a native lock, and to her horror she found inside it a surreptitious keg of raw negro rum. She took the keg out, put it conspicuously in the midst of the storeroom, and said nothing. That night she heard John in the jungle behind the yard, and looking out, she saw dimly that he was hacking the keg to pieces vehemently with an axe. After that he was even kinder and tenderer to her than usual for the next week, but Ethel vaguely remembered that once or twice before, he had seemed a little odd in his manner, and that it was on those days that she had seen gleams of the savage nature peeping through. Perhaps, she thought, with a shiver, his civilization was only a veneer, and a glass of raw rum or so was enough to wash it off.

Twelve months after their first arrival, Ethel came home very feverish one evening from her girls' school, and found John gone from the hut. Searching about in the room for the quinine bottle, she came once more upon a rum-keg, and this time it was empty. A nameless terror drove her into the little bedroom. There, on the bed, torn into a hundred shreds, lay John Creedy's black coat and European clothing. The room whirled around her, and though she had never heard of such a thing before, the terrible truth flashed across her bewildered mind like a hideous dream. She went out, alone, at night, as she had never done before since she came to Africa, into the broad lane between the huts which constituted the chief street of Butabué. So far away from home, so utterly solitary among all those black faces, so sick at heart with that burning and devouring horror! She reeled and staggered down the street, not knowing how or where she went, till at the end, beneath the two tall date-palms, she saw lights flashing and heard the noise of shouts and laughter. A group of natives, men and women together, were dancing and howling round a dancing and howling negro. The central figure was dressed in the native fashion, with arms and legs bare, and he was shouting a loud song at the top of his voice in the Fantee language, while he shook a tom-tom. There was a huskiness as of drink in his throat, and his steps were unsteady and doubtful. Great heavens! could that reeling, shrieking black savage be John Creedy?

Yes, instinct had gained the day over civilization; the savage in John Creedy had broken out; he had torn up his English clothes and, in West African parlance, "had gone Fantee." Ethel gazed at him, white with horror, stood still and gazed, and never cried nor fainted, nor said a word. The crowd of negroes divided to right and left, and John Creedy saw his wife standing there like a marble figure. With one awful cry he came to himself again, and rushed to her side. She did not repel him, as he expected; she did not speak; she was mute and cold like a corpse, not like a living woman. He took her up in his strong arms, laid her head on his shoulder, and carried her home through the long line of thatched huts, erect and steady as when he first walked up the aisle of Walton Magna church. Then he laid her down gently on the bed, and called the wife of the catechist. "She has the fever," he said in Fantee. "Sit by her."

The catechist's wife looked at her, and said, "Yes; the yellow fever."

And so she had. Even before she saw John the fever had been upon her, and that awful revelation had brought it out suddenly in full force. She lay unconscious upon the bed, her eyes open, staring ghastlily, but not a trace of colour in her cheek nor a sign of life upon her face.

John Creedy wrote a few words on a piece of paper, which he folded in his hand, gave a few directions in Fantee to the woman at the bedside, and then hurried out like one on fire into the darkness outside.

III

It was thirty miles through the jungle, by a native trackway, to the nearest mission station at Effuenta. There were two Methodist missionaries stationed there, John Creedy knew, for he had gone round by boat more than once to see them. When he first came to Africa he could no more have found his way across the neck of the river fork by that tangled jungle track than he could have flown bodily over the top of the cocoa palms; but now, half naked, barefooted, and inspired with an overpowering emotion, he threaded his path through the darkness among the creepers and lianas of the forest in true African fashion. Stooping here, creeping on all fours there, running in the open at full speed anon, he never once stopped to draw breath till he had covered the whole thirty miles, and knocked in the early dawn at the door of the mission hut at Effuenta.

One of the missionaries opened the barred door cautiously. "What do you want?" he asked in Fantee of the bare-legged savage, who stood crouching by the threshold.

"I bring a message from Missionary John Creedy," the bare-legged savage answered, also in Fantee. "He wants European clothes."

"Has he sent a letter?" asked the missionary.

John Creedy took the folded piece of paper from his palm. The missionary read it. It told him in a few words how the Butabué people had pillaged John's hut at night and stolen his clothing, and how he could not go outside his door till he got some European dress again.

"This is strange," said the missionary. "Brother Felton died three days ago of the fever. You can take his clothes to Brother Creedy, if you will."

The bare-limbed savage nodded acquiescence. The missionary looked hard at him, and fancied he had seen his face before, but he never even for a moment suspected that he was speaking to John Creedy himself.

A bundle was soon made of dead Brother Felton's clothes, and the bare-limbed man took it in his arms and prepared to run back again the whole way to Butabué.

"You have had nothing to eat," said the lonely missionary. "Won't you take something to help you on your way?"

"Give me some plantain paste," answered John Creedy. "I can eat it as I go." And when they gave it him he forgot himself for the moment, and answered, "Thank you" in English. The missionary stared, but thought it was only a single phrase that he had picked up at Butabué, and that he was anxious, negro-fashion, to air his knowledge.

Back through the jungle, with the bundle in his arms, John Creedy wormed his way once more, like a snake or a tiger, never pausing or halting on the road till he found himself again in the open space outside the village of Butabué. There he stayed awhile, and behind a clump of wild ginger, he opened the bundle and arrayed himself once more from head to foot in English clerical dress. That done, too proud to slink, he walked bold and erect down the main alley, and quietly entered his own hut. It was high noon, the baking high noon of Africa, as he did so.

Ethel lay unconscious still upon the bed. The negro woman crouched, half asleep after her night's watching, at the foot. John Creedy looked at his watch, which stood hard by on the little wooden table. "Sixty miles in fourteen hours," he said aloud. "Better time by a great deal than when we walked from Oxford to the White Horse, eighteen months since." And then he sat down silently by Ethel's bedside.

"Has she moved her eyes?" he asked the negress.

"Never, John Creedy," answered the woman. Till last night she had always called him "Master."

He watched the lifeless face for an hour or two. There was no change in it till about four o'clock; then Ethel's eyes began to alter their expression. He saw the dilated pupils contract a little, and know that consciousness was gradually returning.

In a moment more she looked round at him and gave a little cry. "John," she exclaimed, with a sort of awakening hopefulness in her voice, "where on earth did you get those clothes?"

"These clothes?" he answered softly. "Why, you must be wandering in your mind, Ethie dearest, to ask such a question now. At Standen's, in the High at Oxford, my darling." And he passed his black hand gently across her loose hair.

Ethel gave a great cry of joy. "Then it was a dream, a horrid dream, John, or a terrible mistake? Oh, John, say it was a dream!"

John drew his hand across his forehead slowly. "Ethie darling," he said, "you are wandering, I'm afraid. You have a bad fever. I don't know what you mean."

"Then you didn't tear them up, and wear a Fantee dress, and dance with a tom-tom down the street? Oh, John!"

"Oh, Ethel! No. What a terrible delirium you must have had!"

"It is all well," she said. "I don't mind if I die now." And she sank back exhausted into a sort of feverish sleep.

"John Creedy," said the black catechist's wife solemnly, in Fantee, "you will have to answer for that lie to a dying woman with your soul!"

"My soul!" cried John Creedy passionately, smiting both breasts with his clenched fists. "My soul! Do you think, you negro wench, I wouldn't give my poor, miserable, black soul to eternal torments a thousand times over, if only I could give her little white heart one moment's forgetfulness before she dies?"

For five days longer Ethel lingered in the burning fever, sometimes conscious for a minute or two, but for the most part delirious or drowsy all the time. She never said another word to John about her terrible dream, and John never said another word to her. But he sat by her side and tended her like a woman, doing everything that was possible for her in the bare little hut, and devouring his full heart with a horrible gnawing remorse too deep for pen or tongue to probe and fathom. For civilization with John Creedy was really at bottom far more than a mere veneer; though the savage instincts might break out with him now and again, such outbursts no more affected his adult and acquired nature than a single bump supper or wine party at college affects the nature of many a gentle-minded English lad. The truest John Creedy of all was the gentle, tender, English clergyman.

As he sat by her bedside sleepless and agonized, night and day for five days together, one prayer only rose to his lips time after time: "Heaven grant she may die!" He had depth enough in the civilized side of his soul to feel that that was the only way to save her from a lifelong shame. "If she gets well," he said to himself, trembling, "I will leave this accursed Africa at once. I will work my way back to England as a common sailor, and send her home by the mail with my remaining money. I will never inflict my presence upon her again, for she cannot be persuaded, if once she recovers, that she did not see me, as she did see me, a bare-limbed heathen Fantee brandishing a devilish tom-tom. But I shall get work in England, not a parson's; that I can never be again, but clerk's work, labourer's work, navvy's work, anything! Look at my arms: I rowed five in the Magdalen eight: I could hold a spade as well as any man. I will toil, and slave, and save, and keep her still like a lady, if I starve for it myself, but she shall never see my face again, if once she recovers. Even then it will be a living death for her, poor angel! There is only one hope—Heaven grant she may die!"

On the fifth day she opened her eyes once. John saw that his prayer was about to be fulfilled. "John," she said feebly—"John, tell me, on your honour, it was only my delirium."

And John, raising his hand to heaven, splendide mendax, answered in a firm voice, "I swear it."

Ethel smiled and shut her eyes. It was for the last time.

Next morning, John Creedy, tearless, but parched and dry in the mouth, like one stunned and unmanned, took a pickaxe and hewed out a rude grave in the loose soil near the river. Then he fashioned a rough coffin from twisted canes with his own hands, and in it he reverently placed the sacred body. He allowed no one to help him or come near him, not even his fellow-Christians, the catechist and his wife: Ethel was too holy a thing for their African hands to touch. Next he put on his white surplice, and for the first and only time in his life he read, without a quaver in his voice, the Church of England burial service over the open grave. And when he had finished he went back to his desolate hut, and cried with a loud voice of utter despair, "The one thing that bound me to civilization is gone. Henceforth I shall never speak another word of English. I go to my own people." So saying, he solemnly tore up his European clothes once more, bound a cotton loin-cloth round his waist, covered his head with dirt, and sat fasting and wailing piteously, like a broken-hearted child, in his cabin.

Nowadays, the old half-caste Portuguese rum-dealer at Butabué can point out to any English pioneer who comes up the river which one, among a crowd of dilapidated negroes who lie basking in the soft dust outside his hut, was once the Reverend John Creedy, B.A., of Magdalen College, Oxford.

DR. GREATREX'S ENGAGEMENT

Everybody knows by name at least the celebrated Dr. Greatrex, the discoverer of that abstruse molecular theory of the interrelations of forces and energies. He is a comparatively young man still, as times go, for a person of such scientific distinction, for he is now barely forty; but to look at his tall, spare, earnest figure, and his clear-cut, delicate, intellectual face, you would scarcely imagine that he had once been the hero of a singularly strange and romantic story. Yet there have been few lives more romantic than Arthur Greatrex's, and few histories stranger in their way than this of his engagement. After all, why should not a scientific light have a romance of his own as well as other people?

Fifteen years ago Arthur Greatrex, then a young Cambridge fellow, had just come up to begin his medical studies at a London hospital. He was tall in those days, of course, but not nearly so slender or so pale as now; for he had rowed seven in his college boat, and was a fine, athletic young man of the true English university pattern. Handsome, too, then and always, but with a more human-looking and ordinary handsomeness when he was young than in these latter times of his scientific eminence. Indeed, any one who met Arthur Greatrex at that time would merely have noticed him as a fine, intelligent young English gentleman, with a marked taste for manly sports, and a decided opinion of his own about most passing matters of public interest.

Already, even in those days, the young medical student was very deeply engaged in recondite speculations on the question of energy. His active mind, always dwelling upon wide points of cosmical significance, had hit upon the germ of that great revolutionary idea which was afterwards to change the whole course of modern physics. But, as often happens with young men of twenty-five, there was another subject which divided his attention with the grand theory of his life: and that subject was the pretty daughter of his friend and instructor, Dr. Abury, the eminent authority on the treatment of the insane. In all London you couldn't have found a sweeter or prettier girl than Hetty Abury. Young Greatrex thought her clever, too; and, though that is perhaps saying rather too much, she was certainly a good deal above the average of ordinary London girls in intellect and accomplishments.

"They say, Arthur," she said to him on the day after their formal engagement, "that the course of true love never did run smooth; and yet it seems somehow as if ours was wonderfully smoothed over for us by everybody and everything. I am the happiest and proudest girl in all the world to have won the love of such a man as you for my future husband."

Arthur Greatrex stroked the back of her white little hand with his, and answered gently, "I hope nothing will ever arise to make the course of our love run any the rougher; for certainly we do seem to have every happiness laid out most temptingly before us. It almost feels to me as if my paradise had been too easily won, and I ought to have something harder to do before I enter it."

"Don't say that, Arthur," Hetty put in hastily. "It sounds too much like an evil omen."

"You superstitious little woman!" the young doctor replied with a smile. "Talking to a scientific man about signs and portents!" And he kissed her wee hand tenderly, and went home to his bachelor lodging with that strange exhilaration in heart and step which only the ecstasy of first love can ever bring one.

"No," he thought to himself, as he sat down in his own easy-chair, and lighted his cigar; "I don't believe any cloud can ever arise between me and Hetty. We have everything in our favour, means to live upon, love for one another, a mutual respect, kind relations, and hearts that were meant by nature each for the other. Hetty is certainly the very sweetest little girl that ever lived; and she's as good as she's sweet, and as loving as she's beautiful. What a dreadful thing it is for a man in love to have to read up medicine for his next examination!" and he took a medical book down from the shelf with a sigh, and pretended to be deeply interested in the diagnosis of scarlet fever till his cigar was finished. But, if the truth must be told, the words really swam before him, and all the letters on the page apparently conspired together to make up but a single name a thousand times over, Hetty, Hetty, Hetty, Hetty. At last he laid the volume down as hopeless, and turned dreamily into his bedroom, only to lie awake half the night and think perpetually on that one theme of Hetty.

Next day was Dr. Abury's weekly lecture on diseases of the brain and nervous system; and Arthur Greatrex, convinced that he really must make an effort, went to hear it. The subject was one that always interested him; and partly by dint of mental attention, partly out of sheer desire to master the matter, he managed to hear it through, and even take in the greater part of its import. As he left the room to go down the hospital stairs, he had his mind fairly distracted between the premonitory symptoms of insanity and Hetty Abury. "Was there ever such an unfortunate profession as medicine for a man in love?" he asked himself, half angrily. "Why didn't I go and be a parson or a barrister, or anything else that would have kept me from mixing up such incongruous associations? And yet, when one comes to think of it, too, there's no particular natural connection after all between 'Chitty on Contract' and dearest Hetty."

Musing thus, he turned to walk down the great central staircase of the hospital. As he did so, his attention was attracted for a moment by a singular person who was descending the opposite stair towards the same landing. This person was tall and not ill-looking; but, as he came down the steps, he kept pursing up his mouth and cheeks into the most extraordinary and hideous grimaces; in fact, he was obviously making insulting faces at Arthur Greatrex. Arthur was so much preoccupied at the moment, however, that he hardly had time to notice the eccentric stranger; and, as he took him for one of the harmless lunatic patients in the mental-diseases ward, he would have passed on without further observing the man but for an odd circumstance which occurred as they both reached the great central landing together. Arthur happened to drop the book he was carrying from under his arm, and instinctively stooped to pick it up. At the same moment the grimacing stranger dropped his own book also, not in imitation, but by obvious coincidence, and stooped to pick it up with the self-same gesture. Struck by the oddity of the situation, Arthur turned to look at the curious patient. To his utter horror and surprise, he discovered that the man he had been observing was his own reflection.

In one second the real state of the case flashed like lightning across his bewildered brain. There was no opposite staircase, as he knew very well, for he had been down those steps a hundred times before: nothing but a big mirror, which reflected and doubled the one-sided flight from top to bottom. It was only his momentary preoccupation which had made him for a minute fall into the obvious delusion. The man whom he saw descending towards him was really himself, Arthur Greatrex.

Even so, he did not at once grasp the full strangeness of the scene he had just witnessed. It was only as he turned to descend again that he caught another glimpse of himself in the big mirror, and saw that he was still making the most horrible and ghastliest grimaces, grimaces such as he had never seen equalled save by the monkeys at the Zoo, and (horridest thought of all!) by the worst patients in the mental-disease ward. He pulled himself up in speechless horror, and looked once more into the big mirror. Yes, there was positively no mistaking the fact: it was he, Arthur Greatrex, fellow of Catherine's, who was making these hideous and meaningless distortions of his own countenance.

With a terrible effort of will he pulled his face quite straight again, and assumed his usual grave and quiet demeanour. For a full minute he stood looking at himself in the glass; and then, fearful that someone else would come and surprise him, he hurried down the remaining steps, and rushed out into the streets of London. Which way he turned he did not know or care; all he knew was that he was repressing by sheer force of muscular strain a deadly impulse to pucker up his mouth and draw down the corners of his lips into one-sided grimaces. As he passed down the streets, he watched his own image faintly reflected in the panes of the windows, and saw that he was maintaining outward decorum, but only with a conscious and evident struggle. At one doorstep a little child was playing with a kitten; Arthur Greatrex, who was a naturally kindly man, looked down at her and smiled, in spite of his preoccupation: instead of smiling back, the child uttered a scream of terror, and rushed back into the house to hide her face in her mother's apron. He felt instinctively that, in place of smiling, he had looked at the child with one of his awful faces. It was horrible, unendurable, and he walked on through the streets and across the bridges, pulling himself together all the time, till at last, half-unconsciously, he found himself near Pimlico, where the Aburys were then living.

Looking around him, he saw that he had come nearly to the corner where Hetty's little drawing-room faced the road. The accustomed place seemed to draw him off for a moment from thinking of himself, and he remembered that he had promised Hetty to come in for luncheon. But dare he go in such a state of mind and body as he then found himself in? Well, Hetty would be expecting him; Hetty would be disappointed if he didn't come; he certainly mustn't break his engagement with dear little Hetty. After all, he began to say to himself, what was it but a mere twitching of his face, probably a slight nervous affection? Young doctors are always nervous about themselves, they say; they find all their own symptoms accurately described in all the text-books. His face wasn't twitching now, of that he was certain; the nearer he got to Hetty's, the calmer he grew, and the more he was conscious he could relax his attention without finding his muscles were playing tricks upon him. He would turn in and have luncheon, and soon forgot all about it.

Hetty saw him coming, and ran lightly to open the door for him, and as he took his seat beside her at the table, he forgot straightway his whole trouble, and found himself at once in Paradise once more. All through lunch they talked about other things, happy plans for the future, and the small prettinesses that lovers find so perennially delightful; and long before Arthur went away the twitching in his face had altogether ceased to trouble him. Once or twice, indeed, in the course of the afternoon he happened to glance casually at the looking-glass above the drawing-room fireplace (those were the pre-Morrisian days when overmantels as yet were not), and he saw to his great comfort that his face was resting in its usual handsome repose and peacefulness. A bright, earnest, strong face it was, with all the promise of greatness already in it; and so Hetty thought as she looked up at it from the low footstool where she sat by his side, and half whispered into his ear the little timid confidences of early betrothal.

Five o'clock tea came all too soon, and then Arthur felt he must really be going and must get home to do a little reading. On his way, he fancied once he saw a street boy start in evident surprise as he approached him, but it might be fancy; and when the street boy stuck his tongue into the corner of his cheek and uttered derisive shouts from a safe distance, Arthur concluded he was only doing after the manner of his kind out of pure gratuitous insolence. He went home to his lodgings and sat down to an hour's work; but after he had read up several pages more of "Stuckey on Gout," he laid down the book in disgust, and took out Helmholtz and Joule instead, indulging himself with a little desultory reading in his favourite study of the higher physics.

As he read and read the theory of correlation, the great idea as to the real nature of energy, which had escaped all these learned physicists, and which was then slowly forming itself in his own mind, grew gradually clearer and clearer still before his mental vision. Helmholtz was wrong here, because he had not thoroughly appreciated the disjunctive nature of electric energy; Joule was wrong here, because he had failed to understand the real antithesis between potential and kinetic. He laid down the books, paced up and down the room thoughtfully, and beheld the whole concrete theory of interrelation embodying itself visibly before his very eyes. At last he grew fired with the stupendous grandeur of his own conception, seized a quire of foolscap, and sat down eagerly at the table to give written form to the splendid phantom that was floating before him in so distinct a fashion. He would make a great name, for Hetty's sake; and, when he had made it, his dearest reward would be to know that Hetty was proud of him.

Hour after hour he sat and wrote, as if inspired, at his little table. The landlady knocked at the door to tell him dinner was ready, but he would have none of it, he said; let her bring him up a good cup of strong tea and a few plain biscuits. So he wrote and wrote in feverish haste, drinking cup after cup of tea, and turning off page after page of foolscap, till long past midnight. The whole theory had come up so distinctly before his mind's eye, under the exceptional exaltation of first love, and the powerful stimulus of the day's excitement, that he wrote it off as though he had it by heart; omitting only the mathematical calculations, which he left blank, not because he had not got them clearly in his head, but because he would not stop his flying pen to copy them all out then and there at full length, for fear of losing the main thread of his argument. When he had finished, about forty sheets of foolscap lay huddled together on the table before him, written in a hasty hand, and scarcely legible; but they contained the first rough draft and central principle of that immortal work, the "Transcendental Dynamics."

Arthur Greatrex rose from the table, where his grand discovery was first formulated, well satisfied with himself and his theory, and fully determined to submit it shortly to the critical judgment of the Royal Society. As he took up his bedroom candle, however, he went over to the mantelpiece to kiss Hetty's photograph, as he always did (for even men of science are human) every evening before retiring. He lifted the portrait reverently to his lips, and was just about to kiss it, when suddenly in the mirror before him he saw the same horrible mocking face which had greeted him so unexpectedly that morning on the hospital staircase. It was a face of inhuman devilry; the face of a mediæval demon, a hideous, grinning, distorted ghoul, a very caricature and insult upon the features of humanity. In his dismay he dropped the frame and the photograph, shivering the glass that covered it into a thousand atoms. Summoning up all his resolution, he looked again. Yes, there was no mistaking it: a face was gibing and jeering at him from the mirror with diabolical ingenuity of distorted hideousness; a disgusting face which even the direct evidence of his senses would scarcely permit him to believe was really the reflection of his own features. It was overpowering, it was awful, it was wholly incredible; and, utterly unmanned by the sight, he sank back into his easy-chair and buried his face bitterly between the shelter of his trembling hands.

At that moment Arthur Greatrex felt sure he knew the real meaning of the horror that surrounded him. He was going mad.

For ten minutes or more he sat there motionless, hot tears boiling up from his eyes and falling silently between his fingers. Then at last he rose nervously from his seat, and reached down a volume from the shelf behind him. It was Prang's "Treatise on the Physiology of the Brain." He turned it over hurriedly for a few pages, till he came to the passage he was looking for.

"Ah, I thought so," he said to himself, half aloud: "'Premonitory symptoms: facial distortions; infirmity of the will; inability to distinguish muscular movements.' Let's see what Prang has to say about it. 'A not uncommon concomitant of these early stages'—Great heavens, how calmly the man talks about losing your reason!-'is an unconscious or semi-conscious tendency to produce a series of extraordinary facial distortions. At times, the sufferer is not aware of the movements thus initiated; at other times they are quite voluntary, and are accompanied by bodily gestures of contempt or derision for passing strangers.' Why, that's what must have happened with that boy this morning! 'Symptoms of this character usually result from excessive activity of the brain, and are most frequent among mathematicians or scholars who have overworked their intellectual faculties. They may be regarded as the immediate precursors of acute dementia.' Acute dementia! Oh, Hetty! Oh, heavens! What have I done to deserve such a blow as this?"

He laid his face between his hands once more, and sobbed like a broken-hearted child for a few minutes. Then he turned accidentally towards his tumbled manuscript. "No, no," he said to himself, reassuringly; "I can't be going mad. My brain was never clearer in my life. I couldn't have done a piece of good work like that, bristling with equations and figures and formulas, if my head was really giving way. I seemed to grasp the subject as I never grasped it in my life before. I never worked so well at Cambridge; this is a discovery, a genuine discovery. It's impossible that a man who was going mad could ever see anything so visibly and distinctly as I see that universal principle. Let's look again at what Prang has to say upon that subject."

He turned over the volume a few pages further, and glanced lightly at the contents at the head of each chapter, till at last a few words in the title struck his eye, and he hurried on to the paragraph they indicated, with feverish eagerness. As he did so, these were the words which met his bewildered gaze.

"In certain cases, especially among men of unusual intelligence and high attainments, the exaltation of incipient madness takes rather the guise of a scientific or philosophic enthusiasm. Instead of imagining himself the possessor of untold wealth, or the absolute despot of a servile people, the patient deludes himself with the belief that he has made a great discovery or lighted upon a splendid generalization of the deepest and most universal importance. He sees new truths crowding upon him with the most startling and vivid objectivity. He perceives intimate relations of things which he never before suspected. He destroys at one blow the Newtonian theory of gravitation; he discovers obvious flaws in the nebular hypothesis of Laplace; he gives a scholar's-mate to Kant in the very fundamental points of the 'Critique of Pure Reason.' The more serious the attack, the more utterly convinced is the patient of the exceptional clearness of his own intelligence at that particular moment. He writes pamphlets whose scientific value he ridiculously over-estimates; and he is sure to be very angry with any one who tries rationally to combat his newly found authority. Mathematical reasoners are specially liable to this form of incipient mental disease, which, when combined with the facial distortions already alluded to in a previous section, is peculiarly apt to terminate in acute dementia."

"Acute dementia again!" Arthur Greatrex cried with a gesture of horror, flinging the book from him as if it were a poisonous serpent. "Acute dementia, acute dementia, acute dementia; nothing but acute dementia ahead of me, whichever way I happen to turn. Oh, this is too horrible! I shall never be able to marry Hetty! And yet I shall never be able to break it to Hetty! Great heavens, that such a phantom as this should have risen between me and paradise only since this very morning!"

In his agony he caught up the papers on which he had written the rough draft of his grand discovery, and crumpled them up fiercely in his fingers. "The cursed things!" he groaned between his teeth, tossing them with a gesture of impatient disgust into the waste-paper basket; "how could I ever have deluded myself into thinking I had hit off-hand upon a grand truth which had escaped such men as Helmholtz, and Mayer, and Joule, and Thomson! The thing's preposterous upon the very face of it; I must be going mad, indeed, ever to have dreamt of it!"

He took up his candle once more, kissed the portrait in the broken frame with intense fervour a dozen times over, and then went up gloomily into his own bedroom. There he did not attempt to undress, but merely pulled off his boots, lay down in his clothes upon the bed, and hastily blew out the candle. For a long time he lay tossing and turning in unspeakable terror; but at last, after perhaps two hours or so, he fell into a troubled sleep, and dreamed a hideous nightmare, in which somebody or other in shadowy outlines was trying perpetually to tear him away by main force from poor pale and weeping Hetty.

It was daylight when Arthur woke again, and he lay for some time upon his bed, thinking over his last night's scare, which seemed much less serious, as such things always do, now that the sun had risen upon it. After a while his mind got round to the energy question; and, as he thought it over once more, the conviction forced itself afresh upon him that he was right upon the matter after all, and that if he was going mad there was at least method in his madness. So firmly was he convinced upon this point now (though he recognized that that very certainty might be merely a symptom of his coming malady) that he got up hurriedly, before the lodging-house servant came to clean up his little sitting-room, so as to rescue his crumpled foolscap from the waste-paper basket. After that, a bath and breakfast almost made him laugh at his evening terrors.

All the morning Arthur Greatrex sat down at his table again, working in the algebraical calculations which he had omitted from his paper overnight, and finishing it in full form as if for presentation to a learned society. But he did not mean now to offer it to any society: he had a far deeper and more personal interest in the matter at present than that. He wanted to settle first of all the question whether he was going mad or not. Afterwards, there would be plenty of time to settle such minor theoretical problems as the general physical constitution of the universe.

As soon as he had finished his calculations he took the paper in his hands, and went out with it to make two calls on scientific acquaintances. The first man he called upon was that distinguished specialist, Professor Linklight, one of the greatest authorities of his own day on all questions of molecular physics. Poor man! he is almost forgotten now, for he died ten years ago; and his scientific reputation was, after all, of that flashy sort which bases itself chiefly upon giving good dinners to leading fellows of the Royal Society. But fifteen years ago Professor Linklight, with his cut-and-dried dogmatic notions, and his narrow technical accuracy, was universally considered the principal physical philosopher in all England. To him, then, Arthur Greatrex—a far deeper and clearer thinker—took in all humility the first manuscript of his marvellous discovery; not to ask him whether it was true or not, but to find out whether it was physical science at all or pure insanity. The professor received him kindly; and when Arthur, who had of course his own reasons for attempting a little modest concealment, asked him to look over a friend's paper for him, with a view to its presentation to the Royal Society, he cheerfully promised to do his best. "Though you will admit, my dear Mr. Greatrex," he said with his blandest smile, "that your friend's manuscript certainly does not err on the side of excessive brevity." From Linklight's, Arthur walked on tremulously to the house of another great scientific magnate, Dr. Warminster, of being the first living authority on the treatment of the insane in the United Kingdom. Before Dr. Warminster, Arthur made no attempt to conceal his apprehensions. He told out all his symptoms and fears without reserve, even exaggerating them a little, as a man is prone to do through over-anxiety not to put too favourable a face upon his own ailments. Dr. Warminster listened attentively and with a gathering interest to all that Arthur told him, and at the end of his account he shook his head gloomily, and answered in a very grave and sympathetic tone.

"My dear Greatrex," he said gently, holding his arm with a kindly pressure, "I should be dealing wrongly with you if I did not candidly tell you that your case gives ground for very serious apprehensions. You are a young man, and with steady attention to curative means and surroundings, it is possible that you may ward off this threatened danger. Society, amusement, relaxation, complete cessation of scientific work, absence, as far as possible, of mental anxiety in any form, may enable you to tide over the turning point. But that there is danger threatened, it would be unkind and untrue not to warn you. It is very unusual for a patient to consult us in person about these matters. More often it is the friends who notice the coming change; but, as you ask me directly for an opinion, I can't help telling you that I regard your case as not without real cause for the strictest care and for a preventive regimen."

Arthur thanked him for the numerous directions he gave as to things which should be done or things which should be avoided, and hurried out into the street with his brain swimming and reeling. "Absence of mental anxiety!" he said to himself bitterly. "How calmly they talk about mental anxiety! How can I possibly be free from anxiety when I know I may go mad at any moment, and that the blow would kill Hetty outright? For myself, I should not care a farthing; but for Hetty! It is too terrible."

He had not the heart to call at the Aburys' that afternoon, though he had promised to do so; and he tortured himself with the thought that Hetty would think him neglectful. He could not call again while the present suspense lasted; and if his worst fears were confirmed he could never call again, except once, to take leave of Hetty forever. For, deeply as Arthur Greatrex loved her, he loved her too well ever to dream of marrying her if the possible shadow of madness was to cloud her future life with its perpetual presence. Better she should bear the shock, even if it killed her at once, than that both should live in ceaseless apprehension of that horrible possibility, and should become the parents of children upon whom that hereditary curse might rest for a lifetime, reflecting itself back with the added sting of conscientious remorse on the father who had brought them into the world against his own clear judgment of right and justice.

Next morning Arthur went round once more to Professor Linklight's. The professor had promised to read through the paper immediately, and give his opinion of its chances for presentation to the Royal Society. He was sitting at his breakfast-table, in his flowered dressing-gown and slippers, when Arthur called upon him, and, with a cup of coffee in one hand, was actually skimming the last few pages through his critical eyeglass as his visitor entered.

"Good-morning, Mr. Greatrex!" he said, with one of his most gracious smiles, indicative of the warm welcome attended by acknowledged wisdom towards rising talent. "You see I have been reading your friend's paper, as I promised. Well, my dear sir, not to put too fine a point upon it, it won't hold water. In fact, it's a mere rigmarole. Excuse my asking you, Greatrex, but have you any idea, my dear fellow, whether your friend is inclined to be a little cracky?"

Arthur swallowed a groan with the greatest difficulty, and answered in as unconcerned a tone as possible, "Well, to tell you the truth, Mr. Linklight, some doubts have been cast upon his perfect sanity."

"Ah, I should have thought so," the professor went on in his airiest manner; "I should have thought so. The fact is, this paper is fitter for the Transactions of the Colney Hatch Academy than for those of the Royal Society. It has a delusive outer appearance of physical thinking, but there's no real meaning in it of any sort. It's gassy, unsubstantial, purely imaginative." And the professor waved his hand in the air to indicate its utter gaseousness. "If you were to ask my own opinion about it, I should say it's the sort of thing that might be produced by a young man of some mathematical training with a very superficial knowledge of modern physics, just as he was on the point of lapsing into complete insanity. It's the maddest bit of writing that has ever yet fallen under my critical notice."

"Your opinion is of course conclusive," Arthur answered with unfeigned humility, his eyes almost bursting with the tears he would not let come to the surface. "It will be a great disappointment to my friend, but I have no doubt he will accept your verdict."

"Not a bit of it, my dear sir," the professor put in quickly. "Not a bit of it. These crazy fellows always stick to their own opinions, and think you a perfect fool for disagreeing with them. Mark my words, Mr. Greatrex, your friend will still go on believing, in spite of everything, that his roundabout reasoning upon that preposterous square-root-of-Pi theorem is sound mathematics."

And Arthur, looking within, felt with a glow of horror that the theorem in question seemed to him at that moment more obviously true and certain in all its deductions than it had ever done before since the first day that he conceived it. How very mad he must be after all.

He thanked Professor Linklight as well as he was able for his kindness in looking over the paper, and groped his way blindly through the passage to the front door and out into the square. Thence he staggered home wearily, convinced that it was all over between him and Hetty, and that he must make up his mind forthwith to his horrible destiny.

If he had only known at that moment that forty years earlier Professor Linklight had used almost the same words about Young's theory of undulations, and had since used them about every new discovery from that day to the one on which he then saw him, he might have attached less importance than he actually did to this supposed final proof of his own insanity.

As Arthur entered his lodgings he hung his hat up on the stand in the passage. There was a little strip of mirror in the middle of the stand, and glancing at it casually he saw once more that awful face—his own—distorted and almost diabolical, which he had learnt so soon to hate instinctively as if it were a felon's and a murderer's. He rushed away wildly into his little sitting-room, and flung his manuscript on the table, almost without observing that his friend Freeling, the rising physiologist, was quietly seated on the sofa opposite.

"What's this, Arthur?" Freeling asked, taking it up carelessly and glancing at the title. "You don't mean to say that you've finally written out that splendid idea of yours about the interrelations of energy?"

"Yes, I have, Harry: I have, and I wish to heaven I hadn't, for it's all mad and silly and foolish and meaningless!"

"If it is, then I'm mad too, my dear fellow, for I think it's the most convincing thing in physics I ever listened to. Let me have the manuscript to look over, and see how you've worked out those beautiful calculations about the square root of Pi, will you?"

"Take the thing, for heaven's sake, and leave me, Harry, for if I'm not left alone I shall break down and cry before you." And as he spoke he buried his head in his arm and sobbed like a woman.

Dr. Freeling knew Arthur was in love, and was aware that people sometimes act very unaccountably under such circumstances; so he did the wisest thing to be done then and there: he grasped his friend's arm gently with his hand, spoke never a word, and, taking up his hat and the manuscript, walked quietly out into the passage. Then he told the landlady to make Mr. Greatrex a strong cup of tea, with a dash of brandy in it, and turned away, leaving Arthur to solitude and his own reflections.

That evening's post brought Arthur Greatrex two letters, which finally completed his utter prostration. The first he opened was from Dr. Abury. He broke the envelope with a terrible misgiving, and read the letter through with a deepening and sickening feeling of horror. It was not he alone, then, who had distorted the secret of his own incipient insanity. Dr. Abury's practised eye had also detected the rising symptoms. The doctor wrote kindly and with evident grief; but there was no mistaking the firm purport of his intentions. Conferring this morning with his professional friend Warminster, a case had been mentioned to him, without a name, which he at once recognized as Arthur's. He recalled certain symptoms he had himself observed, and his suspicions were thus vividly aroused. Happening accidentally to follow Arthur in the street he was convinced that his surmise was correct, and he thought it his duty both to inform Arthur of the danger that encompassed him, and to assure him that, deeply as it grieved him to withdraw the consent he had so gladly given, he could not allow his only daughter to marry a man bearing on his face the evident marks of an insane tendency. The letter contained much more of regret and condolence; but that was the pith that Arthur Greatrex picked out of it all through the blinding tears, that dimmed his vision.

The second letter was from Hetty. Half guessing its contents, he had left it purposely till the last, and he tore it open now with a fearful sinking feeling in his bosom. It was indeed a heart-broken, heart-breaking letter. What could be the secret which papa would not tell her? Why had not Arthur come yesterday? Why could she never marry him? Why was papa so cruel as not to tell her the reason? He couldn't have done anything in the slightest degree dishonourable, far less anything wicked: of that she felt sure; but, if not, what could be this horrible, mysterious, unknown barrier that was so suddenly raised between them? "Do write, dearest Arthur, and relieve me from this terrible, incomprehensible suspense; do let me know what has happened to make papa so determined against you. I could bear to lose you—at least I could bear it as other women have done—but I can't bear this awful uncertainty, this awful doubt as to your love or your constancy. For heaven's sake, darling, send me a note somehow! send me a line to tell me you love me. Your heart-broken

"HETTY."

Arthur took his hat, and, unable to endure this agony, set out at once for the Aburys'. When he reached the door, the servant who answered his ring at the bell told him he could not see the doctor; he was engaged with two other doctors in a consultation about Miss Hetty. What was the matter with Miss Hetty, then? What, didn't he know that? Oh, Miss Hetty had had a fit, and Dr. Freeling and Dr. MacKinlay had been called in to see her. Arthur did not wait for a moment, but walked upstairs unannounced, and into the consulting room.

Was it a very serious matter? Yes, Freeling answered, very serious. It seemed Miss Abury had had a great shock—a great shock to her affections—which, he added in a lower voice, "you yourself can perhaps best explain to me. She will certainly have a long illness. Perhaps she may never recover."

"Come out into the conservatory, Harry," said Arthur to his friend. "I can tell you there what it is all about."

In a few words Arthur told him the nature of the shock, but without describing the particular symptoms on which the opinion of his supposed approaching insanity was based. Freeling listened with an incredulous smile, and at the end he said to his friend gently, "My dear Arthur, I wish you had told me all this before. If you had done so, we might have saved Miss Abury a shock which may perhaps be fatal. You are no more going mad than I am; on the contrary, you're about the sanest and most clear-headed fellow of my acquaintance. But these mad-doctors are always finding madness everywhere. If you had come to me and told me the symptoms that troubled you, I should soon have set you right again in your own opinion. To have gone to Warminster was most unfortunate, but it can't be helped now. What we have to do at present is to take care of Miss Abury."

Arthur shook his head sadly. "Ah," he said, "you don't know the real gravity of the symptoms I am suffering from. I shall tell you all about them some other time. However, as you say, what we have to think about now is Hetty. Can you let me see her? I am sure if I could see her it would reassure her and do her good."

Dr. Abury was at first very unwilling to let Arthur visit Hetty, who was now lying unconscious on the sofa in her own boudoir; but Freeling's opinion that it might possibly do her good at last prevailed with him, and he gave his permission grudgingly.

Arthur went into the room silently and took his seat beside the low couch where the motherless girl was lying. Her face was very white, and her hands pale and bloodless. He took one hand in his: the pulse was hardly perceptible. He laid it down upon her breast, and leaned back to watch for any sign of returning life in her pallid cheek and closed eyelids.

For hours and hours he sat there watching, and no sign came. Dr. Abury sat at the bottom of the couch, watching with him; and as they watched, Arthur felt from time to time that his face was again twitching horribly. However, he had only thoughts for one thing now: would Hetty die or would she recover? The servants brought them a little cake and wine. They sat and drank in silence, looking at one another, but each absorbed in his own thoughts, and speaking never a word for good or evil.

At last Hetty's eyes opened. Arthur noticed the change first, and took her hand in his gently. Her staring gaze fell upon him for a moment, and she asked feebly, "Arthur, Arthur, do you still love me?"

"Love you, Hetty? With all my heart and soul, as I have always loved you!"

She smiled, and said nothing. Dr. Abury gave her a little wine in a teaspoon, and she drank it quietly. Then she shut her eyes again, but this time she was sleeping.

All night Arthur watched still by the bedside where they put her a little later, and Dr. Abury and a nurse watched with him. In the morning she woke slightly better, and when she saw Arthur still there, she smiled again, and said that if he was with her, she was happy. When Freeling came to inquire after the patient, he found her so much stronger, and Arthur so worn with fear and sleeplessness, that he insisted upon carrying off his friend in his brougham to his own house, and giving him a slight restorative. He might come back at once, he said; but only after he had had a dose of mixture, a glass of brandy and seltzer, and at least a mouthful of something for breakfast.

As Freeling was drawing the cork of the seltzer, Arthur's eye happened to light on a monkey, which was chained to a post in the little area plot outside the consulting-room. Arthur was accustomed to see monkeys there, for Freeling often had invalids from the Zoo to observe side by side with human patients; but this particular monkey fascinated him even in his present shattered state of nerves, because there was a something in its face which seemed strangely and horribly familiar to him. As he looked, he recognized with a feeling of unspeakable aversion what it was of which the monkey reminded him. It was making a series of hideous and apparently mocking grimaces—the very self-same grimaces which he had seen on his own features in the mirror during the last day or two! Horrible idea! He was descending to the level of the very monkeys!

The more he watched, the more absolutely identical the two sets of grimaces appeared to him to be. Could it be fancy or was it reality? Or might it be one more delusion, showing that his brain was now giving way entirely? He rubbed his eyes, steadied his attention, and looked again with the deepest interest. No, he could not be mistaken. The monkey was acting in every respect precisely as he himself had acted.

"Harry," he said, in a low and frightened tone, "look at this monkey. Is he mad? Tell me."

"My dear Arthur," replied his friend, with just a shade of expostulation in his voice, "you have really got madness on the brain at present. No, he isn't mad at all. He's as sane as you are, and that's saying a good deal, I can assure you."

"But, Harry, you can't have seen what he's doing. He's grimacing and contorting himself in the most extraordinary fashion."

"Well, monkeys often do grimace, don't they?" Harry Freeling answered coolly. "Take this brandy and you'll soon feel better."

"But they don't grimace like this one," Arthur persisted.

"No, not like this one, certainly. That's why I've got him here. I'm going to operate upon him for it under chloroform, and cure him immediately."

Arthur leaped from his seat like one demented. "Operate upon him, cure him!" he cried hastily. "What on earth do you mean, Harry?"

"My dear boy, don't be so excited," said Freeling. "This suspense and sleeplessness have been too much for you. This is antivivisection carried ad absurdum. You don't mean to say you object to operations upon a monkey for his own benefit, do you? If I don't cut a nerve, tetanus will finally set in, and he'll die of it in great agony. Drink off your brandy, and you'll feel better after it."

"But, Harry, what's the matter with the monkey? For heaven's sake, tell me!"

Harry Freeling looked at his friend for the first time a little suspiciously. Could Warminster be right after all, and could Arthur really be going mad? It was so ridiculous of him to get into such a state of flurry about the ailments of a tame monkey, and at such a moment, too! "Well," he answered slowly, "the monkey has got facial distortions due to a slight local paralysis of the inhibitory nerves supplied to the buccal and pharyngeal muscles, with a tendency to end in tetanus. If I cut a small ganglion behind the ear, and exhibit santonin, the muscles will be relaxed; and though they won't act so freely as before, they won't jerk and grimace any longer."

"Does it ever occur in human beings?" Arthur asked eagerly.

"Occur in human beings? Bless my soul, yes! I've seen dozens of cases. Why, goodness gracious, Arthur, it's positively occurring in your own face at this very moment!"

"I know it is," Arthur answered in an agony of suspense. "Do you think this twitching of mine is due to a local paralysis of the inhibitories, such as you speak of?"

"Excuse my laughing, my dear fellow; you really do look so absurdly comical. No, I don't think anything about it. I know it is."

"Then you believe Warminster was wrong in taking it for a symptom of incipient insanity?"

It was Freeling's turn now to jump up in surprise. "You don't mean to tell me, Arthur, that that was the sole ground on which that old fool, Warminster, thought you were going crazy?"

"He didn't see it himself," answered Arthur, with a sigh of unspeakable relief. "I only described it to him, and he drew his inference from what I told him. But the real question is this, Harry: Do you feel quite sure that there's nothing more than that the matter with me?"

"Absolutely certain, my dear fellow. I can cure you in half an hour. I've done it dozens of times before, and know the thing as well as you know an ordinary case of scarlet fever."

Arthur sighed again. "And perhaps," he said bitterly, "this terrible mistake may cost dear Hetty her life!"

He drank off the brandy, ate a few mouthfuls of food as best he might, and hastened back to the Aburys'. When he got there he learned from the servant that Hetty was at least no worse; and with that negative comfort he had for the moment to content himself.

Hetty's illness was long and serious; but before it was over Freeling was able to convince Dr. Abury of his own and his colleague's error, and to prove by a simple piece of surgery that Arthur's hideous grimaces were due to nothing worse than a purely physical impediment. The operation was quite a successful one; but though Greatrex's face has never since been liable to these curious contortions, the consequent relaxation of the muscles has given his features that peculiarly calm and almost impassive expression which everybody must have noticed upon them at the present day, even in moments of the greatest animation. The difficulty was how to break the cause of the temporary mistake to Hetty, and this they were unable to do until she was to a great extent convalescent. When once the needful explanation was over, and Arthur was able once more to kiss her with perfect freedom from any tinge of suspicion on her part, he felt that his paradise was at last attained.

A few days before the deferred date fixed for their wedding, Freeling came into the doctor's drawing-room, where Hetty and Arthur were sitting together, and threw a letter with a French official stamp on its face down upon the table. "There," he said, "I find all the members of the Académie des Sciences at Paris are madmen also!"

Hetty smiled faintly, and said with a little earnestness in her tone, "Ah, Dr. Freeling, that subject has been far too serious a one for both of us to make it pleasant jesting."

"Oh, but look here, Miss Abury," said Freeling; "I have to apologise to Arthur for a great liberty I have ventured to take, and I think it best to begin by explaining to you wherein it consisted. The fact is, before you were ill, Arthur had just written a paper on the interrelations of energy, which he showed to that pompous old nincompoop, Professor Linklight. Well, Linklight being one of those men who can never see an inch beyond his own nose, had the incomprehensible stupidity to tell him there was nothing in it. Thereupon your future husband, who is a modest and self-depreciating sort of fellow, was minded to throw it incontinently into the waste-paper basket. But a friend of his, Harry Freeling, who flatters himself that he can see an inch or two beyond his own nose, read it over, and recognized that it was a brilliant discovery. So what does he go and do—here comes in the apologetic matter—but get this memoir quietly translated into French, affix a motto to it, put it in an envelope, and send it in for the gold medal competition of the Académie. Strange to say, the members of the Académie turned out to be every bit as mad as the author and his friend; for I have just received this letter, addressed to Arthur at my house (which I have taken the further liberty of opening), and it informs me that the Académie decrees its gold medal for physical discovery to M. Arthur Greatrex, of London, which is a subject of congratulation for us three, and a regular slap in the face for pompous old Linklight."

Hetty seized Freeling's two hands in hers. "You have been our good genius, Dr. Freeling," she said with brimming eyes. "I owe Arthur to you; and Arthur owes me to you; and now we both owe you this. What can we ever do to thank you sufficiently?"

Since those days Hetty and Arthur have long been married, and Dr. Greatrex's famous work (in its enlarged form) has been translated into all the civilized languages of the world, as well as into

German; but to this moment, happy as they both are, you can read in their faces the lasting marks of that one terrible anxiety. To many of their friends it seemed afterwards a mere laughing matter; but to those two, who went through it, and especially to Arthur Greatrex, it is a memory too painful to be looked back upon even now without a thrill of terrible recollection.

MR. CHUNG

The first time I ever met poor Chung was at one of Mrs. Bouverie Barton's Thursday evening receptions in Eaton Place. Of course you know Mrs. Bouverie Barton, the cleverest literary hostess at this moment living in London. Herself a well-known novelist, she collects around her all the people worth knowing, at her delightful At Homes; and whenever you go there you are sure to meet somebody whose acquaintance is a treasure and an acquisition for your whole after life.

Well, it so happened on one of those enjoyable Thursday evenings that I was sitting on the circular ottoman in the little back room with Miss Amelia Hogg, the famous woman's-rights advocate. Now, if there is a subject on earth which infinitely bores me, that subject is woman's rights; and if there is a person on earth who can make it absolutely unendurable, that person is Miss Amelia Hogg. So I let her speak on placidly in her own interminable manner about the fortunes of the Bill—she always talks as though her own pet Bill were the only Bill now existing on this sublunary planet—and while I interposed an occasional "Indeed" or "Quite so" for form's sake, I gave myself up in reality to digesting the conversation of two intelligent people who sat back to back with us on the other side of the round ottoman.

"Yes," said one of the speakers, in a peculiarly soft silvery voice which contrasted oddly with Miss Hogg's querulous treble, "his loss is a very severe one to contemporary philosophy. His book on the "Physiology of Perception" is one of the most masterly pieces of analytic work I have ever met with in the whole course of my psychological reading. It was to me, I confess, who approached it fresh from the school of Schelling and Hegel, a perfect revelation of à posteriori thinking. I shall never cease to regret that he did not live long enough to complete the second volume."

Just at this point Miss Hogg had come to a pause in her explanation of the seventy-first clause of the Bill, and I stole a look round the corner to see who my philosophic neighbour might happen to be. An Oxford don, no doubt, I said to myself, or a young Cambridge professor, freshly crammed to the throat with all the learning of the Moral Science Tripos.

Imagine my surprise when, on glancing casually at the silvery-voiced speaker, I discovered him to be a full-blown Chinaman! Yes, a yellow-skinned, almond-eyed, Mongolian-featured Chinaman, with a long pigtail hanging down his back, and attired in the official amber silk robe and purple slippers of a mandarin of the third grade, and the silver button. My curiosity was so fully aroused by this strange discovery that I determined to learn something more about so curious a product of an alien civilization; and therefore, after a few minutes, I managed to give Miss Amelia Hogg the slip by drawing in young Harry Farquhar the artist at the hundred-and-twentieth section, and making my way quietly across the room to Mrs. Bouverie Barton.

"The name of that young Chinaman?" our hostess said in answer to my question. "Oh, certainly; he is Mr. Chung, of the Chinese Legation. A most intelligent and well-educated young man, with a great deal of taste for European literature. Introduce you?—of course, this minute." And she led the way back to where my Oriental phenomenon was still sitting, deep as ever in philosophical problems with

Professor Woolstock, a spectacled old gentleman of German aspect, who was evidently pumping him thoroughly with a view to the materials for Volume Forty of his forthcoming great work on "Ethnical Psychology."

I sat by Mr. Chung for the greater part of what was left of that evening. From the very first he exercised a sort of indescribable fascination over me. His English had hardly a trace of foreign accent, and his voice was one of the sweetest and most exquisitely modulated that I have ever heard. When he looked at you, his deep calm eyes bespoke at once the very essence of transparent sincerity. Before the evening was over, he had told me the whole history of his education and his past life. The son of a well-to-do Pekin mandarin, of distinctly European tastes, he had early passed all his examinations in China, and had been selected by the Celestial Government as one of the first batch of students sent to Europe to acquire the tongues and the sciences of the Western barbarians. Chung's billet was to England; and here, or in France, he had lived with a few intervals ever since he first came to man's estate. He had picked up our language quickly; had taken a degree at London University; and had made himself thoroughly at home in English literature. In fact, he was practically an Englishman in everything but face and clothing. His naturally fine intellect had assimilated European thought and European feeling with extraordinary ease, and it was often almost impossible in talking with him to remember that he was not one of ourselves. If you shut your eyes and listened, you heard a pleasant, cultivated, intelligent young Englishman; when you opened them again, it was always a fresh surprise to find yourself conversing with a genuine yellow-faced pig-tailed Chinaman, in the full costume of the peacock's feather.

"You could never go back to live in China?" I said to him inquiringly after a time. "You could never endure life among your own people after so long a residence in civilized Europe?"

"My dear sir," he answered with a slight shudder of horror, "you do not reflect what my position actually is. My Government may recall me any day. I am simply at their mercy, and I must do as I am bidden."

"But you would not like China," I put in.

"Like it!" he exclaimed with a gesture which for a Chinaman I suppose one must call violent. "I should abhor it. It would be a living death. You who have never been in China can have no idea of what an awful misfortune it would be for a man who has acquired civilized habits and modes of thought to live among such a set of more than mediæval barbarians as my countrymen still remain at the present day. Oh no; God grant I may never have to return there permanently, for it would be more than I could endure. Even a short visit to Pekin is bad enough; the place reeks of cruelty, jobbery, and superstition from end to end; and I always breathe more freely when I have once more got back on to the deck of a European steamer that flies the familiar British flag."

"Then you are not patriotic," I ventured to say.

"Patriotic!" he replied with a slight curl of the lip; "how can a man be patriotic to such a mass of corruption and abomination as our Chinese Government? I can understand a patriotic Russian, a patriotic Egyptian, nay, even a patriotic Turk; but a patriotic Chinaman—why, the very notion is palpably absurd. Listen, my dear sir; you ask me if I could live in China. No, I couldn't; and for the best of all possible reasons—they wouldn't let me. You don't know what the furious prejudice and blind superstition of that awful country really is. Before I had been there three months they would accuse me either of foreign practices or, what comes to much the same thing, of witchcraft; and they would put me to death by one of their most horrible torturing punishments—atrocities which I could not even mention in an English drawing-room. That is the sort of Damocles' sword that is always hanging over the head of every Europeanized Chinaman who returns against his own free will to his native land."

I was startled and surprised. It seemed so natural and simple to be talking under Mrs. Bouverie Barton's big chandelier with this interesting young man, and yet so impossible for a moment to connect him in thought with all the terrible things that one had read in books about the prisons and penal laws of China. That a graduate of London University, a philosopher learned in all the political wisdom of Ricardo, Mill, and Herbert Spencer, should really be subject to that barbaric code of abominable tortures, was more than one could positively realize. I hesitated a moment, and then I said, "But of course they will never recall you."

"I trust not," he said quietly; "I pray not. Very likely they will let me stop here all my lifetime. I am an assistant interpreter to the Embassy, in which capacity I am useful to Pekin; whereas in any home appointment I would of course be an utter failure, a manifest impossibility. But there is really no accounting for the wild vagaries and caprices of the Vermilion Pencil. For aught I know to the contrary, I might even be recalled to-morrow. If once they suspect a man of European sympathies, their first idea is to cut off his head. They regard it as you would regard the first plague-spot of cholera or small-pox in a great city."

"Heaven forbid that they should ever recall you," I said earnestly; for already I had taken a strong fancy to his strange phenomenon of Western education grafted on an immemorial Eastern stock; and I had read enough of China to know that what he said about his probable fate if he returned there permanently was nothing more than the literal truth. The bare idea of such a catastrophe was too horrible to be realized for a moment in Eaton Place.

As we drove home in our little one-horse brougham that evening, my wife and Effie were very anxious to learn what manner of man my Chinese acquaintance might really be; and when I told them what a charming person I had found him, they were both inclined rather to laugh at me for my enthusiastic description. Effie, in particular, jeered much at the notion of an intelligent and earnest-minded Chinaman. "You know, Uncle darling," she said in her bewitching way, "all your geese are always swans. Every woman you meet is absolutely beautiful, and every man is perfectly delightful— till Auntie and I have seen them."

"Perfectly true, Effie," I answered; "it is an amiable weakness of mine, after all."

However, before the week was out Effie and Marian between them would have it that I must call upon Chung and ask him to dine with us at Kensington Park Terrace. Their curiosity was piqued, for one thing; and for another thing, they thought it rather the cheese in these days of expansive cosmopolitanism to be on speaking terms with a Chinese attaché. "Japanese are cheap," said Effie, "horribly cheap of late years—a perfect drug in the market; but a Chinaman is still, thank Heaven, at a social premium." Now, though I am an obedient enough husband, as husbands go, I don't always accede to Marian's wishes in these matters; but everybody takes it for granted that Effie's will is law. Effie, I may mention parenthetically, is more than a daughter to us, for she is poor Tom's only child; and of course everybody connected with dear Tom is doubly precious to us now, as you may easily imagine. So when Effie had made up her mind that Chung was to dine with us, the thing was settled; and I called at his rooms and duly invited him, to the general satisfaction of everybody concerned.

The dinner was a very pleasant one, and, for a wonder, Effie and Marian both coincided entirely in my hastily formed opinion of Mr. Chung. His mellow silvery voice, his frank truthful manner, his perfect freedom from self-consciousness, all pleased and impressed those stern critics, and by the end of the evening they were both quite as much taken with his delightful personality as I myself had originally been. One link leads on to another; and the end of it all was that when we went down for our summer villeggiatura to Abbot's Norbury, nothing would please Marian but that Mr. Chung must be invited down as one of our party. He came willingly enough, and for five or six weeks we had as pleasant a time together as any four people over spent. Chung was a perfect encyclopædia of information, while his good humour and good spirits never for a moment failed him under any circumstances whatsoever.

One day we had made up a little private picnic to Norbury Edge, and were sitting together after luncheon under the shade of the big ash tree, when the conversation happened to turn by accident on the small feet of Chinese ladies. I had often noticed that Chung was very reticent about China; he did not like talking about his native country; and he was most pleased and most at home when we treated him most like a European born. Evidently he hated the provincialism of the Flowery Land, and loved to lose his identity in the wider culture of a Western civilization.

"How funny it will be," said Effie, "to see Mrs. Chung's tiny feet when you bring her to London. I suppose one of these days, on one of your flying visits to Pekin, you will take to yourself a wife in your country?"

"No," Chung answered, with quiet dignity; "I shall never marry—that I have quite decided in my own mind."

"Oh, don't say that," Marian put in quickly; "I hate to hear men say they'll never marry. It is such a terrible mistake. They become so selfish, and frumpish, and old-bachelorish." Dear Marian has a high idea of the services she has rendered to society in saving her own fortunate husband from this miserable and deplorable condition.

"Perhaps so," Chung replied quietly. "No doubt what you say is true as a rule. But, for my own part, I could never marry a Chinawoman; I am too thoroughly Europeanized for that; we should have absolutely no tastes or sympathies in common. You don't know what my countrywomen are like, Mrs. Walters."

"Ah, no," said my wife contemplatively; "I suppose your people are all heathens. Why, goodness gracious, Mr. Chung, if it comes to that, I suppose really you are a heathen yourself!"

Chung parried the question gracefully. "Don't you know," said he, "what Lord Chesterfield answered to the lady who asked him what religion he professed? 'Madam, the religion to which all wise men belong.' 'And what is that?' said she. 'Madam, no wise man ever says.'"

"Never mind Lord Chesterfield," said Effie, smiling, "but let us come back to the future Mrs. Chung. I'm quite disappointed you won't marry a Chinawoman; but at any rate I suppose you'll marry somebody?"

"Well, not a European, of course," Marian put in.

"Oh, of course not," Chung echoed with true Oriental imperturbability.

"Why of course?" Effie asked half unconsciously; and yet the very unconsciousness with which she asked the question showed in itself that she instinctively felt the gulf as much as any of us. If Chung had been a white man instead of a yellow one, she would hardly have discussed the question at issue with so much simplicity and obvious innocence.

"Well, I will tell you why," Chung answered. "Because, even supposing any European lady were to consent to become my wife—which is in the first place eminently improbable—I could never think of putting her in the terribly false position that she would have to occupy under existing circumstances. To begin with, her place in English society would be a peculiar and a trying one. But that is not all. You must remember that I am still a subject of the Chinese Empire, and a member of the Chinese Civil Service. I may any day be recalled to China, and of course—I say 'of course' this time advisedly—it would be absolutely impossible for me to take an English wife to Pekin with me. So I am placed in this awkward dilemma. I would never care to marry anybody except a European lady; and to marry a European lady would be an act of injustice to her which I could never dream of committing. But considering the justifiable contempt which all Europeans rightly feel for us poor John Chinamen, I don't think it probable in any case that the temptation is at all likely to arise. And so, if you please, as the newspapers always put it, 'the subject then dropped.'"

We all saw that Chung was in earnest as to his wish that no more should be said about the matter, and we respected his feelings accordingly; but that evening, as we sat smoking in the arbour after the ladies had retired, I said to him quietly, "Tell me, Chung, if you really dislike China so very much, and are so anxious not to return there, why don't you throw off your allegiance altogether, become a British subject, and settle down among us for good and all?"

"My dear fellow," he said, smiling, "you don't think of the difficulties, I may say the impossibilities, in the way of any such plan as you propose. It is easy enough for a European to throw off his nationality whenever he chooses; it is a very different thing for an Asiatic to do so. Moreover, I am a member of a Legation. My Government would never willingly let me become a naturalized Englishman; and if I tried to manage it against their will they would demand my extradition, and would carry their point, too, as a matter of international courtesy, for one nation could never interfere with the accredited representative of another, or with any of his suite. Even if I were to abscond and get rid of my personality altogether, what would be the use of it? Nobody in England could find any employment for a Chinaman. I have no property of my own; I depend entirely upon my salary for support; my position is therefore quite hopeless. I must simply let things go their own way, and trust to chance not to be recalled to Pekin."

During all the rest of Chung's visit we let him roam pretty much as he liked about the place, and Effie and I generally went with him. Of course we never for a moment fancied it possible that Effie could conceivably take a fancy to a yellow man like him; the very notion was too preposterously absurd. And yet, just towards the end of his stay with us, it began to strike me uneasily that after all even a Chinaman is human. And when a Chinaman happens to have perfect manners, noble ideas, delicate sensibility, and a chivalrous respect for English ladies, it is perhaps just within the bounds of conceivability that at some odd moments an English girl might for a second partially forget his oblique eyelids and his yellow skin. I was sometimes half afraid that it might be so with Effie; and though I don't think she would ever herself have dreamed of marrying such a man—the physical barrier between the races is far too profound for that—I fancy she occasionally pitied poor Chung's loneliness with that womanly pity which so easily glides into a deeper and closer sentiment. Certainly she felt his isolation greatly, and often hoped he would never really be obliged to go back for ever to that hateful China.

One lovely summer evening, a few days before Chung's holiday was to end, and his chief at the Embassy expected him back again, Marian and I had gone out for a stroll together, and in coming home happened to walk above the little arbour in the shrubbery by the upper path. A seat let into the hedge bank overhung the summer-house, and here we both sat down silently to rest after our walking. As we did so, we heard Chung's voice in the arbour close below, so near and so clear that every word was quite distinctly audible.

"For the last time in England," he was saying, with a softly regretful cadence in his tone, as we came upon him.

"The last time, Mr. Chung!" The other voice was Effie's. "What on earth do you mean by that?"

"What I say, Miss Walters. I am recalled to China; I got the letters of recall the day before yesterday."

"The day before yesterday, and you never told us! Why didn't you let us know before?"

"I did not know you would interest yourselves in my private affairs."

"Mr. Chung!" There was a deep air of reproach in Effie's tone.

"Well, Miss Walters, that is not quite true. I ought not to have said it to friends so kind as you have all shown yourselves to be. No; my real reason was that I did not wish to grieve you unnecessarily, and even now I would not have done so, only—"

"Only—?"

At this moment I for my part felt we had heard too much. I blushed up to my eyes at the thought that we should have unwittingly played the spy upon these two innocent young people. I was just going to call out and rush down the little path to them; but as I made a slight movement forward, Marian held my wrist with an imploring gesture, and earnestly put her finger on my lips. I was overborne, and I regret to say I stopped and listened. Marian did not utter a word, but speaking rapidly on her fingers, as we all had learnt to do for poor Tom, she said impressively, "For God's sake, not a sound. This is serious. We must and ought to hear it out." Marian is a very clever woman in these matters; and when she thinks anything a point of duty to poor Tom's girl, I always give way to her implicitly. But I confess I didn't like it.

"Only—?" Effie had said.

"Only I felt compelled to now. I could not leave without telling you how deeply I had appreciated all your kindness."

"But, Mr. Chung, tell me one thing," she asked earnestly; "why have they recalled you to Pekin?"

"I had rather not tell you."

"I insist."

"Because they are displeased with my foreign tastes and habits, which have been reported to them by some of my fellow-attachés."

"But, Mr. Chung, Uncle says there is no knowing what they will do to you. They may kill you on some absurd charge or other of witchcraft or something equally meaningless."

"I am afraid," he answered imperturbably, "that may be the case. I don't mind at all on my own account—we Chinese are an apathetic race, you know—but I should be sorry to be a cause of grief to any of the dear friends I have made in England."

"Mr. Chung!" This time the tone was one of unspeakable horror.

"Don't speak like that," Chung said quickly. "There is no use in taking trouble at interest. I may come to no harm; at any rate, it will not matter much to any one but myself. Now let us go back to the house. I ought not to have stopped here with you so long, and it is nearly dinner time."

"No," said Effie firmly; "we will not go back. I must understand more about this. There is plenty of time before dinner: and if not, dinner must wait."

"But, Miss Walters, I don't think I ought to have brought you out here, and I am quite sure I ought not to stay any longer. Do return. Your Aunt will be annoyed."

"Bother Aunt! She is the best woman in the world, but I must hear all about this. Mr. Chung, why don't you say you won't go, and stay in England in spite of them?"

Nobody ever disobeys Effie, and so Chung wavered visibly. "I will tell you why," he answered slowly; "because I cannot. I am a servant of the Chinese Government, and if they choose to recall me, I must go."

"But they couldn't enforce their demand."

"Yes, they could. Your Government would give me up."

"But Mr. Chung, couldn't you run away and hide for a while, and then come out again, and live like an Englishman?"

"No," he answered quietly; "it is quite impossible. A Chinaman couldn't get work in England as a clerk or anything of that sort, and I have nothing of my own to live upon."

There was a silence of a few minutes. Both were evidently thinking it out. Effie broke the silence first.

"Oh, Mr Chung, do you think they will really put you to death?"

"I don't think it; I know it."

"You know it?"

"Yes."

Again a silence, and this time Chung broke it first. "Miss Effie," he said, "one Chinaman more or less in the world does not matter much, and I shall never forgive myself for having been led to grieve you for a moment, even though this is the last time I shall be able to speak to you. But I see you are sorry for me, and now—Chinaman as I am, I must speak out—I can't leave you without having told you all I feel. I am going to a terrible end, and I know it—so you will forgive me. We shall never meet again, so what I am going to say need never cause you any embarrassment in future. That I am recalled does not much trouble me; that I am going to die does not much trouble me; but that I can never, could never possibly have called you my wife, troubles me and cuts me to the very quick. It is the deepest drop in my cup of humiliation."

"I knew it," said Effie, with wonderful composure.

"You knew it?"

"Yes, I knew it. I saw it from the second week you were here; and I liked you for it. But of course it was impossible, so there is nothing more to be said about it."

"Of course," said Chung. "Ah, that terrible of course! I feel it; you feel it; we all feel it; and yet what a horrible thing it is. I am so human in everything else, but there is that one impassable barrier between us, and I myself cannot fail to recognize it. I could not even wish you to feel that you could marry a Chinaman."

At that moment—for a moment only—I almost felt as if I could have said to Effie, "Take him!" but the thing was too impossible—a something within us rises against it—and I said nothing.

"So now," Chung continued, "I must go. We must both go back to the house. I have said more than I ought to have said, and I am ashamed of myself for having done so. Yet, in spite of the measureless gulf that parts us, I felt I could not return to China without having told you. Will you forgive me?"

"I am glad you did," said Effie; "it will relieve you."

She stood a minute irresolute, and then she began again: "Mr. Chung, I am too horrified to know what I ought to do. I can't grasp it and take it all in so quickly. If you had money of your own, would you be able to run away and live somehow?"

"I might possibly," Chung answered, "but not probably. A Chinaman, even if he wears European clothing, is too marked a person ever to escape. The only chance would be by going to Mauritius or California, where I might get lost in the crowd."

"But, Mr. Chung, I have money of my own. What can I do? Help me, tell me. I can't let a fellow-creature die for a mere prejudice of race and colour. If I were your wife it would be yours. Isn't it my duty?"

"No," said Chung. "It is more sacrifice than any woman ought to make for any man. You like me, but that is all."

"If I shut my eyes and only heard you, I think I could love you."

"Miss Effie," said Chung suddenly, "this is wrong, very wrong of me. I have let my weakness overcome me. I won't stop any longer. I have done what I ought not to have done, and I shall go this minute. Just once, before I go, shut your eyes and let me kiss the tips of your fingers. Thank you. No, I will not stop," and without another word he was gone.

Marian and I stared at one another in blank horror. What on earth was to be done? All solutions were equally impossible. Even to meet Chung at dinner was terrible. We both knew in our heart of hearts that if Chung had been an Englishman, remaining in heart and soul the very self-same man he was, we would willingly have chosen him for Effie's husband. But a Chinaman! Reason about the prejudice as you like, there it is, a thing not to be got over, and at bottom so real that even the very notion of getting over it is terribly repugnant to our natural instincts. On the other hand, was poor Chung, with his fine delicate feelings, his courteous manners, his cultivated intellect, his English chivalry, to go back among the savage semi-barbarians of Pekin, and to be put to death in Heaven knows what inhuman manner for the atrocious crime of having outstripped his race and nation? The thing was too awful to contemplate either way.

We walked home together without a word. Chung had taken the lower path; we took the upper one and followed him at a distance. Effie remained behind for a while in the summer-house. I don't know how we managed to dress for dinner, but we did somehow; and when we went down into the little drawing-room at eight o'clock, we were not surprised to hear that Miss Effie had a headache and did not want any dinner that evening. I was more surprised, however, when, shortly before the gong sounded, one of the servants brought me a little twisted note from Chung, written hurriedly in pencil, and sent, she said, by a porter from the railway station. It ran thus:—

"DEAR MR. WALTERS,

"Excuse great haste. Compelled to return to town immediately. Shall write more fully to-morrow. Just in time to catch up express.

"Yours ever,   "CHUNG."

Evidently, instead of returning to the house, he had gone straight to the station. After all, Chung had the true feelings of a gentleman. He could not meet Effie again after what had passed, and he cut the Gordian knot in the only way possible.

Effie said nothing to us, and we said nothing to Effie, except to show her Chung's note next morning in a casual, off-hand fashion. Two days later a note came for us from the Embassy in Chung's pretty incisive handwriting. It contained copious excuses for his hasty departure, and a few lines to say that he was ordered back to China by the next mail, which started two days later. Marian and I talked it all over, but we could think of nothing that could be of any use; and after all, we said to one another, poor Chung might be mistaken about the probable fate that was in store for him.

"I don't think," Effie said, when we showed her the letter, "I ever met such a nice man as Mr. Chung. I believe he is really a hero." We pretended not to understand what she could mean by it.

The days went by, and we went back again to the dull round of London society. We heard nothing more of Chung for many weeks; till at last one morning I found a letter on the table bearing the Hong Kong postmark. I opened it hastily. As I supposed, it was a note from Chung. It was written in a very small hand on a tiny square of rice-paper, and it ran as follows:—

"Thien-Shan Prison, Pekin, Dec. 8.

"MY DEAR FRIEND,

"Immediately on my return here I was arrested on a charge of witchcraft, and of complicity with the Foreign Devils to introduce the Western barbarism into China. I have now been in a loathsome prison in Pekin for three weeks, in the midst of sights and sounds which I dare not describe to you. Already I have suffered more than I can tell; and I have very little doubt that I shall be brought to trial and executed within a few weeks. I write now begging you not to let Miss Effie hear of this, and if my name happens to be mentioned in the English papers, to keep my fate a secret from her as far as possible. I trust to chance for the opportunity of getting this letter forwarded to Hong Kong, and I have had to write it secretly, for I am not allowed pen, ink, or paper. Thank you much for your very great kindness to me. I am not sorry to die, for it is a mistake for a man to have lived outside the life of his own people, and there was no place left for me on earth. Good-bye.

"Ever yours gratefully, "CHUNG."

The letter almost drove me wild with ineffectual remorse and regret. Why had I not tried to persuade Chung to remain in England? Why had I not managed to smuggle him out of the way, and to find him some kind of light employment, such as even a Chinaman might easily have performed? But it was no use regretting now. The impassable gulf was fixed between us; and it was hardly possible even then to realize that this amiable young student, versed in all the science and philosophy of the nineteenth century, had been handed over alive to the tender mercies of a worse than mediæval barbarism and superstition. My heart sank within me, and I did not venture to show the letter even to Marian.

For some weeks the days passed heavily indeed. I could not get Chung out of my mind, and I saw that Effie could not either. We never mentioned his name; but I noticed that Effie had got from Mudie's all the books about China that she could hear of, and that she was reading up with a sort of awful interest all the chapters that related to Chinese law and Chinese criminal punishments. Poor child, the subject evidently enthralled her with a terrible fascination; and I feared that the excitement she was in might bring on a brain fever.

One morning, early in April, we were all seated in the little breakfast-room about ten o'clock, and Effie had taken up the outside sheet of the Times, while I was engaged in looking over the telegrams on the central pages. Suddenly she gave a cry of horror, flung down the paper with a gesture of awful repugnance, and fell from her chair as stiff and white as a corpse. I knew instinctively what had happened, and I took her up in my arms and carried her to her room. After the doctor had come, and Effie had recovered a little from the first shock, I took up the paper from the ground where it lay and read the curt little paragraph which contained the news that seemed to us so terrible:—

"The numerous persons who made the acquaintance of Chung Fo Tsiou, late assistant interpreter to the Chinese Embassy in London, will learn with regret that this unfortunate member of the Civil Service has been accused of witchcraft and executed at Pekin by the frightful Chinese method known as the Heavy Death. Chung Fo Tsiou was well known in London and Paris, where he spent many years of his official life, and attracted some attention by his natural inclination to European society and manners."

Poor Chung! His end was too horrible for an English reader even to hear of it. But Effie knew it all, and I did not wonder that the news should have affected her so deeply.

Effie was some weeks ill, and at first we almost feared her mind would give way under the pressure. Not that she had more than merely liked poor Chung, but the sense of horror was too great for her easily to cast it off. Even I myself did not sleep lightly for many and many a day after I heard the terrible truth. But while Effie was still ill, a second letter reached us, written this time in blood with a piece of stick, apparently on a scrap of coarse English paper, such as that which is used for wrapping up tobacco. It was no more than this:—

"Execution to-day. Keep it from Miss Effie. Cannot forgive myself for having spoken to her. Will you forgive me? It was the weakness of a moment: but even Chinamen have hearts. I could not die without telling her.—CHUNG."

I showed Effie the scrap afterwards—it had come without a line of explanation from Shanghao—and she has kept it ever since locked up in her little desk as a sacred memento. I don't doubt that some of these days Effie will marry; but as long as she lives she will bear the impress of what she has suffered about poor Chung. An English girl could not conceivably marry a Chinaman; but now that Chung is dead, Effie cannot help admiring the steadfastness, the bravery, and the noble qualities of her Chinese lover. It is an awful state of things which sometimes brings the nineteenth century and primitive barbarism into such close and horrible juxtaposition.

THE CURATE OF CHURNSIDE

I

Walter Dene, deacon, in his faultless Oxford clerical coat and broad felt hat, strolled along slowly, sunning himself as he went, after his wont, down the pretty central lane of West Churnside. It was just the idyllic village best suited to the taste of such an idyllic young curate as Walter Dene. There were cottages with low-thatched roofs, thickly overgrown with yellow stonecrop and pink house-leek; there were trellis-work porches up which the scented dog-rose and the fainter honeysuckle clambered together in sisterly rivalry; there were pargeted gable-ends of Elizabethan farmhouses, quaintly varied with black oak joists and moulded plaster panels. At the end of all, between an avenue of ancient elm trees, the heavy square tower of the old church closed in the little vista—a church with a round Norman doorway and dog-tooth arches, melting into Early English lancets in the aisle, and finishing up with a great Decorated east window by the broken cross and yew tree. Not a trace of Perpendicularity about it anywhere, thank goodness: "for if it were Perpendicular," said Walter Dene to himself often, "I really think, in spite of my uncle, I should have to look out for another curacy."

Yes, it was a charming village, and a charming country; but, above all, it was rendered habitable and pleasurable for a man of taste by the informing presence of Christina Eliot. "I don't think I shall propose to Christina this week after all," thought Walter Dene as he strolled along lazily. "The most delightful part of love-making is certainly its first beginning. The little tremor of hope and expectation; the half-needless doubt you feel as to whether she really loves you; the pains you take to pierce the thin veil of maidenly reserve; the triumph of detecting her at a blush or a flutter when she sees you coming—all these are delicate little morsels to be rolled daintily on the critical palate, and not to be swallowed down coarsely at one vulgar gulp. Poor child, she is on tenter-hooks of hesitation and expectancy all the time, I know; for I'm sure she loves me now, I'm sure she loves me; but I must wait a week yet: she will be grateful to me for it hereafter. We mustn't kill the goose that lays the golden eggs; we mustn't eat up all our capital at one extravagant feast, and then lament the want of our interest ever afterward. Let us live another week in our first fool's paradise before we enter on the safer but less tremulous pleasures of sure possession. We can enjoy first love but once in a lifetime; let us enjoy it now while we can, and not fling away the chance prematurely by mere childish haste and girlish precipitancy." Thinking which thing, Walter Dene halted a moment by the churchyard wall, picked a long spray of scented wild thyme from a mossy cranny, and gazed into the blue sky above at the graceful swifts who nested in the old tower, as they curved and circled through the yielding air on their evenly poised and powerful pinions.

Just at that moment old Mary Long came out of her cottage to speak with the young parson. "If ye plaze, Maister Dene," she said in her native west-country dialect, "our Nully would like to zee 'ee. She's main ill to-day, zur, and she be like to die a'most, I'm thinking."

"Poor child, poor child," said Walter Dene tenderly. "She's a dear little thing, Mrs. Long, is your Nellie, and I hope she may yet be spared to you. I'll come and see her at once, and try if I can do anything to ease her."

He crossed the road compassionately with the tottering old grandmother, giving her his helping hand over the kerbstone, and following her with bated breath into the close little sick-room. Then he flung open the tiny casement with its diamond-leaded panes, so as to let in the fresh summer air, and picked a few sprigs of sweet-briar from the porch, which he joined with the geranium from his own button-hole to make a tiny nosegay for the bare bedside. After that, he sat and talked awhile gently in an undertone to pale, pretty little Nellie herself, and went away at last promising to send her some jelly and some soup immediately from the vicarage kitchen.

"She's a sweet little child," he said to himself musingly, "though I'm afraid she's not long for this world now; and the poor like these small attentions dearly. They get them seldom, and value them for the sake of the thoughtfulness they imply, rather than for the sake of the mere things themselves. I can order a bottle of calf's-foot at the grocer's, and Carter can set it in a mould without any trouble; while as for the soup, some tinned mock-turtle and a little fresh stock makes a really capital mixture for this sort of thing. It costs so little to give these poor souls pleasure, and it is a great luxury to oneself undeniably. But, after all, what a funny trade it is to set an educated man to do! They send us up to Oxford or Cambridge, give us a distinct taste for Æschylus and Catullus, Dante and Milton, Mendelssohn and Chopin, good claret and olives farcies, and then bring us down to a country village, to look after the bodily and spiritual ailments of rheumatic old washerwomen! If it were not for poetry, flowers, and Christina, I really think I should succumb entirely under the infliction."

"He's a dear, good man, that he is, is young passon," murmured old Miry Long as Walter disappeared between the elm trees; "and he do love the poor and the zick, the same as if he was their own brother. God bless his zoul, the dear, good vulla, vor all his kindness to our Nully."

Halfway down the main lane Walter came across Christina Eliot. As she saw him she smiled and coloured a little, and held out her small gloved hand prettily. Walter took it with a certain courtly and graceful chivalry. "An exquisite day, Miss Eliot," he said; "such a depth of sapphire in the sky, such a faint undertone of green on the clouds by the horizon, such a lovely humming of bees over the flickering hot meadows! On days like this, one feels that Schopenhauer is wrong after all, and that life is sometimes really worth living."

"It seems to me often worth living," Christina answered; "if not for oneself, at least for others. But you pretend to be more of a pessimist than you really are, I fancy, Mr. Dene. Any one who finds so much beauty in the world as you do can hardly think life poor or meagre. You seem to catch the loveliest points in everything you look at, and to throw a little literary or artistic reflection over them which makes them even lovelier than they are in themselves."

"Well, no doubt one can increase one's possibilities of enjoyment by carefully cultivating one's own faculties of admiration and appreciation," said the curate thoughtfully; "but, after all, life has only a few chapters that are thoroughly interesting and enthralling in all its history. We oughtn't to hurry over them too lightly, Miss Eliot; we ought to linger on them lovingly, and make the most of their potentialities; we ought to dwell upon them like "linked sweetness long drawn out." It is the mistake of the world at large to hurry too rapidly over the pleasantest episodes, just as children pick all the plums at once out of the pudding. I often think that, from the purely selfish and temporal point of view, the real value of a life to its subject may be measured by the space of time over which he has managed to spread the enjoyment of its greatest pleasures. Look, for example, at poetry, now."

A faint shade of disappointment passed across Christina's face as he turned from what seemed another groove into that indifferent subject; but she answered at once, "Yes, of course one feels that with the higher pleasures at least; but there are others in which the interest of plot is greater, and then one looks naturally rather to the end. When you begin a good novel, you can't help hurrying through it in order to find out what becomes of everybody at last."

"Ah, but the highest artistic interest goes beyond mere plot interest. I like rather to read for the pleasure of reading, and to loiter over the passages that please me, quite irrespective of what goes before or what comes after; just as you, for your part, like to sketch a beautiful scene for its own worth to you, irrespective of what may happen to the leaves in autumn, or to the cottage roof in twenty years from this. By the way, have you finished that little water-colour of the mill yet? It's the prettiest thing of yours I've ever seen, and I want to look how you've managed the light on your foreground."

"Come in and see it," said Christina. "It's finished now, and, to tell you the truth, I'm very well pleased with it myself."

"Then I know it must be good," the curate answered; "for you are always your own harshest critic." And he turned in at the little gate with her, and entered the village doctor's tiny drawing-room.

Christina placed the sketch on an easel near the window—a low window opening to the ground, with long lithe festoons of faint-scented jasmine encroaching on it from outside—and let the light fall on it aslant in the right direction. It was a pretty and a clever sketch certainly, with more than a mere amateur's sense of form and colour; and Walter Dene, who had a true eye for pictures, could conscientiously praise it for its artistic depth and fulness. Indeed, on that head at least, Walter Dene's veracity was unimpeachable, however lax in other matters; nothing on earth would have induced him to praise as good a picture or a sculpture in which he saw no real merit. He sat a little while criticizing and discussing it, suggesting an improvement here or an alteration there, and then he rose hurriedly, remembering all at once his forgotten promise to little Nellie. "Dear me," he said, "your daughter's picture has almost made me overlook my proper duties, Mrs. Eliot. I promised to send some jelly and things at once to poor little Nellie Long at her grandmother's. How very wrong of me to let my natural inclinations keep me loitering here, when I ought to have been thinking of the poor of my parish!" And he went out with just a gentle pressure on Christina's hand, and a look from his eyes that her heart knew how to read aright at the first glance of it.

"Do you know, Christie," said her father, "I sometimes fancy when I hear that new parson fellow talk about his artistic feelings, and so on, that he's just a trifle selfish, or at least self-centred. He always dwells so much on his own enjoyment of things, you know."

"Oh no, papa," cried Christina warmly. "He's anything but selfish, I'm sure. Look how kind he is to all the poor in the village, and how much he thinks about their comfort and welfare. And whenever he's talking with one, he seems so anxious to make you feel happy and contented with yourself. He has a sort of little subtle flattery of manner about him that's all pure kindliness; and he's always thinking what he can say or do to please you, and to help you onward. What you say about his dwelling on enjoyment so much is really only his artistic sensibility. He feels things so keenly, and enjoys beauty so deeply, that he can't help talking enthusiastically about it even a little out of season. He has more feelings to display than most men, and I'm sure that's the reason why he displays them so much. A ploughboy could only talk enthusiastically about roast beef and dumplings; Mr. Dene can talk about everything that's beautiful and sublime on earth or in heaven."

Meanwhile, Walter Dene was walking quickly with his measured tread—the even, regular tread of a cultivated gentleman—down the lane toward the village grocer's, saying to himself as he went, "There was never such a girl in all the world as my Christina. She may be only a country surgeon's daughter—a rosebud on a hedgerow bush—but she has the soul and the eye of a queen among women for all that. Every lover has deceived himself with the same sweet dream, to be sure—how over-analytic we have become nowadays, when I must needs half argue myself out of the sweets of first love!—but then they hadn't so much to go upon as I have. She has a wonderful touch in music, she has an exquisite eye in painting, she has an Italian charm in manner and conversation. I'm something of a connoisseur, after all, and no more likely to be deceived in a woman than I am in a wine or a picture. And next week I shall really propose formally to Christina, though I know by this time it will be nothing more than the merest formality. Her eyes are too eloquent not to have told me that long ago. It will be a delightful pleasure to live for her, and in order to make her happy. I frankly recognize that I am naturally a little selfish—not coarsely and vulgarly selfish; from that disgusting and piggish vice I may conscientiously congratulate myself that I'm fairly free; but still selfish in a refined and cultivated manner. Now, living with Christina and for Christina will correct this defect in my nature, will tend to bring me nearer to a true standard of perfection. When I am by her side, and then only, I feel that I am thinking entirely of her, and not at all of myself. To her I show my best side; with her, that best side would be always uppermost. The companionship of such a woman makes life something purer, and higher, and better worth having. The one thing that stands in our way is this horrid practical question of what to live upon. I don't suppose Uncle Arthur will be inclined to allow me anything, and I can't marry on my own paltry income and my curacy only. Yet I can't bear to keep Christina waiting indefinitely till some thick-headed squire or other chooses to take it into his opaque brain to give me a decent living."

From the grocer's the curate walked on, carrying the two tins in his hand, as far as the vicarage. He went into the library, sat down by his own desk, and rang the bell. "Will you be kind enough to give those things to Carter, John?" he said in his bland voice; "and tell her to put the jelly in a mould, and let it set. The soup must be warmed with a little fresh stock, and seasoned. Then take them both, with my compliments, to old Mary Long the washerwoman, for her grandchild. Is my uncle in?"

"No, Master Walter," answered the man—he was always "Master Walter" to the old servants at his uncle's—"the vicar have gone over by train to Churminster. He told me to tell you he wouldn't be back till evening, after dinner."

"Did you see him off, John?"

"Yes, Master Walter. I took his portmantew to the station."

"This will be a good chance, then," thought Walter Dene to himself. "Very well, John," he went on aloud: "I shall write my sermon now. Don't let anybody come to disturb me."

John nodded and withdrew. Walter Dene locked the door after him carefully, as he often did when writing sermons, and then lit a cigar, which was also a not infrequent concomitant of his exegetical labours. After that he walked once or twice up and down the room, paused a moment to look at his parchment-covered Rabelais and Villon on the bookshelf, peered out of the dulled glass windows with the crest in their centre, and finally drew a curious bent iron instrument out of his waistcoat pocket. With it in his hands, he went up quietly to his uncle's desk, and began fumbling at the lock in an experienced manner. As a matter of fact, it was not his first trial of skill in lock-picking; for Walter Dene was a painstaking and methodical man, and having made up his mind that he would get at and read his uncle's will, he took good care to begin by fastening all the drawers in his own bedroom, and trying his prentice hand at unfastening them again in the solitude of his chamber.

After half a minute's twisting and turning, the wards gave way gently to his dexterous pressure, and the lid of the desk lay open before him. Walter Dene took out the different papers one by one— there was no need for hurry, and he was not a nervous person—till he came to a roll of parchment, which he recognized at once as the expected will. He unrolled it carefully and quietly, without any womanish trembling or excitement—"thank Heaven," he said to himself, "I'm above such nonsense as that"—and sat down leisurely to read it in the big, low, velvet-covered study chair. As he did so, he did not forget to lay a notched foot-rest for his feet, and to put the little Japanese dish on the tiny table by his side to hold his cigar ash. "And now," he said, "for the important question whether Uncle Arthur has left his money to me, or to Arthur, or to both of us equally. He ought, of course, to leave at least half to me, seeing I have become a curate on purpose to please him, instead of following my natural vocation to the Bar; but I shouldn't be a bit surprised if he had left it all to Arthur. He's a pig-headed and illogical old man, the vicar; and he can never forgive me, I believe, because, being the eldest son, I wasn't called after him by my father and mother. As if that was my fault! Some people's ideas of personal responsibility are so ridiculously muddled."

He composed himself quietly in the arm-chair, and glanced rapidly at the will through the meaningless preliminaries till he came to the significant clauses. These he read more carefully. "All my estate in the county of Dorset, and the messuage or tenement known as Redlands, in the parish of Lode, in the county of Devon, to my dear nephew, Arthur Dene," he said to himself slowly: "Oh, this will never do." "And I give and bequeath to my said nephew, Arthur Dene, the sum of ten thousand pounds, three per cent. consolidated annuities, now standing in my name."—"Oh this is atrocious, quite atrocious! What's this?" "And I give and bequeath to my dear nephew, Walter Dene, the residue of my personal estate"—"and so forth. Oh no. That's quite sufficient. This must be rectified. The residuary legatee would only come in for a few hundreds or so. It's quite preposterous. The vicar was always an ill-tempered, cantankerous, unaccountable person, but I wonder he has the face to sit opposite me at dinner after that."

He hummed an air from Schubert, and sat a moment looking thoughtfully at the will. Then he said to himself quietly, "The simplest thing to do would be merely to scrape out or take out with chemicals the name Arthur, substituting the name Walter, and vice versâ. That's a very small matter; a man who draws as well as I do ought to be able easily to imitate a copying clerk's engrossing hand. But it would be madness to attempt it now and here; I want a little practice first. At the same time, I mustn't keep the will out a moment longer than is necessary; my uncle may return by some accident before I expect him; and the true philosophy of life consists in invariably minimizing the adverse chances. This will was evidently drawn up by Watson and Blenkiron, of Chancery Lane. I'll write to-morrow and get them to draw up a will for me, leaving all I possess to Arthur. The same clerk is pretty sure to engross it, and that'll give me a model for the two names on which I can do a little preliminary practice. Besides, I can try the stuff Wharton told me about, for making ink fade on the same parchment. That will be killing two birds with one stone, certainly. And now if I don't make haste I shan't have time to write my sermon."

He replaced the will calmly in the desk, fastened the lock again with a delicate twirl of the pick, and sat down in his arm-chair to compose his discourse for to-morrow's evensong. "It's not a bad bit of rhetoric," he said to himself as he read it over for correction, "but I'm not sure that I haven't plagiarized a little too freely from Montaigne and dear old Burton. What a pity it must be thrown away upon a Churnside congregation! Not a soul in the whole place will appreciate a word of it, except Christina. Well, well, that alone is enough reward for any man." And he knocked off his ash pensively into the Japanese ash-pan.

During the course of the next week Walter practised diligently the art of imitating handwriting. He got his will drawn up and engrossed at Watson and Blenkiron's (without signing it, bien entendu); and he spent many solitary hours in writing the two names "Walter" and "Arthur" on the spare end of parchment, after the manner of the engrossing clerk. He also tested the stuff for making the ink fade to his own perfect satisfaction. And on the next occasion when his uncle was safely off the premises for three hours, he took the will once more deliberately from the desk, removed the obnoxious letters with scrupulous care, and wrote in his own name in place of Arthur's, so that even the engrossing clerk himself would hardly have known the difference. "There," he said to himself approvingly, as he took down quiet old George Herbert from the shelf and sat down to enjoy an hour's smoke after the business was over, "that's one good deed well done, anyhow. I have the calm satisfaction of a clear conscience. The vicar's proposed arrangement was really most unfair; I have substituted for it what Aristotle would have rightly called true distributive justice. For though I've left all the property to myself, by the unfortunate necessity of the case, of course I won't take it all. I'll be juster than the vicar. Arthur shall have his fair share, which is more, I believe, than he'd have done for me; but I hate squalid money-grubbing. If brothers can't be generous and brotherly to one another, what a wretched, sordid little life this of ours would really be!"

Next Sunday morning the vicar preached, and Walter sat looking up at him reflectively from his place in the chancel. A beautiful clear-cut face, the curate's, and seen to great advantage from the doctor's pew, set off by the white surplice, and upturned in quiet meditation towards the elder priest in the pulpit. Walter was revolving many things in his mind, and most of all one adverse chance which he could not just then see his way to minimize. Any day his uncle might take it into his head to read over the will and discover the—ah, well, the rectification. Walter was a man of too much delicacy of feeling even to think of it to himself as a fraud or a forgery. Then, again, the vicar was not a very old man after all; he might live for an indefinite period, and Christina and himself might lose all the best years of their life waiting for a useless person's natural removal. What a pity that threescore was not the utmost limit of human life! For his own part, like the Psalmist, Walter had no desire to outlive his own highest tastes and powers of enjoyment. Ah, well, well, man's prerogative is to better and improve upon nature. If people do not die when they ought, then it becomes clearly necessary for philosophically minded juniors to help them on their way artificially.

It was an ugly necessity, certainly; Walter frankly recognized that fact from the very beginning, and he shrank even from contemplating it; but there was no other way out of the difficulty. The old man had always been a selfish bachelor, with no love for anybody or anything on earth except his books, his coins, his garden, and his dinner; he was growing tired of all except the last; would it not be better for the world at large, on strict utilitarian principles, that he should go at once? True, such steps are usually to be deprecated; but the wise man is a law unto himself, and instead of laying down the wooden, hard-and-fast lines that make conventional morality so much a rule of thumb, he judges every individual case on its own particular merits. Here was Christina's happiness and his own on the one hand, with many collateral advantages to other people, set in the scale against the feeble remnant of a selfish old man's days on the other. Walter Dene had a constitutional horror of taking life in any form, and especially of shedding blood; but he flattered himself that if anything of the sort became clearly necessary, he was not the man to shrink from taking the needful measures to ensure it, at any sacrifice of personal comfort.

All through the next week Walter turned over the subject in his own mind; and the more he thought about it, the more the plan gained in definiteness and consistency as detail after detail suggested itself to him. First he thought of poison. That was the cleanest and neatest way of managing the thing, he considered; and it involved the least unpleasant consequences. To stick a knife or shoot a bullet into any sentient creature was a horrid and revolting act; to put a little tasteless powder into a cup of coffee and let a man sleep off his life quietly was really nothing more than helping him involuntarily to a delightful euthanasia. "I wish any one would do as much for me at his age, without telling me about it," Walter said to himself seriously. But then the chances of detection would be much increased by using poison, and Walter felt it an imperative duty to do nothing which would expose Christina to the shock of a discovery. She would not see the matter in the same practical light as he did; women never do; their morality is purely conventional and a wise man will do nothing on earth to shake it. You cannot buy poison without the risk of exciting question. There remained, then, only shooting or stabbing. But shooting makes an awkward noise, and attracts attention at the moment; so the one thing possible was a knife, unpleasant as that conclusion seemed to all his more delicate feelings.

Having thus decided, Walter Dene proceeded to lay his plans with deliberate caution. He had no intention whatsoever of being detected, though his method of action was simplicity itself. It was only bunglers and clumsy fools who got caught; he knew that a man of his intelligence and ability would not make such an idiot of himself as—well, as common ruffians always do. He took his old American bowie-knife, bought years ago as a curiosity, out of the drawer where it had lain so long. It was very rusty, but it would be safer to sharpen it privately on his own hone and strop than to go asking for a new knife at a shop for the express purpose of enabling the shopman afterwards to identify him. He sharpened it for safety's sake during sermon-hour in the library, with the door locked as usual. It took a long time to get off all the rust, and his arm got quickly tired. One morning as he was polishing away at it, he was stopped for a moment by a butterfly which flapped and fluttered against the dulled window-panes. "Poor thing," he said to himself, "it will beat its feathery wings to pieces in its struggles;" and he put a vase of Venetian glass on top of it, lifted the sash carefully, and let the creature fly away outside in the broad sunshine. At the same moment the vicar, who was strolling with his King Charlie on the lawn, came up and looked in at the window. He could not have seen in before, because of the dulled and painted diamonds.

"That's a murderous-looking weapon, Wally," he said, with a smile, as his glance fell upon the bowie and hone. "What do you use it for?"

"Oh, it's an American bowie," Walter answered carelessly. "I bought it long ago for a curiosity, and now I'm sharpening it up to help me in carving that block of walnut wood." And he ran his finger lightly along the edge of the blade to test its keenness. What a lucky thing that it was the vicar himself, and not the gardener! If he had been caught by anybody else the fact would have been fatal evidence after all was over. "Méfiez-vous des papillons," he hummed to himself, after Béranger, as he shut down the window. "One more butterfly, and I must give up the game as useless."

Meanwhile, as Walter meant to make a clean job of it—hacking and hewing clumsily was repulsive to all his finer feelings—he began also to study carefully the anatomy of the human back. He took down all the books on the subject in the library, and by their aid discovered exactly under which ribs the heart lay. A little observation of the vicar, compared with the plates in Quain's "Anatomy," showed him precisely at what point in his clerical coat the most vulnerable interstice was situated. "It's a horrid thing to have to do," he thought over and over again as he planned it, "but it's the only way to secure Christina's happiness." And so, by a certain bright Friday evening in August, Walter Dene had fully completed all his preparations.

That afternoon, as on all bright afternoons in summer, the vicar went for a walk in the grounds, attended only by little King Charlie. He was squire and parson at once in Churnside, and he loved to make the round of his own estate. At a certain gate by Selbury Copse the vicar always halted to rest awhile, leaning on the bar and looking at the view across the valley. It was a safe and lonely spot. Walter remained at home (he was to take the regular Friday evensong) and went into the study by himself. After a while he took his hat, not without trembling, strolled across the garden, and then made the short cut through the copse, so as to meet the vicar by the gate. On his way he heard the noise of the Dennings in the farm opposite, out rabbit-shooting with their guns and ferrets in the warren. His very soul shrank within him at the sound of that brutal sport. "Great heavens!" he said to himself, with a shudder; "to think how I loathe and shrink from the necessity of almost painlessly killing this one selfish old man for an obviously good reason, and those creatures there will go out massacring innocent animals with the aid of a hideous beast of prey, not only without remorse, but actually by way of amusement! I thank Heaven I am not even as they are." Near the gate he came upon his uncle quietly and naturally, though it would be absurd to deny that at that supreme moment even Walter Dene's equable heart throbbed hard, and his breath went and came tremulously. "Alone," he thought to himself, "and nobody near; this is quite providential," using even then, in thought, the familiar phraseology of his profession.

"A lovely afternoon, Uncle Arthur," he said as composedly as he could, accurately measuring the spot on the vicar's coat with his eye meanwhile. "The valley looks beautiful in this light."

"Yes, a lovely afternoon, Wally, my boy, and an exquisite glimpse down yonder into the churchyard."

As he spoke, Walter half leaned upon the gate beside him, and adjusted the knife behind the vicar's back scientifically. Then, without a word more, in spite of a natural shrinking, he drove it home up to the haft, with a terrible effort of will, at the exact spot on the back that the books had pointed out to him. It was a painful thing to do, but he did it carefully and well. The effect of Walter Dene's scientific prevision was even more instantaneous than he had anticipated. Without a single cry, without a sob or a contortion, the vicar's lifeless body fell over heavily by the side of the gate. It rolled down like a log into the dry ditch beneath. Walter knelt trembling on the ground close by, felt the pulse for a moment to assure himself that his uncle was really dead, and having fully satisfied himself on this all-important point, proceeded to draw the knife neatly out of the wound. He had let it fall in the body, in order to extricate it more easily afterward, and not risk pulling it out carelessly so as to get himself covered needlessly by tell-tale drops of blood, like ordinary clumsy assassins. But he had forgotten to reckon with little King Charlie. The dog jumped piteously upon the body of his master, licked the wound with his tongue, and refused to allow Walter to withdraw the knife. It would be unsafe to leave it there, for it might be recognized. "Minimize the adverse chances," he muttered still; but there was no inducing King Charlie to move. A struggle might result in getting drops of blood upon his coat, and then, great heavens, what a terrible awakening for Christina! "Oh, Christina, Christina, Christina," he said to himself piteously, "it is for you only that I could ever have ventured to do this hideous thing." The blood was still oozing out of the narrow slit, and saturating the black coat, and Walter Dene with his delicate nerves could hardly bear to look upon it.

At last he summoned up resolution to draw out the knife from the ugly wound, in spite of King Charlie, and as he did so, oh, horror! the little dog jumped at it, and cut his left fore-leg against the sharp edge deep to the bone. Here was a pretty accident indeed! If Walter Dene had been a common heartless murderer he would have snatched up the knife immediately, left the poor lame dog to watch and bleed beside his dead master, and skulked off hurriedly from the mute witness to his accomplished crime. But Walter was made of very different mould from that; he could not find it in his heart to leave a poor dumb animal wounded and bleeding for hours together, alone and untended. Just at first, indeed, he tried sophistically to persuade himself his duty to Christina demanded that he should go away at once, and never mind the sufferings of a mere spaniel; but his better nature told him the next moment that such sophisms were indefensible, and his humane instincts overcame even the profound instinct of self-preservation. He sat down quietly beside the warm corpse. "Thank goodness," he said, with a slight shiver of disgust, "I'm not one of those weak-minded people who are troubled by remorse. They would be so overcome by terror at what they had done that they would want to run away from the body immediately, at any price. But I don't think I could feel remorse. It is an incident of lower natures—natures that are capable of doing actions under one set of impulses, which they regret when another set comes uppermost in turn. That implies a want of balance, an imperfect co-ordination of parts and passions. The perfect character is consistent with itself; shame and repentance are confessions of weakness. For my part, I never do anything without having first deliberately decided that it is the best or the only thing to do; and having so done it, I do not draw back like a girl from the necessary consequences of my own act. No fluttering or running away for me. Still, I must admit that all that blood does look very ghastly. Poor old gentleman! I believe he really died almost without knowing it, and that is certainly a great comfort to one under the circumstances."

He took King Charlie tenderly in his hands, without touching the wounded leg, and drew his pocket handkerchief softly from his pocket. "Poor beastie," he said aloud, holding out the cut limb before him, "you are badly hurt, I'm afraid; but it wasn't my fault. We must see what we can do for you." Then he wrapped the handkerchief deftly around it, without letting any blood show through, pressed the dog close against his breast, and picked up the knife gingerly by the reeking handle. "A fool of a fellow would throw it into the river," he thought, with a curl of his graceful lip. "They always dredge the river after these incidents. I shall just stick it down a hole in the hedge a hundred yards off. The police have no invention, dull donkeys; they never dredge the hedges." And he thrust it well down a disused rabbit burrow, filling in the top neatly with loose mould.

Walter Dene meant to have gone home quietly and said evensong, leaving the discovery of the body to be made at haphazard by others, but this unfortunate accident to King Charlie compelled him against his will to give the first alarm. It was absolutely necessary to take the dog to the veterinary at once, or the poor little fellow might bleed to death incontinently. "One's best efforts," he thought, "are always liable to these unfortunate contretemps. I meant merely to remove a superfluous person from an uncongenial environment; yet I can't manage it without at the same time seriously injuring a harmless little creature that I really love." And with one last glance at the lifeless thing behind him, he took his way regretfully along the ordinary path back towards the peaceful village of Churnside.

Halfway down the lane, at the entrance to the village, he met one of his parishioners. "Tom," he said boldly, "have you seen anything of the vicar? I'm afraid he's got hurt somehow. Here's poor little King Charlie come limping back with his leg cut."

"He went down the road, zur, 'arf an hour zince, and I arn't zeen him afterwards."

"Tell the servants at the vicarage to look around the grounds, then; I'm afraid he has fallen and hurt himself. I must take the dog at once to Perkins's, or else I shall be late for evensong."

The man went off straight toward the vicarage, and Walter Dene turned immediately with the dog in his arms into the village veterinary's.

II

The servants from the vicarage were not the first persons to hit upon the dead body of the vicar. Joe Harley, the poacher, was out reconnoitring that afternoon in the vicar's preserves; and five minutes after Walter Dene had passed down the far side of the hedge, Joe Harley skulked noiselessly from the orchard up to the cover of the gate by Selbury Copse. He crept through the open end by the post (for it was against Joe's principles under any circumstances to climb over an obstacle of any sort, and so needlessly expose himself), and he was just going to slink off along the other hedge, having wires and traps in his pocket, when his boot struck violently against a soft object in the ditch underfoot. It struck so violently that it crushed in the object with the force of the impact; and when Joe came to look at what the object might be, he found to his horror that it was the bruised and livid face of the old parson. Joe had had a brush with keepers more than once, and had spent several months of seclusion in Dorchester Gaol; but, in spite of his familiarity with minor forms of lawlessness, he was moved enough in all conscience by this awful and unexpected discovery. He turned the body over clumsily with his hands, and saw that it had been stabbed in the back once only. In doing so he trod in a little blood, and got a drop or two on his sleeve and trousers; for the pool was bigger now, and Joe was not so handy or dainty with his fingers as the idyllic curate.

It was an awful dilemma, indeed, for a confirmed and convicted poacher. Should he give the alarm then and there, boldly, trusting to his innocence for vindication, and helping the police to discover the murderer? Why, that would be sheer suicide, no doubt; "for who but would believe," he thought, "'twas me as done it?" Or should he slink away quietly and say nothing, leaving others to find the body as best they might? That was dangerous enough in its way if anybody saw him, but not so dangerous as the other course. In an evil hour for his own chances Joe Harley chose that worse counsel, and slank off in his familiar crouching fashion towards the opposite corner of the copse.

On the way he heard John's voice holloaing for his master, and kept close to the hedge till he had quite turned the corner. But John had caught a glimpse of him too, and John did not forget it when, a few minutes later, he came upon the horrid sight beside the gate of Selbury Copse.

Meanwhile Walter had taken King Charlie to the veterinary's, and had his leg bound and bandaged securely. He had also gone down to the church, got out his surplice, and begun to put it on in the vestry for evensong, when a messenger came at hot haste from the vicarage, with news that Master Walter must come up at once, for the vicar was murdered.

"Murdered!" Walter Dene said to himself slowly half aloud; "murdered! how horrible! Murdered!" It was an ugly word, and he turned it over with a genuine thrill of horror. That was what they would say of him if ever the thing came to be discovered! What an inappropriate classification!

He threw aside the surplice, and rushed up hurriedly to the vicarage. Already the servants had brought in the body, and laid it out in the clothes it wore, on the vicar's own bed. Walter Dene went in, shuddering, to look at it. To his utter amazement, the face was battered in horribly and almost unrecognizably by a blow or kick! What could that hideous mutilation mean? He could not imagine. It was an awful mystery. Great heavens! just fancy if any one were to take it into his head that he, Walter Dene, had done that—had kicked a defenceless old gentleman brutally about the face like a common London ruffian! The idea was too horrible to be borne for a moment. It unmanned him utterly, and he hid his face between his two hands and sobbed aloud like one broken-hearted. "This day's work has been too much for my nerves," he thought to himself between the sobs; "but perhaps it is just as well I should give way now completely."

That night was mainly taken up with the formalities of all such cases; and when at last Walter Dene went off, tired and nerve-worn, to bed, about midnight, he could not sleep much for thinking of the mystery. The murder itself didn't trouble him greatly; that was over and past now, and he felt sure his precautions had been amply sufficient to protect him even from the barest suspicion; but he couldn't fathom the mystery of that battered and mutilated face! Somebody must have seen the corpse between the time of the murder and the discovery! Who could that somebody have been? and what possible motive could he have had for such a horrible piece of purposeless brutality?

As for the servants, in solemn conclave in the hall, they had unanimously but one theory to account for all the facts: some poacher or other, for choice Joe Harley, had come across the vicar in the copse, with gun and traps in hand. The wretch had seen he was discovered, had felled the poor old vicar by a blow in the face with the butt-end of his rifle, and after he fell, fainting, had stabbed him for greater security in the back. That was such an obvious solution of the difficulty, that nobody in the servants' hall had a moment's hesitation in accepting it.

When Walter heard next morning early that Joe Harley had been arrested overnight, on John's information, his horror and surprise at the news were wholly unaffected. Here was another new difficulty, indeed. "When I did the thing," he said to himself, "I never thought of that possibility. I took it for granted it would be a mystery, a problem for the local police (who, of course, could no more solve it than they could solve the pons-asinorum), but it never struck me they would arrest an innocent person on the charge instead of me. This is horrible. It's so easy to make out a case against a poacher, and hang him for it, on suspicion. One's whole sense of justice revolts against the thing. After all, there's a great deal to be said in favour of the ordinary commonplace morality: it prevents complications. A man of delicate sensibilities oughtn't to kill anybody; he lets himself in for all kinds of unexpected contingencies, without knowing it."

At the coroner's inquest things looked very black indeed for Joe Harley. Walter gave his evidence first, showing how he had found King Charlie wounded in the lane; and then the others gave theirs, as to the search for and finding of the body. John in particular swore to having seen a man's back and head slinking away by the hedge while they were looking for the vicar; and that back and head he felt sure were Joe Harley's. To Walter's infinite horror and disgust, the coroner's jury returned a verdict of wilful murder against the poor poacher. What other verdict could they possibly have given in accordance with such evidence?

The trial of Joe Harley for the wilful murder of the Reverend Arthur Dene was fixed for the next Dorchester Assizes. In the interval, Walter Dene, for the first time in his placid life, knew what it was to undergo a mental struggle. Whatever happened, he could not let Joe Harley be hanged for this murder. His whole soul rose up within him in loathing for such an act of hideous injustice. For though Walter Dene's code of morality was certainly not the conventional one, as he so often boasted to himself, he was not by any means without any code of morals of any sort. He could commit a murder where he thought it necessary, but he could not let an innocent man suffer in his stead. His ethical judgment on that point was just as clear and categorical as the judgment which told him he was in duty bound to murder his uncle. For Walter did not argue with himself on moral questions: he perceived the right and necessary thing intuitively; he was a law to himself, and he obeyed his own law implicitly, for good or for evil. Such men are capable of horrible and diabolically deliberate crimes; but they are capable of great and genuine self-sacrifices also.

Walter made no secret in the village of his disinclination to believe in Joe Harley's guilt. Joe was a rough fellow, he said, certainly, and he had no objection to taking a pheasant or two, and even to having a free fight with the keepers; but, after all, our game laws were an outrageous piece of class legislation, and he could easily understand how the poor, whose sense of justice they outraged, should be so set against them. He could not think Joe Harley was capable of a detestable crime. Besides, he had seen him himself within a few minutes before and after the murder. Everybody thought it such a proof of the young parson's generous and kindly disposition; he had certainly the charity which thinketh no evil. Even though his own uncle had been brutally murdered on his own estate, he checked his natural feelings of resentment, and refused to believe that one of his own parishioners could have been guilty of the crime. Nay, more, so anxious was he that substantial justice should be done the accused, and so confident was he of his innocence, that he promised to provide counsel for him at his own expense; and he provided two of the ablest barristers on the Western circuit.

Before the trial, Walter Dene had come, after a terrible internal struggle, to an awful resolution. He would do everything he could for Joe Harley; but if the verdict went against him, he was resolved, then and there, in open court, to confess, before judge and jury, the whole truth. It would be a horrible thing for Christina; he knew that; but he could not love Christina so much, "loved he not honour more;" and honour, after his own fashion, he certainly loved dearly. Though he might be false to all that all the world thought right, it was ingrained in the very fibre of his soul to be true to his own inner nature at least. Night after night he lay awake, tossing on his bed, and picturing to his mind's eye every detail of that terrible disclosure. The jury would bring in a verdict of guilty: then, before the judge put on his black cap, he, Walter, would stand up, and tell them that he could not let another man hang for his crime; he would have the whole truth out before them; and then he would die, for he would have taken a little bottle of poison at the first sound of the verdict. As for Christina—oh, Christina!—Walter Dene could not dare to let himself think upon that. It was horrible; it was unendurable; it was torture a thousand times worse than dying: but still, he must and would face it. For in certain phases, Walter Dene, forger and murderer as he was, could be positively heroic.

The day of the trial came, and Walter Dene, pale and haggard with much vigil, walked in a dream and faintly from his hotel to the court-house. Everybody present noticed what a deep effect the shock of his uncle's death had had upon him. He was thinner and more bloodless than usual, and his dulled eyes looked black and sunken in their sockets. Indeed, he seemed to have suffered far more intensely than the prisoner himself, who walked in firmer and more erect, and took his seat doggedly in the familiar dock. He had been there more than once before, to say the truth, though never before on such an errand. Yet mere habit, when he got there, made him at once assume the hang-dog look of the consciously guilty.

Walter sat and watched and listened, still in a dream, but without once betraying in his face the real depth of his innermost feelings. In the body of the court he saw Joe's wife, weeping profusely and ostentatiously, after the fashion considered to be correct by her class; and though he pitied her from the bottom of his heart, he could only think by contrast of Christina. What were that good woman's fears and sorrows by the side of the grief and shame and unspeakable horror he might have to bring upon his Christina? Pray Heaven the shock, if it came, might kill her outright; that would at least be better than that she should live long years to remember. More than judge, or jury, or prisoner, Walter Dene saw everywhere, behind the visible shadows that thronged the court, that one persistent prospective picture of heart-broken Christina.

The evidence for the prosecution told with damning force against the prisoner. He was a notorious poacher; the vicar was a game-preserver. He had poached more than once on the ground of the vicarage. He was shown by numerous witnesses to have had an animus against the vicar. He had been seen, not in the face, to be sure, but still seen and recognized, slinking away, immediately after the fact, from the scene of the murder. And the prosecution had found stains of blood, believed by scientific experts to be human, on the clothing he had worn when he was arrested. Walter Dene listened now with terrible, unabated earnestness, for he knew that in reality it was he himself who was upon his trial. He himself, and Christina's happiness; for if the poacher were found guilty, he was firmly resolved, beyond hope of respite, to tell all, and face the unspeakable.

The defence seemed indeed a weak and feeble theory. Somebody unknown had committed the murder, and this somebody, seen from behind, had been mistaken by John for Joe Harley. The blood-stains need not be human, as the cross-examination went to show, but were only known by counter-experts to be mammalian—perhaps a rabbit's. Every poacher—and it was admitted that Joe was a poacher—was liable to get his clothes blood-stained. Grant they were human, Joe, it appeared, had himself once shot off his little finger. All these points came out from the examination of the earlier witnesses. At last, counsel put the curate himself into the box, and proceeded to examine him briefly as a witness for the defence.

Walter Dene stepped, pale and haggard still, into the witness-box. He had made up his mind to make one final effort "for Christina's happiness." He fumbled nervously all the time at a small glass phial in his pocket, but he answered all questions without a moment's hesitation, and he kept down his emotions with a wonderful composure which excited the admiration of everybody present. There was a general hush to hear him. Did he see the prisoner, Joseph Harley, on the day of the murder? Yes, three times. When was the first occasion? From the library window, just before the vicar left the house. What was Joseph Harley then doing? Walking in the opposite direction from the copse. Did Joseph Harley recognize him? Yes, he touched his hat to him. When was the second occasion? About ten minutes later, when he, Walter, was leaving the vicarage for a stroll. Did Joseph Harley then recognize him? Yes, he touched his hat again, and the curate said, "Good morning, Joe; a fine day for walking." When was the third time? Ten minutes later again, when he was returning from the lane, carrying wounded little King Charlie. Would it have been physically possible for the prisoner to go from the vicarage to the spot where the murder was committed, and back again, in the interval between the first two occasions? It would not. Would it have been physically possible for the prisoner to do so in the interval between the second and third occasions? It would not.

"Then in your opinion, Mr. Dene, it is physically impossible that Joseph Harley can have committed this murder?"

"In my opinion, it is physically impossible."

While Walter Dene solemnly swore amid dead silence to this treble lie, he did not dare to look Joe Harley once in the face; and while Joe Harley listened in amazement to this unexpected assistance to his case—for counsel, suspecting a mistaken identity, had not questioned him too closely on the subject—he had presence of mind enough not to let his astonishment show upon his stolid features. But when Walter had finished his evidence in chief, he stole a glance at Joe; and for a moment their eyes met. Then Walter's fell in utter self-humiliation; and he said to himself fiercely, "I would not so have debased and degraded myself before any man to save my own life—what is my life worth me, after all?—but to save Christina, to save Christina, to save Christina! I have brought all this upon myself for Christina's sake."

Meanwhile, Joe Harley was asking himself curiously what could be the meaning of this new move on parson's part. It was deliberate perjury, Joe felt sure, for parson could not have mistaken another person for him three times over; but what good end for himself could parson hope to gain by it? If it was he who had murdered the vicar (as Joe strongly suspected), why did he not try to press the charge home against the first person who happened to be accused, instead of committing a distinct perjury on purpose to compass his acquittal? Joe Harley, with his simple everyday criminal mind, could not be expected to unravel the intricacies of so complex a personality as Walter Dene's. But even there, on trial for his life, he could not help wondering what on earth young parson could be driving at in this business.

The judge summed up with the usual luminously obvious alternate platitudes. If the jury thought that John had really seen Joe Harley, and that the curate was mistaken in the person whom he thrice saw, or was mistaken once only out of the thrice, or had miscalculated the time between each occurrence, or the time necessary to cover the ground to the gate, then they would find the prisoner guilty of wilful murder. If, on the other hand, they believed John had judged hastily, and that the curate had really seen the prisoner three separate times, and that he had rightly calculated all the intervals, then they would find the prisoner not guilty. The prisoner's case rested entirely upon the alibi. Supposing they thought there was a doubt in the matter, they should give the prisoner the benefit of the doubt. Walter noticed that the judge said in every other case, "If you believe the witness So-and-so," but that in his case he made no such discourteous reservation. As a matter of fact, the one person whose conduct nobody for a moment dreamt of calling in question was the real murderer.

The jury retired for more than an hour. During all that time two men stood there in mortal suspense, intent and haggard, both upon their trial, but not both equally. The prisoner in the dock fixed his arms in a dogged and sullen attitude, the colour half gone from his brown cheek, and his eyes straining with excitement, but showing no outward sign of any emotion except the craven fear of death. Walter Dene stood almost fainting in the body of the court, his bloodless fingers still fumbling nervously at the little phial, and his face deadly pale with the awful pallor of a devouring horror. His heart scarcely beat at all, but at each long slow pulsation he could feel it throb distinctly within his bosom. He saw or heard nothing before him, but kept his aching eyes fixed steadily on the door by which the jury were to enter. Junior counsel nudged one another to notice his agitation, and whispered that that poor young curate had evidently never seen a man tried for his life before.

At last the jury entered. Joe and Walter waited, each in his own manner, breathless for the verdict. "Do you find the prisoner at the bar guilty or not guilty of wilful murder?" Walter took the little phial from his pocket, and held it carefully between his finger and thumb. The awful moment had come; the next word would decide the fate of himself and Christina. The foreman of the jury looked up solemnly, and answered with slow distinctness, "Not guilty." The prisoner leaned back vacantly, and wiped his forehead; but there was an awful cry of relief from one mouth in the body of the court, and Walter Dene sank back into the arms of the bystanders, exhausted with suspense and overcome by the reaction. The crowd remarked among themselves that young Parson Dene was too tender-hearted a man to come into court at a criminal trial. He would break his heart to see even a dog hanged, let alone his fellow-Christians. As for Joe Harley, it was universally admitted that he had had a narrow squeak of it, and that he had got off better than he deserved. The jury gave him the benefit of the doubt.

As soon as all the persons concerned had returned to Churnside, Walter sent at once for Joe Harley. The poacher came to see him in the vicarage library. He was elated and coarsely exultant with his victory, as a relief from the strain he had suffered, after the manner of all vulgar natures.

"Joe," said the clergyman slowly, motioning him into a chair at the other side of the desk, "I know that after this trial Churnside will not be a pleasant place to hold you. All your neighbours believe, in spite of the verdict, that you killed the vicar. I feel sure, however, that you did not commit this murder. Therefore, as some compensation for the suffering of mind to which you have been put, I think it well to send you and your wife and family to Australia or Canada, whichever you like best. I propose also to make you a present of a hundred pounds, to set you up in your new home."

"Make it five hundred, passon," Joe said, looking at him significantly.

Walter smiled quietly, and did not flinch in any way. "I said a hundred," he continued calmly, "and I will make it only a hundred. I should have had no objection to making it five, except for the manner in which you ask it. But you evidently mistake the motive of my gift. I give it out of pure compassion for you, and not out of any other feeling whatsoever."

"Very well, passon," said Joe sullenly, "I accept it."

"You mistake again," Walter went on blandly, for he was himself again now. "You are not to accept it as terms; you are to thank me for it as a pure present. I see we two partially understand each other; but it is important you should understand me exactly as I mean it. Joe Harley, listen to me seriously. I have saved your life. If I had been a man of a coarse and vulgar nature, if I had been like you in a similar predicament, I would have pressed the case against you for obvious personal reasons, and you would have been hanged for it. But I did not press it, because I felt convinced of your innocence, and my sense of justice rose irresistibly against it. I did the best I could to save you; I risked my own reputation to save you; and I have no hesitation now in telling you that to the best of my belief, if the verdict had gone against you, the person who really killed the vicar, accidentally or intentionally, meant to have given himself up to the police, rather than let an innocent man suffer."

"Passon," said Joe Harley, looking at him intently, "I believe as you're tellin' me the truth. I zeen as much in that person's face afore the verdict."

There was a solemn pause for a moment; and then Walter Dene said slowly, "Now that you have withdrawn your claim as a claim, I will stretch a point and make it five hundred. It is little enough for what you have suffered. But I, too, have suffered terribly, terribly."

"Thank you, passon," Joe answered. "I zeen as you were turble anxious."

There was again a moment's pause. Then Walter Dene asked quietly, "How did the vicar's face come to be so bruised and battered?"

"I stumbled up agin 'im accidental like, and didn't know I'd kicked 'un till I'd done it. Must 'a been just a few minutes after you'd 'a left 'un."

"Joe," said the curate in his calmest tone, "you had better go; the money will be sent to you shortly. But if you ever see my face again, or speak or write a word of this to me, you shall not have a penny of it, but shall be prosecuted for intimidation. A hundred before you leave, four hundred in Australia. Now go."

"Very well, passon," Joe answered; and he went.

"Pah!" said the curate with a face of disgust, shutting the door after him, and lighting a perfumed pastille in his little Chinese porcelain incense-burner, as if to fumigate the room from the poacher's offensive presence. "Pah! to think that these affairs should compel one to humiliate and abase one's self before a vulgar clod like that! To think that all his life long that fellow will virtually know—and misinterpret—my secret. He is incapable of understanding that I did it as a duty to Christina. Well, he will never dare to tell it, that's certain, for nobody would believe him if he did; and he may congratulate himself heartily that he's got well out of this difficulty. It will be the luckiest thing in the end that ever happened to him. And now I hope this little episode is finally over."

When the Churnside public learned that Walter Dene meant to carry his belief in Joe Harley's innocence so far as to send him and his family at his own expense out to Australia, they held that the young parson's charity and guilelessness was really, as the doctor said, almost Quixotic. And when, in his anxiety to detect and punish the real murderer, he offered a reward of five hundred pounds from his own pocket for any information leading to the arrest and conviction of the criminal, the Churnside people laughed quietly at his extraordinary childlike simplicity of heart. The real murderer had been caught and tried at Dorchester Assizes, they said, and had only got off by the skin of his teeth because Walter himself had come forward and sworn to a quite improbable and inconclusive alibi. There was plenty of time for Joe to have got to the gate by the short cut, and that he did so everybody at Churnside felt morally certain. Indeed, a few years later a blood-stained bowie-knife was found in the hedge not far from the scene of the murder, and the gamekeeper "could almost 'a took his Bible oath he'd zeen just such a knife along o' Joe Harley."

That was not the end of Walter Dene's Quixotisms, however. When the will was read, it turned out that almost everything was left to the young parson; and who could deserve it better, or spend it more charitably? But Walter, though he would not for the world seem to cast any slight or disrespect upon his dear uncle's memory, did not approve of customs of primogeniture, and felt bound to share the estate equally with his brother Arthur. "Strange," said the head of the firm of Watson and Blenkiron to himself, when he read the little paragraph about this generous conduct in the paper; "I thought the instructions were to leave it to his nephew Arthur, not to his nephew Walter; but there, one forgets and confuses names of people that one does not know so easily." "Gracious goodness!" thought the engrossing clerk; "surely it was the other way on. I wonder if I can have gone and copied the wrong names in the wrong places?" But in a big London business, nobody notes these things as they would have been noted in Churnside; the vicar was always a changeable, pernickety, huffy old fellow, and very likely he had had a reverse will drawn up afterwards by his country lawyer. All the world only thought that Walter Dene's generosity was really almost ridiculous, even in a parson. When he was married to Christina, six months afterwards, everybody said so charming a girl was well mated with so excellent and admirable a husband.

And he really did make a very tender and loving husband and father. Christina believed in him always, for he did his best to foster and keep alive her faith. He would have given up active clerical duty if he could, never having liked it (for he was above hypocrisy), but Christina was against the project, and his bishop would not hear of it. The Church could ill afford to lose such a man as Mr. Dene, the bishop said, in these troubled times; and he begged him as a personal favour to accept the living of Churnside, which was in his gift. But Walter did not like the place, and asked for another living instead, which, being of less value—"so like Mr. Dene to think nothing of the temporalities,"— the bishop even more graciously granted. He has since published a small volume of dainty little poems on uncut paper, considered by some critics as rather pagan in tone for a clergyman, but universally allowed to be extremely graceful, the perfection of poetical form with much delicate mastery of poetical matter. And everybody knows that the author is almost certain to be offered the first vacant canonry in his own cathedral. As for the little episode, he himself has almost forgotten all about it; for those who think a murderer must feel remorse his whole life long, are trying to read their own emotional nature into the wholly dispassionate character of Walter Dene.

AN EPISODE IN HIGH LIFE

Sir Henry Vardon, K.C.B., electrician to the Admiralty, whose title, as everybody knows, was gazetted some six weeks since, is at this moment the youngest living member of the British knighthood. He is now only just thirty, and he has obtained his present high distinction by those remarkable inventions of his in the matter of electrical signalling and lighthouse arrangements which have been so much talked about in Nature this year, and which gained him the gold medal of the Royal Society in 1881. Lady Vardon is one of the youngest and prettiest hostesses in London, and if you would care to hear the history of their courtship here it is.

When Harry Vardon left Oxford, only seven years ago, none of his friends could imagine what he meant by throwing up all his chances of University success. The son of a poor country parson in Devonshire, who had strained his little income to the uttermost to send him to college, Vardon of Magdalen had done credit to his father and himself in all the schools. He gained the best demyship of his year; got a first in classical mods.; and then unaccountably took to reading science, in which he carried everything before him. At the end of his four years, he walked into a scientific fellowship at Balliol as a matter of course; and then, after twelve months' residence, he suddenly surprised the world of Oxford by accepting a tutorship to the young Earl of Surrey, at that time, as you doubtless remember, a minor, aged about sixteen.

But Harry Vardon had good reasons of his own for taking this tutorship. Six months after he became a fellow of Balliol, the old vicar had died unexpectedly, leaving his only other child, Edith, alone and unprovided for, as was indeed natural; for the expenses of Harry's college life had quite eaten up the meagre savings of twenty years at Little Hinton. In order to provide a home for Edith, it was necessary that Harry should find something or other to do which would bring in an immediate income. School-mastering, that refuge of the destitute graduate, was not much to his mind; and so when the senior tutor of Boniface wrote a little note to ask whether he would care to accept the charge of a cub nobleman, as he disrespectfully phrased it, Harry jumped at the offer, and took the proposed salary of 400l. a year with the greatest alacrity. That would far more than suffice for all Edith's simple needs, and he himself could live upon the proceeds of his fellowship, besides finding time to continue his electrical researches. For I will not disguise the fact that Harry only accepted the cub nobleman as a stop-gap, and that he meant even then to make his fortune in the end by those splendid electrical discoveries which will undoubtedly immortalize his name in future ages.

It was summer term when the appointment was made; and the Surrey people (who were poor for their station) had just gone down to Colyford Abbey, the family seat, in the valley of the Axe near Seaton. You have visited the house, I dare say—open to visitors every Tuesday, when the family is absent—a fine somewhat modernized mansion, with some good perpendicular work about it still, in spite of the havoc wrought in it by Inigo Jones, who converted the chapel and refectory of the old Cistercians into a banqueting-hall and ballroom for the first Lord Surrey of the present creation. It was lovely weather when Harry Vardon went down there; and the Abbey, and the terrace, and the park, and the beautiful valley beyond were looking their very best. Harry fell in love with the view at once, and almost fell in love with the inmates too at the first glance.

Lady Surrey, the mother, was sitting on a garden seat in front of the house as the carriage which met him at Colyford station drove up to the door. She was much younger and more beautiful than Harry had at all expected. He had pictured the dowager to himself as a stately old lady of sixty, with white hair and a grand manner; instead of which he found himself face to face with a well-preserved beauty of something less than forty, not above medium height, and still strikingly pretty in a round-faced, mature, but very delicate fashion. She had wavy chestnut hair, regular features, an exquisite set of pearly teeth, full cheeks whose natural roses were perhaps just a trifle increased by not wholly ungraceful art, and above all a lovely complexion quite unspoilt as yet by years. She was dressed as such a person should be dressed, with no affectation of girlishness, but in the style that best shows off ripe beauty and a womanly figure. Harry was always a very impressionable fellow; and I really believe that if Lady Surrey had been alone he would have fallen over head and ears in love with her at first sight.

But there was something which kept him from falling in love at once with Lady Surrey, and that was the girl who sat half reclining on a tiger-skin at her feet, with a little sketching tablet on her lap. He could hardly take full stock of the mother because he was so busy looking at the daughter as well. I shall not attempt to describe Lady Gladys Durant; all pretty girls fall under one of some half-dozen heads, and description at best can really do no more than classify them. Lady Gladys belonged to the tall and graceful aristocratic class, and she was a good specimen of the type at seventeen. Not that Harry Vardon fell in love with her at once; he was really in the pleasing condition of Captain Macheath, too much engaged in looking at two pretty women to be capable even mentally of making a choice between them. Mother and daughter were both almost equally beautiful, each in her own distinct style.

The countess half rose to greet him—it is condescension on the part of a countess to notice the tutor at all, I believe; but though I am no lover of lords myself, I will do the Durants the justice to say that their treatment of Harry was always the very kindliest that could possibly be expected from people of their ideas and traditions.

"Mr. Vardon?" she said interrogatively, as she held out her hand to the new tutor. Harry bowed assent. "I'm glad you have such a lovely day to make your first acquaintance with Colyford. It's a pretty place, isn't it? Gladys, this is Mr. Vardon, who is kindly going to take charge of Surrey for us."

"I'm afraid you don't know what you're going to undertake," said Gladys, smiling and holding out her hand. "He's a dreadful pickle. Do you know this part of the world before, Mr. Vardon?"

"Not just hereabouts," Harry answered; "my father's parish was in North Devon, but I know the greater part of the county very well."

"That's a good thing," said Gladys quickly; "we're all Devonshire people here, and we believe in the county with all our hearts. I wish Surrey took his title from it. It's so absurd to take your title from a place you don't care about only because you've got land there. I love Devonshire people best of any."

"Mr. Vardon would probably like to see his rooms," said the countess. "Parker, will you show him up?"

The rooms were everything that Harry could wish. There was a prettily furnished sitting-room for himself on the front, looking across the terrace, with a view of the valley and the sea in the distance; there was a study next door, for tutor and pupil to work in; there was a cheerful little bedroom behind; and downstairs at the back there was the large bare room for which Harry had specially stipulated, wherein to put his electrical apparatus, for he meant to experiment and work busily at his own subject in his spare time. There was a special servant, too, told off to wait upon him; and altogether Harry felt that if only the social position could be made endurable, he could live very comfortably for a year or two at Colyford Abbey.

There are some men who could never stand such a life at all. There are others who can stand it because they can stand anything. But Harry Vardon belonged to neither class. He was one of those who feel at home in most places, and who can get on in all society alike. In the first place, he was one of the handsomest fellows you ever saw, with large dark eyes, and that particular black moustache that no woman can ever resist. Then again he was tall and had a good presence, which impressed even those most dangerous of critics for a private tutor, the footmen. Moreover, he was clever, chatty, and agreeable; and it never entered into his head that he was not conferring some distinction upon the Surrey family by consenting to be teacher to their young lordling—which, indeed, was after all the sober fact.

The train was in a little before seven, and there was a bit of a drive from the station, so that Harry had only just had time to dress for dinner when the gong sounded. In the drawing-room he met his future pupil, a good-looking, high-spirited, but evidently lazy boy of sixteen. The family was alone, so the earl took down his mother, while Harry gave his arm to Lady Gladys. Before dinner was over, the new tutor had taken the measure of the trio pretty accurately. The countess was clever, that was certain; she took an interest in books and in art, and she could talk lightly but well upon most current topics in the easy sparkling style of a woman of the world. Gladys was clever too, though not booky; she was full of sketching and music, and was delighted to hear that Harry could paint a little in water-colours, besides being the owner of a good violin. As to the boy, his fancy clearly ran for the most part to dogs, guns, and cricket; and indeed, though he was no doubt a very important person as a future member of the British legislature, I think for the purposes of the present story, which is mainly concerned with Harry Vardon's fortunes, we may safely leave him out of consideration. Harry taught him as much as he could be induced to learn for an hour or two every morning, and looked after him as far as possible when he was anywhere within hearing throughout the rest of the day; but as the lad was almost always out around the place somewhere with a gamekeeper or a stable-boy, he hardly entered practically into the current of Harry's life at all, outside the regular hours of study. As a matter of fact, he never learnt much from anybody or did anything worth speaking of; but he has since married a Birmingham heiress with a million or so of her own, and is now one of the most rising young members of the House of Lords.

After dinner, the countess showed Harry her excellent collection of Bartolozzis, and Harry, who knew something about them, showed the countess that she was wrong as to the authenticity of one or two among them. Then Gladys played passably well, and he sang a duet with her, in a way that made her feel a little ashamed of her own singing. And lastly Harry brought down his violin, at which the countess smiled a little, for she thought it audacious on the first evening; but when he played one of his best pieces she smiled again, for she had a good ear and a great deal of taste. After which they all retired to bed, and Gladys remarked to her maid, in the privacy of her own room, that the new tutor was a very pleasant man, and quite a relief after such a stick as Mr. Wilkinson.

At breakfast next morning the party remained unchanged, but at lunch the two younger girls appeared upon the scene, with their governess, Miss Martindale. Though very different in type from Gladys, Ethel Martindale was in her way an equally pretty girl. She was small and mignonne, with delicate little hands, and a light pretty figure, not too slight, but very gracefully proportioned. Her cheeks and chin were charmingly dimpled, and her complexion was just of that faintly-dark tinge that one sees so often combined with light-brown hair and eyes in the moorland parts of Lancashire. Altogether, she was a perfect foil to Gladys, and it would have been difficult for almost any man as he sat at that table to say which of the three, mother, daughter, or governess, was really the prettiest. For my own part, I give my vote unreservedly for the countess, but then I am getting somewhat grizzled now and have long been bald; so my liking turns naturally towards ripe beauty. I hate your self-conscious chits of seventeen, who can only chat and giggle; I like a woman who has something to say for herself. But Harry was just turned twenty-three, and perhaps his choice might, not unnaturally, have gone otherwise.

The governess talked little at lunch, and seemed altogether a rather subdued and timid girl. Harry noticed with pain that she appeared half afraid of speaking to anybody, and also that the footmen made a marked distinction between their manner to him and their manner to her. He would have liked once or twice to kick the fellows for their insolence. After lunch, Gladys and the little ones went for a stroll down towards the river, and Harry followed after with Miss Martindale.

"Do you come from this part of England?" he asked.

"No," answered Ethel, "I come from Lancashire. My father was rector of a small parish on the moors."

Harry's heart smote him. It might have been Edith. What a little turn of chance had made all the difference! "My father was a parson too," he said, and then checked himself for the half-disrespectful word, "but he lived down here in Devonshire. Do you like Colyford?"

"Oh yes, the place, very much. There are delightful rambles, and Lady Gladys and I go out sketching a great deal. And it's a delightful country for flowers."

The place, but not the life, thought Harry. Poor child, it must be very hard for her.

"Mr. Vardon, come on here, I want you," called out Gladys from the little stone bridge. "You know everything. Can you tell me what this flower is?" and she held out a long spray of waving green-stuff.

"Caper spurge," said Harry, looking at it carelessly.

"Oh no," Miss Martindale put in quickly, "Portland spurge, surely."

"So it is," Harry answered, looking closer. "Then you are a bit of a botanist, Miss Martindale?"

"Not a botanist, but very fond of the flowers."

"Miss Martindale's always picking lots of ugly things and bringing them home," said Gladys laughingly; "aren't you, dear?"

Ethel smiled and nodded. So they went on past the bridge and out upon the opposite side, and back again by the little white railings into the park.

For the next three months Harry enjoyed himself in a busy way immensely. Every morning he had his three hours' teaching, and every afternoon he went a walk, or fished in the river, or worked at his electrical machines. To the household at the Abbey such a man was a perfect godsend. For he was a versatile fellow, able to turn his hand to anything, and the Durants lived in a very quiet way, and were glad of somebody to keep the house lively. The money was all tied up till the boy came of age, and even then there wouldn't be much of it. Surrey had been sent to Eton for a month or two and then removed, by request, to prevent more violent measures; after which he was sent to two or three other schools, always with the same result. So he was brought home again and handed over to the domestic persuasion of a private tutor. The only thing that kept him moderately quiet was the possibility of running around the place with the keepers; and the only person who ever taught him anything was Harry Vardon, though even he, I must admit, did not succeed in impressing any very valuable lessons upon the lad's volatile brain. The countess saw few visitors, and so a man like Harry was a real acquisition to the little circle. He was perpetually being wanted by everybody, everywhere, and at the end of three months he was simply indispensable.

Lady Surrey was always consulting him as to the proper place to plant the new wellingtonias, the right aspect for deodars, the best plan for mounting water-colours, and the correct date of all the neighbouring churches. It was so delightful to drive about with somebody who really understood the history and geology and antiquities of the county, she said; and she began to develop an extraordinary interest in prehistoric archæology, and to listen patiently to Harry's disquisitions on the difference between long barrows and round barrows, or on the true nature of the earthworks that cap the top of Membury Hill. Harry for his part was quite ready to discourse volubly on all these subjects, for it was his hobby to impart information, whereof he had plenty; and he liked knocking about the country, examining castles or churches, and laying down the law about matters architectural with much authority to two pretty women. The countess even took an interest in his great electrical investigation, and came into his workshop to hear all about the uses of his mysterious batteries. As for Lady Gladys, she was forever wanting Mr. Vardon's opinion about the exact colour for that shadow by the cottage, Mr. Vardon's aid in practising that difficult bit of Chopin, Mr. Vardon's counsel about the decorative treatment of the passion-flower on that lovely piece of crewel-work. Indeed, contrary to Miss Martindale's express admonition, and all the dictates of propriety, she was always running off to Harry's little sitting-room to ask his advice about five hundred different things, five hundred times in every twenty-four hours.

There was only one person in the household who seemed at all shy of Harry, and that was Miss Martindale. Do what he could, he could never get her to feel at home with him. She seemed always anxious to keep out of his way, and never ready to join in any of his plans. This was annoying, because Harry really liked the poor girl and felt sorry for her lonely position. But as she would have nothing to say to him, why, there was nothing else to be done; so he contented himself with being as polite to her as possible, while respecting her evident wish to be let alone.

One afternoon, when the four had been out for a drive together to visit the old ruins near Cowhayne, and Harry had been sketching with Gladys and lecturing to the countess to his heart's content, he was sitting on the bench by the red cedars, when to his surprise he saw the governess strolling carelessly across the terrace towards him. "Mr. Vardon," she said, standing beside the bench, "I want to say something to you. You mustn't mind my saying it, but I feel it is part of my duty. Do you think you ought to pay so much attention to Gladys? You and I come into a family of this sort on peculiar terms, you know. They don't think we are quite the same sort of human beings as themselves. Now, I'm half afraid—I don't like to say so, but I think it better I should say it than my lady—I'm half afraid that Gladys is getting her head too much filled with you. Whatever she does, you are always helping her. She is forever running off to see you about something or other. She is very young; she meets very few other men; and you have been extremely attentive to her. But when people like these admit you into their family, they do so on the tacit understanding that you will not do what they would call abusing the position. To-day, I half fancied that my lady looked at you once or twice when you were talking to Gladys, and I thought I would try to be brave enough to speak to you about it. If I don't, I think she will."

"Really, Miss Martindale," said Harry, rising and walking by her side towards the laburnum alley, "I'm very glad you have unburdened your mind about this matter. For myself, you know, I don't acknowledge the obligation. I should marry any girl I liked, if she would have me, whatever her artificial position might be; and I should never let any barriers of that sort stand in my way. But I don't know that I have the slightest intention of ever trying to marry Lady Gladys or anybody else of the sort; so while I remain undecided on that point, I shall do as you wish me. By the way, it strikes me now that you have been trying to keep her away from me as much as possible."

"As part of my duty, I think I ought to do so. Yes."

"Well, you may rely upon it, I will give you no more cause for anxiety," said Harry; "so the less we say about it the better. What a lovely sunset, and what a glorious colour on the cliffs at Axmouth!" And he walked down the alley with her two or three times, talking about various indifferent subjects. Somehow he had never managed to get on so well with her before. She was a very nice girl, he thought, really a very nice girl; what a pity she would never take any notice of him in any way! However, he enjoyed that quiet half-hour immensely, and was quite sorry when Lady Surrey came out a little later and joined them, exactly as if she wanted to interrupt their conversation. But what a beautiful woman Lady Surrey was too, as she came across the lawn just then in her garden hat and the pale blue Umritzur shawl thrown loosely across her shapely shoulders! By Jove, she was as handsome a woman, after all, as he had ever seen.

After dinner that evening Lady Surrey sent Gladys off to Miss Martindale's room on some small pretext, and then put Harry down on the sofa beside her to help in arranging those interminable ferns of hers. Evening dress suited the countess best, and she knew it. She was looking even more beautiful than before, with her hair prettily dressed, and the little simple turquoise necklet setting off her white neck; and she talked a great deal to Harry, and was really very charming. No more fascinating widow, he thought, to be found anywhere within a hundred miles. At last she stopped, leaning over the ferns, and sat back a little on the sofa, half fronting him. "Mr. Vardon," she said suddenly, "there is something I wish to speak to you about, privately."

"Certainly," said Harry, half expecting the topic.

"Do you know, I think you ought not to pay such marked attention to Lady Gladys. Two or three times I have fancied I noticed it, and have meant to mention it to you, but I thought it might be unnecessary. On many accounts, however, I think it is best not to let it pass any longer. The difference of station—"

"Excuse me," said Harry, "I'm sorry to differ from you, but I don't acknowledge differences of station."

"Well," said the countess, in a conciliatory tone, "under certain circumstances that may be perfectly correct. A young man in your position and with your talents has of course the whole world before him. He can make himself whatever he pleases. I don't think, Mr. Vardon, I have ever under-estimated the worth of brains. I do feel that knowledge and culture are much greater things after all than mere position. Now, in justice to me, don't you think I do?"

Harry looked at her—she was really a very beautiful woman—and then said, "Yes, I think you have certainly better and more rational tastes than most other people circumstanced as you are."

"I'm so glad you do," the countess answered, heartily. "I don't care for a life of perfect frivolity and fashion, such as one gets in London. If it were not for Gladys's sake I sometimes think I would give it up entirely. Do you know, I often wish my life had been cast very differently—cast among another set of people from the people I have always mixed among. Whenever I meet clever people—literary people and scholars—I always feel so sorry I haven't moved all my life in their world. From one point of view, I quite recognize what you said just now, that these artificial distinctions should not exist between people who are really equals in intellect and culture."

"Naturally not," said Harry, to whom this proposition sounded like a familiar truism.

"But in Lady Gladys's case, I feel I ought to guard her against seeing too much of anybody in particular just at present. She is only seventeen, and she is of course impressionable. Now, you know a great many mothers would not have spoken to you as I do; but I like you, Mr. Vardon, and I feel at home with you. You will promise me not to pay so much attention to Gladys in future, won't you?"

As she looked at him full in the face with her beautiful eyes, Harry felt he could just then have promised her anything. "Yes," he said, "I will promise."

"Thank you," said the countess, looking at him again; "I am very much obliged to you." And then for a moment there was an awkward pause, and they both looked full into one another's eyes without saying a word.

In a minute the countess began again, and said a good many things about what a dreadful waste of life people generally made; and what a privilege it was to know clever people; and what a reality and purpose there was in their lives. A great deal of this sort she said, and in a low pleasant voice. And then there was another awkward pause, and they looked at one another once more.

Harry certainly thought the countess very beautiful, and he liked her very much. She was really kind-hearted and friendly; she was interested in the subjects that pleased him; and she was after all a pretty woman, still young as men count youth, and very agreeable—nay, anxious to please. And then she had said what she said about the artificiality of class distinctions so markedly and pointedly, with such a commentary from her eyes, that Harry half fancied—well, I don't quite know what he fancied. As he sat there beside her on the sofa, with the ferns before him, looking straight into her eyes, and she into his, it must be clear to all my readers that if he had any special proposition to make to her on any abstract subject of human speculation, the time had obviously arrived to make it. But something or other inscrutable kept him back. "Lady Surrey—" he said, and the words stuck in his throat.

"Yes," she answered softly. "Shall ... shall we go on with the ferns?" Lady Surrey gave a little short breath, brought back her eyes from dreamland, and turned with a sudden smile back to the portfolio. For the rest of the evening, the candid historian must admit that they both felt like a pair of fools. Conversation lagged, and I don't think either of them was sorry when the time came for retiring.

It is useless for the clumsy male psychologist to pretend that he can see into the heart of a woman, especially when the normal action of said heart is complicated by such queer conventionalities as that of a countess who feels a distinct liking for her son's tutor: but if I may venture to attempt that impossible feat of clairvoyance without rebuke, I should be inclined to diagnose Lady Surrey's condition as she lay sleepless for an hour or so on her pillow that night somewhat as follows. She thought that Harry Vardon was really a very clever and a very pleasant fellow. She thought that men in society were generally dreadfully empty-headed and horribly vain. She thought that the importance of disparity in age had, as a rule, been immensely overrated. She thought that rank was after all much less valuable than she used to think it when first she married poor dear Surrey, who was really the kindest of men, and a thorough gentleman, but certainly not at all brilliant. She thought that a young man of Harry's talent might, if well connected, get into Parliament and rise, like Beaconsfield, to any position. She thought he was very frank, and open, and gentlemanly; and very handsome too. She thought he had half hesitated whether he should propose to her or not, and had then drawn back because he was not certain of the consequences. She thought that if he had proposed to her—well, perhaps—why, yes, she might even possibly have accepted him. She thought he would probably propose in earnest, before long, as soon as he saw that she was not wholly averse to his attentions. She thought in that case she might perhaps provisionally accept him, and get him to try what he could do in the way of obtaining some sort of position—she didn't exactly know what—where he could more easily marry her with the least possible shock to the feelings of society. And she thought that she really didn't know before for twenty years at least how great a goose she positively was.

Next morning, after breakfast, Lady Surrey sent for Gladys to come to her in her boudoir. Then she put her daughter in a chair by the window, drew her own close to it, laid her hand kindly on her shoulder—she was a nice little woman at heart, was the countess—and said to her gently, "My dear

Gladys, there's a little matter I want to talk to you about. You are still very young, you know, dear; and I think you ought to be very careful about not letting your feelings be played upon in any way, however unconsciously. Now, you walk and talk a great deal too much, dear, with Mr. Vardon. In many ways, it would be well that you should. Mr. Vardon is very clever, and very well informed, and a very instructive companion. I like you to talk to intelligent people, and to hear intelligent people talk; it gives you something that mere books can never give. But you know, Gladys, you should always remember the disparity in your stations. I don't deny that there's a great deal in all that sort of thing that's very conventional and absurd, my dear; but still, girls are girls, and if they're thrown too much with any one young man"—Lady Surrey was going to add, "especially when he's handsome and agreeable," but she checked herself in time—"they're very apt to form an affection for him. Of course I'm not suggesting that you're likely to do anything of the sort with Mr. Vardon—I don't for a moment suppose you would—but a girl can never be too careful. I hope you know your position too well;" here Lady Surrey was conscious of certain internal qualms; "and indeed whether it was Mr. Vardon or anybody else, you are much too young to fill your head with such notions at your age. Of course, if some really good offer had been made to you even in your first season—say Lord St. Ives or Sir Montague—I don't say it might not have been prudent to accept it; but under ordinary circumstances, a girl does best to think as little as possible about such things until she is twenty at least. However, I hope in future you'll remember that I don't wish you to be quite so familiar in your intercourse with Mr. Vardon."

"Very well, mamma," said Gladys quietly, drawing herself up; "I have heard what you want to say, and I shall try to do as you wish. But I should like to say something in return, if you'll be so kind as to listen to me."

"Certainly, darling," Lady Surrey answered, with a vague foreboding of something wrong.

"I don't say I care anymore for Mr. Vardon than for anybody else; I haven't seen enough of him to know whether I care for him or not. But if ever I do care for anybody, it will be for somebody like him, and not for somebody like Lord St. Ives or Monty Fitzroy. I don't like the men I meet in town; they all talk to us as if we were dolls or babies. I don't want to marry a man who says to himself, as Surrey says already, 'Ah, I shall look out for some rich girl or other and make her a countess, if she's a good girl, and if she suits me.' I'd rather have a man like Mr. Vardon than any of the men we ever meet in London."

"But, my darling," said Lady Surrey, quite alarmed at Gladys' too serious tone, "surely there are gentlemen quite as clever and quite as intellectual as Mr. Vardon."

"Mamma!" cried Gladys, rising, "do you mean to say Mr. Vardon is not a gentleman?"

"Gladys, Gladys! sit down, dear. Don't get so excited. Of course he is. I trust I have as great a respect as anybody for talent and culture. But what I meant to say was this—can't you find as much talent and culture among people of our own station as—as among people of Mr. Vardon's?"

"No," said Gladys shortly.

"Really, my dear, you are too hard upon the peerage."

"Well, mamma, can you mention any one that we know who is?" asked the peremptory girl.

"Not exactly in our own set," said Lady Surrey hesitatingly; "but surely there must be some."

"I don't know them," Gladys replied quietly, "and till I do know them, I shall remain of my own opinion still. If you wish me not to see so much of Mr. Vardon, I shall try to do as you say; but if I happen to like any particular person, whether he's a peer or a ploughboy, I can't help liking him, so there's an end of it." And Gladys kissed her mother demurely on the forehead, and walked with a stately sweep out of the room.

"It's perfectly clear," said Lady Surrey to herself, "that that girl's in love with Mr. Vardon, and what on earth I'm to do about it is to me a mystery." And indeed Lady Surrey's position was by no means an easy one. On the one hand, she felt that whatever she herself, who was a person of mature years, might happen to do, it would be positively wicked in her to allow a young girl like Gladys to throw herself away on a man in Harry Vardon's position. Without any shadow of an arrière pensée, that was her genuine feeling as a mother and a member of society. But then, on the other hand, how could she oppose it, if she really ever thought herself, even conditionally, of marrying Harry Vardon? Could she endure that her daughter should think she had acted as her rival? Could she press the point about Harry's conventional disadvantages, when she herself had some vague idea that if Harry offered himself as Gladys' step-father, she would not be wholly disinclined to consider his proposal? Could she set it down as a crime in her daughter to form the very self-same affection which she herself had well-nigh formed? Moreover, she couldn't help feeling in her heart that Gladys was right, after all; and that the daughter's defiance of conventionality was implicitly inherited from the mother. If she had met Harry Vardon twenty years ago, she would have thought and spoken much like Gladys; in fact, though she didn't speak, she thought so, very nearly, even now. I am sorry that I am obliged to write out these faint outlines of ideas in all the brutal plainness of the English language as spoken by men; I cannot give all those fine shades of unspoken reservations and womanly self-deceptive subterfuges by which the poor little countess half disguised her own meaning even from herself; but at least you will not be surprised to hear that in the end she lay down on the little couch in the corner, covered her face with chagrin and disappointment, and had a good cry. Then she got up an hour later, washed her eyes carefully to take off the redness, put on her pretty dove-coloured morning gown with the lace trimming—she looked charming in lace—and went down smiling to lunch, as pleasant and cheery a little widow of thirty-seven as ever you would wish to see. Upon my soul, Harry Vardon, I really almost think you will be a fool if you don't finally marry the countess!

"Gladys," said little Lord Surrey to his sister that evening, when she came into his room on her way upstairs to bed—"Gladys, it's my opinion you're getting too sweet on this fellow Vardon."

"I shall be obliged, Surrey, if you'll mind your own business, and allow me to mind mine."

"Oh, it's no use coming the high and mighty over me, I can tell you, so don't you try it on. Besides, I have something I want to speak to you about particularly. It's my opinion also that my lady's doing the very same thing."

"What nonsense, Surrey!" cried Gladys, colouring up to her eyebrows in a second: "how dare you say such a thing about mamma?" But a light broke in upon her suddenly all the same, and a number of little unnoticed circumstances flashed back at once upon her memory with a fresh flood of meaning.

"Nonsense or not, it's true, I know; and what I want to say to you is this—If old Vardon's to marry either of you, it ought to be you, because that would save mamma at any rate from making a fool of herself. As far as I'm concerned, I'd rather neither of you did; for I don't see why either of you should want to marry a beggarly fellow of a tutor"—Gladys' eyes flashed fire—"though Vardon's a decent enough chap in his way, if that was all; but at any rate, as one or other of you's cock-sure to do it, I don't want him for a step-father. So you see, as far as that goes, I back the filly. Now, say no more about it, but go to bed like a good girl, and mind, whatever you do, you don't forget to say your prayers. Good night, old girl."

"I wouldn't marry a fellow like Surrey," said Gladys to herself, as she went upstairs, "no, not if he was the premier duke of England!"

For the next three weeks there was such a comedy of errors and cross-purposes at Colyford Abbey as was never seen before anywhere outside of one of Mr. Gilbert's clever extravaganzas. Lady Surrey tried to keep Gladys in every possible way out of Harry's sight; while her brother tried in every possible way to throw them together. Gladys on her part half avoided him, and yet grew somewhat more confidential than ever whenever she happened to talk with him. Harry did not feel quite so much at home as before with Lady Surrey; he had an uncomfortable sense that he had failed to acquit himself as he ought to have done; while Lady Surrey had a half suspicion that she had let him see her unfledged secret a little too early and too openly. The natural consequence of all this was that Harry was cast far more than before upon the society of Ethel Martindale, with whom he often strolled about the shrubbery till very close upon the dressing gong. Ethel did not come down to dinner—she dined with the little ones at the family luncheon; and that horrid galling distinction cut Harry to the quick every night when he left her to go in. Every day, too, it began to dawn upon him more clearly that the vague reason which had kept him back from proposing to Lady Surrey on that eventful night was just this—that Ethel Martindale had made herself a certain vacant niche in his unfurnished heart. She was a dear, quiet, unassuming little girl, but so very graceful, so very tender, so very womanly, that she crept into his affections unawares without possibility of resistance. The countess was a beautiful and accomplished woman of the world, with a real heart left in her still, but not quite the sort of tender, shrinking, girlish heart that Harry wanted. Gladys was a lovely girl with stately manners and a wonderfully formed character, but too great and too redolent of society for Harry. He admired them both, each in her own way, but he couldn't possibly have lived a lifetime with either. But Ethel, dear, meek, pretty, gentle little Ethel—well, there, I'm not going to repeat for you all the raptures that Harry went into over that perennial and ever rejuvenescent theme. For, to tell you the truth, about three weeks after the night when Harry did not propose to the countess, he actually did propose to Ethel Martindale. And Ethel, after many timid protests, after much demure self-depreciation and declaration of utter unworthiness for such a man—which made Harry wild with indignation—did finally let him put her little hand to his lips, and whispered a sort of broken and blushing "Yes."

What a fool he had been, he thought that evening, to suppose for half a second that Lady Surrey had ever meant to regard him in any other light than as her son's tutor. He hated himself for his own nonsensical vanity. Who was he that he should fancy all the women in England were in love with him?

Next morning's Times contained that curious announcement about its being the intention of the Government to appoint an electrician to the Admiralty, and inviting applications from distinguished men of science. Now Harry, young as he was, had just perfected his great system of the double-revolving commutator and back-action rheostat (Patent Office, No. 18,237,504), and had sent in a paper on the subject which had been read with great success at the Royal Society. The famous Professor Brusegay himself had described it as a remarkable invention, likely to prove of immense practical importance to telegraphy and electrical science generally. So when Harry saw the announcement that morning, he made up his mind to apply for the appointment at once; and he thought that if he got it, as the salary was a good one, he might before long marry Ethel, and yet manage to keep Edith in the same comfort as before.

Lady Surrey saw the paragraph too, and had her own ideas about what it might be made to do. It was the very opening that Harry wanted, and if he got it, why then no doubt he might make the proposal which he evidently felt afraid to make, poor fellow, in his present position. So she went into her boudoir immediately after breakfast, and wrote two careful and cautiously worded little notes. One was to Dr. Brusegay, whom she knew well, mentioning to him that her son's tutor was the author of that remarkable paper on commutators, and that she thought he would probably be admirably fitted for the post, but that on that point the Professor himself was the best judge; the other was to her cousin, Lord Ardenleigh, who was a great man in the government of the day, suggesting casually that he should look into the claims of her friend, Mr. Vardon, for this new place at the Admiralty. Two nicer little notes, written with better tact and judgment, it would be difficult to find.

At that very moment Harry was also sitting down in his own room, after five minutes' consultation with Ethel, to make formal application for the new post. And after lunch the same day he spoke to Lady Surrey upon the subject.

"There is one special reason," he said, "why I should like to get this post, and I think I ought to let you know it now." Poor little Lady Surrey's heart fluttered like a girl's. "The fact is, I am anxious to obtain a position which would enable me to marry." ("How very bluntly he puts it," said the countess to herself.) "I ought to tell you, I think, that I have proposed to Miss Martindale, and she has accepted me."

Miss Martindale! Great heavens, how the room reeled round the poor little woman, as she stood with her hand on the table, trying to balance herself, trying to conceal her shame and mortification, trying to look as if the announcement did not concern her in any way. Poor, dear, good little countess; from my heart I pity you. Miss Martindale! why, she had never even thought of her. A mere governess, a nobody; and Harry Vardon, with his magnificent intellect and splendid prospects, was going to throw himself away on that girl! She could hardly control herself to answer him, but with a great effort she gulped down her feelings, and remarked that Ethel Martindale was a very good girl, and would doubtless make an admirable wife. And then she walked quietly out of the room, stepped up the stairs somewhat faster, rushed into her boudoir, double-locked the door, and burst into a perfect flood of hot scalding tears. At that moment she began to realize the fact that she had in truth liked Harry Vardon much more than a little.

By-and-by she got up, went over to her desk, took out the two unposted notes, tore them into fragments, and then carefully burnt them up piece by piece, in a perfect holocaust of white paper. What a wicked vindictive little countess! Was she going to spoil these two young people's lives, to throw every possible obstacle in the way of their marriage? Not a bit of it. As soon as her eyes allowed her, she sat down and wrote two more notes, a great deal stronger and better than before; for this time she need not fear the possibility of after reflections from an unkind world. She said a great deal in a casual half-hinting fashion about Harry's merits, and remarked upon the loss that she should sustain in the removal of such a tutor from Lord Surrey; but she felt that sooner or later his talents must get him a higher recognition, and she hoped Dr. Brusegay and her cousin would use their influence to obtain him the appointment. Then she went downstairs feeling like a Christian martyr, kissed and congratulated Ethel, talked gaily about Bartolozzi to Harry, and tried to make believe that she took the engagement as a matter of course. Nothing in fact, as she remarked to Gladys, could possibly be more suitable. Gladys bit her tongue, and answered shortly that she didn't herself perceive any special natural congruity about the match, but perhaps her mother was better informed on the subject.

Now, we all know that in the matter of public appointment anything like backstairs influence or indirect canvassing is positively fatal to the success of a candidate. Accordingly, it may surprise you to learn that when Professor Brusegay (who held the appointment virtually in his hands) opened his letters next morning he said to his wife, "Why, Maria, that young fellow Vardon who wrote that astonishingly clever paper on commutators, you know, is tutor at Lady Surrey's, and she wants him to get this place at the Admiralty. We must really see what we can do about it. Lady Surrey is such a very useful person to know, and besides it's so important to keep on good terms with her, for the Paulsons would be absolutely intolerable if we hadn't its acquaintance in the peerage to play off against their Lord Poodlebury." And when the Professor shortly afterwards mentioned Harry's name to Lord Ardenleigh, his lordship remarked immediately, "Why, bless my soul, that's the very man Amelia wrote to me about. He shall have the place, by all means." And they both wrote back nice little notes to Lady Surrey, to say that she might consider the matter settled, but that she mustn't mention it to Harry until the appointment was regularly announced. Anything so remarkable in this age of purity I for my part have seldom heard of.

Lady Surrey never did mention the matter to Harry from that day to this; and Sir Henry Vardon, K.C.B., does not for a moment imagine even now that he owes his advancement to anything but his own native merits. He married Ethel shortly after, and a prettier or more blushing bride you never saw. Lady Surrey has been their best friend in society, and still sighs occasionally when she sees Harry a great magnate in his way, and thinks of the narrow escape he had that night at Colyford. As to Gladys, she consistently refused several promising heirs, at least twenty younger sons, and a score or so of wealthy young men whose papas were something in the City, her first five seasons; and then, to Lord Surrey's horror, she married a young Scotchman from Glasgow, who was merely a writer for some London paper, and had nothing on earth but a head on his shoulders to bless himself with. His lordship himself "bagged an heiress" as he expressively puts it, with several thousands a year of her own, and is now one of the most respected members of his party, who may be counted upon always to vote straight, and never to have any opinions of his own upon any subject except the improvement of the British racehorse. He often wishes Gladys had taken his advice and married Vardon, who is at least in respectable society, instead of that shock-headed Scotch fellow—but there, the girl was always full of fancies, and never would behave like other people.

For myself, I am a horrid radical, and republican, and all that sort of thing, and have a perfectly rabid hatred of titles and so forth, don't you know?—but still, on the first day when Ethel went to call on the countess dowager after Harry was knighted, I happened to be present (purely on business), and heard her duly announced as "Lady Vardon:" and I give you my word of honour I could not find it in my heart to grudge the dear little woman the flush of pride that rose upon her cheek as she entered the room for the first time in her new position. It was a pleasure to me (who know the whole story) to see Lady Surrey kiss the little ex-governess warmly on her cheek and say to her, "My dear Lady Vardon, I am so glad, so very very glad." And I really believe she meant it. After all, in spite of her little weakness, there is a great deal of human nature left in the countess.

MY NEW YEARS EVE AMONG THE MUMMIES

I have been a wanderer and a vagabond on the face of the earth for a good many years now, and I have certainly had some odd adventures in my time; but I can assure you, I never spent twenty-four queerer hours than those which I passed some twelve months since in the great unopened Pyramid of Abu Yilla.

The way I got there was itself a very strange one. I had come to Egypt for a winter tour with the Fitz-Simkinses, to whose daughter Editha I was at that precise moment engaged. You will probably remember that old Fitz-Simkins belonged originally to the wealthy firm of Simkinson and Stokoe, worshipful vintners; but when the senior partner retired from the business and got his knighthood, the College of Heralds opportunely discovered that his ancestors had changed their fine old Norman name for its English equivalent some time about the reign of King Richard I.; and they immediately authorized the old gentleman to resume the patronymic and the armorial bearings of his distinguished forefathers. It's really quite astonishing how often these curious coincidences crop up at the College of Heralds.

Of course it was a great catch for a landless and briefless barrister like myself—dependent on a small fortune in South American securities, and my precarious earnings as a writer of burlesque—to secure such a valuable prospective property as Editha Fitz-Simkins. To be sure, the girl was undeniably plain; but I have known plainer girls than she was, whom forty thousand pounds converted into My Ladies: and if Editha hadn't really fallen over head and ears in love with me, I suppose old Fitz-Simkins would never have consented to such a match. As it was, however, we had flirted so openly and so desperately during the Scarborough season, that it would have been difficult for Sir Peter to break it off: and so I had come to Egypt on a tour of insurance to secure my prize, following in the wake of my future mother-in-law, whose lungs were supposed to require a genial climate—though in my private opinion they were really as creditable a pair of pulmonary appendages as ever drew breath.

Nevertheless, the course of our true love did not run so smoothly as might have been expected. Editha found me less ardent than a devoted squire should be; and on the very last night of the old year she got up a regulation lovers' quarrel, because I had sneaked away from the boat that afternoon, under the guidance of our dragoman, to witness the seductive performances of some fair Ghawázi, the dancing girls of a neighbouring town. How she found it out heaven only knows, for I gave that rascal Dimitri five piastres to hold his tongue: but she did find it out somehow, and chose to regard it as an offence of the first magnitude: a mortal sin only to be expiated by three days of penance and humiliation.

I went to bed that night, in my hammock on deck, with feelings far from satisfactory. We were moored against the bank at Abu Yilla, the most pestiferous hole between thee cataracts and the Delta. The mosquitoes were worse than the ordinary mosquitoes of Egypt, and that is saying a great deal. The heat was oppressive even at night, and the malaria from the lotus beds rose like a palpable mist before my eyes. Above all, I was getting doubtful whether Editha Fitz-Simkins might not after all slip between my fingers. I felt wretched and feverish: and yet I had delightful interlusive recollections, in between, of that lovely little Gháziyah, who danced that exquisite, marvellous, entrancing, delicious, and awfully oriental dance that I saw in the afternoon.

By Jove, she was a beautiful creature. Eyes like two full moons; hair like Milton's Penseroso; movements like a poem of Swinburne's set to action. If Editha was only a faint picture of that girl now! Upon my word, I was falling in love with a Gháziyah!

Then the mosquitoes came again. Buzz—buzz—buzz. I make a lunge at the loudest and biggest, a sort of prima donna in their infernal opera. I kill the prima donna, but ten more shrill performers come in its place. The frogs croak dismally in the reedy shallows. The night grows hotter and hotter still. At last, I can stand it no longer. I rise up, dress myself lightly, and jump ashore to find some way of passing the time.

Yonder, across the flat, lies the great unopened Pyramid of Abu Yilla. We are going to-morrow to climb to the top; but I will take a turn to reconnoitre in that direction now. I walk across the moonlit fields, my soul still divided between Editha and the Gháziyah, and approach the solemn mass of huge, antiquated granite-blocks standing out so grimly against the pale horizon. I feel half awake, half asleep, and altogether feverish: but I poke about the base in an aimless sort of way, with a vague idea that I may perhaps discover by chance the secret of its sealed entrance, which has ere now baffled so many pertinacious explorers and learned Egyptologists.

As I walk along the base, I remember old Herodotus's story, like a page from the "Arabian Nights," of how King Rhampsinitus built himself a treasury, wherein one stone turned on a pivot like a door; and how the builder availed himself of this his cunning device to steal gold from the king's storehouse. Suppose the entrance to the unopened Pyramid should be by such a door. It would be curious if I should chance to light upon the very spot.

I stood in the broad moonlight, near the north-east angle of the great pile, at the twelfth stone from the corner. A random fancy struck me, that I might turn this stone by pushing it inward on the left side. I leant against it with all my weight, and tried to move it on the imaginary pivot. Did it give way a fraction of an inch? No, it must have been mere fancy. Let me try again. Surely it is yielding! Gracious Osiris, it has moved an inch or more! My heart beats fast, either with fever or excitement, and I try a third time. The rust of centuries on the pivot wears slowly off, and the stone turns ponderously round, giving access to a low dark passage.

It must have been madness which led me to enter the forgotten corridor, alone, without torch or match, at that hour of the evening; but at any rate I entered. The passage was tall enough for a man to walk erect, and I could feel, as I groped slowly along, that the wall was composed of smooth polished granite, while the floor sloped away downward with a slight but regular descent. I walked with trembling heart and faltering feet for some forty or fifty yards down the mysterious vestibule: and then I felt myself brought suddenly to a standstill by a block of stone placed right across the pathway. I had had nearly enough for one evening, and I was preparing to return to the boat, agog with my new discovery, when my attention was suddenly arrested by an incredible, a perfectly miraculous fact.

The block of stone which barred the passage was faintly visible as a square, by means of a struggling belt of light streaming through the seams. There must be a lamp or other flame burning within. What if this were a door like the outer one, leading into a chamber perhaps inhabited by some dangerous band of outcasts? The light was a sure evidence of human occupation: and yet the outer door swung rustily on its pivot as though it had never been opened for ages. I paused a moment in fear before I ventured to try the stone: and then, urged on once more by some insane impulse, I turned the massive block with all my might to the left. It gave way slowly like its neighbour, and finally opened into the central hall.

Never as long as I live shall I forget the ecstasy of terror, astonishment, and blank dismay which seized upon me when I stepped into that seemingly enchanted chamber. A blaze of light first burst upon my eyes, from jets of gas arranged in regular rows tier above tier, upon the columns and walls of the vast apartment. Huge pillars, richly painted with red, yellow, blue, and green decorations, stretched in endless succession down the dazzling aisles. A floor of polished syenite reflected the splendour of the lamps, and afforded a base for red granite sphinxes and dark purple images in porphyry of the cat-faced goddess Pasht, whose form I knew so well at the Louvre and the British Museum. But I had no eyes for any of these lesser marvels, being wholly absorbed in the greatest marvel of all: for there, in royal state and with mitred head, a living Egyptian king, surrounded by his coiffured court, was banqueting in the flesh upon a real throne, before a table laden with Memphian delicacies!

I stood transfixed with awe and amazement, my tongue and my feet alike forgetting their office, and my brain whirling round and round, as I remember it used to whirl when my health broke down utterly at Cambridge after the Classical Tripos. I gazed fixedly at the strange picture before me, taking in all its details in a confused way, yet quite incapable of understanding or realizing any part of its true import. I saw the king in the centre of the hall, raised on a throne of granite inlaid with gold and ivory; his head crowned with the peaked cap of Rameses, and his curled hair flowing down his shoulders in a set and formal frizz. I saw priests and warriors on either side, dressed in the costumes which I had often carefully noted in our great collections; while bronze-skinned maids, with light garments round their waists, and limbs displayed in graceful picturesqueness, waited upon them, half nude, as in the wall paintings which we had lately examined at Karnak and Syene. I saw the ladies, clothed from head to foot in dyed linen garments, sitting apart in the background, banqueting by themselves at a separate table; while dancing girls, like older representatives of my yesternoon friends, the Ghawázi, tumbled before them in strange attitudes, to the music of four-stringed harps and long straight pipes. In short, I beheld as in a dream the whole drama of everyday Egyptian royal life, playing itself out anew under my eyes, in its real original properties and personages.

Gradually, as I looked, I became aware that my hosts were no less surprised at the appearance of their anachronistic guest than was the guest himself at the strange living panorama which met his eyes. In a moment music and dancing ceased; the banquet paused in its course, and the king and his nobles stood up in undisguised astonishment to survey the strange intruder.

Some minutes passed before any one moved forward on either side. At last a young girl of royal appearance, yet strangely resembling the Gháziyah of Abu Yilla, and recalling in part the laughing maiden in the foreground of Mr. Long's great canvas at the previous Academy, stepped out before the throng.

"May I ask you," she said in Ancient Egyptian, "who you are, and why you come hither to disturb us?"

I was never aware before that I spoke or understood the language of the hieroglyphics: yet I found I had not the slightest difficulty in comprehending or answering her question. To say the truth, Ancient Egyptian, though an extremely tough tongue to decipher in its written form, becomes as easy as love-making when spoken by a pair of lips like that Pharaonic princess's. It is really very much the same as English, pronounced in a rapid and somewhat indefinite whisper, and with all the vowels left out.

"I beg ten thousand pardons for my intrusion," I answered apologetically; "but I did not know that this Pyramid was inhabited, or I should not have entered your residence so rudely. As for the points you wish to know, I am an English tourist, and you will find my name upon this card;" saying which I handed her one from the case which I had fortunately put into my pocket, with conciliatory politeness. The princess examined it closely, but evidently did not understand its import.

"In return," I continued, "may I ask you in what august presence I now find myself by accident?"

A court official stood forth from the throng, and answered in a set heraldic tone: "In the presence of the illustrious monarch, Brother of the Sun, Thothmes the Twenty-seventh, king of the Eighteenth Dynasty."

"Salute the Lord of the World," put in another official in the same regulation drone.

I bowed low to his Majesty, and stepped out into the hall. Apparently my obeisance did not come up to Egyptian standards of courtesy, for a suppressed titter broke audibly from the ranks of bronze-skinned waiting-women. But the king graciously smiled at my attempt, and turning to the nearest nobleman, observed in a voice of great sweetness and self-contained majesty: "This stranger, Ombos, is certainly a very curious person. His appearance does not at all resemble that of an Ethiopian or other savage, nor does he look like the pale-faced sailors who come to us from the Achaian land beyond the sea. His features, to be sure, are not very different from theirs; but his extraordinary and singularly inartistic dress shows him to belong to some other barbaric race."

I glanced down at my waistcoat, and saw that I was wearing my tourist's check suit, of grey and mud colour, with which a Bond Street tailor had supplied me just before leaving town, as the latest thing out in fancy tweeds. Evidently these Egyptians must have a very curious standard of taste not to admire our pretty and graceful style of male attire.

"If the dust beneath your Majesty's feet may venture upon a suggestion," put in the officer whom the king had addressed, "I would hint that this young man is probably a stray visitor from the utterly uncivilized lands of the North. The head-gear which he carries in his hand obviously betrays an Arctic habitat."

I had instinctively taken off my round felt hat in the first moment of surprise, when I found myself in the midst of this strange throng, and I standing now in a somewhat embarrassed posture, holding it awkwardly before me like a shield to protect my chest.

"Let the stranger cover himself," said the king.

"Barbarian intruder, cover yourself," cried the herald. I noticed throughout that the king never directly addressed anybody save the higher officials around him.

I put on my hat as desired. "A most uncomfortable and silly form of tiara indeed," said the great Thothmes.

"Very unlike your noble and awe-spiring mitre, Lion of Egypt," answered Ombos.

"Ask the stranger his name," the king continued.

It was useless to offer another card, so I mentioned it in a clear voice.

"An uncouth and almost unpronounceable designation truly," commented his Majesty to the Grand Chamberlain beside him. "These savages speak strange languages, widely different from the flowing tongue of Memnon and Sesostris."

The chamberlain bowed his assent with three low genuflexions. I began to feel a little abashed at these personal remarks, and I almost think (though I shouldn't like it to be mentioned in the Temple) that a blush rose to my cheek.

The beautiful princess, who had been standing near me meanwhile in an attitude of statuesque repose, now appeared anxious to change the current of the conversation. "Dear father," she said with a respectful inclination, "surely the stranger, barbarian though he be, cannot relish such pointed allusions to his person and costume. We must let him feel the grace and delicacy of Egyptian refinement. Then he may perhaps carry back with him some faint echo of its cultured beauty to his northern wilds."

"Nonsense, Hatasou," replied Thothmes XXVII. testily. "Savages have no feelings, and they are as incapable of appreciating Egyptian sensibility as the chattering crow is incapable of attaining the dignified reserve of the sacred crocodile."

"Your Majesty is mistaken," I said, recovering my self-possession gradually and realizing my position as a free-born Englishman before the court of a foreign despot—though I must allow that I felt rather less confident than usual, owing to the fact that we were not represented in the Pyramid by a British Consul—"I am an English tourist, a visitor from a modern land whose civilization far surpasses the rude culture of early Egypt; and I am accustomed to respectful treatment from all other nationalities, as becomes a citizen of the First Naval Power in the World."

My answer created a profound impression. "He has spoken to the Brother of the Sun," cried Ombos in evident perturbation. "He must be of the Blood Royal in his own tribe, or he would never have dared to do so!"

"Otherwise," added a person whose dress I recognized as that of a priest, "he must be offered up in expiation to Amon-Ra immediately."

As a rule I am a decently truthful person, but under these alarming circumstances I ventured to tell a slight fib with an air of nonchalant boldness. "I am a younger brother of our reigning king," I said without a moment's hesitation; for there was nobody present to gainsay me, and I tried to salve my conscience by reflecting that at any rate I was only claiming consanguinity with an imaginary personage.

"In that case," said King Thothmes, with more geniality in his tone, "there can be no impropriety in my addressing you personally. Will you take a place at our table next to myself, and we can converse together without interrupting a banquet which must be brief enough in any circumstances? Hatasou, my dear, you may seat yourself next to the barbarian prince."

I felt a visible swelling to the proper dimensions of a Royal Highness as I sat down by the king's right hand. The nobles resumed their places, the bronze-skinned waitresses left off standing like soldiers in a row and staring straight at my humble self, the goblets went round once more, and a comely maid soon brought me meat, bread, fruits, and date wine.

All this time I was naturally burning with curiosity to inquire who my strange hosts might be, and how they had preserved their existence for so many centuries in this undiscovered hall; but I was obliged to wait until I had satisfied his Majesty of my own nationality, the means by which I had entered the Pyramid, the general state of affairs throughout the world at the present moment, and fifty thousand other matters of a similar sort. Thothmes utterly refused to believe my reiterated assertion that our existing civilization was far superior to the Egyptian; "because," said he, "I see from your dress that your nation is utterly devoid of taste or invention;" but he listened with great interest to my account of modern society, the steam-engine, the Permissive Prohibitory Bill, the telegraph, the House of Commons, Home Rule, and the other blessings of our advanced era, as well as to a brief résumé of European history from the rise of the Greek culture to the Russo-Turkish war. At last his questions were nearly exhausted, and I got a chance of making a few counter inquiries on my own account.

"And now," I said, turning to the charming Hatasou, whom I thought a more pleasing informant than her august papa, "I should like to know who you are."

"What, don't you know?" she cried with unaffected surprise. "Why, we're mummies."

She made this astounding statement with just the same quiet unconsciousness as if she had said, "we're French," or "we're Americans." I glanced round the walls, and observed behind the columns, what I had not noticed till then—a large number of empty mummy-cases, with their lids placed carelessly by their sides.

"But what are you doing here?" I asked in a bewildered way.

"Is it possible," said Hatasou, "that you don't really know the object of embalming? Though your manners show you to be an agreeable and well-bred young man, you must excuse my saying that you are shockingly ignorant. We are made into mummies in order to preserve our immortality. Once in every thousand years we wake up for twenty-four hours, recover our flesh and blood, and banquet once more upon the mummied dishes and other good things laid by for us in the Pyramid. To-day is the first day of a millennium, and so we have waked up for the sixth time since we were first embalmed."

"The sixth time?" I inquired incredulously. "Then you must have been dead six thousand years."

"Exactly so."

"But the world has not yet existed so long," I cried, in a fervour of orthodox horror.

"Excuse me, barbarian prince. This is the first day of the three hundred and twenty-seven thousandth millennium."

My orthodoxy received a severe shock. However, I had been accustomed to geological calculations, and was somewhat inclined to accept the antiquity of man; so I swallowed the statement without more ado. Besides, if such a charming girl as Hatasou had asked me at that moment to turn Mohammedan, or to worship Osiris, I believe I should incontinently have done so.

"You wake up only for a single day and night, then?" I said.

"Only for a single day and night. After that, we go to sleep for another millennium."

"Unless you are meanwhile burned as fuel on the Cairo Railway," I added mentally. "But how," I continued aloud, "do you get these lights?"

"The Pyramid is built above a spring of inflammable gas. We have a reservoir in one of the side chambers in which it collects during the thousand years. As soon as we awake, we turn it on at once from the tap, and light it with a lucifer match."

"Upon my word," I interposed, "I had no notion you Ancient Egyptians were acquainted with the use of matches."

"Very likely not. 'There are more things in heaven and earth, Cephrenes, than are dreamt of in your philosophy,' as the bard of Philæ puts it."

Further inquiries brought out all the secrets of that strange tomb-house, and kept me fully interested till the close of the banquet. Then the chief priest solemnly rose, offered a small fragment of meat to a deified crocodile, who sat in a meditative manner by the side of his deserted mummy-case, and declared the feast concluded for the night. All rose from their places, wandered away into the long corridors or side-aisles, and formed little groups of talkers under the brilliant gas-lamps.

For my part, I scrolled off with Hatasou down the least illuminated of the colonnades, and took my seat beside a marble fountain, where several fish (gods of great sanctity, Hatasou assured me) were disporting themselves in a porphyry basin. How long we sat there I cannot tell, but I know that we talked a good deal about fish, and gods, and Egyptian habits, and Egyptian philosophy, and, above all, Egyptian love-making. The last-named subject we found very interesting, and when once we got fully started upon it, no diversion afterwards occurred to break the even tenour of the conversation. Hatasou was a lovely figure, tall, queenly, with smooth dark arms and neck of polished bronze: her big black eyes full of tenderness, and her long hair bound up into a bright Egyptian headdress, that harmonized to a tone with her complexion and her robe. The more we talked, the more desperately did I fall in love, and the more utterly oblivious did I become of my duty to Editha Fitz-Simkins. The mere ugly daughter of a rich and vulgar brand-new knight, forsooth, to show off her airs before me, when here was a Princess of the Blood Royal of Egypt, obviously sensible to the attentions which I was paying her, and not unwilling to receive them with a coy and modest grace.

Well, I went on saying pretty things to Hatasou, and Hatasou went on deprecating them in a pretty little way, as who should say, "I don't mean what I pretend to mean one bit;" until at last I may confess that we were both evidently as far gone in the disease of the heart called love as it is possible for two young people on first acquaintance to become. Therefore, when Hatasou pulled forth her watch—another piece of mechanism with which antiquaries used never to credit the Egyptian people—and declared that she had only three more hours to live, at least for the next thousand years, I fairly broke down, took out my handkerchief, and began to sob like a child of five years old.

Hatasou was deeply moved. Decorum forbade that she should console me with too much empressement; but she ventured to remove the handkerchief gently from my face, and suggested that there was yet one course open by which we might enjoy a little more of one another's society. "Suppose," she said quietly, "you were to become a mummy. You would then wake up, as we do, every thousand years; and after you have tried it once, you will find it just as natural to sleep for a millennium as for eight hours. Of course," she added with a slight blush, "during the next three or four solar cycles there would be plenty of time to conclude any other arrangements you might possibly contemplate, before the occurrence of another glacial epoch."

This mode of regarding time was certainly novel and somewhat bewildering to people who ordinarily reckon its lapse by weeks and months; and I had a vague consciousness that my relations with Editha imposed upon me a moral necessity of returning to the outer world, instead of becoming a millennial mummy. Besides, there was the awkward chance of being converted into fuel and dissipated into space before the arrival of the next waking day. But I took one look at Hatasou, whose eyes were filling in turn with sympathetic tears, and that look decided me. I flung Editha, life, and duty to the dogs, and resolved at once to become a mummy.

There was no time to be lost. Only three hours remained to us, and the process of embalming, even in the most hasty manner, would take up fully two. We rushed off to the chief priest, who had charge of the particular department in question. He at once acceded to my wishes, and briefly explained the mode in which they usually treated the corpse.

That word suddenly aroused me. "The corpse!" I cried; "but I am alive. You can't embalm me living."

"We can," replied the priest, "under chloroform."

"Chloroform!" I echoed, growing more and more astonished: "I had no idea you Egyptians knew anything about it."

"Ignorant barbarian!" he answered with a curl of the lip; "you imagine yourself much wiser than the teachers of the world. If you were versed in all the wisdom of the Egyptians, you would know that chloroform is one of our simplest and commonest anæsthetics."

I put myself at once under the hands of the priest. He brought out the chloroform, and placed it beneath my nostrils, as I lay on a soft couch under the central court. Hatasou held my hand in hers, and watched my breathing with an anxious eye. I saw the priest leaning over me, with a clouded phial in his hand, and I experienced a vague sensation of smelling myrrh and spikenard. Next, I lost myself for a few moments, and when I again recovered my senses in a temporary break, the priest was holding a small greenstone knife, dabbled with blood, and I felt that a gash had been made across my breast. Then they applied the chloroform once more; I felt Hatasou give my hand a gentle squeeze; the whole panorama faded finally from my view; and I went to sleep for a seemingly endless time.

When I awoke again, my first impression led me to believe that the thousand years were over, and that I had come to life once more to feast with Hatasou and Thothmes in the Pyramid of Abu Yilla. But second thoughts, combined with closer observation of the surroundings, convinced me that I was really lying in a bedroom of Shepheard's Hotel at Cairo. An hospital nurse leant over me, instead of a chief priest; and I noticed no tokens of Editha Fitz-Simkins's presence. But when I endeavoured to make inquiries upon the subject of my whereabouts, I was peremptorily informed that I mustn't speak, as I was only just recovering from a severe fever, and might endanger my life by talking.

Some weeks later I learned the sequel of my night's adventure. The Fitz-Simkinses, missing me from the boat in the morning, at first imagined that I might have gone ashore for an early stroll. But after breakfast time, lunch time, and dinner time had gone past, they began to grow alarmed, and sent to look for me in all directions. One of their scouts, happening to pass the Pyramid, noticed that one of the stones near the north-east angle had been displaced, so as to give access to a dark passage, hitherto unknown. Calling several of his friends, for he was afraid to venture in alone, he passed down the corridor, and through a second gateway into the central hall. There the Fellahin found me, lying on the ground, bleeding profusely from a wound on the breast, and in an advanced stage of malarious fever. They brought me back to the boat, and the Fitz-Simkinses conveyed me at once to Cairo, for medical attendance and proper nursing.

Editha was at first convinced that I had attempted to commit suicide because I could not endure having caused her pain, and she accordingly resolved to tend me with the utmost care through my illness. But she found that my delirious remarks, besides bearing frequent reference to a princess, with whom I appeared to have been on unexpectedly intimate terms, also related very largely to our casus belli itself, the dancing girls of Abu Yilla. Even this trial she might have borne, setting down the moral degeneracy which led me to patronize so degrading an exhibition as a first symptom of my approaching malady: but certain unfortunate observations, containing pointed and by no means flattering allusions to her personal appearance—which I contrasted, much to her disadvantage, with that of the unknown princess—these, I say, were things which she could not forgive; and she left Cairo abruptly with her parents for the Riviera, leaving behind a stinging note, in which she denounced my perfidy and empty-heartedness with all the flowers of feminine eloquence. From that day to this I have never seen her.

When I returned to London and proposed to lay this account before the Society of Antiquaries, all my friends dissuaded me on the ground of its apparent incredibility. They declare that I must have gone to the Pyramid already in a state of delirium, discovered the entrance by accident, and sunk exhausted when I reached the inner chamber. In answer, I would point out three facts. In the first place, I undoubtedly found my way into the unknown passage—for which achievement I afterwards received the gold medal of the Sociétée Khédiviale, and of which I retain a clear recollection, differing in no way from my recollection of the subsequent events. In the second place, I had in my pocket, when found, a ring of Hatasou's, which I drew from her finger just before I took the chloroform, and put into my pocket as a keepsake. And in the third place, I had on my breast the wound which I saw the priest inflict with a knife of greenstone, and the scar may be seen on the spot to the present day. The absurd hypothesis of my medical friends, that I was wounded by falling against a sharp edge of rock, I must at once reject as unworthy a moment's consideration.

My own theory is either that the priest had not time to complete the operation, or else that the arrival of the Fitz-Simkins' scouts frightened back the mummies to their cases an hour or so too soon. At any rate, there they all were, ranged around the walls undisturbed, the moment the Fellahin entered.

Unfortunately, the truth of my account cannot be tested for another thousand years. But as a copy of this book will be preserved for the benefit of posterity in the British Museum, I hereby solemnly call upon Collective Humanity to try the veracity of this history by sending a deputation of archæologists to the Pyramid of Abu Yilla, on the last day of December, Two thousand eight hundred and seventy-seven. If they do not then find Thothmes and Hatasou feasting in the central hall exactly as I have described, I shall willingly admit that the story of my New Year's Eve among the Mummies is a vain hallucination, unworthy of credence at the hands of the scientific world.

THE FOUNDERING OF THE "FORTUNA."

I

I am going to spin you the yarn of the foundering of the Fortuna exactly as an old lake captain on a Huron steamer once span it for me by Great Manitoulin Island. It is a strange and a weird story; and if I can't give you the dialect in which he told it, you must forgive an English tongue its native accent for the sake of the curious Yankee tale that underlies it.

Captain Montague Beresford Pierpoint was hardly the sort of man you would have expected to find behind the counter of a small shanty bank at Aylmer's Pike, Colorado. There was an engaging English frankness, an obvious honesty and refinement of manner about him, which suited very oddly with the rough habits and rougher western speech of the mining population in whose midst he lived. And yet, Captain Pierpoint had succeeded in gaining the confidence and respect of those strange outcasts of civilization by some indescribable charm of address and some invisible talisman of quiet good-fellowship, which caused him to be more universally believed in than any other man whatsoever at Aylmer's Pike. Indeed, to say so much is rather to underrate the uniqueness of his position; for it might, perhaps, be truer to say that Captain Pierpoint was the only man in the place in whom any one believed at all in any way. He was an honest-spoken, quiet, unobtrusive sort of man, who walked about fearlessly without a revolver, and never gambled either in mining shares or at poker; so that, to the simple-minded, unsophisticated rogues and vagabonds of Aylmer's Pike, he seemed the very incarnation of incorruptible commercial honour. They would have trusted all their earnings and winnings without hesitation to Captain Pierpoint's bare word; and when they did so, they knew that Captain Pierpoint had always had the money forthcoming, on demand, without a moment's delay or a single prevarication.

Captain Pierpoint walked very straight and erect, as becomes a man of conspicuous uprightness; and there was a certain tinge of military bearing in his manner which seemed at first sight sufficiently to justify his popular title. But he himself made no false pretences upon that head; he freely acknowledged that he had acquired the position of captain, not in her Britannic Majesty's Guards, as the gossip of Aylmer's Pike sometimes asserted, but in the course of his earlier professional engagements as skipper of a Lake Superior grain-vessel. Though he hinted at times that he was by no means distantly connected with the three distinguished families whose names he bore, he did not attempt to exalt his rank or birth unduly, admitting that he was only a Canadian sailor by trade, thrown by a series of singular circumstances into the position of a Colorado banker. The one thing he really understood, he would tell his mining friends, was the grain-trade on the upper lakes; for finance he had but a single recommendation, and that was that if people trusted him he could never deceive them.

If any man had set up a bank in Aylmer's Point with an iron strong-room, a lot of electric bells, and an obtrusive display of fire-arms and weapons, it is tolerably certain that that bank would have been promptly robbed and gutted within its first week of existence by open violence. Five or six of the boys would have banded themselves together into a body of housebreakers, and would have shot down the banker and burst into his strong-room, without thought of the electric bells or other feeble resources of civilization to that end appointed. But when a quiet, unobtrusive, brave man, like Captain Montague Pierpoint, settled himself in a shanty in their midst, and won their confidence by his straightforward honesty, scarcely a miner in the lot would ever have dreamt of attempting to rob him. Captain Pierpoint had not come to Aylmer's Pike at first with any settled idea of making himself the financier of the rough little community; he intended to dig on his own account, and the rôle of banker was only slowly thrust upon him by the unanimous voice of the whole diggings. He had begun by lending men money out of his own pocket—men who were unlucky in their claims, men who had lost everything at monte, men who had come penniless to the Pike, and expected to find silver growing freely and openly on the surface. He had lent to them in a friendly way, without interest, and had been forced to accept a small present, in addition to the sum advanced, when the tide began to turn, and luck at last led the penniless ones to a remunerative placer or pocket. Gradually the diggers got into the habit of regarding this as Captain Pierpoint's natural function, and Captain Pierpoint, being himself but an indifferent digger, acquiesced so readily that at last, yielding to the persuasion of his clients, he put up a wooden counter, and painted over his rough door the magnificent notice, "Aylmer's Pike Bank: Montague Pierpoint, Manager." He got a large iron safe from Carson City, and in that safe, which stood by his own bedside, all the silver and other securities of the whole village were duly deposited. "Any one of the boys could easily shoot me and open that safe any night," Captain Pierpoint used to say pleasantly; "but if he did, by George! he'd have to reckon afterwards with every man on the Pike; and I should be sorry to stand in his shoes—that I would, any time." Indeed, the entire Pike looked upon Captain Pierpoint's safe as "Our Bank;" and, united in a single front by that simple social contract, they agreed to respect the safe as a sacred object, protected by the collective guarantee of three hundred mutually suspicious revolver-bearing outcasts.

However, even at Aylmer's Pike, there were degrees and stages of comparative unscrupulousness. Two men, new-comers to the Pike, by name Hiram Coffin and Pete Morris, at last wickedly and feloniously conspired together to rob Captain Pierpoint's bank. Their plan was simplicity itself. They would go at midnight, very quietly, to the Captain's house, cut his throat as he slept, rob the precious safe, and ride off straight for the east, thus getting a clear night's start of any possible pursuer. It was an easy enough thing to do; and they were really surprised in their own minds that nobody else had ever been cute enough to seize upon such an obvious and excellent path to wealth and security.

The day before the night the two burglars had fixed upon for their enterprise, Captain Pierpoint himself appeared to be in unusual spirits. Pete Morris called in at the bank during the course of the morning, to reconnoitre the premises, under pretence of paying in a few dollars' worth of silver, and he found the Captain very lively indeed. When Pete handed him the silver across the counter, the Captain weighed it with a smile, gave a receipt for the amount—he always gave receipts as a matter of form—and actually invited Pete into the little back room, which was at once kitchen, bedroom, and parlour, to have a drink. Then, before Pete's very eyes, he opened the safe, bursting with papers, and placed the silver in a bag on a shelf by itself, sticking the key into his waistcoat pocket. "He is delivering himself up into our hands," thought Pete to himself, as the Captain poured out two glasses of old Bourbon, and handed one to the miner opposite. "Here's success to all our enterprises!" cried the Captain gaily. "Here's success, pard!" Pete answered, with a sinister look, which even the Captain could not help noting in a sidelong fashion.

That night, about two o'clock, when all Aylmer's Pike was quietly dreaming its own sordid, drunken dreams, two sober men rose up from their cabin and stole out softly to the wooden bank house. Two horses were ready saddled with Mexican saddle-bags, and tied to a tree outside the digging, and in half an hour Pete and Hiram hoped to find themselves in full possession of all Captain Pierpoint's securities, and well on their road towards the nearest station of the Pacific Railway. They groped along to the door of the bank shanty, and began fumbling with their wire picks at the rough lock. After a moment's exploration of the wards, Pete Morris drew back in surprise.

"Pard," he murmured in a low whisper, "here's suthin' rather extraordinary; this 'ere lock's not fastened."

They turned the handle gently, and found that the door opened without an effort. Both men looked at one another in the dim light incredulously. Was there ever such a simple, trustful fool as that fellow Pierpoint! He actually slept in the bank shanty with his outer door unfastened!

The two robbers passed through the outer room and into the little back bedroom-parlour. Hiram held the dark lantern, and turned it full on to the bed. To their immense astonishment they found it empty.

Their first impulse was to suppose that the Captain had somehow anticipated their coming, and had gone out to rouse the boys. For a moment they almost contemplated running away, without the money. But a second glance reassured them; the bed had not been slept in. The Captain was a man of very regular habits. He made his bed in civilized fashion every morning after breakfast, and he retired every evening at a little after eleven. Where he could be stopping so late they couldn't imagine. But they hadn't come there to make a study of the Captain's personal habits, and, as he was away, the best thing they could do was to open the safe immediately, before he came back. They weren't particular about murder, Pete and Hiram; still, if you could do your robbery without bloodshed, it was certainly all the better to do it so.

Hiram held the lantern, carefully shaded by his hand, towards the door of the safe. Pete looked cautiously at the lock, and began pushing it about with his wire pick; he had hoped to get the key out of Captain Pierpoint's pocket, but as that easy scheme was so unexpectedly foiled, he trusted to his skill in picking to force the lock open. Once more a fresh surprise awaited him. The door opened almost of its own accord! Pete looked at Hiram, and Hiram looked at Pete. There was no mistaking the strange fact that met their gaze—the safe was empty!

"What on airth do you suppose is the meaning of this, Pete?" Hiram whispered hoarsely. But Pete did not whisper; the whole truth flashed upon him in a moment, and he answered aloud, with a string of oaths, "The Cap'n has gone and made tracks hisself for Madison Depôt. And he's taken every red cent in the safe along with him, too! the mean, low, dirty scoundrel! He's taken even my silver that he give me a receipt for this very morning!"

Hiram stared at Pete in blank amazement. That such base treachery could exist on earth almost surpassed his powers of comprehension; he could understand that a man should rob and murder, simply and naturally, as he was prepared to do, out of pure, guileless depravity of heart, but that a man should plan and plot for a couple of years to impose upon the simplicity of a dishonest community by a consistent show of respectability, with the ultimate object of stealing its whole wealth at one fell swoop, was scarcely within the limits of his narrow intelligence. He stared blankly at the empty safe, and whispered once more to Pete in a timid undertone, "Perhaps he's got wind of this, and took off the plate to somebody else's hut. If the boys was to come and catch us here, it 'ud be derned awkward for you an' me, Pete." But Pete answered gruffly and loudly, "Never you mind about the plate, pard. The Cap'n's gone, and the plate's gone with him; and what we've got to do now is to rouse the boys and ride after him like greased lightnin'. The mean swindler, to go and swindle me out of the silver that I've been and dug out of that there claim yonder with my own pick!" For the sense of personal injustice to one's self rises perennially in the human breast, however depraved, and the man who would murder another without a scruple is always genuinely aghast with just indignation when he finds the counsel for the prosecution pressing a point against him with what seems to him unfair persistency.

Pete flung his lock-pick out among the agave scrub that faced the bank shanty and ran out wildly into the midst of the dusty white road that led down the row of huts which the people of Aylmer's Pike euphemistically described as the Main Street. There he raised such an unearthly whoop as roused the sleepers in the nearest huts to turn over in their beds and listen in wonder, with a vague idea that "the Injuns" were coming down on a scalping-trail upon the diggings. Next, he hurried down the street, beating heavily with his fist on every frame door, and kicking hard at the log walls of the successive shanties. In a few minutes the whole Pike was out and alive. Unwholesome-looking men, in unwashed flannel shirts and loose trousers, mostly barefooted in their haste, came forth to inquire, with an unnecessary wealth of expletives, what the something was stirring. Pete, breathless and wrathful in the midst, livid with rage and disappointment, could only shriek aloud, "Cap'n Pierpoint has cleared out of camp, and taken all the plate with him!" There was at first an incredulous shouting and crying; then a general stampede towards the bank shanty; and, finally, as the truth became apparent to everybody, a deep and angry howl for vengeance on the traitor. In one moment Captain Pierpoint's smooth-faced villany dawned as clear as day to all Aylmer's Pike; and the whole chorus of gamblers, rascals, and blacklegs stood awe-struck with horror and indignation at the more plausible rogue who had succeeded in swindling even them. The clean-washed, white-shirted, fair-spoken villain! they would have his blood for this, if the United States Marshal had every mother's son of them strung up in a row for it after the pesky business was once fairly over.

Nobody inquired how Pete and Hiram came by the news. Nobody asked how they had happened to notice that the shanty was empty and the safe rifled. All they thought of was how to catch and punish the public robber. He must have made for the nearest depôt, Madison Clearing, on the Union

Pacific Line, and he would take the first cars east for St. Louis—that was certain. Every horse in the Pike was promptly requisitioned by the fastest riders, and a rough cavalcade, revolvers in hand, made down the gulch and across the plain, full tilt to Madison. But when, in the garish blaze of early morning, they reached the white wooden depôt in the valley and asked the ticket-clerk whether a man answering to their description had gone on by the east mail at 4.30, the ticket-clerk swore, in reply, that not a soul had left the depôt by any train either way that blessed night. Pete Morris proposed to hold a revolver to his head and force him to confess. But even that strong measure failed to induce a satisfactory retractation. By way of general precaution, two of the boys went on by the day train to St. Louis, but neither of them could hear anything of Captain Pierpoint. Indeed, as a matter of fact, the late manager and present appropriator of the Aylmer's Pike Bank had simply turned his horse's head in the opposite direction, towards the further station at Cheyenne Gap, and had gone westward to San Francisco, intending to make his way back to New York viâ Panama and the Isthmus Railway.

When the boys really understood that they had been completely duped, they swore vengeance in solemn fashion, and they picked out two of themselves to carry out the oath in a regular assembly. Each contributed of his substance what he was able; and Pete and Hiram, being more stirred with righteous wrath than all the rest put together, were unanimously deputed to follow the Captain's tracks to San Francisco, and to have his life wherever and whenever they might chance to find him. Pete and Hiram accepted the task thrust upon them, con amore, and went forth zealously to hunt up the doomed life of Captain Montague Beresford Pierpoint.

II

Society in Sarnia admitted that Captain Pierpoint was really quite an acquisition. An English gentleman by birth, well educated, and of pleasant manners, he had made a little money out west by mining, it was understood, and had now retired to the City of Sarnia, in the Province of Ontario and Dominion of Canada, to increase it by a quiet bit of speculative grain trading. He had been in the grain trade already, and people on the lake remembered him well; for Captain Pierpoint, in his honest, straightforward fashion, disdained the vulgar trickiness of an alias, and bore throughout the string of names which he had originally received from his godfathers and godmothers at his baptism. A thorough good fellow Captain Pierpoint had been at Aylmer's Pike; a perfect gentleman he was at Sarnia. As a matter of fact, indeed, the Captain was decently well-born, the son of an English country clergyman, educated at a respectable grammar school, and capable of being all things to all men in whatever station of life it might please Providence to place him. Society at Sarnia had no prejudice against the grain trade; if it had, the prejudice would have been distinctly self-regarding, for everybody in the little town did something in grain; and if Captain Pierpoint chose sometimes to navigate his own vessels, that was a fad which struck nobody as out of the way in an easy-going, money-getting, Canadian city.

Somehow or other, everything seemed to go wrong with Captain Pierpoint's cargoes. He was always losing a scow laden with best fall wheat from Chicago for Buffalo; or running a lumber vessel ashore on the shoals of Lake Erie; or getting a four-master jammed in the ice packs on the St. Clair river: and though the insurance companies continually declared that Captain Pierpoint had got the better of them, the Captain himself was wont to complain that no insurance could ever possibly cover the losses he sustained by the carelessness of his subordinates or the constant perversity of wind and waters. He was obliged to take his own ships down, he would have it, because nobody else could take them safely for him; and though he met with quite as many accidents himself as many of his deputies did, he continued to convey his grain in person, hoping, as he said, that luck would turn some day, and that a good speculation would finally enable him honourably to retrieve his shattered fortunes.

However this might be, it happened curiously enough that, in spite of all his losses, Captain Pierpoint seemed to grow richer and richer, visibly to the naked eye, with each reverse of his trading efforts. He took a handsome house, set up a carriage and pair, and made love to the prettiest and sweetest girl in all Sarnia. The prettiest and sweetest girl was not proof against Captain Pierpoint's suave tongue and handsome house; and she married him in very good faith, honestly believing in him as a good woman will in a scoundrel, and clinging to him fervently with all her heart and soul. No happier and more loving pair in all Sarnia than Captain and Mrs. Pierpoint.

Some months after the marriage, Captain Pierpoint arranged to take down a scow or flat-bottomed boat, laden with grain, from Milwaukee for the Erie Canal. He took up the scow himself, and before he started for the voyage, it was a curious fact that he went in person down into the hold, bored eight large holes right through the bottom, and filled each up, as he drew out the auger, with a caulked plug made exactly to fit it, and hammered firmly into place with a wooden mallet. There was a ring in each plug, by which it could be pulled out again without much difficulty; and the whole eight were all placed along the gangway of the hold, where no cargo would lie on top of them. The scow's name was the Fortuna: "sit faustum omen et felix," murmured Captain Pierpoint to himself; for among his other accomplishments he had not wholly neglected nor entirely forgotten the classical languages.

It took only two men and the skipper to navigate the scow; for lake craft towed by steam propellers are always very lightly manned: and when Captain Pierpoint reached Milwaukee, where he was to take in cargo, he dismissed the two sailors who had come with him from Sarnia, and engaged two fresh hands at the harbour. Rough, miner-looking men they were, with very little of the sailor about them; but Captain Pierpoint's sharp eye soon told him they were the right sort of men for his purpose, and he engaged them on the spot, without a moment's hesitation. Pete and Hiram had had some difficulty in tracking him, for they never thought he would return to the lakes, but they had tracked him at last, and were ready now to take their revenge.

They had disguised themselves as well as they were able, and in their clumsy knavery they thought they had completely deceived the Captain. But almost from the moment the Captain saw them, he knew who they were, and he took his measures accordingly. "Stupid louts," he said to himself, with the fine contempt of an educated scoundrel for the unsophisticated natural ruffian: "here's a fine chance of killing two birds with one stone!" And when the Captain said the word "killing," he said it in his own mind with a delicate sinister emphasis which meant business.

The scow was duly loaded, and with a heavy cargo of grain aboard, she proceeded to make her way slowly, by the aid of a tug, out of Milwaukee Harbour.

As soon as she was once clear of the wharf, and while the busy shipping of the great port still surrounded them on every side, Captain Pierpoint calmly drew his revolver, and took his stand beside the hatches. "Pete and Hiram," he said quietly to his two assistants, "I want to have a little serious talk with you two before we go any further."

If he had fired upon them outright instead of merely calling them by their own names, the two common conspirators could not have started more unfeignedly, or looked more unspeakably cowed, than they did at that moment. Their first impulse was to draw their own revolvers in return; but they saw in a second that the Captain was beforehand with them, and that they had better not try to shoot him before the very eyes of all Milwaukee.

"Now, boys," the Captain went on steadily, with his finger on the trigger and his eye fixed straight on the men's faces, "we three quite understand one another. I took your savings for reasons of my own; and you have shipped here to-day to murder me on the voyage. But I recognized you before I engaged you: and I have left word at Milwaukee that if anything happens to me on this journey, you two have a grudge against me, and must be hanged for it. I've taken care that if this scow comes into any port along the lakes without me aboard, you two are to be promptly arrested." (This was false, of course; but to Captain Pierpoint a small matter like that was a mere trifle.) "And I've shipped myself along with you, just to show you I'm not afraid of you. But if either of you disobeys my orders in anything for one minute, I shoot at once, and no jury in Canada or the States will touch a hair of my head for doing it. I'm a respectable shipowner and grain merchant, you're a pair of disreputable skulking miners, pretending to be sailors, and you've shipped aboard here on purpose to murder and rob me. If you shoot me, it's murder: if I shoot you, it's justifiable homicide. Now, boys, do you understand that?"

Pete looked at Hiram and was beginning to speak, when the captain interrupted him in the calm tone of one having authority. "Look here, Pete," he said, drawing a chalk line amidships across the deck; "you stand this side of that line, and you stand there, Hiram. Now, mind, if either of you chooses to step across that line or to confer with the other, I shoot you, whether it's here before all the eyes of Milwaukee, or alone in the middle of Huron. You must each take your own counsel, and do as you like for yourselves. But I've got a little plan of my own on, and if you choose willingly to help me in it, your fortune's made. Look at the thing, squarely, boys; what's the use of your killing me? Sooner or later you'll get hung for it, and it's a very unpleasant thing, I can assure you, hanging." As the Captain spoke, he placed his unoccupied hand loosely on his throat, and pressed it gently backward. Pete and Hiram shuddered a little as he did so. "Well, what's the good of ending your lives that way, eh? But I'm doing a little speculative business on these lakes, where I want just such a couple of men as you two—men that'll do as they're told in a matter of business and ask no squeamish questions. If you care to help me in this business, stop and make your fortunes; if you don't, you can go back to Milwaukee with the tug."

"You speak fair enough," said Pete, dubitatively; "but you know, Cap'n, you ain't a man to be trusted. I owe you one already for stealing my silver."

"Very little silver," the Captain answered, with a wave of the hand and a graceful smile. "Bonds, United States bonds and greenbacks most of it, converted beforehand for easier conveyance by horseback. These, however, are business details which needn't stand in the way between you and me, partner. I always was straightforward in all my dealings, and I'll come to the point at once, so that you can know whether you'll help me or not. This scow's plugged at bottom. My intention is, first, to part the rope that ties us to the tug; next, to transfer the cargo by night to a small shanty I've got on Manitoulin Island; and then to pull the plugs and sink the scow on Manitoulin rocks. That way I get insurance for the cargo and scow, and carry on the grain in the slack season. If you consent to help me unload, and sink the ship, you shall have half profits between you; if you don't, you can go back to Milwaukee like a couple of fools, and I'll put into port again to get a couple of pluckier fellows. Answer each for yourselves. Hiram, will you go with me?"

"How shall I know you'll keep your promise?" asked Hiram.

"For the best of all possible reasons," replied the Captain, jauntily; "because, if I don't, you can inform upon me to the insurance people."

In Hiram Coffin's sordid soul there was a moment's turning over of the chances; and then greed prevailed over revenge, and he said, grudgingly—

"Well, Cap'n, I'll go with you."

The Captain smiled the smile of calm self-approbation, and turned half round to Pete.

"And you?" he asked.

"If Hiram goes, I go too," Pete answered, half hoping that some chance might occur for conferring with his neighbour on the road, and following out their original conspiracy. But Captain Pierpoint had been too much for him: he had followed the excellent rule "divide et impera" and he remained clearly master of the situation.

As soon as they were well outside Milwaukee Harbour, the tug dragged them into the open lake, all unconscious of the strange scene that had passed on the deck so close to it; and the oddly mated crew made its way, practically alone, down the busy waters of Lake Michigan.

Captain Pierpoint certainly didn't spend a comfortable time during his voyage down the lake, or through the Straits of Mackinaw. To say the truth, he could hardly sleep at all, and he was very fagged and weary when they arrived at Manitoulin Island. But Pete and Hiram, though they had many chances of talking together, could not see their way to kill him in safety; and Hiram at least, in his own mind, had come to the conclusion that it was better to make a little money than to risk one's neck for a foolish revenge. So in the dead of night, on the second day out, when a rough wind had risen from the north, and a fog had come over them, the Captain quietly began to cut away at the rope that tied them to the tug. He cut the rope all round, leaving a sound core in the centre; and when the next gust of wind came, the rope strained and parted quite naturally, so that the people on the tug never suspected the genuineness of the transaction. They looked about in the fog and storm for the scow, but of course they couldn't find her, for Captain Pierpoint, who knew his ground well, had driven her straight ashore before the wind and beached her on a small shelving cove on Manitoulin Island. There they found five men waiting for them, who helped unload the cargo with startling rapidity, for it was all arranged in sacks, not in bulk, and a high slide fixed on the gangway enabled them to slip it quickly down into an underground granary excavated below the level of the beach. After unloading, they made their way down before the breeze towards the jagged rocks of Manitoulin.

It was eleven o'clock on a stormy moonlight night when the Fortuna arrived off the jutting point of the great island. A "black squall," as they call it on the lakes, was blowing down from the Sault Ste. Marie. The scow drove about aimlessly, under very little canvas, and the boat was ready to be lowered, "in case," the Captain said humorously, "of any accident." Close to the end of the point the Captain ordered Pete and Hiram down into the hold. He had shown them beforehand the way to draw the plugs, and had explained that the water would rise very slowly, and they would have plenty of time to get up the companion-ladder long before there was a foot deep of water in the hold. At the last moment Pete hung back a little. The Captain took him quietly by the shoulders, and, without an oath (an omission which told eloquently on Pete), thrust him down the ladder, and told him in his calmest manner to do his duty. Hiram held the light in his hand, and both went down together into the black abyss. There was no time to be lost; they were well off the point, and in another moment the wreck would have lost all show of reasonable probability.

As the two miners went down into the hold, Captain Pierpoint drew quietly from his pocket a large hammer and a packet of five-inch nails. They were good stout nails, and would resist a considerable pressure. He looked carefully down into the hold, and saw the two men draw the first plug. One after another he watched them till the fourth was drawn, and then he turned away, and took one of the nails firmly between his thumb and forefinger.

Next week everybody at Sarnia was grieved to hear that another of Captain Pierpoint's vessels had gone down off Manitoulin Point in that dreadful black squall on Thursday evening. Both the sailors on board had been drowned, but the Captain himself had managed to make good his escape in the jolly boat. He would be a heavy loser, it was understood, on the value of the cargo, for insurance never covers the loss of grain. Still, it was a fortunate thing that such a delightful man as the Captain had not perished in the foundering of the Fortuna.

III

Somehow, after that wreck, Captain Pierpoint never cared for the water again. His nerves were shattered, he said, and he couldn't stand danger as he used to do when he was younger and stronger. So he went on the lake no more, and confined his attention more strictly to the "futures" business. He was a thriving and prosperous person, in spite of his losses; and the underwriters had begun to look a little askance at his insurances even before this late foundering case. Some whispered ominously in underwriting circles that they had their doubts about the Fortuna.

One summer, a few years later, the water on Lake Huron sank lower than it had ever been known to sink before. It was a very dry season in the back country, and the rivers brought down very diminished streams into the great basins. Foot by foot, the level of the lake fell slowly, till many of the wharves were left high and dry, and the vessels could only come alongside in very few deep places. Captain Pierpoint had suffered much from sleeplessness, combined with Canadian ague, for some years past, but this particular summer his mind was very evidently much troubled. For some unaccountable reason, he watched the falling of the river with the intensest anxiety, and after it had passed a certain point, his interest in the question became painfully keen. Though the fever and the ague gained upon him from day to day, and his doctor counselled perfect quiet, he was perpetually consulting charts, and making measurements of the configuration which the coast had now reached, especially at the upper end of Lake Huron. At last, his mind seemed almost to give way, and weak and feverish as he was, he insisted, the first time for many seasons, that he must take a trip upon the water. Remonstrance was quite useless; he would go on the lake again, he said, if it killed him. So he hired one of the little steam pleasure yachts which are always to let in numbers at Detroit, and started with his wife and her brother, a young surgeon, for a month's cruise into Lake Superior.

As the yacht neared Manitoulin Island, Captain Pierpoint insisted upon being brought up on deck in a chair—he was too ill to stand—and swept all the coast with his binocular. Close to the point, a flat-topped object lay mouldering in the sun, half out of water, on the shoals by the bank. "What is it, Ernest?" asked the Captain, trembling, of his brother-in-law.

"A wreck, I should say," the brother-in-law answered, carelessly. "By Jove, now I look at it with the glass, I can read the name, 'Fortuna, Sarnia.'"

Captain Pierpoint seized the glass with a shaking hand, and read the name on the stern, himself, in a dazed fashion. "Take me downstairs," he said feebly, "and let me die quietly; and for Heaven's sake, Ernest, never let her know about it all."

They took him downstairs into the little cabin, and gave him quinine; but he called for brandy. They let him have it, and he drank a glassful. Then he lay down, and the shivering seized him; and with his wife's hand in his, he died that night in raving delirium, about eleven. A black squall was blowing down from the Sault Ste. Marie; and they lay at anchor out in the lake, tossing and pitching, opposite the green mouldering hull of the Fortuna.

They took him back and buried him at Sarnia; and all the world went to attend his funeral, as of a man who died justly respected for his wealth and other socially admired qualities. But the brother-in-law knew there was a mystery somewhere in the wreck of the Fortuna; and as soon as the funeral was over, he went back with the yacht, and took its skipper with him to examine the stranded vessel. When they came to look at the bottom, they found eight holes in it. Six of them were wide open; one was still plugged, and the remaining one had the plug pulled half out, inward, as if the persons who were pulling it had abandoned the attempt for the fear of the rising water. That was bad enough, and they did not wonder that Captain Pierpoint had shrunk in horror from the revealing of the secret of the Fortuna.

But when they scrambled on the deck, they discovered another fact which gave a more terrible meaning to the dead man's tragedy. The covering of the hatchway by the companion-ladder was battened down, and nailed from the side with five-inch nails. The skipper loosened the rusty iron with his knife, and after a while they lifted the lid off, and descended carefully into the empty hold below. As they suspected, there was no damaged grain in it; but at the foot of the companion-ladder, left behind by the retreating water, two half-cleaned skeletons in sailor clothes lay huddled together loosely on the floor. That was all that remained of Pete and Hiram. Evidently the Captain had nailed the hatch down on top of them, and left them there terror-stricken to drown as the water rushed in and rose around them.

For a while the skipper and the brother-in-law kept the dead man's secret; but they did not try to destroy or conceal the proofs of his guilt, and in time others visited the wreck, till, bit by bit, the horrible story leaked out in its entirety. Nowadays, as you pass the Great Manitoulin Island, every sailor on the lake route is ready to tell you this strange and ghastly yarn of the foundering of the Fortuna.

THE BACKSLIDER

i

There was much stir and commotion on the night of Thursday, January the 14th, 1874, in the Gideonite Apostolic Church, number 47, Walworth Lane, Peckham, S.E. Anybody could see at a glance that some important business was under consideration; for the Apostle was there himself, in his chair of presidency, and the twelve Episcops were there, and the forty-eight Presbyters, and a large and earnest gathering of the Gideonite laity. It was only a small bare school-room, fitted with wooden benches, was that headquarters station of the young Church; but you could not look around it once without seeing that its occupants were of the sort by whom great religious revolutions may be made or marred. For the Gideonites were one of those strange enthusiastic hole-and-corner sects that spring up naturally in the outlying suburbs of great thinking centres. They gather around the marked personality of someone ardent, vigorous, half-educated visionary; and they consist for the most part of intelligent, half-reasoning people, who are bold enough to cast overboard the dogmatic beliefs of their fathers, but not so bold as to exercise their logical faculty upon the fundamental basis on which the dogmas originally rested. The Gideonites had thus collected around the fixed centre of their Apostle, a retired attorney, Murgess by name, whose teaching commended itself to their groping reason as the pure outcome of faithful Biblical research; and they had chosen their name because, though they were but three hundred in number, they had full confidence that when the time came they would blow their trumpets, and all the host of Midian would be scattered before them. In fact, they divided the world generally into Gideonite and Midianite, for they knew that he that was not with them was against them. And no wonder, for the people of Peckham did not love the struggling Church. Its chief doctrine was one of absolute celibacy, like the Shakers of America; and to this doctrine the Church had testified in the Old Kent Road and elsewhere after a vigorous practical fashion that roused the spirit of South-eastern London into the fiercest opposition. The young men and maidens, said the Apostle, must no longer marry or be given in marriage; the wives and husbands must dwell asunder; and the earth must be made as an image of heaven. These were heterodox opinions, indeed, which South-eastern London could only receive with a strenuous counterblast of orthodox brickbats and sound Anglican road metal.

The fleece of wool was duly laid upon the floor; the trumpet and the lamp were placed upon the bare wooden reading desk; and the Apostle, rising slowly from his seat, began to address the assembled Gideonites.

"Friends," he said, in a low, clear, impressive voice, with a musical ring tempering its slow distinctness, "we have met together to-night to take counsel with one another upon a high matter. It is plain to all of us that the work of the Church in the world does not prosper as it might prosper were the charge of it in worthier hands. We have to contend against great difficulties. We are not among the rich or the mighty of the earth; and the poor whom we have always with us do not listen to us. It is expedient, therefore, that we should set some one among us aside to be instructed thoroughly in those things that are most commonly taught among the Midianites at Oxford or Cambridge. To some of you it may seem, as it seemed at first to me, that such a course would involve going back upon the very principles of our constitution. We are not to overcome Midian by our own hand, nor by the strength of two and thirty thousand, but by the trumpet, and the pitcher, and the cake of barley bread. Yet, when I searched and inquired after this matter, it seemed to me that we might also err by overmuch confidence on the other side. For Moses, who led the people out of Egypt, was made ready for the task by being learned in all the learning of the Egyptians. Daniel, who testified in the captivity, was cunning in knowledge, and understanding science, and instructed in the wisdom and tongue of the Chaldeans. Paul, who was the apostle of the Gentiles, had not only sat at the feet of Gamaliel, but was also able from their own poets and philosophers to confute the sophisms and subtleties of the Grecians themselves. These things show us that we should not too lightly despise even worldly learning and worldly science. Perhaps we have gone wrong in thinking too little of such dross, and being puffed up with spiritual pride. The world might listen to us more readily if we had one who could speak the word for us in the tongues understanded of the world."

As he paused, a hum of acquiescence went round the room.

"It has seemed to me, then," the Apostle went on, "that we ought to choose someone among our younger brethren, upon whose shoulders the cares and duties of the Apostolate might hereafter fall. We are a poor people, but by subscription among ourselves we might raise a sufficient sum to send the chosen person first to a good school here in London, and afterwards to the University of Oxford. It may seem a doubtful and a hazardous thing thus to stake our future upon any one young man; but then we must remember that the choice will not be wholly or even mainly ours; we will be guided and directed as we ever are in the laying on of hands. To me, considering this matter thus, it has seemed that there is one youth in our body who is specially pointed out for this work. Only one child has ever been born into the Church: he, as you know, is the son of brother John Owen and sister Margaret Owen, who were received into the fold just six days before his birth. Paul Owen's very name seems to many of us, who take nothing for chance but all things for divinely ordered, to mark him out at once as a foreordained Apostle. Is it your wish, then, Presbyter John Owen, to dedicate your only son to this ministry?"

Presbyter John Owen rose from the row of seats assigned to the forty-eight, and moved hesitatingly towards the platform. He was an intelligent-looking, honest-faced, sunburnt working man, a mason by trade, who had come into the Church from the Baptist society; and he was awkwardly dressed in his Sunday clothes, with the scrupulous clumsy neatness of a respectable artisan who expects to take part in an important ceremony. He spoke nervously and with hesitation, but with all the transparent earnestness of a simple, enthusiastic nature.

"Apostle and friends," he said, "it ain't very easy for me to disentangle my feelin's on this subjec' from one another. I hope I ain't moved by any worldly feelin', an' yet I hardly know how to keep such considerations out, for there's no denyin' that it would be a great pleasure to me and to his mother to see our Paul becomin' a teacher in Israel, and receivin' an education such as you, Apostle, has pinted out. But we hope, too, we ain't insensible to the good of the Church and the advantage that it might derive from our Paul's support and preachin'. We can't help seein' ourselves that the lad has got abilities; and we've tried to train him up from his youth upward, like Timothy, for the furtherance of the right doctrine. If the Church thinks he's fit for the work laid upon him, his mother and me'll be glad to dedicate him to the service."

He sat down awkwardly, and the Church again hummed its approbation in a suppressed murmur. The Apostle rose once more, and briefly called on Paul Owen to stand forward.

In answer to the call, a tall, handsome, earnest-eyed boy advanced timidly to the platform. It was no wonder that those enthusiastic Gideonite visionaries should have seen in his face the visible stamp of the Apostleship. Paul Owen had a rich crop of dark-brown glossy and curly hair, cut something after the Florentine Cinque-cento fashion—not because his parents wished him to look artistic, but because that was the way in which they had seen the hair dressed in all the sacred pictures that they knew; and Margaret Owen, the daughter of some Wesleyan Spitalfields weaver folk, with the imaginative Huguenot blood still strong in her veins, had made up her mind ever since she became Convinced of the Truth (as their phrase ran) that her Paul was called from his cradle to a great work. His features were delicately chiselled, and showed rather natural culture, like his mother's, than rough honesty, like John Owen's, or strong individuality, like the masterful Apostle's. His eyes were peculiarly deep and luminous, with a far-away look which might have reminded an artist of the central boyish figure in Holman Hunt's picture of the Doctors in the Temple. And yet Paul Owen had a healthy colour in his cheek and a general sturdiness of limb and muscle which showed that he was none of your nervous, bloodless, sickly idealists, but a wholesome English peasant boy of native refinement and delicate sensibilities. He moved forward with some natural hesitation before the eyes of so many people—ay, and what was more terrible, of the entire Church upon earth; but he was not awkward and constrained in his action like his father. One could see that he was sustained in the prominent part he took that morning by the consciousness of a duty he had to perform and a mission laid upon him which he must not reject.

"Are you willing, my son Paul," asked the Apostle, gravely, "to take upon yourself the task that the Church proposes?"

"I am willing," answered the boy in a low voice, "grace preventing me."

"Does all the Church unanimously approve the election of our brother Paul to this office?" the Apostle asked formally; for it was a rule with the Gideonites that nothing should be done except by the unanimous and spontaneous action of the whole body, acting under direct and immediate inspiration; and all important matters were accordingly arranged beforehand by the Apostle in private interviews with every member of the Church individually, so that everything that took place in public assembly had the appearance of being wholly unquestioned. They took counsel first with one another, and consulted the Scripture together; and when all private doubts were satisfied, they met as a Church to ratify in solemn conclave their separate conclusions. It was not often that the Apostle did not have his own way. Not only had he the most marked personality and the strongest will, but he alone also had Greek and Hebrew enough to appeal always to the original word; and that mysterious amount of learning, slight as it really was, sufficed almost invariably to settle the scruples of his wholly ignorant and pliant disciples. Reverence for the literal Scripture in its primitive language was the corner-stone of the Gideonite Church; and for all practical purposes, its one depositary and exponent for them was the Apostle himself. Even the Rev. Albert Barnes's Commentary was held to possess an inferior authority.

"The Church approves," was the unanimous answer.

"Then, Episcops, Presbyters, and brethren," said the Apostle, taking up a roll of names, "I have to ask that you will each mark down on this paper opposite your own names how much a year you can spare of your substance for six years to come as a guarantee fund for this great work. You must remember that the ministry of this Church has cost you nothing; freely I have received and freely given; do you now bear your part in equipping a new aspirant for the succession to the Apostolate."

The two senior Episcops took two rolls from his hand, and went round the benches with a stylographic pen (so strangely do the ages mingle—Apostles and stylographs) silently asking each to put down his voluntary subscription. Meanwhile the Apostle read slowly and reverently a few appropriate sentences of Scripture. Some of the richer members—well-to-do small tradesmen of Peckham—put down a pound or even two pounds apiece; the poorer brethren wrote themselves down for ten shillings or even five. In the end the guarantee list amounted to 195l. a year. The Apostle reckoned it up rapidly to himself, and then announced the result to the assembly, with a gentle smile relaxing his austere countenance. He was well pleased, for the sum was quite sufficient to keep Paul Owen two years at school in London and then send him comfortably if not splendidly to Oxford. The boy had already had a fair education in Latin and some Greek, at the Birkbeck Schools; and with two years' further study he might even gain a scholarship (for he was a bright lad), which would materially lessen the expense to the young Church. Unlike many prophets and enthusiasts, the Apostle was a good man of business; and he had taken pains to learn all about these favourable chances before embarking his people on so very doubtful a speculation.

The Assembly was just about to close, when one of the Presbyters rose unexpectedly to put a question which, contrary to the usual practice, had not already been submitted for approbation to the Apostle. He was a hard-headed, thickset, vulgar-looking man, a greengrocer at Denmark Hill, and the Apostle always looked upon him as a thorn in his side, promoted by inscrutable wisdom to the Presbytery for the special purpose of keeping down the Apostle's spiritual pride.

"One more pint, Apostle," he said abruptly, "afore we close. It seems to me that even in the Church's work we'd ought to be business-like. Now, it ain't business-like to let this young man, Brother Paul, get his eddication out of us, if I may so speak afore the Church, on spec. It's all very well our sayin' he's to be eddicated and take on the Apostleship, but how do we know but what when he's had his eddication he may fall away and become a backslider, like Demas and like others among ourselves that we could mention? He may go to Oxford among a lot of Midianites, and them of the great an' mighty of the earth too, and how do we know but what he may round upon the Church, and go back upon us after we've paid for his eddication? So what I want to ask is just this, can't we bind him down in a bond that if he don't take the Apostleship with the consent of the Church when it falls vacant he'll pay us back our money, so as we can eddicate up another as'll be more worthy?"

The Apostle moved uneasily in his chair; but before he could speak, Paul Owen's indignation found voice, and he said out his say boldly before the whole assembly, blushing crimson with mingled shame and excitement as he did so. "If Brother Grimshaw and all the brethren think so ill of me that they cannot trust my honesty and honour," he said, "they need not be at the pains of educating me. I will sign no bond and enter into no compact. But if you suppose that I will be a backslider, you do not know me, and I will confer no more with you upon the subject."

"My son Paul is right," the Apostle said, flushing up in turn at the boy's audacity; "we will not make the affairs of the Spirit a matter for bonds and earthly arrangements. If the Church thinks as I do, you will all rise up."

All rose except Presbyter Grimshaw. For a moment there was some hesitation, for the rule of the Church in favour of unanimity was absolute; but the Apostle fixed his piercing eyes on Job Grimshaw, and after a minute or so Job Grimshaw too rose slowly, like one compelled by an unseen power, and cast in his vote grudgingly with the rest. There was nothing more said about signing an agreement.

II

Meenie Bolton had counted a great deal upon her visit to Oxford, and she found it quite as delightful as she had anticipated. Her brother knew such a nice set of men, especially Mr. Owen, of Christchurch. Meenie had never been so near falling in love with anybody in her life as she was with Paul Owen. He was so handsome and so clever, and then there was something so romantic about this strange Church they said he belonged to. Meenie's father was a country parson, and the way in which Paul shrank from talking about the rector, as if his office were something wicked or uncanny, piqued and amused her. There was an heretical tinge about him which made him doubly interesting to the Rector's daughter. The afternoon water party that eventful Thursday, down to Nuneham, she looked forward to with the deepest interest. For her aunt, the Professor's wife, who was to take charge of them, was certainly the most delightful and most sensible of chaperons.

"Is it really true, Mr. Owen," she said, as they sat together for ten minutes alone after their picnic luncheon, by the side of the weir under the shadow of the Nuneham beeches—"is it really true that this Church of yours doesn't allow people to marry?"

Paul coloured up to his eyes as he answered, "Well, Miss Bolton, I don't know that you should identify me too absolutely with my Church. I was very young when they selected me to go to Oxford, and my opinions have decidedly wavered a good deal lately. But the Church certainly does forbid marriage. I have always been brought up to look upon it as sinful."

Meenie laughed aloud; and Paul, to whom the question was no laughing matter, but a serious point of conscientious scruple, could hardly help laughing with her, so infectious was that pleasant ripple. He checked himself with an effort, and tried to look serious. "Do you know," he said, "when I first came to Christchurch, I doubted even whether I ought to make your brother's acquaintance because he was a clergyman's son. I was taught to describe clergymen always as priests of Midian." He never talked about his Church to anybody at Oxford, and it was a sort of relief to him to speak on the subject to Meenie, in spite of her laughing eyes and undisguised amusement. The other men would have laughed at him too, but their laughter would have been less sympathetic.

"And do you think them priests of Midian still?" asked Meenie.

"Miss Bolton," said Paul suddenly, as one who relieves his overburdened mind by a great effort, "I am almost moved to make a confidante of you."

"There is nothing I love better than confidences," Meenie answered; and she might truthfully have added, "particularly from you."

"Well, I have been passing lately through a great many doubts and difficulties. I was brought up by my Church to become its next Apostle, and I have been educated at their expense both in London and here. You know," Paul added with his innate love of telling out the whole truth, "I am not a gentleman; I am the son of poor working people in London."

"Tom told me who your parents were," Meenie answered simply; "but he told me, too, you were none the less a true gentleman born for that; and I see myself he told me right."

Paul flushed again—he had a most unmanly trick of flushing up—and bowed a little timid bow. "Thank you," he said quietly. "Well, while I was in London I lived entirely among my own people, and never heard anything talked about except our own doctrines. I thought our Apostle the most learned, the wisest, and the greatest of men. I had not a doubt about the absolute infallibility of our own opinions. But ever since I came to Oxford I have slowly begun to hesitate and to falter. When I came up first, the men laughed at me a good deal in a good-humoured way, because I wouldn't do as they did. Then I thought myself persecuted for the truth's sake, and was glad. But the men were really very kind and forbearing to me; they never argued with me or bullied me; they respected my scruples, and said nothing more about it as soon as they found out what they really were. That was my first stumbling-block. If they had fought me and debated with me, I might have stuck to my own opinions by force of opposition. But they turned me in upon myself completely by their silence, and mastered me by their kindly forbearance. Point by point I began to give in, till now I hardly know where I am standing."

"You wouldn't join the cricket club at first, Tom says."

"No, I wouldn't. I thought it wrong to walk in the ways of Midian. But gradually I began to argue myself out of my scruples, and now I positively pull six in the boat, and wear a Christchurch ribbon on my hat. I have given up protesting against having my letters addressed to me as Esquire (though I have really no right to the title), and I nearly went the other day to have some cards engraved with my name as 'Mr. Paul Owen.' I am afraid I'm backsliding terribly."

Meenie laughed again. "If that is all you have to burden your conscience with," she said, "I don't think you need spend many sleepless nights."

"Quite so," Paul answered, smiling; "I think so myself. But that is not all. I have begun to have serious doubts about the Apostle himself and the whole Church altogether. I have been three years at Oxford now; and while I was reading for Mods, I don't think I was so unsettled in my mind. But since I have begun reading philosophy for my Greats, I have had to go into all sorts of deep books—Mill, and Spencer, and Bain, and all kinds of fellows who really think about things, you know, down to the very bottom—and an awful truth begins to dawn upon me, that our Apostle is after all only a very third-rate type of a thinker. Now that, you know, is really terrible."

"I don't see why," Meenie answered demurely. She was beginning to get genuinely interested.

"That is because you have never had to call in question a cherished and almost ingrown faith. You have never realized any similar circumstances. Here am I, brought up by these good, honest, earnest people, with their own hard-earned money, as a pillar of their belief. I have been taught to look upon myself as the chosen advocate of their creed, and on the Apostle as an almost divinely inspired man. My whole life has been bound up in it; I have worked and read night and day in order to pass high and do honour to the Church; and now what do I begin to find the Church really is? A petty group of poor, devoted, enthusiastic, ignorant people, led blindly by a decently instructed but narrow-minded teacher, who has mixed up his own headstrong self-conceit and self-importance with his own peculiar ideas of abstract religion." Paul paused, half surprised at himself, for, though he had doubted before, he had never ventured till that day to formulate his doubts, even to himself, in such plain and straightforward language.

"I see," said Meenie, gravely; "you have come into a wider world; you have mixed with wider ideas; and the wider world has converted you, instead of your converting the world. Well, that is only natural. Others beside you have had to change their opinions."

"Yes, yes; but for me it is harder—oh! so much harder."

"Because you have looked forward to being an Apostle?"

"Miss Bolton, you do me injustice—not in what you say, but in the tone you say it in. No, it is not the giving up of the Apostleship that troubles me, though I did hope that I might help in my way to make the world a new earth; but it is the shock and downfall of their hopes to all those good earnest people, and especially—oh! especially, Miss Bolton, to my own dear father and mother." His eyes filled with tears as he spoke.

"I can understand," said Meenie, sympathetically, her eyes dimming a little in response. "They have set their hearts all their lives long on your accomplishing this work, and it will be to them the disappointment of a cherished romance."

They looked at one another a few minutes in silence.

"How long have you begun to have your doubts?" Meenie asked after the pause.

"A long time, but most of all since I saw you. It has made me—it has made me hesitate more about the fundamental article of our faith. Even now, I am not sure whether it is not wrong of me to be talking so with you about such matters."

"I see," said Meenie, a little more archly; "it comes perilously near—" and she broke off, for she felt she had gone a step too far.

"Perilously near falling in love," Paul continued boldly, turning his big eyes full upon her. "Yes, perilously near."

Their eyes met; Meenie's fell; and they said no more. But they both felt they understood one another. Just at that moment the Professor's wife came up to interrupt the tête-à-tête; "for that young Owen," she said to herself, "is really getting quite too confidential with dear Meenie."

That same evening Paul paced up and down his rooms in Peckwater with all his soul strangely upheaved within him and tossed and racked by a dozen conflicting doubts and passions. Had he gone too far? Had he yielded like Adam to the woman who beguiled him? Had he given way like Samson to the snares of Delilah? For the old Scripture phraseology and imagery, so long burned into his very nature, clung to him still in spite of all his faltering changes of opinion. Had he said more than he thought and felt about the Apostle? Even if he was going to revise his views, was it right, was it candid, was it loyal to the truth, that he should revise them under the biassing influence of Meenie's eyes? If only he could have separated the two questions—the Apostle's mission, and the something which he felt growing up within him! But he could not—and, as he suspected, for a most excellent reason, because the two were intimately bound up in the very warp and woof of his existence. Nature was asserting herself against the religious asceticism of the Apostle; it could not be so wrong for him to feel those feelings that had thrilled every heart in all his ancestors for innumerable generations.

He was in love with Meenie: he knew that clearly now. And this love was after all not such a wicked and terrible feeling; on the contrary, he felt all the better and the purer for it already. But then that might merely be the horrible seductiveness of the thing. Was it not always typified by the cup of Circe, by the song of the Sirens, by all that was alluring and beautiful and hollow? He paced up and down for half an hour, and then (he had sported his oak long ago) he lit his little reading lamp and sat down in the big chair by the bay window. Running his eyes over his bookshelf, he took out, half by chance, Spencer's "Sociology." Then, from sheer weariness, he read on for a while, hardly heeding what he read. At last he got interested, and finished a chapter. When he had finished it, he put the book down, and felt that the struggle was over. Strange that side by side in the same world, in the same London, there should exist two such utterly different types of man as Herbert Spencer and the Gideonite Apostle. The last seemed to belong to the sixteenth century, the first to some new and hitherto uncreated social world. In an age which produced thinkers like that, how could he ever have mistaken the poor, bigoted, narrow, half-instructed Apostle for a divinely inspired teacher! So far as Paul Owen was concerned, the Gideonite Church and all that belonged to it had melted utterly into thin air.

Three days later, after the Eights in the early evening, Paul found an opportunity of speaking again alone with Meenie. He had taken their party on to the Christchurch barge to see the race, and he was strolling with them afterwards round the meadow walk by the bank of the Cherwell. Paul managed to get a little in front with Meenie, and entered at once upon the subject of his late embarrassments.

"I have thought it all over since, Miss Bolton," he said—he half hesitated whether he should say "Meenie" or not, and she was half disappointed that he didn't, for they were both very young, and very young people fall in love so unaffectedly—"I have thought it all over, and I have come to the conclusion that there is no help for it: I must break openly with the Church."

"Of course," said Meenie, simply. "That I understood."

He smiled at her ingenuousness. Such a very forward young person! And yet he liked it. "Well, the next thing is, what to do about it. You see, I have really been obtaining my education, so to speak, under false pretences. I can't continue taking these good people's money after I have ceased to believe in their doctrines. I ought to have faced the question sooner. It was wrong of me to wait until—until it was forced upon me by other considerations."

This time it was Meenie who blushed. "But you don't mean to leave Oxford without taking your degree?" she asked quickly.

"No, I think it will be better not. To stop here and try for a fellowship is my best chance of repaying these poor people the money which I have taken from them for no purpose."

"I never thought of that," said Meenie. "You are bound in honour to pay them back, of course."

Paul liked the instantaneous honesty of that "of course." It marked the naturally honourable character; for "of course," too, they must wait to marry (young people jump so) till all that money was paid off. "Fortunately," he said, "I have lived economically, and have not spent nearly as much as they guaranteed. I got scholarships up to a hundred a year of my own, and I only took a hundred a year of theirs. They offered me two hundred. But there's five years at a hundred, that makes five hundred pounds—a big debt to begin life with."

"Never mind," said Meenie. "You will get a fellowship, and in a few years you can pay it off."

"Yes," said Paul, "I can pay it off. But I can never pay off the hopes and aspirations I have blighted. I must become a schoolmaster, or a barrister, or something of that sort, and never repay them for their self-sacrifice and devotion in making me whatever I shall become. They may get back their money, but they will have lost their cherished Apostle for ever."

"Mr. Owen," Meenie answered solemnly, "the seal of the Apostolate lies far deeper than that. It was born in you, and no act of yours can shake it off."

"Meenie," he said, looking at her gently, with a changed expression—"Meenie, we shall have to wait many years."

"Never mind, Paul," she replied, as naturally as if he had been Paul to her all her life long, "I can wait if you can. But what will you do for the immediate present?"

"I have my scholarship," he said; "I can get on partly upon that; and then I can take pupils; and I have only one year more of it."

So before they parted that night it was all well understood between them that Paul was to declare his defection from the Church at the earliest opportunity; that he was to live as best he might till he could take his degree; that he was then to pay off all the back debt; and that after all these things he and Meenie might get comfortably married whenever they were able. As to the Rector and his wife, or any other parental authorities, they both left them out in the cold as wholly as young people always do leave their elders out on all similar occasions.

"Maria's a born fool!" said the Rector to his wife a week after Meenie's return; "I always knew she was a fool, but I never knew she was quite such a fool as to permit a thing like this. So far as I can get it out of Edie, and so far as Edie can get it out of Meenie, I understand that she has allowed Meenie to go and get herself engaged to some Dissenter fellow, a Shaker, or a Mormon, or a Communist, or something of the sort, who is the son of a common labourer, and has been sent up to Oxford, Tom tells me, by his own sect, to be made into a gentleman, so as to give some sort or colour of respectability to their absurd doctrines. I shall send the girl to town at once to Emily's, and she shall stop there all next season, to see if she can't manage to get engaged to some young man in decent society at any rate."

III

When Paul Owen returned to Peckham for the long vacation, it was with a heavy heart that he ventured back slowly to his father's cottage. Margaret Owen had put everything straight and neat in the little living room, as she always did, to welcome home her son who had grown into a gentleman; and honest John stood at the threshold beaming with pleasure to wring Paul's hand in his firm grip, just back unwashed from his day's labour. After the first kissings and greetings were over, John Owen said rather solemnly, "I have bad news for you, Paul. The Apostle is sick, even unto death."

When Paul heard that, he was sorely tempted to put off the disclosure for the present; but he felt he must not. So that same night, as they sat together in the dusk near the window where the geraniums stood, he began to unburden his whole mind, gently and tentatively, so as to spare their feelings as much as possible, to his father and mother. He told them how, since he went to Oxford, he had learned to think somewhat differently about many things; how his ideas had gradually deepened and broadened; how he had begun to inquire into fundamentals for himself; how he had feared that the Gideonites took too much for granted, and reposed too implicitly on the supposed critical learning of their Apostle. As he spoke his mother listened in tearful silence; but his father murmured from time to time, "I was afeard of this already, Paul; I seen it coming, now and again, long ago." There was pity and regret in his tone, but not a shade of reproachfulness.

At last, however, Paul came to speak, timidly and reservedly, of Meenie. Then his father's eye began to flash a little, and his breath came deeper and harder. When Paul told him briefly that he was engaged to her, the strong man could stand it no longer. He rose up in righteous wrath, and thrust his son at arm's length from him. "What!" he cried fiercely, "you don't mean to tell me you have fallen into sin and looked upon the daughters of Midian! It was no Scriptural doubts that druv you on, then, but the desire of the flesh and the lust of the eyes that has lost you! You dare to stand up there, Paul Owen, and tell me that you throw over the Church and the Apostle for the sake of a girl, like a poor miserable Samson! You are no son of mine, and I have nothin' more to say to you."

But Margaret Owen put her hand on his shoulder and said softly, "John, let us hear him out." And John, recalled by that gentle touch, listened once more. Then Paul pleaded his case powerfully again. He quoted Scripture to them; he argued with them, after their own fashion, and down to their own comprehension, text by text; he pitted his own critical and exegetical faculty against the Apostle's. Last of all, he turned to his mother, who, tearful still and heart-broken with disappointment, yet looked admiringly upon her learned, eloquent boy, and said to her tenderly, "Remember, mother, you yourself were once in love. You yourself once stood, night after night, leaning on the gate, waiting with your heart beating for a footstep that you knew so well. You yourself once counted the days and the hours and the minutes till the next meeting came." And Margaret Owen, touched to the heart by that simple appeal, kissed him fervently a dozen times over, the hot tears dropping on his cheek meanwhile; and then, contrary to all the rules of their austere Church, she flung her arms round her husband too, and kissed him passionately the first time for twenty years, with all the fervour of a floodgate loosed. Paul Owen's apostolate had surely borne its first fruit.

The father stood for a moment in doubt and terror, like one stunned or dazed, and then, in a moment of sudden remembrance, stepped forward and returned the kiss. The spell was broken, and the Apostle's power was no more. What else passed in the cottage that night, when John Owen fell upon his knees and wrestled in spirit, was too wholly internal to the man's own soul for telling here. Next day John and Margaret Owen felt the dream of their lives was gone; but the mother in her heart rejoiced to think her boy might know the depths of love, and might bring home a real lady for his wife.

On Sunday it was rumoured that the Apostle's ailment was very serious; but young Brother Paul Owen would address the Church. He did so, though not exactly in the way the Church expected. He told them simply and plainly how he had changed his views about certain matters; how he thanked them from his heart for the loan of their money (he was careful to emphasize the word loan), which had helped him to carry on his education at Oxford; and how he would repay them the principal and interest, though he could never repay them the kindness, at the earliest possible opportunity. He was so grave, so earnest, so transparently true, that, in spite of the downfall of their dearest hopes, he carried the whole meeting with him, all save one man. That man was Job Grimshaw. Job rose from his place with a look of undisguised triumph as soon as Paul had finished, and, mounting the platform quietly, said his say.

"I knew, Episcops, Presbyters, and Brethren," he began, "how this 'ere young man would finish. I saw it the day he was appinted. He's flushing up now the same as he flushed up then when I spoke to him; and it ain't sperritual, it's worldly pride and headstrongness, that's what it is. He's had our money, and he's had his eddication, and now he's going to round on us, just as I said he would. It's all very well talking about paying us back: how's a young man like him to get five hundred pounds, I should like to know. And if he did even, what sort o' repayment would that be to many of the brethren, who've saved and scraped for five year to let him live like a gentleman among the great and the mighty o' Midian? He's got his eddication out of us, and he can keep that whatever happens, and make a living out of it, too; and now he's going back on us, same as I said he would, and, having got all he can out of the Church, he's going to chuck it away like a sucked orange. I detest such backsliding and such ungratefulness."

Paul's cup of humiliation was full, but he bit his lip till the blood almost came, and made no answer.

"He boasted in his own strength," Job went on mercilessly, "that he wasn't going to be a backslider, and he wasn't going to sign no bond, and he wasn't going to confer with us, but we must trust his honour and honesty, and such like. I've got his very words written down in my notebook 'ere; for I made a note of 'em, foreseeing this. If we'd 'a' bound him down, as I proposed, he wouldn't 'a' dared to go backsliding and rounding on us, as I don't doubt but what he's been doing." Paul's tell-tale face showed him at once that he had struck by accident on the right chord. "But if he ever goes bringing a daughter of Midian here to Peckham," Job continued, "we'll show her these very notes, and ask her what she thinks of such dishonourable conduct. The Apostle's dying, that's clear; and before he dies I warrant he shall know this treachery."

Paul could not stand that last threat. Though he had lost faith in the Apostle as an Apostle, he could never forget the allegiance he had once borne him as a father, or the spell which his powerful individuality had once thrown around him as a teacher. To have embittered that man's dying bed with the shadow of a terrible disappointment would be to Paul a lifelong subject of deep remorse. "I did not intend to open my mouth in answer to you, Mr. Grimshaw," he said (for the first time breaking through the customary address of Brother), "but I pray you, I entreat you, I beseech you, not to harass the Apostle in his last moments with such a subject."

"Oh yes, I suppose so," Job Grimshaw answered maliciously, all the ingrained coarseness of the man breaking out in the wrinkles of his face. "No wonder you don't want him enlightened about your goings on with the daughters of Midian, when you must know as well as I do that his life ain't worth a day's purchase, and that he's a man of independent means, and has left you every penny he's got in his will, because he believes you're a fit successor to the Apostolate. I know it, for I signed as a witness, and I read it through, being a short one, while the other witness was signing. And you must know it as well as I do. I suppose you don't think he'll make another will now; but there's time enough to burn that one anyhow."

Paul Owen stood aghast at the vulgar baseness of which this lewd fellow supposed him capable. He had never thought of it before; and yet it flashed across his mind in a moment how obvious it was now. Of course the Apostle would leave him his money. He was being educated for the Apostolate, and the Apostolate could not be carried on without the sinews of war. But that Job Grimshaw should think him guilty of angling for the Apostle's money, and then throwing the Church overboard—the bare notion of it was so horrible to him that he could not even hold up his head to answer the taunt. He sat down and buried his crimson face in his hands; and Job Grimshaw, taking up his hat sturdily, with the air of a man who has to perform an unpleasant duty, left the meeting-room abruptly without another word.

There was a gloomy Sunday dinner that morning in the mason's cottage, and nobody seemed much inclined to speak in any way. But as they were in the midst of their solemn meal, a neighbour who was also a Gideonite came in hurriedly. "It's all over," he said, breathless—"all over with us and with the Church. The Apostle is dead. He died this morning."

Margaret Owen found voice to ask, "Before Job Grimshaw saw him?"

The neighbour nodded, "Yes."

"Thank heaven for that!" cried Paul. "Then he did not die misunderstanding me!"

"And you'll get his money," added the neighbour, "for I was the other witness."

Paul drew a long breath. "I wish Meenie was here," he said. "I must see her about this."

IV

A few days later the Apostle was buried, and his will was read over before the assembled Church. By earnest persuasion of his father, Paul consented to be present, though he feared another humiliation from Job Grimshaw. But two days before he had taken the law into his own hands, by writing to Meenie, at her aunt's in Eaton Place; and that very indiscreet young lady, in response, had actually consented to meet him in Kensington Gardens alone the next afternoon. There he sat with her on one of the benches by the Serpentine, and talked the whole matter over with her to his heart's content.

"If the money is really left to me," he said, "I must in honour refuse it. It was left to me to carry on the Apostolate, and I can't take it on any other ground. But what ought I to do with it? I can't give it over to the Church, for in three days there will be no Church left to give it to. What shall I do with it?"

"Why," said Meenie, thoughtfully, "if I were you I should do this. First, pay back everybody who contributed towards your support in full, principal and interest; then borrow from the remainder as much as you require to complete your Oxford course; and finally, pay back all that and the other money to the fund when you are able, and hand it over for the purpose of doing some good work in Peckham itself, where your Church was originally founded. If the ideal can't be fulfilled, let the money do something good for the actual."

"You are quite right, Meenie," said Paul, "except in one particular. I will not borrow from the fund for my own support. I will not touch a penny of it, temporarily or permanently, for myself in any way. If it comes to me, I shall make it over to trustees at once for some good object, as you suggest, and shall borrow from them five hundred pounds to repay my own poor people, giving the trustees my bond to repay the fund hereafter. I shall fight my own battle henceforth unaided."

"You will do as you ought to do, Paul, and I am proud of it."

So next morning, when the meeting took place, Paul felt somewhat happier in his own mind as to the course he should pursue with reference to Job Grimshaw.

The Senior Episcop opened and read the last will and testament of Arthur Murgess, attorney-at-law. It provided in a few words that all his estate, real and personal, should pass unreservedly to his friend, Paul Owen, of Christchurch, Oxford. It was whispered about that, besides the house and grounds, the personalty might be sworn at £8000, a vast sum to those simple people.

When the reading was finished, Paul rose and addressed the assembly. He told them briefly the plan he had formed, and insisted on his determination that not a penny of the money should be put to his own uses. He would face the world for himself, and thanks to their kindness he could face it easily enough. He would still earn and pay back all that he owed them. He would use the fund, first for the good of those who had been members of the Church, and afterwards for the good of the people of Peckham generally. And he thanked them from the bottom of his heart for the kindness they had shown him.

Even Job Grimshaw could only mutter to himself that this was not sperritual grace, but mere worldly pride and stubbornness, lest the lad should betray his evil designs, which had thus availed him nothing. "He has lost his own soul and wrecked the Church for the sake of the money," Job said, "and now he dassn't touch a farden of it."

Next John Owen rose and said slowly, "Friends, it seems to me we may as well all confess that this Church has gone to pieces. I can't stop in it myself any longer, for I see it's clear agin nature, and what's agin nature can't be true." And though the assembly said nothing, it was plain that there were many waverers in the little body whom the affairs of the last week had shaken sadly in their simple faith. Indeed, as a matter of fact, before the end of the month the Gideonite Church had melted away, member by member, till nobody at all was left of the whole assembly but Job Grimshaw.

"My dear," said the Rector to his wife a few weeks later, laying down his Illustrated, "this is really a very curious thing. That young fellow Owen, of Christchurch, that Meenie fancied herself engaged to, has just come into a little landed property and eight or nine thousand pounds on his own account. He must be better connected than Tom imagines. Perhaps we might make inquiries about him after all."

The Rector did make inquiries in the course of the week, and with such results that he returned to the rectory in blank amazement. "That fellow's mad, Amelia," he said, "stark mad, if ever anybody was. The leader of his Little Bethel, or Ebenezer, or whatever it may be, has left him all his property absolutely, without conditions; and the idiot of a boy declares he won't touch a penny of it, because he's ceased to believe in their particular shibboleth, and he thinks the leader wanted him to succeed him. Very right and proper of him, of course, to leave the sect if he can't reconcile it with his conscience, but perfectly Quixotic of him to give up the money and beggar himself outright. Even if his connection was otherwise desirable (which it is far from being), it would be absurd to think of letting Meenie marry such a ridiculous hair-brained fellow."

Paul and Meenie, however, went their own way, as young people often will, in spite of the Rector. Paul returned next term to Oxford, penniless, but full of resolution, and by dint of taking pupils managed to eke out his scholarship for the next year. At the end of that time he took his first in Greats, and shortly after gained a fellowship. From the very first day he began saving money to pay off that dead weight of five hundred pounds. The kindly ex-Gideonites had mostly protested against his repaying them at all, but in vain: Paul would not make his entry into life, he said, under false pretences. It was a hard pull, but he did it. He took pupils, he lectured, he wrote well and vigorously for the press, he worked late and early with volcanic energy; and by the end of three years he had not only saved the whole of the sum advanced by the Gideonites, but had also begun to put away a little nest-egg against his marriage with Meenie. And when the editor of a great morning paper in London offered him a permanent place upon the staff, at a large salary, he actually went down to Worcestershire, saw the formidable Rector himself in his own parish, and demanded Meenie outright in marriage. And the Rector observed to his wife that this young Owen seemed a well-behaved and amiable young man; that after all one needn't know anything about his relations if one didn't like; and that as Meenie had quite made up her mind, and was as headstrong as a mule, there was no use trying to oppose her any longer.

Down in Peckham, where Paul Owen lives, and is loved by half the poor of the district, no one has forgotten who was the real founder of the Murgess Institute, which does so much good in encouraging thrift, and is so admirably managed by the founder and his wife. He would take a house nowhere but at Peckham, he said. To the Peckham people he owed his education, and for the Peckham people he would watch the working of his little Institute. There is no better work being done anywhere in that great squalid desert, the east and south-east of London; there is no influence more magnetic than the founder's. John and Margaret Owen have recovered their hopes for their boy, only they run now in another and more feasible direction; and those who witness the good that is being done by the Institute among the poor of Peckham, or who have read that remarkable and brilliant economical work lately published on "The Future of Co-operation in the East End, by P. O.," venture to believe that Meenie was right after all, and that even the great social world itself has not yet heard the last of young Paul Owen's lay apostolate.

THE MYSTERIOUS OCCURRENCE IN PICCADILLY

I

I really never felt so profoundly ashamed of myself in my whole life as when my father-in-law, Professor W. Bryce Murray, of Oriel College, Oxford, sent me the last number of the Proceedings of the Society for the Investigation of Supernatural Phenomena. As I opened the pamphlet, a horrible foreboding seized me that I should find in it, detailed at full length, with my name and address in plain printing (not even asterisks), that extraordinary story of his about the mysterious occurrence in Piccadilly. I turned anxiously to page 14, which I saw was neatly folded over at the corner; and there, sure enough, I came upon the Professor's remarkable narrative, which I shall simply extract here, by way of introduction, in his own admirable and perspicuous language.

"I wish to communicate to the Society," says my respected relation, "a curious case of wraiths or doubles, which came under my own personal observation, and for which I can vouch on my own authority, and that of my son-in-law, Dr. Owen Mansfield, keeper of Accadian Antiquities at the British Museum. It is seldom, indeed, that so strange an example of a supernatural phenomenon can be independently attested by two trustworthy scientific observers, both still living.

"On the 12th of May, 1873—I made a note of the circumstance at the time, and am therefore able to feel perfect confidence as to the strict accuracy of my facts—I was walking down Piccadilly about four o'clock in the afternoon, when I saw a simulacrum or image approaching me from the opposite direction, exactly resembling in outer appearance an undergraduate of Oriel College, of the name of Owen Mansfield. It must be carefully borne in mind that at this time I was not related or connected with Mr. Mansfield in any way, his marriage with my daughter having taken place some eleven months later: I only knew him then as a promising junior member of my own College. I was just about to approach and address Mr. Mansfield, when a most singular and mysterious event took place. The simulacrum appeared spontaneously to glide up towards me with a peculiarly rapid and noiseless motion, waved a wand or staff which it bore in its hands thrice round my head, and then vanished hastily in the direction of an hotel which stands at the corner of Albemarle Street. I followed it quickly to the door, but on inquiry of the porter, I learned that he himself had observed nobody enter. The simulacrum seems to have dissipated itself or become invisible suddenly in the very act of passing through the folding glass portals which give access to the hotel from Piccadilly.

"That same evening, by the last post, I received a hastily-written note from Mr. Mansfield, bearing the Oxford postmark, dated Oriel College, 5 p.m., and relating the facts of an exactly similar apparition which had manifested itself to him, with absolute simultaneity of occurrence. On the very day and hour when I had seen Mr. Mansfield's wraith in Piccadilly, Mr. Mansfield himself was walking down the Corn Market in Oxford, in the direction of the Taylor Institute. As he approached the corner, he saw what he took to be a vision or image of myself, his tutor, moving towards him in my usual leisurely manner. Suddenly, as he was on the point of addressing me with regard to my Aristotle lecture the next morning, the image glided up to him in a rapid and evasive manner, shook a green silk umbrella with a rhinoceros-horn handle three times around his head, and then disappeared incomprehensibly through the door of the Randolph Hotel. Returning to college in a state of breathless alarm and surprise, at what he took to be an act of incipient insanity or extreme inebriation on my part, Mr. Mansfield learnt from the porter, to his intense astonishment, that I was at that moment actually in London. Unable to conceal his amazement at this strange event, he wrote me a full account of the facts while they were still fresh in his memory: and as I preserve his note to this day, I append a copy of it to my present communication, for publication in the Society's Transactions.

"There is one small point in the above narrative to which I would wish to call special attention, and that is the accurate description given by Mr. Mansfield of the umbrella carried by the apparition he observed in Oxford. This umbrella exactly coincided in every particular with the one I was then actually carrying in Piccadilly. But what is truly remarkable, and what stamps the occurrence as a genuine case of supernatural intervention, is the fact that Mr. Mansfield could not possibly ever have seen that umbrella in my hands, because I had only just that afternoon purchased it at a shop in Bond Street. This, to my mind, conclusively proves that no mere effort of fancy or visual delusion based upon previous memories, vague or conscious, could have had anything whatsoever to do with Mr. Mansfield's observation at least. It was, in short, distinctly an objective apparition, as distinguished from a mere subjective reminiscence or hallucination."

As I laid down the Proceedings on the breakfast table with a sigh, I said to my wife (who had been looking over my shoulder while I read): "Now, Nora, we're really in for it. What on earth do you suppose I'd better do?"

Nora looked at me with her laughing eyes laughing harder and brighter than ever. "My dear Owen," she said, putting the Proceedings promptly into the waste paper basket, "there's really nothing on earth possible now, except to make a clean breast of it."

I groaned. "I suppose you're right," I answered, "but it's a precious awkward thing to have to do. However, here goes." So I sat down at once with pen, ink, and paper at my desk, to draw up this present narrative as to the real facts about the "Mysterious Occurrence in Piccadilly."

II

In 1873 I was a fourth-year man, going in for my Greats at the June examination. But as if Aristotle and Mill and the affair of Corcyra were not enough to occupy one young fellow's head at the age of twenty-three, I had foolishly gone and fallen in love, undergraduate fashion, with the only really pretty girl (I insist upon putting it, though Nora has struck it out with her pen) in all Oxford. She was the daughter of my tutor, Professor Bryce Murray, and her name (as the astute reader will already have inferred) was Nora.

The Professor had lost his wife some years before, and he was left to bring up Nora by his own devices, with the aid of his sister, Miss Lydia Amelia Murray, the well-known advocate of female education, woman's rights, anti-vaccination, vegetarianism, the Tichborne claimant, and psychic force. Nora, however, had no fancy for any of these multifarious interests of her aunt's: I have reason to believe she takes rather after her mother's family: and Miss Lydia Amelia Murray early decided that she was a girl of no intellectual tastes of any sort, who had better be kept at school at South Kensington as much as possible. Especially did Aunt Lydia hold it to be undesirable that Nora should ever come in contact with that very objectionable and wholly antagonistic animal, the Oriel undergraduate. Undergraduates were well known to laugh openly at woman's rights, to devour underdone beefsteaks with savage persistence, and to utter most irreverent and ribald jests about psychic force.

Still, it is quite impossible to keep the orbit of a Professor's daughter from occasionally crossing that of a stray meteoric undergraduate. Nora only came home to Oxford in vacation time: but during the preceding Long I had stopped up for the sake of pursuing my Accadian studies in a quiet spot, and it was then that I first quite accidentally met Nora. I was canoeing on the Cherwell one afternoon, when I came across the Professor and his daughter in a punt, and saw the prettiest girl in all Oxford actually holding the pole in her own pretty little hands, while that lazy old man lolled back at his ease with a book, on the luxurious cushions in the stern. As I passed the punt, I capped the Professor, of course, and looking back a minute later I observed that the pretty daughter had got her pole stuck fast in the mud, and couldn't, with all her force, pull it out again. In another minute she had lost her hold of it, and the punt began to drift of itself down the river towards Iffley.

Common politeness naturally made me put back my canoe, extricate the pole, and hand it as gracefully as I could to the Professor's daughter. As I did so, I attempted to raise my straw hat cautiously with one hand, while I gave back the pole with the other: an attempt which of course compelled me to lay down my paddle on the front, of the canoe, as I happen to be only provided with two hands, instead of four like our earlier ancestors. I don't know whether it was my instantaneous admiration for Nora's pretty blush, which distracted my attention from the purely practical question of equilibrium, or whether it was her own awkwardness and modesty in taking the pole, or finally whether it was my tutor's freezing look that utterly disconcerted me, but at any rate, just at that moment, something unluckily (or rather luckily) caused me to lose my balance altogether. Now, everybody knows that a canoe is very easily upset: and in a moment, before I knew exactly where I was, I found the canoe floating bottom upward about three yards away from me, and myself standing, safe and dry, in my tutor's punt, beside his pretty blushing daughter. I had felt the canoe turning over as I handed back the pole, and had instinctively jumped into the safer refuge of the punt, which saved me at least the ignominy of appearing before Miss Nora Murray in the ungraceful attitude of clambering back, wet and dripping, into an upset canoe.

The inexorable logic of facts had thus convinced the Professor of the impossibility of keeping all undergraduates permanently at a safe distance: and there was nothing open for him now except resignedly to acquiesce in the situation so created for him. However much he might object to my presence, he could hardly, as a Christian and a gentleman, request me to jump in and swim after my canoe, or even, when we had at last successfully brought it alongside with the aid of the pole, to seat myself once more on the soaking cushions. After all, my mishap had come about in the endeavour to render him a service: so he was fain with what grace he could to let me relieve his daughter of the pole, and punt him back as far as the barges, with my own moist and uncomfortable bark trailing casually from the stern.

As for Nora, being thus thrown unexpectedly into the dangerous society of that gruesome animal, the Oriel undergraduate, I think I may venture to say (from my subsequent experience) that she was not wholly disposed to regard the creature as either so objectionable or so ferocious as she had been previously led to imagine. We got on together so well that I could see the Professor growing visibly wrathful about the corners of the mouth: and by the time we reached the barges, he could barely be civil enough to say Good morning to me when we parted.

An introduction, however, no matter how obtained, is really in these matters absolutely everything. As long as you don't know a pretty girl, you don't know her, and you can't take a step in advance without an introduction. But when once you do know her, heaven and earth and aunts and fathers may try their hardest to prevent you, and yet whatever they try they can't keep you out. I was so far struck with Nora, that I boldly ventured whenever I met her out walking with her father or her aunt, to join myself to the party: and though they never hesitated to show me that my presence was not rapturously welcomed, they couldn't well say to me point-blank, "Have the goodness, Mr. Mansfield, to go away and not to speak to me again in future." So the end of it was, that before the beginning of October term, Nora and I understood one another perfectly, and had even managed, in a few minutes' tête-à-tête in the parks, to whisper to one another the ingenuous vows of sweet seventeen and two-and-twenty.

When the Professor discovered that I had actually written a letter to his daughter, marked "Private and Confidential," his wrath knew no bounds. He sent for me to his rooms, and spoke to me severely. "I've half a mind, Mansfield," he said, "to bring the matter before a college meeting. At any rate, this conduct must not be repeated. If it is, Sir,"—he didn't finish the sentence, preferring to terrify me by the effective figure of speech which commentators describe as an aposiopesis: and I left him with a vague sense that if it was repeated I should probably incur the penalties of præmunire (whatever they may be), or be hanged, drawn, and quartered, with my head finally stuck as an adornment on the acute wings of the Griffin, vice Temple Bar removed.

Next day, Nora met me casually at a confectioner's in the High, where I will frankly confess that I was engaged in experimenting upon the relative merits of raspberry cream and lemon water ices. She gave me her hand timidly, and whispered to me half under her breath, "Papa's so dreadfully angry, Owen, and I'm afraid I shall never be able to meet you any more, for he's going to send me back this very afternoon to South Kensington, and keep me away from Oxford altogether in future." I saw her eyes were red with crying, and that she really thought our little romance was entirely at an end.

"My darling Nora," I replied in an undertone, "even South Kensington is not so unutterably remote that I shall never be able to see you there. Write to me whenever you are able, and let me know where I can write to you. My dear little Nora, if there were a hundred papas and a thousand Aunt

Lydias interposed in a square between us, don't you know we should manage all the same to love one another and to overcome all difficulties?"

Nora smiled and half cried at once, and then discreetly turned to order half a pound of glacé cherries. And that was the last that I saw of her for the time at Oxford.

During the next term or two, I'm afraid I must admit that the relations between my tutor and myself were distinctly strained, so much so as continually to threaten the breaking out of open hostilities. It wasn't merely that Nora was in question, but the Professor also suspected me of jeering in private at his psychical investigations. And if the truth must be told, I will admit that his suspicions were not wholly without justification. It began to be whispered among the undergraduates just then that the Professor and his sister had taken to turning planchettes, interrogating easy-chairs, and obtaining interesting details about the present abode of Shakespeare or Milton from intelligent and well-informed five-o'clock tea-tables. It had long been well known that the Professor took a deep interest in haunted houses, considered that the portents recorded by Livy must have something in them, and declared himself unable to be sceptical as to facts which had convinced such great men as Plato, Seneca, and Samuel Johnson. But the table-turning was a new fad, and we noisy undergraduates occasionally amused ourselves by getting up an amateur séance, in imitation of the Professor, and eliciting psychical truths, often couched in a surprisingly slangy or even indecorous dialect, from a very lively though painfully irreverent spirit, who discoursed to us through the material intervention of a rickety what-not. However, as the only mediums we employed were the very unprofessional ones of two plain decanters, respectively containing port and sherry, the Professor (who was a teetotaler, and who paid five guineas a séance for the services of that distinguished psychical specialist, Dr. Grade) considered the interesting results we obtained as wholly beneath the dignity of scientific inquiry. He even most unworthily endeavoured to stifle research by gating us all one evening when a materialized spirit, assuming the outer form of the junior exhibitioner, sang a comic song of the period in a loud voice with the windows open, and accompanied itself noisily with a psychical tattoo on the rickety what-not. The Professor went so far as to observe sarcastically that our results appeared to him to be rather spirituous than spiritual.

On May 11, 1873 (I will endeavour to rival the Professor in accuracy and preciseness), I got a short note from dear Nora, dated from South Kensington, which I, too (though not from psychical motives), have carefully preserved. I will not publish it, however, either here or in the Society's Proceedings, for reasons which will probably be obvious to any of my readers who happen ever to have been placed in similar circumstances themselves. Disengaging the kernel of fact from the irrelevant matter in which it was imbedded, I may state that Nora wrote me somewhat to this effect. She was going next day to the Academy with the parents of some schoolfellow; could I manage to run up to town for the day, go to the Academy myself, and meet her "quite accidentally, you know, dear," in the Water-colour room about half-past eleven?

This was rather awkward; for next day, as it happened, was precisely the Professor's morning for the Herodotus lecture; but circumstances like mine at that moment know no law. So I succeeded in excusing myself from attendance somehow or other (I hope truthfully) and took the nine a.m. express up to town. Shortly after eleven I was at the Academy, and waiting anxiously for Nora's arrival. That dear little hypocrite, the moment she saw me approach, assumed such an inimitable air of infantile surprise and innocent pleasure at my unexpected appearance that I positively blushed for her wicked powers of deception.

"You here, Mr. Mansfield!" she cried in a tone of the most apparently unaffected astonishment, "why, I thought it was full term time; surely you ought to be up at Oriel."

"So I am," I answered, "officially; but in my private capacity I've come up for the day to look at the pictures."

"Oh, how nice!" said that shocking little Nora, with a smile that was childlike and bland. "Mr. Mansfield is such a great critic, Mrs. Worplesdon; he knows all about art, and artists, and so on. He'll be able to tell us which pictures we ought to admire, you know, and which aren't worth looking at. Mr. Worplesdon, let me introduce you; Mrs. Worplesdon—Miss Worplesdon. How very lucky we should have happened to come across you, Mr. Mansfield!"

The Worplesdons fell immediately, like lambs, into the trap so ingenuously spread for them. Indeed, I have always noticed that ninety-nine per cent. of the British public, when turned into an art-gallery, are only too glad to accept the opinion of anybody whatsoever, who is bold enough to have one, and to express it openly. Having thus been thrust by Nora into the arduous position of critic by appointment to the Worplesdon party, I delivered myself ex cathedrâ forthwith upon the merits and demerits of the entire exhibition; and I was so successful in my critical views that I not only produced an immense impression upon Mr. Worplesdon himself, but also observed many ladies in the neighbourhood nudge one another as they gazed intently backward and forward between wall and catalogue, and heard them whisper audibly among themselves, "A gentleman here says the flesh tones on that shoulder are simply marvellous;" or, "That artist in the tweed suit behind us thinks the careless painting of the ferns in the foreground quite unworthy of such a colourist as Daubiton." So highly was my criticism appreciated, in fact, that Mr. Worplesdon even invited me to lunch with Nora and his party at a neighbouring restaurant, where I spent the most delightful hour I had passed for the last half-year, in the company of that naughty mendacious little schemer.

About four o'clock, however, the Worplesdons departed, taking Nora with them to South Kensington; and I prepared to walk back in the direction of Paddington, meaning to catch an evening train, and return to Oxford. I was strolling in a leisurely fashion along Piccadilly towards the Park, and looking into all the photographers' windows, when suddenly an awful apparition loomed upon me— the Professor himself, coming round the corner from Bond Street, folding up a new rhinoceros-handled umbrella as he walked along. In a moment I felt that all was lost. I was up in town without leave; the Professor would certainly see me and recognize me; he would ask me how and why I had left the University, contrary to rules; and I must then either tell him the whole truth, which would get Nora into a fearful scrape, or else run the risk of being sent down in disgrace, which might prevent me from taking a degree, and would at least cause my father and mother an immense deal of unmerited trouble.

Like a flash of lightning, a wild idea shot instantaneously across my brain. Might I pretend to be my own double? The Professor was profoundly superstitious on the subject of wraiths, apparitions, ghosts, brain-waves, and supernatural appearances generally; if I could only manage to impose upon him for a moment by doing something outrageously uncommon or eccentric, I might succeed in stifling further inquiry by setting him from the beginning on a false track which he was naturally prone to follow. Before I had time to reflect upon the consequences of my act, the wild idea had taken possession of me, body and soul, and had worked itself out in action with all the rapidity of a mad impulse. I rushed frantically up to the Professor, with my eyes fixed in a vacant stare on a point in space somewhere above the tops of the chimney-pots: I waved my stick three times mysteriously around his head; and then, without giving him time to recover from his surprise or to address a single word to me, I bolted off in a Red Indian dance to the nearest corner.

There was an hotel there, which I had often noticed before, though I had never entered it; and I rushed wildly in, meaning to get out as best I could when the Professor (who is very short-sighted) had passed on along Piccadilly in search of me. But fortune, as usual, favoured the bold. Luckily, it was a corner house, and, to my surprise, I found when I got inside it, that the hall opened both ways, with a door on to the side street. The porter was looking away as I entered; so I merely ran in of one door and out of the other, never stopping till I met a hansom, into which I jumped and ordered the man to drive to Paddington. I just caught the 4.35 to Oxford, and by a little over six o'clock I was in my own rooms at Oriel.

It was very wrong of me, indeed; I acknowledge it now; but the whole thing had flashed across my undergraduate mind so rapidly that I carried it out in a moment, before I could at all realize what a very foolish act I was really committing. To take a rise out of the Professor, and to save Nora an angry interview, were the only ideas that occurred to me at the second: when I began to reflect upon it afterwards, I was conscious that I had really practised a very gross and wicked deception. However, there was no help for it now; and as I rolled along in the train to Oxford, I felt that to save myself and Nora from utter disgrace, I must carry the plot out to the end without flinching. It then occurred to me that a double apparition would be more in accordance with all recognized principles of psychical manifestation than a single one. At Reading, therefore, I regret to say, I bought a pencil, and a sheet of paper, and an envelope; and before I reached Oxford station, I had written to the Professor what I now blush to acknowledge as a tissue of shocking fables, in which I paralleled every particular of my own behaviour to him by a similar imaginary piece of behaviour on his part to me, only changing the scene to Oxford. It was awfully wrong, I admit. At the time, however, being yet but little more than a schoolboy, after all, I regarded it simply in the light of a capital practical joke. I informed the Professor gravely how I had seen him at four o'clock in the Corn Market, and how astonished I was when I found him waving his green silk umbrella three times wildly, around my head.

The moment I arrived at Oxford, I dashed up to college in a hansom, and got the Professor's address in London from the porter. He had gone up to town for the night, it seemed, probably to visit Nora, and would not be back in college till the next morning. Then I rushed down to the post-office, where I was just in time (with an extra stamp) to catch the last post for that night's delivery. The moment the letter was in the box, I repented, and began to fear I had gone too far: and when I got back to my own rooms at last, and went down late for dinner in hall, I confess I trembled not a little, as to the possible effect of my quite too bold and palpable imposition.

Next morning by the second post I got a long letter from the Professor, which completely relieved me from all immediate anxiety as to his interpretation of my conduct. He rose to the fly with a charming simplicity which showed how delighted he was at this personal confirmation of all his own most cherished superstitions. "My dear Mansfield," his letter began, "now hear what, at the very self-same hour and minute, happened to me in Piccadilly." In fact, he had swallowed the whole thing entire, without a single moment's scepticism or hesitation.

From what I heard afterwards, it was indeed a lucky thing for me that I had played him this shocking trick, for Nora believes he was then actually on his way to South Kensington on purpose to forbid her most stringently from holding any further communication with me in any way. But as soon as this mysterious event took place, he began to change his mind about me altogether. So remarkable an apparition could not have happened except for some good and weighty reason, he argued: and he suspected that the reason might have something to do with my intentions towards Nora. Why, when he was on his way to warn her against me, should a vision, bearing my outer and bodily shape, come straight across his path, and by vehement signs of displeasure, endeavour to turn him from his purpose, unless it were clearly well for Nora that my attentions should not be discouraged?

From that day forth the Professor began to ask me to his rooms and address me far more cordially than he used to do before: he even, on the strength of my singular adventure, invited me to assist at one or two of his psychical séances. Here, I must confess, I was not entirely successful: the distinguished medium complained that I exerted a repellent effect upon the spirits, who seemed to be hurt by my want of generous confidence in their good intentions, and by my suspicious habit of keeping my eyes too sharply fixed upon the legs of the tables. He declared that when I was present, an adverse influence seemed to pervade the room, due, apparently, to my painful lack of spiritual sympathies. But the Professor condoned my failure in the regular psychical line, in consideration of my brilliant success as a beholder of wraiths and visions. After I took my degree that summer, he used all his influence to procure me the post of keeper of the Accadian Antiquities at the Museum, for which my previous studies had excellently fitted me: and by his friendly aid I was enabled to obtain the post, though I regret to say that, in spite of his credulity in supernatural matters, he still refuses to believe in the correctness of my conjectural interpretation of the celebrated Amalekite cylinders imported by Mr. Ananias, which I have deciphered in so very simple and satisfactory a manner. As everybody knows, my translation may be regarded as perfectly certain, if only one makes the very modest assumption that the cylinders were originally engraved upside down by an Aztec captive, who had learned broken Accadian, with a bad accent, from a Chinese exile, and who occasionally employed Egyptian hieroglyphics in incorrect senses, to piece out his own very imperfect idiom and doubtful spelling of the early Babylonian language. The solitary real doubt in the matter is whether certain extraordinary marks in the upper left-hand corner of the cylinder are to be interpreted as accidental scratches, or as a picture representing the triumph of a king over seven bound prisoners, or, finally, as an Accadian sentence in cuneiforms which may be translated either as "To the memory of Om the Great," or else as "Pithor the High Priest dedicates a fat goose to the family dinner on the 25th of the month of mid winter." Every candid and unprejudiced mind must admit that these small discrepancies or alternatives in the opinions of experts can cast no doubt at all upon the general soundness of the method employed. But persons like the Professor, while ready to accept any evidence at all where their own prepossessions are concerned, can never be induced to believe such plain and unvarnished statements of simple scientific knowledge.

However, the end of it all was that before I had been a month at the Museum, I had obtained the Professor's consent to my marriage with Nora: and as I had had Nora's own consent long before, we were duly joined together in holy matrimony early in October at Oxford, and came at once to live in Hampstead. So, as it turned out, I finally owed the sweetest and best little wife in all Christendom to the mysterious occurrence in Piccadilly.

CARVALHO

I

The first time I ever met Ernest Carvalho was just before the regimental dance at Newcastle. I had ridden up the Port Royal mountains that same morning from our decaying sugar estate in the Liguanca plain, and I was to stop in cantonments with the Major's wife, fat little Mrs. Venn, who had promised my mother that she would undertake to chaperon me to this my earliest military party. I won't deny that I looked forward to it immensely, for I was then a girl of only eighteen, fresh out from school in England, where I had been living away from our family ever since I was twelve years old. Dear mamma was a Jamaican lady of the old school, completely overpowered by the ingrained West Indian indolence; and if I had waited to go to a dance till I could get her to accompany me, I might have waited till Doomsday, or probably later. So I was glad enough to accept fat little Mrs. Venn's proffered protection, and to go up the hills on my sure-footed mountain pony; while Isaac, the black stable-boy, ran up behind me carrying on his thick head the small portmanteau that contained my plain white ball-dress.

As I went up the steep mountain-path alone—for ladies ride only with such an unmounted domestic escort in Jamaica—I happened to overtake a tall gentleman with a handsome rather Jewish face and a pair of extremely lustrous black eyes, who was mounted on a beautiful chestnut mare just in front of me. The horse-paths in the Port Royal mountains are very narrow, being mere zigzag ledges cut half-way up the precipitous green slopes of fern and club-moss, so that there is seldom room for two horses to pass abreast, and it is necessary to wait at some convenient corner whenever you see another rider coming in the opposite direction. At the first opportunity the tall Jewish-looking gentleman drew aside in such a corner, and waited for me to pass. "Pray don't wait," I said, as soon as I saw what he meant; "your horse will get up faster than my pony, and if I go in front I shall keep you back unnecessarily."

"Not at all," he answered, raising his hat gracefully; "you are a stranger in the hills, I see. It is the rule of these mountain-paths always to give a lady the lead. If I go first and my mare breaks into a canter on a bit of level, your pony will try to catch her up on the steep slopes, and that is always dangerous."

Seeing he did not intend to move till I did, I waived the point at last and took the lead. From that moment I don't know what on earth came over my lazy old pony. He refused to go at more than a walk, or at best a jog-trot, the whole way to Newcastle. Now the rise from the plain to the cantonments is about four thousand feet, I think (I am a dreadfully bad hand at remembering figures), and the distance can't be much less, I suppose, than seven miles. During all that time you never see a soul, except a few negro pickaninnies playing in the dustheaps, not a human habitation, except a few huts embowered in mangoes, hibiscus-bushes, and tree-ferns. At first we kept a decorous silence, not having been introduced to one another; but the stranger's mare followed close at my pony's heels, pull her in as he would, and it seemed really too ridiculous to be solemnly pacing after one another, single file, in this way for a couple of hours, without speaking a word, out of pure punctiliousness. So at last we broke the ice, and long before we got to Newcastle we had struck up quite an acquaintance with one another. It is wonderful how well two people can get mutually known in the course of two hours' tête-à-tête, especially under such peculiar circumstances. You are just near enough to one another for friendly chat, and yet not too near for casual strangers. And then Isaac with the portmanteau behind was quite sufficient escort to satisfy the convenances. In England, one's groom would have to be mounted, which always seems to me, in my simplicity, a distinction without a difference.

Mr. Carvalho was on his way up to Newcastle on the same errand as myself, to go to the dance. He might have been twenty, I suppose; and, to a girl of eighteen, boys of twenty seem quite men already. He was a clerk in a Government Office in Kingston, and was going to stop with a sub at Newcastle for a week or two, on leave. I did not know much about men in those days, but I needed little knowledge of the subject to tell me that Ernest Carvalho was decidedly clever. As soon as the first chill wore off our conversation, he kept me amused the whole way by his bright sketchy talk about the petty dignitaries of a colonial capital. There was his Excellency for the time being, and there was the Right Reverend of that day, and there was the Honourable Colonial Secretary, and there was the Honourable Director of Roads, and there were a number of other assorted Honourables, whose queer little peculiarities he hit off dexterously in the quaintest manner. Not that there was any unkindly satire in his brilliant conversation; on the contrary, he evidently liked most of the men he talked about, and seemed only to read and realize their characters so thoroughly that they spoke for themselves in his dramatic anecdotes. He appeared to me a more genial copy of Thackeray in a colonial society, with all the sting gone, and only the skilful delineation of men and women left. I had never met anybody before, and I have never met anybody since, who struck me so instantaneously with the idea of innate genius as Ernest Carvalho.

"You have been in England, of course," I said, as we were nearing Newcastle.

"No, never," he answered; "I am a Jamaican born and bred, I have never been out of the island."

I was surprised, for he seemed so different from any of the young planters I had met at our house, most of whom had never opened a book, apparently, in the course of their lives, while Mr. Carvalho's talk was full of indefinite literary flavour. "Where were you educated, then?" I asked.

"I never was educated anywhere," he answered, laughing. "I went to a small school at Port Antonio during my father's life, but for the most part I have picked up whatever I know (and that's not much) wholly by myself. Of course French, like reading and writing, comes by nature, and I got enough Spanish to dip into Cervantes from the Cuban refugees. Latin one has to grind up out of books, naturally; and as for Greek, I'm sorry to say I know very little, though, of course, I can spell out Homer a bit, and even Æschylus. But my hobby is natural science, and there a fellow has to make his own way here, for hardly anything has been done at the beasts and the flowers in the West Indies yet. But if I live, I mean to work them up in time, and I've made a fair beginning already."

This reasonable list of accomplishments, given modestly, not boastfully, by a young man of twenty, wholly self-taught, fairly took my breath away. I was inspired at once with a secret admiration for Mr. Carvalho. He was so handsome and so clever that I think I was half-inclined to fall in love with him at first sight. To say the truth, I believe almost all love is love at first sight; and for my own part, I wouldn't give you a thank-you for any other kind.

"Here we must part," he said, as we reached a fork in the narrow path just outside the steep hog's back on which Newcastle stands, "unless you will allow me to see you safely as far as Mrs. Venn's. The path to the right leads to the Major's quarters; this on the left takes me to my friend Cameron's hut. May I see you to the Major's door?"

"No, thank you," I answered decidedly; "Isaac is escort enough. We shall meet again this evening."

"Perhaps then," he suggested, "I may have the pleasure of a dance with you. Of course it's quite irregular of me to ask you now, but we shall be formally introduced no doubt to-night, and I'm afraid if you lunch at the Venns' your card will be filled up by the 99th men before I can edge myself in anywhere for a dance. Will you allow me?"

"Certainly," I said; "what shall it be? The first waltz?"

"You are very kind," he answered, taking out a pencil. "You know my name—Carvalho; what may I put down for yours? I haven't heard it yet."

"Miss Hazleden," I replied, "of Palmettos."

Mr. Carvalho gave a little start of surprise. "Miss Hazleden of Palmettos," he said half to himself, with a rather pained expression. "Miss Hazleden! Then, perhaps, I'd better—well, why not? why not, indeed? Palmettos—Yes, I will." Turning to me, he said, louder, "Thank you; till this evening, then;" and, raising his hat, he hurried sharply round the corner of the hill.

What was there in my name, I wondered, which made him so evidently hesitate and falter?

Fat little Mrs. Venn was very kind, and not a very strict chaperon, but I judged it best not to mention to her this romantic episode of the handsome stranger. However, during the course of lunch, I ventured casually to ask her husband whether he knew of any family in Jamaica of the name of Carvalho.

"Carvalho," answered the Major, "bless my soul, yes. Old settled family in the island; Jews; live down Savannah-la-Mar way; been here ever since the Spanish time; doocid clever fellows, too, and rich, most of them."

"Jews," I thought; "ah, yes, Mr. Carvalho had a very handsome Jewish type of face and dark eyes; but, why, yes, surely I heard him speak several times of having been to church, and once of the Cathedral at Spanish Town. This was curious."

"Are any of them Christians?" I asked again.

"Not a man," answered the Major; "not a man, my dear. Good old Jewish family; Jews in Jamaica never turn Christians; nothing to gain by it."

The dance took place in the big mess-room, looking out on the fan-palms and tree-ferns of the regimental garden. It was a lovely tropical night, moonlight of course, for all Jamaican entertainments are given at full moon, so as to let the people who ride from a distance get to and fro safely over the breakneck mountain horse-paths. The windows, which open down to the ground, were flung wide for the sake of ventilation; and thus the terrace and garden were made into a sort of vestibule where partners might promenade and cool themselves among the tropical flowers after the heat of dancing. And yet, I don't know how it is, though the climate is so hot in Jamaica, I never danced anywhere so much or felt the heat so little oppressive.

Before the first waltz, Mr. Carvalho came up, accompanied by my old friend Dr. Wade, and was properly introduced to me. By that time my card was pretty full, for of course I was a belle in those days, and being just fresh out from England was rather run after. But I will confess that I had taken the liberty of filling in three later waltzes (unasked) with Mr. Carvalho's name, for I knew by his very look that he could waltz divinely, and I do love a good partner. He did waltz divinely, but at the end of the dance I was really afraid he didn't mean to ask me again. When he did, a little hesitatingly, I said I had still three vacancies, and found he had not yet asked anybody else. I enjoyed those four dances more than any others that evening, the more so, perhaps, as I saw my cousin, Harry Verner of Agualta, was dying with jealousy because I danced so much with Mr. Carvalho.

I must just say a word or two about Harry Verner. He was a planter pur sang, and Agualta was one of the few really flourishing sugar estates then left on the island. Harry was, therefore, naturally regarded as rather a catch; but, for my part, I could never care for any man who has only three subjects of conversation—himself, vacuum-pan sugar, and the wickedness of the French bounty system, which keeps the poor planter out of his own. So I danced away with Mr. Carvalho, partly because I liked him just a little, you know, but partly, also, I will frankly admit, because I saw it annoyed Harry Verner.

At the end of our fourth dance, I was strolling with Mr. Carvalho among the great bushy poinsettias and plumbagos on the terrace, under the beautiful soft green light of that tropical moon, when Harry Verner came from one of the windows directly upon us. "I suppose you've forgotten, Edith," he said, "that you're engaged to me for the next lancers. Mr. Carvalho, I know you are to dance with Miss Wade; hadn't you better go and look for your partner?"

He spoke pointedly, almost rudely, and Mr. Carvalho took the hint at once. As soon as he was gone, Harry turned round to me fiercely and said in a low angry voice, "You shall not dance this lancers, you shall sit it out with me here in the garden; come over to the seat in the far corner."

He led me resistlessly to the seat, away from the noise of the regimental band and the dancers, and then sat himself down at the far end from me, like a great surly bear that he was.

"A pretty fool you've been making of yourself to-night, Edith," he said in a tone of suppressed anger, "with that fellow Carvalho. Do you know who he is, miss? Do you know who he is?"

"No," I answered faintly, fearing he was going to assure me that my clever new acquaintance was a notorious swindler or a runaway ticket-of-leave man.

"Well, then, I'll tell you," he cried angrily. "I'll tell you. He's a coloured man, miss! that's what he is."

"A coloured man?" I exclaimed in surprise; "why, he's as white as you and I are, every bit as white, Harry."

"So he may be, to look at," answered my cousin; "but a brown man's a brown man, all the same, however much white blood he may have in him; you can never breed the nigger out. Confound his impudence, asking you to dance four times with him in a single evening! You, too, of all girls in the island! Confound his impudence! Why, his mother was a slave girl once on Palmettos estate!"

"Oh, Harry, you don't mean to say so," I cried, for I was West Indian enough in my feelings to have a certain innate horror of coloured blood, and I was really shocked to think I had been so imprudent as to dance four times with a brown man.

"Yes, I do mean it, miss," he answered; "an octaroon slave girl, and Carvalho's her son by old Jacob Carvalho, a Jew merchant at the back of the island, who was fool enough to go and actually marry her. So now you see what a pretty mess you've gone and been and made of it. We shall have it all over Kingston to-morrow, I suppose, that Miss Hazleden, a Hazleden and a Verner, has been flirting violently with a bit of coloured scum off her own grandfather's estate at Palmettos. A nice thing for the family, indeed!"

"But, Harry," I said, pleading, "he's such a perfect gentleman in his manners and conversation, so very much superior to a great many Jamaican young men."

"Hang it all, miss," said Harry—he used a stronger expression, for he was not particular about swearing before ladies, but I won't transcribe all his oaths—"hang it all, that's the way of you girls who have been to England. If I had fifty daughters I'd never send one of 'em home, not I. You go over there, and you get enlightened, as you call it, and you learn a lot of radical fal-lal about equality and a-man-and-a-brother, and all that humbug: and then you come back and despise your own people, who are gentlemen and the sons of gentlemen for fifty generations, from the good old slavery days onward. I wish we had them here again, I do, and I'd tie up that fellow Carvalho to a horse-post and flog him with a cow-hide within an inch of his life."

I was too much accustomed to Harry's manners to make any protest against this vigorous suggestion of reprisals. I took his arm quietly. "Let us go back into the ballroom, Harry," I said as persuasively as I was able, for I loathed the man in my heart, "and for heaven's sake don't make a scene about it. If there is anything on earth I detest, it's scenes."

Next morning I felt rather feverish, and dear fat little Mrs. Venn was quite frightened about me. "If you go down again to Liguanea with this fever on you, my dear," she said, "you'll get yellow Jack as soon as you are home again. Better write and ask your mamma to let you stop a fortnight with us here."

I consented, readily enough, for, of course, no girl of eighteen ever in her heart objects to military society, and the 99th were really very pleasant well-intentioned young fellows. But I made up my mind that if I stayed I would take particular care to see no more of Mr. Carvalho. He was very clever, very fascinating, very nice, but then—he was a brown man! That was a bar that no West Indian girl could ever be expected to get over.

As ill-luck would have it, however—I write as I then felt—about three days after, Mrs. Venn said to me, "I've invited Mr. Cameron, one of our sub-lieutenants, to dine this evening, and I've had to invite his guest, young Carvalho, as well. By the way, Edie, if I were you, I wouldn't talk quite so much as you did the other evening to Mr. Carvalho. You know, dear, though he doesn't look it, he's a brown man."

"I didn't know it," I answered, "till the end of the evening, and then Harry Verner told me. I wouldn't have danced with him more than once if I'd known it."

"Wonderful how that young fellow has managed to edge himself into society," said the major, looking up from his book; "devilish odd. Son of old Jacob Carvalho: Jacob left him all his coin, not very much; picked up his ABC somewhere or other; got into Government service; asked to Governor's dances; goes everywhere now. Can't understand it."

"Well, my dear," says Mrs. Venn, "why do we ask him ourselves?"

"Because we can't help it," says the major, testily. "Cameron goes and picks him up; ought to be in the Engineers, Cameron; too doocid clever for the line and for this regiment. Always picks up some astronomer fellow, or some botanist fellow, or some fellow who understands fortification or something. Competitive examination's ruin of the service. Get all sorts of people into the regiment now. Believe Cameron himself lives upon his pay almost, hanged if I don't."

That evening, Mr. Carvalho came, and I liked him better than ever. Mr. Cameron, who was a brother botanist and a nice ingenuous young Highlander, made him bring his portfolio of Jamaica ferns and flowers, the loveliest things I ever saw—dried specimens and water-colour sketches to accompany them of the plants themselves as they grew naturally. He told us all about them so enthusiastically, and of how he used to employ almost all his holidays in the mountains hunting for specimens. "I'm afraid the fellows at the office think me a dreadful muff for it," he said, "but I can't help it, it's born in me. My mother is a descendant of Sir Hans Sloane's, who lived here for several years—the founder of the British Museum, you know—and all her family have always had a taste for bush, as the negroes call it. You know, a good many mulatto people have the blood of able English families in their veins, and that accounts, I believe, for their usual high average of general intelligence."

I was surprised to hear him speak so unaffectedly of his ancestry on the wrong side of the house, for most light coloured people studiously avoid any reference to their social disabilities. I liked him all the better, however, for the perfect frankness with which he said it. If only he hadn't been a brown man, now! But there, you can't get over those fundamental race prejudices.

Next morning, as the Major and I were out riding, we came again across Mr. Cameron and Mr. Carvalho. Fate really seemed determined to throw us together. We were going to the Fern Walk to gather gold and silver ferns, and Mr. Carvalho was bound in the same direction, to look for some rare hill-top flowers. At the Walk we dismounted, and, while the two officers went hunting about among the bush, Mr. Carvalho and I sat for a while upon a big rock in the shade of a mountain palm. The conversation happened to come round to somewhat the same turn as it had taken the last evening.

"Yes," said Mr Carvalho, in answer to a question of mine, "I do think that mulattos and quadroons are generally cleverer than the average run of white people. You see, mixture of race evidently tends to increase the total amount of brain power. There are peculiar gains of brain on the one side, and other peculiar gains, however small, on the other; and the mixture, I fancy, tends to preserve or increase both. That is why the descendants of Huguenots in England, and the descendants of Italians in France, show generally such great ability."

"Then you yourself ought to be an example," I said, "for your name seems to be Spanish or Portuguese."

"Spanish and Jewish," he answered, laughing, "though I didn't mean to give a side-puff to myself. Yes, I am of very mixed race indeed. On my father's side I am Jewish, though of course the Jews acknowledge nobody who isn't a pure-blooded descendant of Abraham in both lines; and for that reason I have been brought up a Christian. On my mother's side I am partly negro, partly English, partly Haitian French, and, through the Sloanes, partly Dutch as well. So you see I am a very fair mixture."

"And that accounts," I said, "for your being so clever."

He blushed and bowed a little demure bow, but said nothing.

It's no use fighting against fate, and during all that fortnight I did nothing but run up against Mr. Carvalho. Wherever I went, he was sure to be; wherever I was invited, he was invited to meet me. The fact is, I had somehow acquired the reputation of being a clever girl, and, as Mr. Cameron was by common consent the clever man of his regiment, it was considered proper that he (and by inference his guest) should be always asked to entertain me. The more I saw of Mr. Carvalho the better I liked him. He was so clever, and yet so simple and unassuming, that one couldn't help admiring and sympathizing with him. Indeed, if he hadn't been a brown man, I almost think I should have fallen in love with him outright.

At the end of a fortnight I went back to Palmettos. A few days after, who should come to call but old General Farquhar, and with him, of all men in the world, Mr. Carvalho! Mamma was furious. She managed to be frigidly polite as long as they stopped, but when they were gone she went off at once into one of her worst nervous crisises (that's not the regular plural, I'm sure, but no matter). "I know his mother when she was a slave of your grandfather's," she said; "an upstanding proud octaroon girl, who thought herself too good for her place because she was nearly a white woman. She left the estate immediately after that horrid emancipation, to keep a school of brown girls in Kingston. And then she had the insolence to go and get actually married at church to old Jacob Carvalho! Just like those brown people. Their grandmothers never married." For poor mamma always made it a subject of reproach against the respectable coloured folk that they tried to live more decently and properly than their ancestors used to do in slavery times.

Mr. Carvalho never came to Palmettos again, but whenever I went to Kingston to dances I met him, and in spite of mamma I talked to him too. One day I went over to a ball at Government House, and there I saw both him and Harry Verner. For the first time in my life I had two proposals made me, and on the same night. Harry Verner's came first.

"Edie," he said to me, between the dances, as we were strolling out in the gardens, West Indian fashion, "I often think Agualta is rather lonely. It wants a lady to look after the house, while I'm down looking after the cane pieces. We made the best return in sugar of any estate on the island, last year, you know; but a man can't subsist entirely on sugar. He wants sympathy and intellectual companionship." (This was quite an effort for Harry.) "Now, I've not been in a hurry to get married. I've waited till I could find someone whom I could thoroughly respect and admire as well as love. I've looked at all the girls in Jamaica, before making my choice, and I've determined not to be guided by monetary considerations or any other considerations except those of the affections and of real underlying goodness and intellect. I feel that you are the one girl I have met who is far and away my superior in everything worth living for, Edie; and I'm going to ask you whether you will make me proud and happy for ever by becoming the mistress of Agualta."

I felt that Harry was really conceding so very much to me, and honouring me so greatly by offering me a life partnership in that flourishing sugar-estate, that it really went to my heart to have to refuse him. But I told him plainly I could not marry him because I did not love him. Harry seemed quite surprised at my refusal, but answered politely that perhaps I might learn to love him hereafter, that he would not be so foolish as to press me further now, and that he would do his best to deserve my love in future. And with that little speech he led me back to the ballroom, and handed me over to my next partner.

Later on in the evening, Mr. Carvalho too, with an earnest look in his handsome dark eyes, asked leave to take me for a few turns in the garden. We sat down on a bench under the great mango tree, and he began to talk to me in a graver fashion than usual.

"Your mother was annoyed, I fear, Miss Hazleden," he said, "that I should call at Palmettos."

"To tell you the truth," I answered, "I think she was."

"I was afraid she would be—I knew she would be, in fact; and for that very reason I hesitated to do it, as I hesitated to dance with you the first time I met you, as soon as I knew who you really were. But I felt I ought to face it out. You know by this time, no doubt, Miss Hazleden, that my mother was once a slave on your grandfather's estate. Now, it is a theory of mine—a little Quixotic, perhaps, but still a theory of mine—that the guilt and the shame of slavery lay with the slave-owners (forgive me if I must needs speak against your own class), and not with the slaves or their descendants. We have nothing on earth to be ashamed of. Thinking thus, I felt it incumbent upon me to call at Palmettos, partly in defence of my general principles, and partly also because I wished to see whether you shared your mother's ideas on that subject."

"You were quite right in what you did, Mr. Carvalho," I answered; "and I respect you for the boldness with which you cling to what you think your duty."

"Thank you, Miss Hazleden," he answered, "you are very kind. Now, I wish to speak to you about another and more serious question. Forgive my talking about myself for a moment; I feel sure you have kindly interested yourself in me a little. I too am proud of my birth, in my way, for I am the son of an honest able man and of a tender true woman. I come on one side from the oldest and greatest among civilized races, the Jews; and on the other side from many energetic English, French, and

Dutch families whose blood I am vain enough to prize as a precious inheritance even though it came to me through the veins of an octaroon girl. I have lately arrived at the conclusion that it is not well for me to remain in Jamaica. I cannot bear to live in a society which will not receive my dear mother on the same terms as it receives me, and will not receive either of us on the same terms as it receives other people. We are not rich, but we are well enough off to go to live in England; and to England I mean soon to go."

"I am glad and sorry to hear it," I said. "Glad, because I am sure it is the best thing for your own happiness, and the best opening for your great talents; sorry, because there are not many people in Jamaica whose society I shall miss so much."

"What you say encourages me to venture a little further. When I get to England, I intend to go to Cambridge, and take a degree there, so as to put myself on an equality with other educated people. Now, Miss Hazleden, I am going to ask you something which is so great a thing to ask that it makes my heart tremble to ask it. I know no man on earth, least of all myself, dare think himself fit for you, or dare plead his own cause before you without feeling his own unworthiness and pettiness of soul beside you. Yet just because I know how infinitely better and nobler and higher you are than I am, I cannot resist trying, just once, whether I may not hope that perhaps you will consider my appeal, and count my earnestness to me for righteousness. I have watched you and listened to you and admired you till in spite of myself I have not been able to refrain from loving you. I know it is madness; I know it is yearning after the unattainable; but I cannot help it. Oh, don't answer me too soon and crush me, but consider whether perhaps in the future you might not somehow at some time think it possible."

He leaned forward towards me in a supplicating attitude. At that moment I loved him with all the force of my nature. Yet I dared not say so. The spectre of the race-prejudice rose instinctively like a dividing wall between my heart and my lips. "Mr. Carvalho," I said, "take me back to my seat. You must not talk so, please."

"One minute, Miss Hazleden," he went on passionately; "one minute, and then I will be silent forever. Remember, we might live in England, far away from all these unmeaning barriers. I do not ask you to take me now, and as I am; I will do all I can to make myself more worthy of you. Only let me hope; don't answer me no without considering it. I know how little I deserve such happiness; but if you will take me, I will live all my life for no other purpose than to make you see that I am striving to show myself grateful for your love. Oh, Miss Hazleden, do listen to me."

I felt that in another moment I should yield; I could have seized his outstretched hands then, and told him that I loved him, but I dared not. "Mr. Carvalho," I said, "let us go back now. I will write to you to-morrow." He gave me his arm with a deep breath, and we went back slowly to the music.

"Edith," said my mother sharply, when I got home that night, "Harry has been here, and I know two things. He has proposed to you and you have refused him, I'm certain of that; and the other thing is, that young Carvalho has been insolent enough to make you an offer."

I said nothing.

"What did you answer him?"

"That I would reply by letter."

"Sit down, then, and write as I tell you."

I sat down mechanically. Mamma began dictating. I cried as I wrote, but I wrote it. I know now how very shameful and wrong it was of me; but I was only eighteen, and I was accustomed to do as mamma told me in everything. She had a terrible will, you know, and a terrible temper.

"'Dear Mr. Carvalho' (you'd better begin so, or he'll know I dictated it), 'I was too much surprised at your strange conduct last night to give you an answer immediately. On thinking it over, I can only say I am astonished you should have supposed such a thing as you suggested lay within the bounds of possibility. In future, it will be well that we should avoid one another. Our spheres are different. Pray do not repeat your mistake of last evening.—Yours truly, E. Hazleden.' Have you put all that down?"

"Mamma," I cried, "it is abominable. It isn't true. I can't sign it."

"Sign it," said my mother, briefly.

I took the pen and did so. "You will break my heart, mamma," I said. "You will break my heart and kill me."

"It shall go first thing to-morrow," said my mother, taking no notice of my words. "And now, Edith, you shall marry Harry Verner."

II

Seven years are a large slice out of one's life, and the seven years spent in fighting poor dear mamma over that fixed project were not happy ones. But on that point nothing on earth would bend me. I would not marry Harry Verner. At last, after poor mamma's sudden death, I thought it best to sell the remnant of the estate for what it would fetch, and go back to England. I was twenty-five then, and had slowly learnt to have a will of my own meanwhile. But during all that time I hardly ever heard again of Ernest Carvalho. Once or twice, indeed, I was told he had taken a distinguished place at Cambridge, and had gone to the bar in the Temple; but that was all.

A month or two after my return to London my aunt Emily (who was not one of the West Indian side of the house) managed to get me an invitation to Mrs. Bouverie Barton's. Of course you know Mrs. Bouverie Barton, the famous novelist, whose books everybody talks about. Well, Mrs. Barton lives in Eaton Place, and gives charming Thursday evening receptions, which are the recognized rendezvous of all literary and artistic London. If there is a celebrity in town, from Paris or Vienna, Timbuctoo or the South Sea Islands, you are sure to meet him in the little back drawing-room at Eaton Place. The music there is always of the best, and the conversation of the cleverest. But what pleased me most on that occasion was the fact that Mr. Gerard Llewellyn, the author of that singular book "Peter Martindale," was to be the lion of the party on this particular Thursday. I had just been reading "Peter Martindale"—who had not, that season? for it was the rage of the day—and I had never read any novel before which so impressed me by its weird power, its philosophical insight, and its transparent depth of moral earnestness. So I was naturally very much pleased at the prospect of seeing and meeting so famous a man as Mr. Gerard Llewellyn.

When we entered Mrs. Bouverie Barton's handsome rooms, we saw a great crowd of people whom even the most unobservant stranger would instantly have recognized as out of the common run. There was the hostess herself, with her kindly smile and her friendly good-humoured manner, hardly, if at all, concealing the profound intellectual strength that lay latent in her calm grey eyes. There were artistic artists and rugged artists; satirical novelists and gay novelists; heavy professors and deep professors—every possible representative of "literature, science, and art." At first, I was put off with introductions to young poe tasters, and gentlemen with an interest in cuneiform inscriptions; but I had quite made up my mind to get a talk with Mr. Gerard Llewellyn; and to Mr. Gerard Llewellyn our hostess at last promised to introduce me. She crossed the room in search of him near the big fireplace.

A tall, handsome young man, with long moustache and beard, and piercing black eyes, stood somewhat listlessly leaning against the mantelshelf, and talking with an even, brilliant flow to a short, stout, Indian-looking gentleman at his side. I knew in a moment that the short stout gentleman must be Mr. Llewellyn, for in the tall young man, in spite of seven years and the long moustaches, I recognized at once Ernest Carvalho.

But to my surprise Mrs. Bouverie Barton brought the tall young man, and not his neighbour, across the room with her. She must have made a mistake, I thought. "Mr. Carvalho," she said, "I want you to come and be introduced to the lady on the ottoman. Miss Hazleden, Mr. Carvalho!"

"I have met Mr. Carvalho long ago in Jamaica," I said warmly, "but I am very glad indeed to meet him here again. However, I hardly expected to see him here this evening."

"Indeed," said Mrs. Barton, with some surprise in her tone; "I thought you asked to be introduced to the author of 'Peter Martindale.'"

"So I did," I answered; "but I understood his name was Llewellyn."

"Oh!" said Ernest Carvalho, quickly, "that is only my nom de plume. But the authorship is an open secret now, and I suppose Mrs. Barton thought you knew it."

"It is a happy chance, at any rate, Mr. Carvalho," I said, "which has thrown us two again together."

He bowed gravely and with dignity. "You are very kind to say so," he said. "It is always a pleasure to meet old acquaintances from Jamaica."

My heart beat violently. There was a studied coldness in his tone, I thought, and no wonder; but if I had been in love with Ernest Carvalho before, I felt a thousand more times in love with him now as he stood there in his evening dress, a perfect English gentleman. He looked so kinglike with his handsome, slightly Jewish features, his piercing black eyes, his long moustaches, and his beautiful delicate thin-lipped mouth. There was such an air of power in his forehead, such a speaking evidence of high culture in his general expression. And then, he had written "Peter Martindale!" Why, who else could possibly have written it? I wondered at my own stupidity in not having guessed the authorship at once. But, most terrible of all, I had probably lost his love for ever. I might once have called Ernest Carvalho my husband, and I had utterly alienated him by a single culpable act of foolish weakness.

"You are living in London, now?" I asked.

"Yes," he answered, "we have a little home of our own in Kensington. I am working on the staff of the Morning Detonator."

"Mrs. Carvalho is here this evening," said Mrs. Bouverie Barton. "Do you know her? I suppose you do, of course."

Mrs. Carvalho! As I heard the name, I was conscious of a deep but rapid thud, thud, thud in my ear, and after a moment it struck me that the thud came from the quick beating of my own heart. Then Ernest Carvalho was married!

"No," he said in reply, seeing that I did not answer immediately. "Miss Hazleden has never met her, I believe; but I shall be happy to introduce her;" and he turned to a sofa where two or three ladies were chatting together, a little in the corner.

A very queenly old lady, with snow-white hair, prettily covered in part by a dainty and becoming lace cap, held out her small white hand to me with a gracious smile. "My mother," Ernest Carvalho said quietly; and I took the proffered hand with a warmth that must have really surprised the slave-born octaroon. The one thought that was uppermost in my mind was just this, that after all Ernest Carvalho was not married. Once more I heard the thud in my ear, and nothing else.

As soon as I could notice anybody or anything except myself, I began to observe that Mrs. Carvalho was very handsome. She was rather dark, to be sure, but less so than many Spanish or Italian ladies I had seen; and her look and manner were those of a Louis Quinze marquise, with a distinct reminiscence of the stately old Haitian French politeness. She could never have had any education except what she had picked up for herself; but no one would suspect the deficiency now, for she was as clever as all half-castes, and had made the best of her advantages meanwhile, such as they were. When she talked about the literary London in which her son lived and moved, I felt like the colonial-bred ignoramus I really was; and when she told me they had just been to visit Mr. Fradelli's new picture at the studio, I was positively too ashamed to let her see that I had never in my life heard of that famous painter before. To think that that queenly old lady was still a slave girl at Palmettos when my poor dear mother was a little child! And to think, too, that my own family would have kept her a slave all her life long, if only they had had the power! I remembered at once with a blush what Ernest Carvalho had said to me the last time I saw him, about the people with whom the guilt and shame of slavery really rested.

I sat, half in a maze, talking with Mrs. Carvalho all the rest of that evening. Ernest lingered near for a while, as if to see what impression his mother produced upon me, but soon went off, proudly I thought, to another part of the room, where he got into conversation with the German gentleman who wore the big blue wire-guarded spectacles. Yet I fancied he kept looking half anxiously in our direction throughout the evening, and I was sure I saw him catch his mother's eye furtively now and again. As for Mrs. Carvalho, she made a conquest of me at once, and she was evidently well pleased with her conquest. When I rose to leave, she took both my hands in hers, and said to me warmly, "Miss Hazleden, we shall be so pleased to see you whenever you like to come, at Merton Gardens." Had Ernest ever told her of his proposal? I wondered.

Mrs. Bouverie Barton was very kind to me. She kept on asking me to her Thursday evenings, and there time after time I met Ernest Carvalho. At first, he seldom spoke to me much, but at last, partly because I always talked so much to his mother perhaps, he began to thaw a little, and often came up to me in quite a friendly way. "We have left Jamaica and all that behind, Miss Hazleden," he said once, "and here in free England we may at least be friends." Oh, how I longed to explain the whole truth to him, and how impossible an explanation was. Besides, he had seen so many other girls since, and very likely his boyish fancy for me had long since passed away altogether. You can't count much on the love-making of eighteen and twenty.

Mrs. Carvalho asked me often to their pretty little house in Merton Gardens, and I went; but still Ernest never in any way alluded to what had passed. Months went by, and I began to feel that I must crush that little dream entirely out of my heart—if I could. One afternoon I went in to Mrs.

Carvalho's for a cup of five-o'clock tea, and had an uninterrupted tête-à-tête with her for half an hour. We had been exchanging small confidences with one another for a while, and after a pause the old lady laid her gentle hand upon my head and stroked back my hair in such a motherly fashion. "My dear child," she said, half-sighing, "I do wish my Ernest would only take a fancy to a sweet young girl like you."

"Mr. Carvalho does not seem quite a marrying man," I answered, forcing a laugh; "I notice he seldom talks to ladies, but always to men, and those of the solemnest."

"Ah, my dear, he has had a great disappointment, a terrible disappointment," said the mother, unburdening herself. "I can tell you all about it, for you are a Jamaican born, and though you are one of the 'proud Palmettos' people you are not full of prejudices like the rest of them, and so you will understand it. Before we left Jamaica he was in love with a young lady there; he never told me her name, and that is the one secret he has ever kept from me. Well, he talked to her often, and he thought she was above the wicked prejudices of race and colour; she seemed to encourage him and to be fond of his society. At last he proposed to her. Then she wrote him a cruel, cruel letter, a letter that he never showed me, but he told me what was in it; and it drove him away from the island immediately. It was a letter full of wicked reproaches about our octaroon blood, and it broke his heart with the shock of its heartlessness. He has never cared for any woman since."

"Then does he love her still?" I asked, breathless.

"How can he? No! but he says he loves the memory of what he once thought her. He has seen her since, somewhere in London, and spoken to her; but he can never love her again. Yet, do you know, I feel sure he cannot help loving her in spite of himself; and he often goes out at night, I am sure, to watch her door, to see her come in and out, for the sake of the love he once bore her. My Ernest is not the sort of man who can love twice in a lifetime."

"Perhaps," I said, colouring, "if he were to ask her again she might accept him. Things are so different here in England, and he is a famous man now."

Mrs. Carvalho shook her head slowly. "Oh no!" she answered; "he would never importune or trouble her. Though she has rejected him, he is too loyal to the love he once bore her, too careful of wounding her feelings or even her very prejudices, ever to obtrude his love again upon her notice. If she cannot love him of herself and for himself, spontaneously, he would not weary her out with oft asking. He will never marry now; of that I am certain."

My eyes filled with tears. As they did so, I tried to brush them away unseen behind my fan, but Mrs. Carvalho caught my glance, and looked sharply through me with a sudden gleam of discovery. "Why," she said, very slowly and distinctly, with a pause and a stress upon each word, "I believe it must have been you yourself, Miss Hazleden." And as she spoke she held her open hand, palm outward, stretched against me with a gesture of horror, as one might shrink in alarm from a coiled rattlesnake.

"Dear Mrs. Carvalho," I cried, clasping my hands before her, "do hear me, I entreat you; do let me explain to you how it all happened."

"There is no explanation possible," she answered sternly. "Go. You have wrecked a life that might otherwise have been happy and famous, and then you come to a mother with an explanation!"

"That letter was not mine," I said boldly; for I saw that to put the truth shortly in that truest and briefest form was the only way of getting her to listen to me now.

She sank back in a chair and folded her hands faintly one above the other. "Tell me it all," she said in a weak voice. "I will hear you."

So I told her all. I did not try to extenuate my own weakness in writing from my mother's dictation; but I let her see what I had suffered then and what I had suffered since. When I had finished, she drew me towards her gently, and printed one kiss upon my forehead. "It is hard to forget," she said softly, "but you were very young and helpless, and your mother was a terrible woman. The iron has entered into your own soul too. Go home, dear, and I will see about this matter."

We fell upon one another's necks, the Palmettos slave-girl and I, and cried together glad tears for ten minutes. Then I wiped my red eyes dry, covered them with a double fold of my veil, and ran home hurriedly in the dusk to auntie's. It was such a terrible relief to have got it all over.

That evening, about eleven o'clock, auntie had gone to bed, and I was sitting up by myself, musing late over the red cinders in the little back drawing-room grate. I felt as though I couldn't sleep, and so I was waiting up till I got sleepy. Suddenly there came a loud knock and a ring at the bell, after which Amelia ran in to say that a gentleman wanted to see me in the dining-room on urgent business, and would I please come down to speak with him immediately. I knew at once it was Ernest.

The moment I entered the room, he never said a word, but he took my two hands eagerly in his, and then he kissed me fervently on the lips half a dozen times over. "And now, Edith," he said, "we need say no more about the past, for my mother has explained it all to me; we will only think about the future."

I have no distinct recollection what o'clock it was before Ernest left that evening; but I know auntie sent down word twice to say it was high time I went to bed, and poor Amelia looked awfully tired and very sleepy. However, it was settled then and there that Ernest and I should be married early in October.

A few days later, after the engagement had been announced to all our friends, dear Mrs. Bouverie Barton paid me a congratulatory call. "You are a very lucky girl, my dear," she said to me kindly. "We are half envious of you; I wish we could find another such husband as Mr. Carvalho for my Christina. But you have carried off the prize of the season, and you are well worthy of him. It is a very great honour for any girl to win and deserve the love of such a man as Ernest Carvalho."

Will you believe it, so strangely do one's first impressions and early ideas about people cling to one, that though I had often felt before how completely the tables had been turned since we two came to England, it had not struck me till that moment that in the eyes of the world at large it was Ernest who was doing an honour to me and not I who was doing an honour to Ernest. I felt ashamed to think that Mrs. Bouverie Barton should see instinctively the true state of the case, while I, who loved and admired him so greatly, should have let the shadow of that old prejudice stand even now between me and the lover I was so proud to own. But when I took dear old Mrs. Carvalho's hand in mine the day of our wedding, and kissed her, and called her mother for the first time, I felt that I had left the guilt and shame of slavery for ever behind me, and that I should strive ever after to live worthily of Ernest Carvalho's love.

PAUSODYNE: A GREAT CHEMICAL DISCOVERY.

Walking along the Strand one evening last year towards Pall Mall, I was accosted near Charing Cross Station by a strange-looking, middle-aged man in a poor suit of clothes, who surprised and startled me by asking if I could tell him from what inn the coach usually started for York.

"Dear me!" I said, a little puzzled. "I didn't know there was a coach to York. Indeed, I'm almost certain there isn't one."

The man looked puzzled and surprised in turn. "No coach to York?" he muttered to himself, half inarticulately. "No coach to York? How things have changed! I wonder whether nobody ever goes to York nowadays!"

"Pardon me," I said, anxious to discover what could be his meaning; "many people go to York every day, but of course they go by rail."

"Ah, yes," he answered softly, "I see. Yes, of course, they go by rail. They go by rail, no doubt. How very stupid of me!" And he turned on his heel as if to get away from me as quickly as possible.

I can't exactly say why, but I felt instinctively that this curious stranger was trying to conceal from me his ignorance of what a railway really was. I was quite certain from the way in which he spoke that he had not the slightest conception what I meant, and that he was doing his best to hide his confusion by pretending to understand me. Here was indeed a strange mystery. In the latter end of this nineteenth century, in the metropolis of industrial England, within a stone's-throw of Charing Cross terminus, I had met an adult Englishman who apparently did not know of the existence of railways. My curiosity was too much piqued to let the matter rest there. I must find out what he meant by it. I walked after him hastily, as he tried to disappear among the crowd, and laid my hand upon his shoulder, to his evident chagrin.

"Excuse me," I said, drawing him aside down the corner of Craven Street; "you did not understand what I meant when I said people went to York by rail?"

He looked in my face steadily, and then, instead of replying to my remark, he said slowly, "Your name is Spottiswood, I believe?"

Again I gave a start of surprise. "It is," I answered; "but I never remember to have seen you before."

"No," he replied dreamily; "no, we have never met till now, no doubt; but I knew your father, I'm sure; or perhaps it may have been your grandfather."

"Not my grandfather, certainly," said I, "for he was killed at Waterloo."

"At Waterloo! Indeed! How long since, pray?"

I could not refrain from laughing outright. "Why, of course," I answered, "in 1815. There has been nothing particular to kill off any large number of Englishmen at Waterloo since the year of the battle, I suppose."

"True," he muttered, "quite true; so I should have fancied." But I saw again from the cloud of doubt and bewilderment which came over his intelligent face that the name of Waterloo conveyed no idea whatsoever to his mind.

Never in my life had I felt so utterly confused and astonished. In spite of his poor dress, I could easily see from the clear-cut face and the refined accent of my strange acquaintance that he was an educated gentleman—a man accustomed to mix in cultivated society. Yet he clearly knew nothing whatsoever about railways, and was ignorant of the most salient facts in English history. Had I suddenly come across some Caspar Hauser, immured for years in a private prison, and just let loose upon the world by his gaolers? or was my mysterious stranger one of the Seven Sleepers of Ephesus, turned out unexpectedly in modern costume on the streets of London? I don't suppose there exists on earth a man more utterly free than I am from any tinge of superstition, any lingering touch of a love for the miraculous; but I confess for a moment I felt half inclined to suppose that the man before me must have drunk the elixir of life, or must have dropped suddenly upon earth from some distant planet.

The impulse to fathom this mystery was irresistible. I drew my arm through his. "If you knew my father," I said, "you will not object to come into my chambers and take a glass of wine with me."

"Thank you," he answered half suspiciously; "thank you very much. I think you look like a man who can be trusted, and I will go with you."

We walked along the Embankment to Adelphi Terrace, where I took him up to my rooms, and seated him in my easy-chair near the window. As he sat down, one of the trains on the Metropolitan line whirred past the Terrace, snorting steam and whistling shrilly, after the fashion of Metropolitan engines generally. My mysterious stranger jumped back in alarm, and seemed to be afraid of some immediate catastrophe. There was absolutely no possibility of doubting it. The man had obviously never seen a locomotive before.

"Evidently," I said, "you do not know London. I suppose you are a colonist from some remote district, perhaps an Australian from the interior somewhere, just landed at the Tower?"

"No, not an Austrian"—I noted his misapprehension—"but a Londoner born and bred."

"How is it, then, that you seem never to have seen an engine before?"

"Can I trust you?" he asked in a piteously plaintive, half-terrified tone. "If I tell you all about it, will you at least not aid in persecuting and imprisoning me?"

I was touched by his evident grief and terror. "No," I answered, "you may trust me implicitly. I feel sure there is something in your history which entitles you to sympathy and protection."

"Well," he replied, grasping my hand warmly, "I will tell you all my story; but you must be prepared for something almost too startling to be credible."

"My name is Jonathan Spottiswood," he began calmly.

Again I experienced a marvellous start: Jonathan Spottiswood was the name of my great-great-uncle, whose unaccountable disappearance from London just a century since had involved our family in so much protracted litigation as to the succession to his property. In fact, it was Jonathan

Spottiswood's money which at that moment formed the bulk of my little fortune. But I would not interrupt him, so great was my anxiety to hear the story of his life.

"I was born in London," he went on, "in 1750. If you can hear me say that and yet believe that possibly I am not a madman, I will tell you the rest of my tale; if not, I shall go at once and for ever."

"I suspend judgment for the present," I answered. "What you say is extraordinary, but not more extraordinary perhaps than the clear anachronism of your ignorance about locomotives in the midst of the present century."

"So be it, then. Well, I will tell you the facts briefly in as few words as I can. I was always much given to experimental philosophy, and I spent most of my time in the little laboratory which I had built for myself behind my father's house in the Strand. I had a small independent fortune of my own, left me by an uncle who had made successful ventures in the China trade; and as I was indisposed to follow my father's profession of solicitor, I gave myself up almost entirely to the pursuit of natural philosophy, following the researches of the great Mr. Cavendish, our chief English thinker in this kind, as well as of Monsieur Lavoisier, the ingenious French chemist, and of my friend Dr. Priestley, the Birmingham philosopher, whose new theory of phlogiston I have been much concerned to consider and to promulgate. But the especial subject to which I devoted myself was the elucidation of the nature of fixed air. I do not know how far you yourself may happen to have heard respecting these late discoveries in chemical science, but I dare venture to say that you are at least acquainted with the nature of the body to which I refer."

"Perfectly," I answered with a smile, "though your terminology is now a little out of date. Fixed air was, I believe, the old-fashioned name for carbonic acid gas."

"Ah," he cried vehemently, "that accursed word again! Carbonic acid has undone me, clearly. Yes, if you will have it so, that seems to be what they call it in this extraordinary century; but fixed air was the name we used to give it in our time, and fixed air is what I must call it, of course, in telling you my story. Well, I was deeply interested in this curious question, and also in some of the results which I obtained from working with fixed air in combination with a substance I had produced from the essential oil of a weed known to us in England as lady's mantle, but which the learned Mr. Carl Linnæus describes in his system as Alchemilla vulgaris. From that weed I obtained an oil which I combined with a certain decoction of fixed air into a remarkable compound; and to this compound, from its singular properties, I proposed to give the name of Pausodyne. For some years I was almost wholly engaged in investigating the conduct of this remarkable agent; and lest I should weary you by entering into too much detail, I may as well say at once that it possessed the singular power of entirely suspending animation in men or animals for several hours together. It is a highly volatile oil, like ammonia in smell, but much thicker in gravity; and when held to the nose of an animal, it causes immediate stoppage of the heart's action, making the body seem quite dead for long periods at a time. But the moment a mixture of the pausodyne with oil of vitriol and gum resin is presented to the nostrils, the animal instantaneously revives exactly as before, showing no evil effects whatsoever from its temporary simulation of death. To the reviving mixture I have given the appropriate name of Anegeiric.

"Of course you will instantly see the valuable medical applications which may be made of such an agent. I used it at first for experimenting upon the amputation of limbs and other surgical operations. It succeeded admirably. I found that a dog under the influence of pausodyne suffered his leg, which had been broken in a street accident, to be set and spliced without the slightest symptom of feeling or discomfort. A cat, shot with a pistol by a cruel boy, had the bullet extracted without moving a muscle. My assistant, having allowed his little finger to mortify from neglect of a burn, permitted me to try the effect of my discovery upon himself; and I removed the injured joints while he remained in a state of complete insensibility, so that he could hardly believe afterwards in the actual truth of their removal. I felt certain that I had invented a medical process of the very highest and greatest utility.

"All this took place in or before the year 1781. How long ago that may be according to your modern reckoning I cannot say; but to me it seems hardly more than a few months since. Perhaps you would not mind telling me the date of the current year. I have never been able to ascertain it."

"This is 1881," I said, growing every moment more interested in his tale.

"Thank you. I gathered that we must now be somewhere near the close of the nineteenth century, though I could not learn the exact date with certainty. Well, I should tell you, my dear sir, that I had contracted an engagement about the year 1779 with a young lady of most remarkable beauty and attractive mental gifts, a Miss Amelia Spragg, daughter of the well-known General Sir Thomas Spragg, with whose achievements you are doubtless familiar. Pardon me, my friend of another age, pardon me, I beg of you, if I cannot allude to this subject without emotion after a lapse of time which to you doubtless seems like a century, but is to me a matter of some few months only at the utmost. I feel towards her as towards one whom I have but recently lost, though I now find that she has been dead for more than eighty years." As he spoke, the tears came into his eyes profusely; and I could see that under the external calmness and quaintness of his eighteenth century language and demeanour his whole nature was profoundly stirred at the thought of his lost love.

"Look here," he continued, taking from his breast a large, old-fashioned gold locket containing a miniature; "that is her portrait, by Mr. Walker, and a very truthful likeness indeed. They left me that when they took away my clothes at the Asylum, for I would not consent to part with it, and the physician in attendance observed that to deprive me of it might only increase the frequency and violence of my paroxysms. For I will not conceal from you the fact that I have just escaped from a pauper lunatic establishment."

I took the miniature which he handed me, and looked at it closely. It was the picture of a young and beautiful girl, with the features and costume of a Sir Joshua. I recognized the face at once as that of a lady whose portrait by Gainsborough hangs on the walls of my uncle's dining-room at Whittingham Abbey. It was strange indeed to hear a living man speak of himself as the former lover of this, to me, historic personage.

"Sir Thomas, however," he went on, "was much opposed to our union, on the ground of some real or fancied social disparity in our positions; but I at last obtained his conditional consent, if only I could succeed in obtaining the Fellowship of the Royal Society, which might, he thought, be accepted as a passport into that fashionable circle of which he was a member. Spurred on by this ambition, and by the encouragement of my Amelia, I worked day and night at the perfectioning of my great discovery, which I was assured would bring not only honour and dignity to myself, but also the alleviation and assuagement of pain to countless thousands of my fellow-creatures. I concealed the nature of my experiments, however, lest any rival investigator should enter the field with me prematurely, and share the credit to which I alone was really entitled. For some months I was successful in my efforts at concealment; but in March of this year—I mistake; of the year 1781, I should say—an unfortunate circumstance caused me to take special and exceptional precautions against intrusion.

"I was then conducting my experiments upon living animals, and especially upon the extirpation of certain painful internal diseases to which they are subject. I had a number of suffering cats in my laboratory, which I had treated with pausodyne, and stretched out on boards for the purpose of removing the tumours with which they were afflicted. I had no doubt that in this manner, while directly benefiting the animal creation, I should indirectly obtain the necessary skill to operate successfully upon human beings in similar circumstances. Already I had completely cured several cats without any pain whatsoever, and I was anxious to proceed to the human subject. Walking one morning in the Strand, I found a beggar woman outside a gin-shop, quite drunk, with a small, ill-clad child by her side, suffering the most excruciating torments from a perfectly remediable cause. I induced the mother to accompany me to my laboratory, and there I treated the poor little creature with pausodyne, and began to operate upon her with perfect confidence of success.

"Unhappily, my laboratory had excited the suspicion of many ill-disposed persons among the low mob of the neighbourhood. It was whispered abroad that I was what they called a vivisectionist; and these people, who would willingly have attended a bull-baiting or a prize fight, found themselves of a sudden wondrous humane when scientific procedure was under consideration. Besides, I had made myself unpopular by receiving visits from my friend Dr. Priestley, whose religious opinions were not satisfactory to the strict orthodoxy of St. Giles's. I was rumoured to be a philosopher, a torturer of live animals, and an atheist. Whether the former accusation were true or not, let others decide; the two latter, heaven be my witness, were wholly unfounded. However, when the neighbouring rabble saw a drunken woman with a little girl entering my door, a report got abroad at once that I was going to vivisect a Christian child. The mob soon collected in force, and broke into the laboratory. At that moment I was engaged, with my assistant, in operating upon the girl, while several cats, all completely anæstheticised, were bound down on the boards around, awaiting the healing of their wounds after the removal of tumours. At the sight of such apparent tortures the people grew wild with rage, and happening in their transports to fling down a large bottle of the anegeiric, or reviving mixture, the child and the animals all at once recovered consciousness, and began of course to writhe and scream with acute pain. I need not describe to you the scene that ensued. My laboratory was wrecked, my assistant severely injured, and I myself barely escaped with my life.

"After this contretemps I determined to be more cautious. I took the lease of a new house at Hampstead, and in the garden I determined to build myself a subterranean laboratory where I might be absolutely free from intrusion. I hired some labourers from Bath for this purpose, and I explained to them the nature of my wishes, and the absolute necessity of secrecy. A high wall surrounded the garden, and here the workmen worked securely and unseen. I concealed my design even from my dear brother—whose grandson or great-grandson I suppose you must be—and when the building was finished, I sent my men back to Bath, with strict injunctions never to mention the matter to any one. A trap-door in the cellar, artfully concealed, gave access to the passage; a large oak portal, bound with iron, shut me securely in; and my air supply was obtained by means of pipes communicating through blank spaces in the brick wall of the garden with the outer atmosphere. Every arrangement for concealment was perfect; and I resolved in future, till my results were perfectly established, that I would dispense with the aid of an assistant.

"I was in high spirits when I went to visit my Amelia that evening, and I told her confidently that before the end of the year I expected to gain the gold medal of the Royal Society. The dear girl was pleased at my glowing prospects, and gave me every assurance of the delight with which she hailed the probability of our approaching union.

"Next day I began my experiments afresh in my new quarters. I bolted myself into the laboratory, and set to work with renewed vigour. I was experimenting upon an injured dog, and I placed a large bottle of pausodyne beside me as I administered the drug to his nostrils. The rising fumes seemed to affect my head more than usual in that confined space, and I tottered a little as I worked. My arm grew weaker, and at last fell powerless to my side. As it fell it knocked down the large bottle of pausodyne, and I saw the liquid spreading over the floor. That was almost the last thing that I knew. I staggered toward the door, but did not reach it; and then I remember nothing more for a considerable period."

He wiped his forehead with his sleeve—he had no handkerchief—and then proceeded.

"When I woke up again the effects of the pausodyne had worn themselves out, and I felt that I must have remained unconscious for at least a week or a fortnight. My candle had gone out, and I could not find my tinder-box. I rose up slowly and with difficulty, for the air of the room was close and filled with fumes, and made my way in the dark towards the door. To my surprise, the bolt was so stiff with rust that it would hardly move. I opened it after a struggle, and found myself in the passage. Groping my way towards the trap-door of the cellar, I felt it was obstructed by some heavy body. With an immense effort, for my strength seemed but feeble, I pushed it up, and discovered that a heap of sea-coals lay on top of it. I extricated myself into the cellar, and there a fresh surprise awaited me. A new entrance had been made into the front, so that I walked out at once upon the open road, instead of up the stairs into the kitchen. Looking up at the exterior of my house, my brain reeled with bewilderment when I saw that it had disappeared almost entirely, and that a different porch and wholly unfamiliar windows occupied its façade. I must have slept far longer than I at first imagined—perhaps a whole year or more. A vague terror prevented me from walking up the steps of my own home. Possibly my brother, thinking me dead, might have sold the lease; possibly some stranger might resent my intrusion into the house that was now his own. At any rate, I thought it safer to walk into the road. I would go towards London, to my brother's house in St. Mary le Bone. I turned into the Hampstead Road, and directed my steps thitherward.

"Again, another surprise began to affect me with a horrible and ill-defined sense of awe. Not a single object that I saw was really familiar to me. I recognized that I was in the Hampstead Road, but it was not the Hampstead Road which I used to know before my fatal experiments. The houses were far more numerous, the trees were bigger and older. A year, nay, even a few years would not have sufficed for such a change. I began to fear that I had slept away a whole decade.

"It was early morning, and few people were yet abroad. But the costume of those whom I met seemed strange and fantastic to me. Moreover, I noticed that they all turned and looked after me with evident surprise, as though my dress caused them quite as much astonishment as theirs caused me. I was quietly attired in my snuff-coloured suit of small-clothes, with silk stockings and simple buckle shoes, and I had of course no hat; but I gathered that my appearance caused universal amazement and concern, far more than could be justified by the mere accidental absence of head-gear. A dread began to oppress me that I might actually have slept out my whole age and generation. Was my Amelia alive? and if so, would she be still the same Amelia I had known a week or two before? Should I find her an aged woman, still cherishing a reminiscence of her former love; or might she herself perhaps be dead and forgotten, while I remained, alone and solitary, in a world which knew me not?

"I walked along unmolested, but with reeling brain, through streets more and more unfamiliar, till I came near the St. Mary le Bone Road. There, as I hesitated a little and staggered at the crossing, a man in a curious suit of dark blue clothes, with a grotesque felt helmet on his head, whom I afterwards found to be a constable, came up and touched me on the shoulder.

"'Look here,' he said to me in a rough voice, 'what are you a-doin' in this 'ere fancy-dress at this hour in the mornin'? You've lost your way home, I take it.'

"'I was going,' I answered, 'to the St. Mary le Bone Road.'

"'Why, you image,' says he rudely, 'if you mean Marribon, why don't you say Marribon? What house are you a-lookin' for, eh?'

"'My brother lives,' I replied, 'at the Lamb, near St. Mary's Church, and I was going to his residence.'

"'The Lamb!' says he, with a rude laugh; 'there ain't no public of that name in the road. It's my belief,' he goes on after a moment, 'that you're drunk, or mad, or else you've stole them clothes. Anyway, you've got to go along with me to the station, so walk it, will you?'

"'Pardon me,' I said, 'I suppose you are an officer of the law, and I would not attempt to resist your authority'—'You'd better not,' says he, half to himself—'but I should like to go to my brother's house, where I could show you that I am a respectable person.'

"'Well,' says my fellow insolently, 'I'll go along of you if you like, and if it's all right, I suppose you won't mind standing a bob?'

"'A what?' said I.

"'A bob,' says he, laughing; 'a shillin', you know.'

"To get rid of his insolence for a while, I pulled out my purse and handed him a shilling. It was a George II. with milled edges, not like the things I see you use now. He held it up and looked at it, and then he said again, 'Look here, you know, this isn't good. You'd better come along with me straight to the station, and not make a fuss about it. There's three charges against you, that's all. One is, that you're drunk. The second is, that you're mad. And the third is, that you've been trying to utter false coin. Any one of 'em's quite enough to justify me in takin' you into custody.'

"I saw it was no use to resist, and I went along with him.

"I won't trouble you with the whole of the details, but the upshot of it all was, they took me before a magistrate. By this time I had begun to realize the full terror of the situation, and I saw clearly that the real danger lay in the inevitable suspicion of madness under which I must labour. When I got into the court I told the magistrate my story very shortly and simply, as I have told it to you now. He listened to me without a word, and at the end he turned round to his clerk and said, 'This is clearly a case for Dr. Fitz-Jenkins, I think.'

"'Sir,' I said, 'before you send me to a madhouse, which I suppose is what you mean by these words, I trust you will at least examine the evidences of my story. Look at my clothing, look at these coins, look at everything about me.' And I handed him my purse to see for himself.

"He looked at it for a minute, and then he turned towards me very sternly. 'Mr. Spottiswood,' he said, 'or whatever else your real name may be, if this is a joke, it is a very foolish and unbecoming one. Your dress is no doubt very well designed; your small collection of coins is interesting and well-selected; and you have got up your character remarkably well. If you are really sane, which I suspect to be the case, then your studied attempt to waste the time of this court and to make a laughing-stock of its magistrate will meet with the punishment it deserves. I shall remit your case for consideration to our medical officer. If you consent to give him your real name and address, you will be liberated after his examination. Otherwise, it will be necessary to satisfy ourselves as to your identity. Not a word more, sir,' he continued, as I tried to speak on behalf of my story. 'Inspector, remove the prisoner.'

"They took me away, and the surgeon examined me. To cut things short, I was pronounced mad, and three days later the commissioners passed me for a pauper asylum. When I came to be examined, they said I showed no recollection of most subjects of ordinary education.

"'I am a chemist,' said I; 'try me with some chemical questions. You will see that I can answer sanely enough.'

"'How do you mix a grey powder?' said the commissioner.

"'Excuse me,' I said, 'I mean a chemical philosopher, not an apothecary.'

"'Oh, very well, then; what is carbonic acid?'

"'I never heard of it,' I answered in despair. 'It must be something which has come into use since—since I left off learning chemistry.' For I had discovered that my only chance now was to avoid all reference to my past life and the extraordinary calamity which had thus unexpectedly overtaken me. 'Please try me with something else.'

"'Oh, certainly. What is the atomic weight of chlorine?'

"I could only answer that I did not know.

"'This is a very clear case,' said the commissioner. 'Evidently he is a gentleman by birth and education, but he can give no very satisfactory account of his friends, and till they come forward to claim him we can only send him for a time to North Street.'

"'For Heaven's sake, gentlemen,' I cried, 'before you consign me to an asylum, give me one more chance. I am perfectly sane; I remember all I ever knew; but you are asking me questions about subjects on which I never had any information. Ask me anything historical, and see whether I have forgotten or confused any of my facts."

"I will do the commissioner the justice to say that he seemed anxious not to decide upon the case without full consideration. 'Tell me what you can recollect,' he said, 'as to the reign of George IV.'

"'I know nothing at all about it,' I answered, terror-stricken, 'but oh, do pray ask me anything up to the time of George III.'

"'Then please say what you think of the French Revolution.'

"I was thunderstruck. I could make no reply, and the commissioners shortly signed the papers to send me to North Street pauper asylum. They hurried me into the street, and I walked beside my captors towards the prison to which they had consigned me. Yet I did not give up all hope even so of ultimately regaining my freedom. I thought the rationality of my demeanour and the obvious soundness of all my reasoning powers would suffice in time to satisfy the medical attendant as to my perfect sanity. I felt sure that people could never long mistake a man so clear-headed and collected as myself for a madman.

"On our way, however, we happened to pass a churchyard where some workmen were engaged in removing a number of old tombstones from the crowded area. Even in my existing agitated condition, I could not help catching the name and date on one mouldering slab which a labourer had just placed upon the edge of the pavement. It ran something like this: 'Sacred to the memory of Amelia, second daughter of the late Sir Thomas Spragg, knight, and beloved wife of Henry McAlister, Esq., by whom this stone is erected. Died May 20, 1799, aged 44 years.' Though I had gathered already that my dear girl must probably have long been dead, yet the reality of the fact had not yet had time to fix itself upon my mind. You must remember, my dear sir, that I had but awaked a few days earlier from my long slumber, and that during those days I had been harassed and agitated by such a flood of incomprehensible complications, that I could not really grasp in all its fulness the complete isolation of my present position. When I saw the tombstone of one whom, as it seemed to me, I had loved passionately but a week or two before, I could not refrain from rushing to embrace it, and covering the insensible stone with my boiling tears. 'Oh, my Amelia, my Amelia,' I cried, 'I shall never again behold thee, then! I shall never again press thee to my heart, or hear thy dear lips pronounce my name!'

"But the unfeeling wretches who had charge of me were far from being moved to sympathy by my bitter grief. 'Died in 1799,' said one of them with a sneer. 'Why, this madman's blubbering over the grave of an old lady who has been buried for about a hundred years!' And the workmen joined in their laughter as my gaolers tore me away to the prison where I was to spend the remainder of my days.

"When we arrived at the asylum, the surgeon in attendance was informed of this circumstance, and the opinion that I was hopelessly mad thus became ingrained in his whole conceptions of my case. I remained five months or more in the asylum, but I never saw any chance of creating a more favourable impression on the minds of the authorities. Mixing as I did only with other patients, I could gain no clear ideas of what had happened since I had taken my fatal sleep; and whenever I endeavoured to question the keepers, they amused themselves by giving me evidently false and inconsistent answers, in order to enjoy my chagrin and confusion. I could not even learn the actual date of the present year, for one keeper would laugh and say it was 2001, while another would confidentially advise me to date my petition to the Commissioners, "Jan. 1, A.D. one million." The surgeon, who never played me any such pranks, yet refused to aid me in any way, lest, as he said, he should strengthen me in my sad delusion. He was convinced that I must be an historical student, whose reason had broken down through too close study of the eighteenth century; and he felt certain that sooner or later my friends would come to claim me. He is a gentle and humane man, against whom I have no personal complaint to make; but his initial misconception prevented him and everybody else from ever paying the least attention to my story. I could not even induce them to make inquiries at my house at Hampstead, where the discovery of the subterranean laboratory would have partially proved the truth of my account.

"Many visitors came to the asylum from time to time, and they were always told that I possessed a minute and remarkable acquaintance with the history of the eighteenth century. They questioned me about facts which are as vivid in my memory as those of the present month, and were much surprised at the accuracy of my replies. But they only thought it strange that so clever a man should be so very mad, and that my information should be so full as to past events, while my notions about the modern world were so utterly chaotic. The surgeon, however, always believed that my reticence about all events posterior to 1781 was a part of my insanity. I had studied the early part of the eighteenth century so fully, he said, that I fancied I had lived in it; and I had persuaded myself that I knew nothing at all about the subsequent state of the world."

The poor fellow stopped a while, and again drew his sleeve across his forehead. It was impossible to look at him and believe for a moment that he was a madman.

"And how did you make your escape from the asylum?" I asked.

"Now, this very evening," he answered; "I simply broke away from the door and ran down toward the Strand, till I came to a place that looked a little like St. Martin's Fields, with a great column and some fountains, and near there I met you. It seemed to me that the best thing to do was to catch the York coach and get away from the town as soon as possible. You met me, and your look and name inspired me with confidence. I believe you must be a descendant of my dear brother."

"I have not the slightest doubt," I answered solemnly, "that every word of your story is true, and that you are really my great-great-uncle. My own knowledge of our family history exactly tallies with what you tell me. I shall spare no endeavour to clear up this extraordinary matter, and to put you once more in your true position."

"And you will protect me?" he cried fervently, clasping my hand in both his own with intense eagerness. "You will not give me up once more to the asylum people?"

"I will do everything on earth that is possible for you," I replied.

He lifted my hand to his lips and kissed it several times, while I felt hot tears falling upon it as he bent over me. It was a strange position, look at it how you will. Grant that I was but the dupe of a madman, yet even to believe for a moment that I, a man of well-nigh fifty, stood there in face of my own great-grandfather's brother, to all appearance some twenty years my junior, was in itself an extraordinary and marvellous thing. Both of us were too overcome to speak. It was a few minutes before we said anything, and then a loud knock at the door made my hunted stranger rise up hastily in terror from his chair.

"Gracious Heavens!" he cried, "they have tracked me hither. They are coming to fetch me. Oh, hide me, hide me, anywhere from these wretches!"

As he spoke, the door opened, and two keepers with a policeman entered my room.

"Ah, here he is!" said one of them, advancing towards the fugitive, who shrank away towards the window as he approached.

"Do not touch him," I exclaimed, throwing myself in the way. "Every word of what he says is true, and he is no more insane than I am."

The keeper laughed a low laugh of vulgar incredulity. "Why, there's a pair of you, I do believe," he said. "You're just as mad yourself as t'other one." And he pushed me aside roughly to get at his charge.

But the poor fellow, seeing him come towards him, seemed suddenly to grow instinct with a terrible vigour, and hurled off the keeper with one hand, as a strong man might do with a little terrier. Then, before we could see what he was meditating, he jumped upon the ledge of the open window, shouted out loudly, "Farewell, farewell!" and leapt with a spring on to the embankment beneath.

All four of us rushed hastily down the three flights of steps to the bottom, and came below upon a crushed and mangled mass on the spattered pavement. He was quite dead. Even the policeman was shocked and horrified at the dreadful way in which the body had been crushed and mutilated in its fall, and at the suddenness and unexpectedness of the tragedy. We took him up and laid him out in my room; and from that room he was interred after the inquest, with all the respect which I should have paid to an undoubted relative. On his grave in Kensal Green Cemetery I have placed a stone bearing the simple inscription, "Jonathan Spottiswood. Died 1881." The hint I had received from the keeper prevented me from saying anything as to my belief in his story, but I asked for leave to undertake the duty of his interment on the ground that he bore my own surname, and that no other person was forthcoming to assume the task. The parochial authorities were glad enough to rid the ratepayers of the expense.

At the inquest I gave my evidence simply and briefly, dwelling mainly upon the accidental nature of our meeting, and the facts as to his fatal leap. I said nothing about the known disappearance of Jonathan Spottiswood in 1781, nor the other points which gave credibility to his strange tale. But from this day forward I give myself up to proving the truth of his story, and realizing the splendid chemical discovery which promises so much benefit to mankind. For the first purpose, I have offered a large reward for the discovery of a trap-door in a coal-cellar at Hampstead, leading into a subterranean passage and laboratory; since, unfortunately, my unhappy visitor did not happen to mention the position of his house. For the second purpose, I have begun a series of experiments upon the properties of the essential oil of alchemilla, and the possibility of successfully treating it with carbonic anhydride; since, unfortunately, he was equally vague as to the nature of his process and the proportions of either constituent. Many people will conclude at once, no doubt, that I myself have become infected with the monomania of my miserable namesake, but I am determined at any rate not to allow so extraordinary an anæsthetic to go unacknowledged, if there be even a remote chance of actually proving its useful nature. Meanwhile, I say nothing even to my dearest friends with regard to the researches upon which I am engaged.

THE EMPRESS OF ANDORRA

All the troubles in Andorra arose from the fact that the town clerk had views of his own respecting the Holy Roman Empire.

Of course everybody knows that for many centuries the Republic of Andorra, situated in an isolated valley among the Pyrenees, has enjoyed the noble and inestimable boon of autonomy. Not that the Andorrans have been accustomed to call it by that name, because, you see, the name was not yet invented; but the thing itself they have long possessed in all its full and glorious significance. The ancient constitution of the Republic may be briefly described as democracy tempered by stiletto. The free and independent citizens did that which seemed right in their own eyes; unless, indeed, it suited their convenience better to do that which seemed wrong; and, in the latter case, they did it unhesitatingly. So every man in Andorra stabbed or shot his neighbour as he willed, especially if he suspected his neighbour of a prior intention to stab or shoot him. The Republic contained no gallows, capital punishment having been entirely abolished, and, for the matter of that, all other punishment into the bargain. In short, the town of Andorra was really a very eligible place of residence for families or gentlemen, provided only they were decently expert in the use of the pistol.

However, in this model little Republic, as elsewhere, society found itself ranged under two camps, the Liberal and the Conservative. And lest any man should herein suspect the present veracious historian of covert satirical intent, or sly allusion to the politics of neighbouring States, it may be well to add that there was not much to choose between the Liberals and the Conservatives of Andorra.

Now, the town clerk was the acknowledged and ostensible head of the Great Liberal Party. His name in full consisted of some twenty high-sounding Spanish prenomens, followed by about the same number of equally high-sounding surnames; but I need only trouble you here with the first and last on the list, which were simply Señor Don Pedro Henriquez. It happened that Don Pedro, being a learned man, took in all the English periodicals; and so I need hardly tell you that he was thoroughly well up in the Holy Roman Empire question. He could have passed a competitive examination on that subject before Mr. Freeman, or held a public discussion with Professor Bryce himself. The town clerk was perfectly aware that the Holy Roman Empire had come to an end, pro tem. at least, in the year eighteen hundred and something, when Francis the First, Second, or Third, renounced for himself and his heirs forever the imperial Roman title. But the town clerk also knew that the Holy Roman Empire had often lain in abeyance for years or even centuries, and had afterwards been resuscitated by some Karl (whom the wicked call Charlemagne), some Otto, or some Henry the Fowler. And the town clerk, a bold and ambitious young man, reflecting on these things, had formed a deep scheme in his inmost heart. The deep scheme was after this wise.

Why not revive the Holy Roman Empire in Andorra?

Nothing could be more simple, more natural, or more in accordance with the facts of history. Even Mr. Freeman could have no plausible argument to urge against it. For observe how well the scheme hangs together. Andorra formed an undoubted and integral portion of the Roman Empire, having been included in Region VII., Diocese 13 (Hispania Citerior VIII.), under the division of Diocletian. But the Empire having gone to pieces at the present day, any fragment of that Empire may re-constitute itself the whole; "just as the tentacle of a hydra polype," said Don Pedro (who, you know, was a very learned man), "may re-constitute itself into a perfect animal, by developing a body, head, mouth, and foot-stalk." (This, as you are well aware, is called the Analogical Method of Political Reasoning.) Therefore, there was no just cause or impediment why Andorra should not set up to be the original and only genuine representative of the Holy Roman Empire, all others being spurious imitations.—Q. E. D.

The town clerk had further determined in his own mind that he himself was the Karl (not Charlemagne) who was destined to raise up this revived and splendid Roman Empire. He had already struck coins in imagination, bearing on the obverse his image and superscription, and the proud title "Imp. Petrus P. F. Aug. Pater Patriæ, Cos. XVIII.;" with a reverse of Victory crowned, and the legend "Renovatio Romanorum." But this part of his scheme he kept as yet deeply buried in the recesses of his own soul.

As regards the details of this Cæsarian plan, much diversity of opinion existed in the minds of the Liberal leaders. Don Pedro himself, as champion of education, proposed that the new Emperor should be elected by competitive examination; in which case he felt sure that his own knowledge of the Holy Roman Empire would easily place him at the head of the list. But his colleague, Don Luis Dacosta, who was the Joseph Hume of Andorran politics, rather favoured the notion of sending in sealed tenders for executing the office of Sovereign, the State not binding itself to accept the lowest or any other tender; and he had himself determined to make an offer for wearing the crown at the modest remuneration of three hundred pounds per annum, payable quarterly. Again, Don Iago Montes, a poetical young man, who believed firmly in prestige, advocated the idea of inviting the younger son of some German Grand-Duke to accept the Imperial Crown, and the faithful hearts of a loyal Andorran people. But these minor points could easily be settled in the future: and the important object for the immediate present, said Don Pedro, was the acceptance in principle of the resuscitated Holy Roman Empire.

Don Pedro's designs, however, met with considerable opposition from the Conservative party in the Folk Mote. (They called it Folk Mote, and not Cortes or Fueros, on purpose to annoy historical critics; and for the same reason they always styled their chief magistrate, not the Alcalde, but the Burgomaster.) The Conservative leader, Don Juan Pereira (first and last names only; intermediate thirty-eight omitted for want of space!) wisely observed that the good old constitution had suited our fathers admirably; that we did not wish to go beyond the wisdom of our ancestors; that young men were apt to prove thoughtless or precipitate; and finally that "Nolumus leges Andorræ mutare." Hereupon, Don Pedro objected that the growing anarchy of the citizens, whose stabbings were increasing by geometrical progression, called for the establishment of a strong government, which should curb the lawless habits of the jeunesse dorée. But Don Juan retorted that stabbing was a very useful practice in its way; that no citizen ever got stabbed unless he had made himself obnoxious to a fellow-citizen, which was a gross and indefensible piece of incivism; and that stilettos had always been considered extremely respectable instruments by a large number of deceased Andorran worthies, whose names he proceeded to recount in a long and somewhat tedious catalogue. (This, you know, is called the Argument from Authority.) The Folk Mote, which consisted of men over forty alone, unanimously adopted Don Juan's views, and at once rejected the town clerk's Bill for the Resuscitation of the Holy Roman Empire.

Thus driven to extremities, the town clerk determined upon a coup d'état. The appeal to the people alone could save Andorran Society. But being as cautious as he was ambitious, he decided not to display his hand too openly at first. Accordingly he resolved to elect an Empress to begin with; and then, by marrying the Empress, to become Emperor-Consort, after which he could easily secure the Imperial crown on his own account.

To ensure the success of this excellent notion, Don Pedro trusted to the emotions of the populace. The way he did it was simply this.

At that particular juncture, a beautiful young prima donna had lately been engaged for the National Italian Opera, Andorra. She was to appear as the Grande Duchesse on the very evening after that on which the Resuscitation Bill had been thrown out on a third reading. This amiable lady bore the name of Signorita Nora Obrienelli. She was of Italian parentage, but born in America, where her father, Signor Patricio Obrienelli, a banished Neapolitan nobleman and patriot, had been better known as Paddy O'Brien; having adopted that disguise to protect himself from the ubiquitous emissaries of King Bomba. However, on her first appearance upon any stage, the Signorita once more resumed her discarded patronymic of Obrienelli; and it is this circumstance alone which has led certain scandalous journalists maliciously to assert that her father was really an Irish chimney-sweep. But not to dwell on these genealogical details, it will suffice to say that Signorita Nora was a beautiful young lady with a magnificent soprano voice. The enthusiastic and gallant Andorrans were already wild at the mere sight of her beauty, and expected great things from her operatic powers.

Don Pedro marked his opportunity. Calling on the prima donna in the afternoon, faultlessly attired in frock-coat, chimney-pot, and lavender kid gloves, the ambitious politician offered her a bouquet worth at least three-and-sixpence, accompanied by a profound bow; and inquired whether the title and position of Empress would suit her views.

"Down to the ground, my dear Don Pedro," replied the impulsive actress. "The resuscitation of the Holy Roman Empire has long been the dream of my existence."

Half an hour sufficed to settle the details. The protocols were signed, the engagements delivered, and the fate of Andorra, with that of the Holy Roman Empire attached, trembled for a moment in the balance. Don Pedro hastily left to organize the coup d'état, and to hire a special body of claqueurs for the occasion.

Evening drew on apace, big with the fate of Pedro and of Rome. The Opera House was crowded. Stalls and boxes glittered with the partisans of the Liberal leader, the expectant hero of a revived

Cæsarism. The claque occupied the pit and gallery. Enthusiasm, real and simulated, knew no bounds. Signorita Obrienelli was almost smothered with bouquets; and the music of catcalls resounded throughout the house. At length, in the second act, when the prima donna entered, crown on head and robes of state trained behind, in the official costume of the Grand-Duchess of Gerolstein, Don Pedro raised himself from his seat and cried in a loud voice, "Long live Nora, Empress of Andorra and of the Holy Roman Empire!"

The whole audience rose as one man. "Long live the Empress," re-echoed from every side of the building. Handkerchiefs waved ecstatically; women sobbed with emotion; old men wept tears of joy that they had lived to behold the Renovation of the Romans. In five minutes the revolution was a fait accompli. Don Juan Pereira obtained early news of the coup d'état, and fled precipitately across the border, to escape the popular vengeance—not a difficult feat, as the boundaries of the quondam Republic extended only five miles in any direction. Thence the broken-hearted old patriot betook himself into France, where he intended at first to commit suicide, in imitation of Cato; but on second thoughts, he decided to proceed to Guernsey, where he entered into negotiations for purchasing Victor Hugo's house, and tried to pose as a kind of pendent to that banished poet and politician.

Although this mode of election was afterwards commented upon as informal by the European Press, Don Pedro successfully defended it in a learned letter to the Times, under the signature of "Historicus Secundus," in which he pointed out that a similar mode has long been practised by the Sacred College, who call it "Electio per Inspirationem."

The very next day, the Bishop of Urgel drove over to Andorra, and crowned the happy prima donna as Empress. Great rejoicings immediately followed, and the illuminations were conducted on so grand a scale that the single tallow-chandler in the town sold out his entire stock-in-trade, and many houses went without candles for a whole week.

Of course the first act of the grateful sovereign was to extend her favour to Don Pedro, who had been so largely instrumental in placing her upon the throne. She immediately created him Chancellor of Andorra and Prince of the Holy Roman Empire. The office of town clerk was abolished in perpetuity; while an hereditary estate of five acres was conferred upon H.E. the Chancellor and his posterity forever.

Don Pedro had now the long-wished-for opportunity of improving the social and political position of that Andorran people whom he had so greatly loved. He determined to endow them with Primary Education, a National Debt, Free Libraries and Museums, the Income Tax, Female Suffrage, Trial by Jury, Permissive Prohibitory Bills, a Plebiscitum, an Extradition Treaty, a Magna Charta Association, and all the other blessings of modern civilization. By these means he hoped to ingratiate himself in the public favour, and thus at length to place himself unopposed upon the Imperial and Holy Roman throne.

His first step was the settlement of the Constitution. And as he was quite determined in his own mind that the poor little Empress should only be a puppet in the hands of her Chancellor, who was to act as Mayor of the Palace (observe how well his historical learning stood him in good stead on all occasions!), he decided that the revived Empire should take the form of a strictly limited monarchy. He had some idea, indeed, of proclaiming it as the "Holy Roman Empire (Limited);" but on second thoughts it occurred to him that the phrase might be misinterpreted as referring to the somewhat exiguous extent of the Andorran territory: and as he wished it to be understood that the new State was an aggressive Power, which contemplated the final absorption of all the other Latin races, he wisely refrained from the equivocal title. However, he settled the Constitution on a broad and liberal basis, after the following fashion. I quote from his rough draft-sketch, the completed document being too long for insertion in full.

"The supreme authority resides in the Sovereign and the Folk Mote. The Sovereign reigns, but does not govern (at present). The Folk Mote has full legislative and deliberative powers. It consists of fourteen members, chosen from the fourteen wards of East and West Andorra. (Members for Spain, France, Portugal, and Italy may hereafter be added, raising the total complement to eighteen.) The right of voting is granted to all persons, male or female, above eighteen years of age. The executive power rests with the Chancellor of the Empire, who acts in the name of the Sovereign. He possesses a right of veto on all acts of the Folk Mote. His office is perpetual. Vivat Imperatrix!"

This Constitution was proposed to a Public Assembly or Comitia of the Andorran people, and was immediately carried. Enthusiasm was the order of the day: Don Pedro was a handsome young man, of personal popularity: the ladies of Andorra were delighted with any scheme of government which offered them a vote: and the men had all a high opinion of Don Pedro's learning. So nobody opposed a single clause of the Constitution on any ground.

The next step to be taken consisted in gaining the affections of the Empress. But here Don Pedro found to his consternation that he had reckoned without his hostess. It is an easy thing to make a revolution in the body politic, but it is much more serious to attempt a revolution in a woman's heart. Her Majesty's had long been bestowed elsewhere. It is true she had encouraged Don Pedro's attentions on his first momentous visit, but that might be largely accounted for on political grounds. It is true also that she was still quite ready to carry on an innocent flirtation with her handsome young Chancellor when he came to deliberate upon matters of state, but that she had often done before with the lout of an actor who took the part of Fritz. "Prince," she would say, with one of her sunny smiles, "do just what you like about the Permissive Prohibitory Bill, and let us have a glass of sparkling Sillery together in the Council Chamber. You and I are too young, and, shall I say, too good-looking, to trouble our poor little heads about politics and such rubbish. Youth, after all, is nothing without champagne and love!"

And yet her heart—her heart was over the sea. During one of her starring engagements among the Central American States, Signorita Obrienelli had made the acquaintance of Don Carlos Montillado, eldest son of the President of Guatemala. A mutual attachment had sprung up between the young couple, and had taken the practical form of bouquets, bracelets, and champagne suppers; but, alas! the difference in their ranks had long hindered the fulfilment of Don Carlos's anxious vows. His Excellency the President constantly declared that nothing could induce him to consent to a marriage between his son and a strolling actress—in such insolent terms did the wretch allude to the future occupant of an Imperial throne! Now, however, all was changed. Fate had smiled upon the happy lovers, and Don Carlos was already on his way to Andorra as Ambassador Extraordinary and Minister Plenipotentiary from the Guatemalan Republic to the renovated Empire. The poor Chancellor discovered too late that he had baited a hook for his own destruction.

However, he did not yet despair. To be sure the Empress, young, beautiful, and with a magnificent soprano voice, had seated herself firmly in the hearts of her susceptible subjects. Besides, her engaging manners, marked by all the charming abandon of the stage, allowed her to make conquests freely among her lieges, each of whom she encouraged in turn, while smiling slily at the discarded rivals. Still, Don Pedro took heart once more. "Revolution enthroned her," he muttered between his teeth, "and counter-revolution shall disenthrone her yet. These silly people will smirk and bow while she pretends to be in love with every one of them from day to day; but when once the young Guatemalan has carried off the prize they will regret their folly, and turn to the Chancellor, whose heart has always been fixed upon the welfare of Andorra."

With this object in view, the astute politician worked harder than ever for the regeneration of the State. His policy falls under two heads, the External and the Internal. Each head deserves a passing mention from the laborious historian.

Don Pedro's External Policy consisted in the annexation of France, Spain, Portugal, and Italy, and the amalgamation of the Latin races. Accordingly, he despatched Ambassadors to the courts of those four Powers, informing them that the Holy Roman Empire had been resuscitated in Andorra, and inviting them to send in their adhesion to the new State. In that case he assured them that each country should possess a representative in the Imperial Folk Mote on the same terms as the several wards of Andorra itself, and that the settlement of local affairs should be left unreservedly to the minor legislatures, while the Chancellor of the Empire in person would manage the military and naval forces and the general executive department of the whole Confederation. As the four Powers refused to take any notice of Don Pedro's manifesto, the Chancellor declared to the Folk Mote his determination of treating them as recalcitrant rebels, and reducing them by force of arms. However, the Andorran army not being thoroughly mobilized, and indeed having fallen into a state of considerable demoralization, the ambitious prince decided to postpone the declaration of war sine die; and his Foreign Policy accordingly stood over for the time being.

Don Pedro's Internal Policy embraced various measures of Finance, Electoral Law, Public Morals, and Police Regulation.

The financial position of Andorra was now truly deplorable. In addition to the expenses of the Imperial Election, and the hire of post-horses for the Bishop of Urgel to attend the coronation, it cannot be denied that the Empress had fallen into most extravagant habits. She insisted upon drinking Veuve Clicquot every day for dinner, and upon ordering large quantities of olives farcies and pâté de foie gras, to which delicacies she was inordinately attached. She also sent to a Parisian milliner for two new bonnets, and had her measure taken for a poult de Lyon dress. These expensive tastes, contracted upon the stage, soon drained the Andorran Exchequer, and the Folk Mote was at its wits' end to devise a Budget. One radical member had even the bad taste to call for a return of Her Majesty's millinery bill; but this motion the House firmly and politely declined to sanction. At last Don Pedro stepped in to solve the difficulty, and proposed an Act for the Inflation of the Currency.

Inflation is a very simple financial process indeed. It consists in writing on a small piece of white paper, "This is a Dollar," or, "This is a Pound," as the case may be, and then compelling your creditors to accept the paper as payment in full for the amount written upon its face. The scheme met with perfect success, and Don Pedro was much bepraised by the press as the glorious regenerator of Andorran Finance.

Among the Chancellor's plans for electoral reform the most important was the Bill for the Promotion of Infant Suffrage. Don Pedro shrewdly argued that if you wished to be popular in the future, you must enlist the sympathies of the rising generation by conferring upon them some signal benefit. Hence his advocacy of Infant Suffrage. In his great speech to the Folk Mote upon this important measure, he pointed out that the brutal doctrine of an appeal to force in the last resort ill befitted the nineteenth century. Many infants owned property; therefore they ought to be represented. Their property was taxed; no taxation without representation; therefore they ought to be represented. Great cruelties were often practised upon them by their parents, which showed how futile was the argument that their parents vicariously represented them; therefore they ought to be directly represented. An honourable member on the Opposition side had suggested that dogs were also taxed, and that great cruelties were occasionally practised upon dogs. Those facts were perfectly true, and he could only say that they proved to him the thorough desirability of insuring representation for dogs at some future day. But we must not move too fast. He was no hasty radical, no violent reconstructionist; he preferred, stone by stone, to build up the sure and perfect fabric of their liberties. So he would waive for the time being the question concerning the rights of dogs, and only move at present the third reading of the Bill for the Promotion of Infant Suffrage. A division was hardly necessary. The House passed the Act by a majority of twelve out of a total of fourteen members.

The Bills for the Gratuitous Distribution of Lollipops, for the Wednesday and Saturday Whole Holidays, and for the Total Abolition of Latin Grammar, followed as a matter of course. The minds of the infant electors were thus thoroughly enlisted on the Chancellor's side.

As to Moral Regeneration, that was mainly ensured by the Act for the Absolute Suppression of the Tea Trade. No man, said the Chancellor, had a right to endanger the health and happiness of his posterity by the pernicious habit of tea-drinking. Alcohol they had suppressed, and tobacco they had suppressed; but tea still remained a plague-spot in their midst. It had been proved that tea and coffee contained poisonous alkaloid principles, known as theine and caffeine (here the Chancellor displayed the full extent of his chemical learning), which were all but absolutely identical with the poisonous principles of opium, prussic acid, and atheistical literature generally. It might be said that this Bill endangered the liberty of the subject. No man had a greater respect for the liberty of the subject than he had; he adored, he idolized, he honoured with absolute apotheosis the liberty of the subject; but in what did it consist? Not, assuredly, in the right to imbibe a venomous drug, which polluted the stream of life for future generations, and was more productive of manifold diseases than even vaccination itself. "Tea," cried the orator passionately, raising his voice till the fresh whitewash on the ceiling of the Council Chamber trembled with sympathetic emotion; "Tea, forsooth! Call it rather strychnine! Call it arsenic! Call it the deadly Upas-tree of Java (Antiaris toxicaria, Linnæus)"—what prodigious learning!—"which poisons with its fatal breath whoever ventures to pass beneath its baleful shadow! I see it driving out of the field the harmless chocolate of our forefathers; I see it forcing its way into the earliest meal of morning, and the latest meal of eve. I see it now once more swarming over the Pyrenees from France, with Paris fashions and bad romances, to desecrate the sacred hour of five o'clock with its newfangled presence. The infant in arms finds it rendered palatable to his tender years by the insidious addition of copious milk and sugar; the hallowed reverence of age forgets itself in disgraceful excesses at the refreshment-room of railway stations. This is the ubiquitous pest which distils its venom into every sex and every age! This is the enchanted chalice of the Cathaian Circe which I ask you to repel to-day from the lips of the young, the pure, and the virtuous!"

It was an able and eloquent effort; but even the Chancellor's powers were all but overtasked in so hard a struggle against ignorance and prejudice. Unhappily, several of the members were themselves secretly addicted to that cup of five o'clock tea to which Don Pedro so feelingly alluded. In the end, however, by taking advantage of the temporary absence of three senators, who had gone to indulge their favourite vice at home, the Bill triumphantly passed its third reading by an overwhelming majority of chocolate drinkers, and became forthwith the law of the Holy Roman Empire.

Meanwhile Don Carlos Montillado had crossed the stormy seas in safety, and arrived by special mule at the city of Andorra. He took up his quarters at the Guatemalan Embassy, and immediately sent his card to the Empress and the Chancellor, requesting the honour of an early interview.

The Empress at once despatched a note requesting Don Carlos to present himself without delay in the private drawing-room of the Palace. The happy lover and ambassador flew to her side, and for half an hour the pair enjoyed the delicious Paradise of a mutual attachment. At the end of that period Don Pedro presented himself at the door.

"Your Majesty," he exclaimed in a tone of surprise, "this is a most irregular proceeding. His Excellency the Guatemalan Ambassador should have called in the first instance upon the Imperial Chancellor."

"Prince," replied the Empress firmly, "I refuse to give you audience at present. I am engaged on private business—on strictly private business—with his Excellency."

"Excuse me," said the Chancellor blandly, "but I must assure your Majesty—"

"Leave the room, Prince," said the Empress, with an impatient gesture. "Leave the room at once!"

"Leave the room, fellow, when a lady speaks to you," cried the impetuous young Guatemalan, drawing his sword, and pushing Don Pedro bodily out of the door.

The die was cast. The Rubicon was crossed. Don Pedro determined on a counter-revolution, and waited for his revenge. Nor had he long to wait.

Half an hour later, as Don Carlos was passing out of the Palace on his way home to dress for dinner, six stout constables seized him by the arms, handcuffed him on the spot, and dragged him off to the Imperial prison. "At the suit of his Excellency the Chancellor," they said in explanation, and hurried him away without another word.

The Empress was furious. "How dare you?" she shrieked to Don Pedro. "What right have you to imprison him—the accredited representative of a Foreign Power?"

"Excuse me," answered Don Pedro, in his smoothest tone. "Article 39 of the Penal Code enacts that the person of the Chancellor is sacred, and that any individual who violently assaults him, with arms in hand, may be immediately committed to prison without trial, by her Majesty's command. Article 40 further provides that Foreign Ambassadors and other privileged persons are not exempt from the penalties of the previous Article."

"But, sir," cried the angry little Empress (she was too excited now to remember that Don Pedro was a Prince), "I never gave any command to have Don Carlos imprisoned. Release him at once, I tell you."

"Your Majesty forgets," replied the Chancellor quietly, "that by Article I of the Constitution the Sovereign reigns but does not govern. The prerogative is solely exercised through the Chancellor. L'état, c'est moi!" And he struck an attitude.

"So you refuse to let him out!" said the Empress. "Mayn't I marry who I like? Mayn't I even settle who shall be my own visitors?"

"Certainly not, your Majesty, if the interests of the State demand that it should be otherwise."

"Then I'll resign," shrieked out the poor little Empress, with a burst of tears. "I'll withdraw. I'll retire. I'll abdicate."

"By all means," said the Chancellor coolly. "We can easily find another Sovereign quite as good."

The shrewd little ex-actress looked hard into Don Pedro's face. She was an adept in the art of reading emotions, and she saw at once what Don Pedro really wished. In a moment she had changed front, and stood up once more every inch an Empress. "No, I won't!" she cried; "I see you would be glad to get rid of me, and I shall stop here to baffle and thwart you; and I shall marry Carlos; and we shall fight it out to the bitter end." So saying, she darted out of the room, red-eyed but majestic, and banged the door after her with a slam as she went.

Henceforward it was open war between them. Don Pedro did not dare to depose the Empress, who had still a considerable body of partisans amongst the Andorran people; but he resolutely refused to release the Guatemalan legate, and decided to accept hostilities with the Central American Republic, in order to divert the minds of the populace from internal politics. If he returned home from the campaign as a successful commander, he did not doubt that he would find himself sufficiently powerful to throw off the mask, and to assume the Imperial purple in name as well as in reality.

Accordingly, before the Guatemalan President could receive the news of his son's imprisonment, Don Pedro resolved to prepare for war. His first care was to strengthen the naval resources of his country. The Opposition—that is to say, the Empress's party—objected that Andorra had no seaboard. But Don Pedro at once overruled that objection, by dint of several parallel instances. The Province of Upper Canada (now Ontario, added the careful historical student) had no seaboard, yet the Canadians placed numerous gunboats on the great lakes during the war of 1812. (What research!) Again, the Nile, the Indus, the Ganges, and many other great rivers had been the scene of important naval engagements as early as B.C. 1082, which he could show from the evidence of papyri now preserved in the British Museum. (What universal knowledge!) The objection was frivolous. But, answered the Opposition, Andorra has neither lakes nor navigable rivers. This, Don Pedro considered, was mere hair-splitting. Perhaps they would tell him next it had no gutters or water-butts. Besides, we must accommodate ourselves to the environment. (This, you see, conclusively proves that the Chancellor had read Mr. Herbert Spencer, and was thoroughly well up in the minutiæ of the Evolutionist Philosophy.) Had they never looked into their Thucydides? Did they not remember the famous holkos, or trench, whereby the Athenian triremes were lifted across the Isthmus of Corinth? Well, he proposed in like manner to order a large number of ironclads from an eminent Glasgow firm, to pull them overland up the Pyrenees, and to plant them on the mountain tops around Andorra as permanent batteries. That was what he meant by adaptation to the environment.

So the order was given to the eminent Glasgow firm, who forthwith supplied the Empire with ten magnificent Clyde-built ironclads, having 14-inch plates, and patent double-security rivets: mounting twelve eighty-ton guns apiece, and fitted up with all the latest Woolwich improvements. These vessels were then hauled up the mountains, as Don Pedro proposed; and there they stood, on the tallest neighbouring summits, in very little danger of going to the bottom, as the ironclads of other Powers are so apt to do. In return, Don Pedro tendered payment by means of five million pounds Inflated Currency, which he assured the eminent ship-builders were quite as good as gold, if not a great deal better. The firm was at first inclined to demur to this mode of payment; but Don Pedro immediately retorted that they did not seem to understand the Currency Question: and as this is an imputation which no gentleman could endure for a moment, the eminent ship-builders pocketed the inflated paper at once, and pretended to think no more about it.

However, there was one man among them who rather mistrusted inflation, because, you see, his education had been sadly neglected, especially as regards the works of American Political Economists, in which Don Pedro was so deeply versed. Now, this ignorant and misguided man went straight off to the Stock Exchange with his share of the five millions, and endeavoured to negotiate a few hundred thousands for pocket-money. But it turned out that all the other Stock Exchange magnates were just as ill-informed as himself with respect to inflation and the Currency Question at large: and they persisted in declaring that a piece of paper is really none the better for having the words "This is a Pound" written across its face. So the eminent ship-builder returned home disconsolate, and next day instituted proceedings in Chancery against the Holy Roman Empire at Andorra for the recovery of five million pounds sterling. What came at last of this important suit you shall hear in the sequel.

Meanwhile, poor Don Carlos remained incarcerated in the Imperial prison, and preparations for war went on with vigour and activity, both in Andorra and Guatemala. Naturally, the greatest excitement prevailed throughout Europe, and especially in the sympathetic Republic of San Marino. Very different views of the situation were expressed by the various periodicals of that effusive State. The Matutinal Agitator declared that Andorra under the Obrienelli dynasty had become a dangerously aggressive Power, and that no peace could be expected in Europe until the Andorrans had been taught to recognize their true position in the scale of nations. The Vespertinal Sentimentalist, on the other hand, looked upon the Guatemalans as wanton disturbers of the public quietude, and considered Andorra in the favourable light of an oppressed nationality. The Hebdomadal Tranquillizer, which treated both sides with contempt—avowing that it held the Andorrans to be little better than lawless brigands, in the last stage of bankruptcy; and the Guatemalans to be mere drunken half-castes, incapable of attack or defence for want of men and money—this lukewarm and mean-spirited journal, I say, was treated with universal contumely as a wretched time-server, devoid of human sympathies and of proper cosmopolitan expansiveness. At length, however, through the good offices of the San Marino Government, both Powers were induced to lay aside the thought of needless bloodshed, and to discuss the terms of a mutual understanding at a Pan-Hispanic Congress to be held in the neutral metropolis of Monaco.

Invitations to attend the Congress were issued to all the Spanish-speaking nations on both sides of the Atlantic. There were a few trifling refusals, it is true, as Spain, Mexico, and the South American States declined to send representatives to the proposed meeting: but still a goodly array of plenipotentiaries met to discuss the terms of peace. Envoys from Andorra, from Guatemala, and from the other Central American Republics—one of whom was of course a Chevalier of the Exalted Order of the Holy Rose of Honduras, while another represented the latest President of Nicaragua—sat down by the side of a coloured marquis from San Domingo, and a mulatto general who presented credentials from the Republic of Cuba—since unhappily extinct. Thus it will be seen at a glance that the Congress wanted nothing which could add to its imposing character, either as an International Parliament or as an expression of military Pan-Hispanic force. Europe felt instinctively that its deliberations were backed up by all the vast terrestrial and naval armaments of its constituent Powers.

But while Don Pedro was pulling the wires of the Monaco convention (by telegraph) from his headquarters at Andorra—he could not himself have attended its meeting, lest his august Sovereign should embrace the opportunity of releasing the captive Guatemalan and so stopping his hopes of future success—he had to contend at home, not only with the covert opposition of the brave little Empress, but also with the open rebellion of a disaffected minority. The five wards which constitute East Andorra had long been at secret variance with the nine wards of West Andorra; and they seized upon this moment of foreign complications to organize a Home Rule party, and set on foot a movement of secession. After a few months of mere parliamentary opposition, they broke at last into overt acts of treason, seized on three of Don Pedro's ironclads, and proclaimed themselves a separate government under the title of the Confederate Wards of Andorra. This last blow almost broke Don Pedro's heart. He had serious thoughts of giving up all for lost, and retiring into a monastery for the term of his natural life.

As it happened, however, the Chancellor was spared the necessity for that final humiliation, and the Pan-Hispanic Congress was relieved of its arduous duties by the sudden intervention of a hitherto passive Power. Great Britain woke at last to a sense of her own prestige and the necessities of the situation. The Court of Chancery decided that the Inflated Currency was not legal tender, and adjudicated the bankrupt state of Andorra to the prosecuting creditors, the firm of eminent ship-builders at Glasgow. A sheriff's officer, backed by a company of British Grenadiers, was despatched to take possession of the territory in the name of the assignees, and to repel any attempt at armed resistance.

Political considerations had no little weight in the decision which led to this imposing military demonstration. It was felt that if we permitted Guatemala to keep up a squadron of ironclads in the Caribbean, a perpetual menace would overshadow our tenure of Jamaica and Barbadoes: while if we suffered Andorra to overrun the Peninsula, our position at Gibraltar would not be worth a fortnight's purchase. For these reasons the above-mentioned expeditionary force was detailed for the purpose of attaching the insolent Empire, liberating the imprisoned Guatemalan, and entirely removing the casus belli. It was hoped that such prompt and vigorous action would deter the Central American States from their extensive military preparations, which had already reached to several pounds of powder and over one hundred stand of Martini-Henry rifles.

Our demonstration was quite as successful as the "little wars" of Great Britain have always been. Don Pedro made some show of resistance with his eighty-ton guns; but finding that the contractors had only supplied them with wooden bores, he deemed it prudent at length to beat a precipitate retreat. As to the poor little Empress, she had long learned to regard herself as a cypher in the realm over which she reigned but did not govern; and she was therefore perfectly ready to abdicate the throne, and resign the crown jewels to the sheriff's officer. She did so with the less regret, because the crown was only aluminium, and the jewels only paste—being, in fact, the identical articles which she had worn in her theatrical character as the Grand-Duchess of Gerolstein. The quondam republic was far from rich, and it had been glad to purchase these convenient regalia from the property-man at the theatre on the eventful morning of the Imperial Coronation.

Don Carlos was immediately liberated by the victorious troops, and rushed at once into the arms of his inamorata. The Bishop of Urgel married them as private persons on the very same afternoon. The ex-Empress returned to the stage, and made her first reappearance in London, where the history of her misfortunes, and the sympathy which the British nation always extends to the conquered, rapidly secured her an unbounded popularity. Don Carlos practised with success on the violin, and joined the orchestra at the same house where his happy little wife appeared as prima donna. Señor Montillado the elder at first announced his intention of cutting off his son with a shilling; but being shortly after expelled from the Presidency of the Guatemalan Republic by one of the triennial revolutions which periodically diversify life in that volcanic state, he changed his mind, took the mail steamer to Southampton, and obtained through his son's influence a remunerative post as pantaloon at a neighbouring theatre.

The eminent ship-builders took possession of East and West Andorra, quelled the insurrectionary movement of the Confederate Wards, and brought back the ten ironclads, together with the crown jewels and other public effects. On the whole, they rather gained than lost by the national bankruptcy, as they let out the conquered territory to the Andorran people at a neat little ground-rent of some £20,000 per annum.

Don Pedro fled across the border to Toulouse, where he obtained congenial employment as clerk to an avoué. He was also promptly elected secretary to the local Academy of Science and Art, a post for which his varied attainments fit him in the highest degree. He has given up all hopes of the resuscitation of the Holy Roman Empire, and is now engaged to a business-like young woman at the Café de l'Univers, who will effectually cure him of all lingering love for transcendental politics.

Finally, if any hypercritical person ventures to assert that this history is based upon a total misconception of the Holy Roman Empire question—that I am completely mistaken about Francis II., utterly wrong about Otto the Great, and hopelessly fogged about Henry the Fowler—I can only answer, that I take these statements as I find them in the note-books of Don Pedro, and the printed debates of the Andorran Folk Mote. Like a veracious historian, I cannot go beyond my authorities. But I think you will agree with me, my courteous reader, that the dogmatic omniscience of these historical critics is really beginning to surpass human endurance.

THE SENIOR PROCTOR'S WOOING: A TALE OF TWO CONTINENTS

I

I was positively blinded. I could hardly read the note, a neatly written little square sheet of paper; and the words seemed to swim before my eyes. It was in the very thick of summer term, and I, Cyril Payne, M.A., Senior Proctor of the University of Oxford, was calmly asked to undertake the sole charge for a week of a wild American girl, travelling alone, and probably expecting me to run about with her just as foolishly as I had done at Nice. There it lay before me, that awful note, in its overwhelming conciseness, without hope of respite or interference. It was simply crushing.

"MY DEAR MR. PAYNE,

"I am coming to Oxford, as you advised me. I shall arrive to-morrow by the 10.15 a.m. train, and mean to stop at the Randolph. I hope you will kindly show me all the lions.

"Yours very sincerely,   "IDA VAN RENSSELAER."

It was dated Tuesday, and this was Wednesday morning. I hadn't opened my letters before seeing last night's charges at nine o'clock; and it was now just ten. In a moment the full terror of the situation flashed upon me. She had started; she was already almost here; there was no possibility of telegraphing to stop her; before I could do anything, she would have arrived, have taken rooms at the Randolph, and have come round in her queer American manner to call upon me. There was not a moment to be lost. I must rush down to the station and meet her—in full academicals, velvet sleeves and all, for a Proctor must never be seen in the morning in mufti. If there had been half an hour more, I could have driven round by the Parks and called for my sister Annie, who was married to the Rev. Theophilus Sheepshanks, Professor of Comparative Osteology, and who might have helped me out of the scrape. But as things stood, I was compelled to burst down the High just as I was, hail a hansom opposite Queen's, and drive furiously to the station in bare time to meet the 10.15 train. At all hazards, Ida Van Rensselaer must not go to the Randolph, and must be carried off to Annie's, whether she would or not. On the way down I had time to arrange my plan of action; and before I reached the station, I thought I saw my way dimly out of the awful scrape which this mad Yankee girl had so inconsiderately got me into.

I had met Ida Van Rensselaer the winter before at Nice. We stopped together at a pension on the Promenade des Anglais; and as I was away from Oxford—for even a Proctor must unbend sometimes—and as she was a pleasant, lively young person with remarkably fine eyes, travelling by herself, I had taken the trouble to instruct her in European scenery and European art. She had a fancy for being original, so I took her to see Eza, and Roccabrunna, and St. Pons, and all the other queer picturesque little places in the Nice district which no American had ever dreamt of going to see before: and when Ida went on to Florence, I happened—quite accidentally, of course—to turn up at the very same pension three days later, where I gave her further lessons in the art of admiring the early mediæval masters and the other treasures of Giotto's city. I was a bit of a collector myself, and in my rooms at Magdalen I flatter myself that I have got the only one genuine Botticelli in a private collection in England. In spite of her untamed American savagery, Ida had a certain taste for these things, and evidently my lessons gave her the first glimpse she had ever had of that real interior Europe whose culture she had not previously suspected. It is pleasant to teach a pretty pupil, and in the impulse of a weak moment—it was in a gondola at Venice—I even told her that she should not leave for America without having seen Oxford. Of course I fancied that she would bring a chaperon. Now she had taken me at my word, but she had come alone. I had brought it all upon myself, undoubtedly; though how the dickens I was ever to get out of it I could not imagine.

As I reached the station, the 10.15 was just coming in. I cast a wild glance right and left, and saw at least a dozen undergraduates, without cap or gown, loitering on the platform in obvious disregard of university law. But I felt far too guilty to proctorize them, and I was terribly conscious that all their eyes were fixed upon me, as I moved up and down the carriages looking for my American friend. She caught my eye in a moment, peering out of a second-class window—she had told me that she was not well off—and I thought I should have sunk in the ground when she jumped lightly out, seized my hand warmly, and cried out quite audibly, in her pretty faintly American voice, "My dear Mr. Payne, I am so glad you've come to meet me. Will you see after my baggage—no, luggage you call it in England, don't you?—and get it sent up to the Randolph, please, at once?"

Was ever Proctor so tried on this earth? But I made an effort to smile it off. "My sister is so sorry she could not come to meet you, Miss Van Rensselaer," I said in my loudest voice, for I saw all those twelve sinister undergraduates watching afar off with eager curiosity; "but she has sent me down to carry you off in her stead, and she begs you won't think of going to the Randolph, but will come and make her house your home as long as you stay in Oxford." I flattered myself that the twelve odious young men, who were now forming a sort of irregular circle around us, would be completely crushed by that masterly stroke: though what on earth Annie would say at being saddled with this Yankee girl for a week I hardly dared to fancy. For Annie was a Professor's wife: and the dignity of a Professor's wife is almost as serious a matter as that of a Senior Proctor himself.

Imagine my horror, then, when Ida answered, with her frank smile and sunny voice, "Your sister! I didn't know you had a sister. And anyhow, I haven't come to see your sister, but yourself. And I'd better go to the Randolph straight, I'm sure, because I shall feel more at home there. You can come round and see me whenever you like, there; and I mean you to show me all Oxford, now I've come here, that's certain."

I glanced furtively at the open-eared undergraduates, and felt that the game was really up. I could never face them again. I must resign everything, take orders, and fly to a country rectory. At least, I thought so on the spur of the moment.

But something must clearly be done. I couldn't stand and argue out the case with Ida before those twelve young fiends, now reinforced by a group of porters; and I determined to act strategically— that is to say, tell a white lie. "You can go to the Randolph, of course, if you wish, Miss Van Rensselaer," I said; "will you come and show me which is your luggage? Here, you, sir," to one of the porters, a little angrily, I fear, "come and get this lady's boxes, will you?"

In a minute I had secured the boxes, and went out for a cab. There was nothing left but a single hansom. Demoralized as I was, I took it, and put Ida inside. "Drive to Lechlade Villa, the Parks," I whispered to the cabby—that was Annie's address—and I jumped in beside my torturer. As we drove up by the Corn-market, I could see the porters and scouts of Balliol and John's all looking eagerly out at the unwonted sight of a Senior Proctor in full academicals, driving through the streets of Oxford in a hansom cab, with a lady by his side. As for Ida, she remained happily unconscious, though I blamed her none the less for it. In her native wilds I knew that such vagaries were permitted by the rules of society; but she ought surely to have known that in Europe they were not admissible.

"Now, Miss Van Rensselaer," I said as we turned the corner of Carfax, "I am taking you to my sister's. Excuse my frankness if I tell you that, according to English, and especially to Oxford etiquette, it would never do for you to go to an hotel. People's sense of decorum would be scandalized if they learnt that a lady had come alone to visit the Senior Proctor, and was stopping at the Randolph. Don't you see yourself how very odd it looks?"

"Well, no," said Ida promptly; "I think you are a dreadfully suspicious people: you seem always to credit everybody with the worst motives. In America, we think people mean no harm, and don't look after them so sharply as you do. But I really can't go to your sister's. I don't know her, and I haven't been invited. Does she know I'm coming?"

"Well, I can't say she does," I answered hesitatingly. "You see, your letter only reached me half an hour ago, and I had no time to see her before I went to meet you."

"Then I certainly won't go, Mr. Payne, that's certain."

"But my dear Miss Van Rensselaer—"

"Not the slightest use, I assure you. I can't go to a house where they don't even know I'm coming. Driver, will you go to the Randolph Hotel, please?"

I sank back paralyzed and unmanned. This girl was one too many for me. "Miss Van Rensselaer," I cried, in a last despairing fit, "do you know that as Senior Proctor of the University I have the power to order you away from Oxford; and that if I told them at the Randolph not to take you in, they wouldn't dare to do it?"

"Well really, Mr. Payne, I dare say you have some extraordinary mediæval customs here, but you can hardly mean to send me away again by main force. I shall go to the Randolph."

And she went. I had to draw up solemnly at the door, to accompany her to the office, and to see her safely provided with a couple of rooms before I could get away hastily to the Ancient House of Convocation, where public business was being delayed by my absence. As I hurried through the Schools Quadrangle, I felt like a convicted malefactor going to face his judges, and self-condemned by his very face.

That afternoon, as soon as I had gulped down a choking lunch, I bolted down to the Parks and saw Annie. At first I thought it was a hopeless task to convince her that Ida Van Rensselaer's conduct was, from an American point of view, nothing extraordinary. She persisted in declaring that such goings-on were not respectable, and that I was bound, as an officer of the University, to remove the young woman at once from the eight-mile radius over which my jurisdiction extended. I pleaded in vain that ladies in America always travelled alone, and that nobody thought anything of it. Annie pertinently remarked that that would be excellent logic in New York, but that it was quite un-Aristotelian in Oxford. "When your American friends come to Rome," she said coldly—as though I were in the habit of importing Yankee girls wholesale—"they must do as Rome does." But when I at last pointed out that Ida, as an American citizen, could appeal to her minister if I attempted to turn her out, and that we might find ourselves the centre of an international quarrel—possibly even a casus belli—she finally yielded with a struggle. "For the sake of respectability," she said solemnly, "I'll go and call on this girl with you; but remember, Cyril, I shall never undertake to help you out of such a disgraceful scrape a second time." I sneaked out into the garden to wait for her, and felt that the burden of a Proctorship was really more than I could endure.

We called duly upon Ida, that very hour, and Ida certainly behaved herself remarkably well. She was so charmingly frank and pretty, she apologized so simply to Annie for her ignorance of English etiquette, and she was so obviously guileless and innocent-hearted in all her talk, that even Annie herself—who is, I must confess, a typical don's wife—was gradually mollified. To my great surprise, Annie even asked her to dinner en famille the same evening, and suggested that I should make an arrangement with the Junior Proctor to take my work, and join the party. I consented, not without serious misgivings; but I felt that if Ida was really going to stop a week, it would be well to put the best face upon it, and to show her up in company with Annie as often as possible. That might just conceivably take the edge off the keen blade of University scandal.

To cut a long story short, Ida did stop her week, and I got through it very creditably after all. Annie behaved like a brick, as soon as the first chill was over; for though she is married to a professor of dry bones (Comparative Osteology sounds very well, but means no more than that, when you come to think of it), she is a woman at heart in spite of it all. Ida had the most winning, charming, confiding manner; and she was so pleased with Oxford, with the colleges, the libraries, the gardens, the river, the boats, the mediæval air, the whole place, that she quite gained Annie over to her side. Nay, my sister even discovered incidentally that Ida had a little fortune of her own, amounting to some £300 a year, which, though it doesn't count for much in America, would be a neat little sum to a man like myself, in England; and she shrewdly observed, in her sensible business-like manner, that it would quite make up for the possible loss of my Magdalen fellowship. I am not exactly what you call a marrying man—at least, I know I had never got married before; but as the week wore on, and I continued boating, flirting, and acting showman to Ida, Annie of course always assisting for propriety's sake, I began to feel that the Proctor was being conquered by the man. I fell most seriously and undoubtedly in love. Ida admired my rooms, was charmed with the pretty view from my windows over Magdalen Bridge and the beautiful gardens, and criticized my Botticelli with real sympathy. I was interested in her; she was so fresh, so real, and so genuinely delighted with the new world which opened before her. It was almost her first glimpse of the true interior Europe, and she was fascinated with it, as all better American minds invariably are when they feel the charm of its contrast with their own hurrying, bustling, mushroom world. The week passed easily and pleasantly enough; and when it was drawing to an end, I had half made up my mind to propose to Ida Van Rensselaer.

The day before she was to leave she told us she would not go out in the afternoon; so I determined to stroll down the river to Iffley by myself in a "tub dingey"—a small boat with room in it for two, if occasion demands. When I reached the Iffley Lock, imagine my horror at seeing Ida in the middle of the stream, quietly engaged in paddling herself down the river in a canoe. I ran my dingey close beside her, drove her remorselessly against the bank, and handed her out on to the meadow, before she could imagine what I was driving at.

"Now, Miss Van Rensselaer," I said sternly, "this will never do. By herculean efforts Annie and I have got over this week without serious scandal; and at the last moment you endeavour to wreck our plans by canoeing down the open river by yourself before the eyes of the whole University. Everybody will talk about the Senior Proctor's visitor having been seen indecorously paddling about in broad daylight in a boat of her own."

"I didn't know there was any harm in it," said Ida penitently; for she was beginning to understand the real seriousness of University etiquette.

"Well," I answered, "it can't be helped now. You must get into my boat at once—I'll send one of Salter's men down to fetch your canoe—and we must row straight back to Oxford immediately."

She obeyed me mechanically, and I began to pull away for very life. "There's nothing for it now," I said pensively, "except to propose to you. I half meant to do it before, and now I've quite made up my mind. Will you have me?"

Ida looked at me without surprise, but with a little pleasure in her face. "What nonsense!" she said quietly. "I knew you were going to propose to me this afternoon, and so I came out alone to keep out of your way. You haven't had time to make up your mind properly yet."

As I looked at her beautiful calm face and lovely eyes I forgot everything. In a moment, I was over head and ears in love again, and conscious of nothing else. "Ida," I cried, looking at her steadily, "Ida!"

"Now, please stop," said Ida, before I could get any further. "I know exactly what you're going to say. You're going to say, 'Ida, I love you.' Don't desecrate the verb to love by draggling it more than it has already been draggled through all the grammars of every European language. I've conjugated to love, myself, in English, French, German, and Italian; and you've conjugated it in Latin and Greek, and for aught I know in Anglo-Saxon and Coptic and Assyrian as well; so now let's have done with it forever, and conjugate some other verb more worthy the attention of two rational and original human beings. Can't you strike out a line for yourself?"

"You're quite mistaken," I answered curtly, for I wasn't going to be browbeaten in that way; "I meant to say nothing of the sort. What I did mean to say—and I'll trouble you to listen to it attentively— was just this. You seem to me about as well suited to my abstract requirements as any other young woman I have ever met: and if you're inclined to take me, we might possibly arrange an engagement."

"What a funny man you are!" she went on innocently. "You don't propose at all en règle. I've had twelve men propose to me separately in a boat in America, and you make up the baker's dozen: but all the others leaned forward lackadaisically, dropped the oars when they were beginning to get serious, and looked at me sentimentally; while you go on rowing all the time as if there was nothing unusual in it."

"Probably," I suggested, "your twelve American admirers attached more importance to the ceremony than I do. But you haven't answered my question yet."

"Let me ask you one instead," she said, more seriously. "Do you think I'm at all the kind of person for a Senior Proctor's wife? You say I suit your abstract requirements, but one can't get married in the abstract, you know. Viewed concretely, don't you fancy I'm about the most unsuitable helpmate you could possibly light upon?"

"The profound consciousness of that indubitable fact," I replied carelessly, "has made me struggle in a hopeless sort of way against the irresistible impulse to propose to you ever since I saw you first. But I suppose Senior Proctors are much the same as other men. They fly like moths about the candle, and can't overcome the temptation of singeing their wings."

"If I had any notion of accepting you," said Ida reflectively, "I should at least have the consolation of knowing that you didn't make anything by your bargain; for my fifteen hundred dollars would just amount to the three hundred a year which you would have to give up with your fellowship."

"Quite so," I answered; "I see you come of a business-like nation; and I, as former bursar of my college, am a man of business myself. So I have no reason for concealing from you the fact that I have a private income of about four hundred a year, besides University appointments worth five hundred more, which would not go with the fellowship."

"Do you really think me sordid enough to care for such considerations?"

"If I did, I wouldn't have taken the trouble to tell you them. I merely mentioned the facts for their general interest, and not as bearing on the question in hand."

"Well, then, Mr. Payne, you shall have my answer.—No."

"Is it final?"

"Is anything human final, except one's twenty-ninth birthday? I choose it to be final for the present, and 'the subject then dropped,' as the papers say about debates in Congress. Let us have done now with this troublesome verb altogether, and conjugate our return to Oxford instead. See what bunches of fritillaries again! I never saw anything prettier, except the orange-lilies in New Hampshire. If you like, you may come to America next season. You would enjoy our woodlands."

"Where shall I find you?"

"At Saratoga."

"When?"

"Any day from July the first."

"Good," I said, after a moment's reflection. "If I stick to my fancy for flying into the candle, you will see me there. If I change my mind, it won't matter much to either of us."

So we paddled back to Oxford, talking all the way of indifferent subjects, of England and our English villages, and enjoying the peaceful greenness of the trees and banks. It was half-past six when we got to Salter's barge, and I walked with Ida as far as the Randolph. Then I returned to college, feeling very much like an undetected sheep-stealer, and had a furtive sort of dinner served up in my own room. Next morning, I confess it was with a sigh of relief that Annie and I saw Ida Van Rensselaer start from the station en route for Liverpool. It was quite a fortnight before I could face my own bulldogs unabashed, and I bowed with a wan and guilty smile upon my face whenever any one of those twelve undergraduates capped me in the High till the end of term. I believe they never missed an opportunity of meeting me if they saw a chance open. I was glad indeed when long vacation came to ease me of my office and my troubles.

Congress Hall in Saratoga is really one of the most comfortable hotels at which I ever stopped. Of course it holds a thousand guests, and covers an unknown extent of area: it measures its passages by the mile and its carpets by the acre. All that goes unsaid, for it is a big American hotel; but it is also a very pleasant and luxurious one, even for America. I was not sorry, on the second of July, to find myself comfortably quartered (by elevator) in room No. 547 on the fifth floor, with a gay look-out on Broadway and the Columbia Spring. After ten days of dismal rolling on the mid-Atlantic, and a week of hurry and bustle in New York, I found it extremely delightful to sit down at my ease in summer quarters, on a broad balcony overlooking the leafy promenade, to sip my iced cobbler like a prince, and to watch that strange, new, and wonderfully holiday life which was unfolding itself before my eyes. Such a phantasmagoria of brightly-dressed women in light but costly silks, of lounging young men in tweed suits and panama hats, of sulkies, carriages, trotting horses, string bands, ice-creams, effervescing drinks, cool fruits, green trees, waving bunting, lilac blossoms, roses, and golden sunshine I had never seen till then, and shall never see again, I doubt me, until I can pay a second visit to Saratoga. It was a midsummer saturnalia of strawberries and acacia flowers, gone mad with excessive mint julep.

"After all," said I to myself, "even if I don't happen to run up against Ida Van Rensselaer, I shall have taken as pleasant a holiday as I could easily have found in old Europe. Everybody is tired of Switzerland and Italy, so, happy thought, try Saratoga. On the other hand, if Ida keeps her tryst, I shall have one more shot at her in the shape of a proposal; and then if she really means no, I shall be none the worse off than if I had stayed in England." In which happy-go-lucky and philosophic frame of mind I sat watching the crowd in the Broadway after dinner, in utrumque paratus, ready either to marry Ida if she would have me, or to go home again in the autumn, a joyous bachelor, if she did not turn up according to her promise. A very cold-blooded attitude that to assume towards the tender passion, no doubt; but after all, why should a sensible man of thirty-five think it necessary to go wild for a year or two like a hobbledehoy, and convert himself into a perambulating statue of melancholy, simply because one particular young woman out of the nine hundred million estimated to inhabit this insignificant planet has refused to print his individual name upon her visiting cards? Ida would make as good a Mrs. Cyril Payne as any other girl of my acquaintance—no doubt; indeed, I am inclined to say, a vast deal a better one; but there are more women than five in the world, and if you strike an average I dare say most of them are pretty much alike.

As I sat and looked, I could not help noticing the extraordinary magnificence of all the toilettes in the promenade. Nowhere in Europe can you behold such a republican dead level of reckless extravagance. Every woman was dressed like a princess, nothing more and nothing less. I began to wonder how poor little Ida, with her simple and tasteful travelling gowns, would feel when she found herself cast in the midst of these gorgeous silks and these costly satin grenadines. Look, for example, at that pair now strolling along from Spring Avenue: a New York exquisite in the very coolest of American summer suits, and a New York élégante (their own word, I assure you) in a splendid but graceful grey silk dress, gold bracelet, diamond ear-rings, and every other item in her costume of the finest and costliest. What would Ida do in a crowd of such women as that?... Why ... gracious heavens! ... can it be?... No, it can't.... Yes, it must.... Well, to be sure, it positively is—Ida herself!

My first impulse was to lean over the balcony and call out to her, as I would have called out to a friend whom I chanced to see passing in Magdalen quad. Not an unnatural impulse either, seeing that (in spite of my own prevarications to myself) I had after all really come across the Atlantic on purpose to see her. But on second thoughts it struck me that even Ida might perhaps find such a proceeding a trifle unconventional, especially now that she was habited in such passing splendour. Besides, what did it all mean? The only rational answer I could give myself, when I fairly squared the question, was that Ida must have got suddenly married to a wealthy fellow-countryman, and that the exquisite in the cool suit was in fact none other than her newly-acquired husband. I had thought my philosophy proof against any such small defeats to my calculation: but when it actually came to the point, I began to perceive that I was after all very unphilosophically in love with Ida Van Rensselaer. The merest undergraduate could not have felt a sillier flutter than that which agitated both auricles and ventricles of my central vascular organ—as a Senior Proctor I must really draw the line at speaking outright of my heart. I seized my hat, rushed down the broad staircase, and walked rapidly along Broadway in the direction the pair had taken. But I could see nothing of them, and I returned to Congress Hall in despair.

That night I thought about many things, and slept very little. It came home to me somewhat vividly that if Ida was really married I should probably feel more grieved and disappointed than a good pessimist philosopher ought ever to feel at the ordinary vexatiousness of the universe. Next morning, however, I rose early, and breakfasted, not without a most unpoetical appetite, on white fish, buckwheat pancakes, and excellent watermelon. After breakfast, refreshed by the meal, I sallied forth, like a true knight-errant, under the shade of a white cotton sun-umbrella instead of a shield, to search for the lady of my choice. Naturally, I turned my steps first towards the Springs; and at the very second of them all, I luckily came upon Ida and the man in the tweed suit, lounging as before, and drinking the waters lazily.

Ida stepped up as if she had fully expected to meet me, extended her daintily-gloved hand with the gold bracelet, and said as unconcernedly as possible, "You have come two days late, Mr. Payne."

"So it seems," I answered. "C'est monsieur votre mari?" And I waved my hand interrogatively towards the stranger, for I hardly knew how to word the question in English.

"À Dieu ne plaise!" she cried heartily, in an undertone, and I felt my vascular system once more the theatre of a most unacademical though more pleasing palpitation. "Allow me to introduce you. Mr. Payne of Oxford; my cousin, Mr. Jefferson Hitchcock."

I charitably inferred that Mr. Hitchcock's early education in modern languages had been unfortunately neglected, or else his companion's energetic mode of denying her supposed conjugal relation with him could hardly have appeared flattering to his vanity.

"My cousin has spoken of you to me, sir," said Mr. Hitchcock solemnly. "I understand that you are one of the most distinguished luminaries of Oxford College, and I am proud to welcome you as such to our country."

I bowed and laughed—I never feel capable of making any other reply than a bow and a laugh to the style of oratory peculiar to American gentlemen—and then I turned to Ida. She was looking as pretty, as piquante, and as fresh as ever; but what her dress could mean was a complete puzzle to me. As she stood, diamonds and all, a jeweller's assistant couldn't have valued her at a penny less than six hundred pounds. In England such a display in morning dress would have been out of taste; but in Saratoga it seemed to be the height of the fashion.

We walked along towards the Grand Union Hotel, where Ida and her cousin were staying, and my astonishment grew upon me at every step. However, we had so much to say to one another about everything in general, and Ida was so unaffectedly pleased at my keeping my engagement, made half in joke, that I found no time to unravel the mystery. When we reached the great doorway, Ida took leave of me for the time, but made me promise to call for her again early the next morning. "Unhappily," she said, "I have to go this afternoon to a most tedious party—a set of Boston people; you know the style; the best European culture, bottled and corked as imported, and let out again by driblets with about as much spontaneousness as champagne the second day. But I must fulfil my social duties here; no canoeing on the Isis at Saratoga. However, we must see a great deal of you now that you've come; so I expect you to call, and drive me down to the lake at ten o'clock to-morrow."

"Is that proceeding within the expansive limits of American proprieties?" I asked dubiously.

"Sir," said Mr. Hitchcock, answering for her, "this is a land of freedom, and every lady can go where she chooses, unmolested by those frivolous bonds of conventionality which bind the feet of your European women as closely as the cramped shoes of the Chinese bind the feet of the celestial females."

Ida smiled at me with a peculiar smile, waved her hand graciously, and ran lightly up the stairs. I was left on the piazza with Mr. Jefferson Hitchcock. His conversation scarcely struck me as in itself enticing, but I was anxious to find out the meaning of Ida's sudden accession to wealth, and so I determined to make the best of his companionship for half an hour. As a sure high road to the American bosom and safe recommendation to the American confidence, I ordered a couple of delectable summer beverages (Mr. Hitchcock advised an "eye-opener," which proved worthy of the commendation he bestowed upon it); and we sat down on the piazza in two convenient rocking-chairs, under the shade of the elms, smoking our havanas and sipping our iced drink. After a little preliminary talk, I struck out upon the subject of Ida.

"When I met Miss Van Rensselaer at Nice," I said, "she was stopping at a very quiet little pension. It is quite a different thing living in a palace like this."

"We are a republican nation, sir," answered Mr. Hitchcock, "and we expect to be all treated on the equal level of a sovereign people. The splendour that you in Europe restrict to princes, we in our country lavish upon the humblest American citizen. Miss Van Rensselaer's wealth, however, entitles her to mix in the highest circles of even your most polished society."

"Indeed?" I said; "I had no idea that she was wealthy."

"No, sir, probably not. Miss Van Rensselaer is a woman of that striking originality only to be met with in our emancipated country. She has shaken off the trammels of female servitude, and prefers to travel in all the simplicity of a humble income. She went to Europe, if I may so speak, incognita, and desired to hide her opulence from the prying gaze of your aristocracy. She did not wish your penniless peers to buzz about her fortune. But she is in reality one of our richest heiresses. The man who secures that woman as a property, sir, will find himself in possession of an income worth as much as one hundred thousand dollars."

Twenty thousand sterling a year! The idea took my breath away, and reduced me once more to a state of helpless incapacity. I couldn't talk much more small-talk to Mr. Hitchcock, so I managed to make some small excuse and returned listlessly to Congress Hall. There, over a luncheon of Saddle-Rock oysters (you see I never allow my feelings to interfere with my appetite), I decided that I must give up all idea of Ida Van Rensselaer.

I have no abstract objection to an income of £20,000 a year; but I could not consent to take it from any woman, or to endure the chance of her supposing that I had been fortune-hunting. It may be and doubtless is a plebeian feeling, which, as Mr. Hitchcock justly hinted, is never shared by the younger sons of our old nobility; but I hate the notion of living off somebody else's money, especially if that somebody were my own wife. So I came to the reluctant conclusion that I must give up the idea for ever; and as it would not be fair to stop any longer at Saratoga under the circumstances, I made up my mind to start for Niagara on the next day but one, after fulfilling my driving engagement with Ida the following morning.

Punctually at ten o'clock the next day I found myself in a handsome carriage waiting at the doors of the Grand Union. Ida came down to meet me splendidly dressed, and looked like a queen as she sat by my side. "We will drive to the lake," she said, as she took her seat, "and you will take me for a row as you did on the Isis at Oxford." So we whirled along comfortably enough over the six miles of splendid avenue leading to the lake; and then we took our places in one of the canopied boats which wait for hire at the little quay.

I rowed out into the middle of the lake, admiring the pretty wooded banks and sandstone cliffs, talking of Saratoga and American society, but keeping to my determination in steering clear of all allusions to my Oxford proposal. Ida was as charming as ever—more provokingly charming, indeed, than even of old, now that I had decided she could not be mine. But I stood by my resolution like a man. Clearly Ida was surprised at my reticence; and when I told her that my time in America being limited, I must start almost at once for Niagara, she was obviously astonished. "It is possible to be even too original," she observed shortly. I turned the boat and rowed back toward the shore.

As I had nearly reached the bank, Ida jumped up from her seat, and asked me suddenly to let her pull for a dozen strokes. I changed places and gave her the oars. To my surprise, she headed the boat around, and pulled once more for the middle of the lake. When we had reached a point at some distance from the shore, she dropped the oars on the thole-pins (they use no rowlocks on American lake or river craft), and looked for a moment full in my face. Then she said abruptly:—

"If you are really going to leave for Niagara to-morrow, Mr. Payne, hadn't we better finish this bit of business out of hand?"

"I was not aware," I answered, "that we had any business transactions to settle."

"Why," she said, "I mean this matter of proposing."

I gazed back at her as straight as I dared. "Ida," I said, with an attempt at firmness, "I don't mean to propose to you again at all. At least, I didn't mean to when I started this morning. I think I thought I had decided not."

"Then why did you come to Saratoga?" she asked quickly. "You oughtn't to have come if you meant nothing by it."

"When I left England I did mean something," I answered, "but I learned a fact yesterday which has altered my intentions." And then I told her about Mr. Hitchcock's revelations, and the reflections to which they had given rise.

Ida listened patiently to all my faint arguments, for I felt my courage quailing under her pretty sympathetic glance, and then she said decisively, "You are quite right and yet quite wrong."

"Explain yourself, O Sphinx," I answered, much relieved by her words.

"Why," she said, "you are quite right to hesitate, quite wrong to decide. I know you don't want my money; I know you don't like it, even: but I ask you to take me in spite of it. Of course that is dreadfully unwomanly and unconventional, and so forth, but it is what I ought to do.... Listen to me, Cyril (may I call you Cyril?). I will tell you why I want you to marry me. Before I went to Europe, I was dissatisfied with all these rich American young men. I hated their wealth, and their selfishness, and their cheap cynicism, and their trotting horses, and their narrow views, and their monotonous tall-talk, all cast in a stereotyped American mould, so that whenever I said A, I knew every one of them would answer B.

"I went to Europe and I met your English young men, with their drawls, and their pigeon-shooting, and their shaggy ulsters, and their conventional wit, and their commonplace chaff, and their utter contempt for women, as though we were all a herd of marketable animals from whom they could pick and choose whichever pleased them best, according to their lordly fancy. I would no more give myself up to one of them than I would marry my cousin, Jefferson Hitchcock. But when I met you first at Nice, I saw you were a different sort of person. You could think and act for yourself, and you could appreciate a real living woman who could think and act too. You taught me what Europe was like. I only knew the outside, you showed me how to get within the husk. You made me admire Eza, and Roccabrunna, and Iffley Church. You roused something within me that I never felt before—a wish to be a different being, a longing for something more worth living for than diamonds and Saratoga. I know I am not good enough for you: I don't know enough or read enough or feel enough; but I don't want to fall back and sink to the level of New York society. So I have a right to ask you to marry me if you will. I don't want to be a blue; but I want not to feel myself a social doll. You know yourself—I see you know it—that I oughtn't to throw away my chance of making the best of what nature I may have in me. I am only a beginner. I scarcely half understand your world yet. I can't properly admire your Botticellis and your Pinturiccios, I know; but I want to admire, I should like to, and I will try. I want you to take me, because I know you understand me and would help me forward instead of letting me sink down to the petty interests of this American desert. You liked me at Nice, you did more than like me at Oxford; but I wouldn't take you then, though I longed to say yes, because I wasn't quite sure whether you really meant it. I knew you liked me for myself, not my money, but I left you to come to Saratoga for two things. I wanted to make sure you were in earnest, not to take you at a moment of weakness. I said, 'If he really cares for me, if he thinks I might become worthy of him, he will come and look for me; if not, I must let the dream go.' And then I wanted to know what effect my fortune would have upon you. Now you know my whole reasons. Why should my money stand in our way? Why should we both make ourselves unhappy on account of it? You would have married me if I was poor: what good reason have you for rejecting me only because I am rich? Whatever my money may do for you (and you have enough of your own), it will be nothing to what you can do for me. Will you tell me to go and make myself an animated peg for hanging jewellery upon, with such a conscious automaton as Jefferson Hitchcock to keep me company through life?"

As she finished, flushed, proud, ashamed, but every inch a woman, I caught her hand in mine. The utter meanness and selfishness of my life burst upon me like a thunderbolt. "Oh, Ida," I cried, "how terribly you make me feel my own pettiness and egotism. You are cutting me to the heart like a knife. I cannot marry you; I dare not marry you; I must not marry you. I am not worthy of such a wife as you. How had I ever the audacity to ask you? My life has been too narrow and egoistic and self-indulgent to deserve such confidence as yours. I am not good enough for you. I really dare not accept it."

"No," she said, a little more calmly, "I hope we are just good enough for one another, and that is why we ought to marry. And as for the hundred thousand dollars, perhaps we might manage to be happy in spite of them."

We had drifted into a little bay, under shelter of a high rocky point. I felt a sudden access of insane boldness, and taking both Ida's hands in mine, I ventured to kiss her open forehead. She took the kiss quietly, but with a certain queenly sense of homage due. "And now," she said, shaking off my hands and smiling archly, "let us row back toward Saratoga, for you know you have to pack up for Niagara."

"No," I answered, "I may as well put off my visit to the Falls till you can accompany me."

"Very well," said Ida quietly, "and then we shall go back to England and live near Oxford. I don't want you to give up the dear old University. I want you to teach me the way you look at things, and show me how to look at them myself. I'm not going to learn any Latin or Greek or stupid nonsense of that sort; and I'm not going to join the Women's Suffrage Association; but I like your English culture, and I should love to live in its midst."

"So you shall, Ida," I answered; "and you shall teach me, too, how to be a little less narrow and self-centred than we Oxford bachelors are apt to become in our foolish isolation."

So we expect to spend our honeymoon at Niagara.

THE CHILD OF THE PHALANSTERY

"Poor little thing," said my strong-minded friend compassionately. "Just look at her! Clubfooted. What a misery to herself and others! In a well-organized state of society, you know, such poor wee cripples as that would be quietly put out of their misery while they were still babies."

"Let me think," said I, "how that would work out in actual practice. I'm not so sure, after all, that we should be altogether the better or the happier for it."

I

They sat together in a corner of the beautiful phalanstery garden, Olive and Clarence, on the marble seat that overhung the mossy dell where the streamlet danced and bickered among its pebbly stickles; they sat there, hand in hand, in lovers' guise, and felt their two bosoms beating and thrilling in some strange, sweet fashion, just like two foolish unregenerate young people of the old antisocial prephalansteric days. Perhaps it was the leaven of their unenlightened ancestors still leavening by heredity the whole lump; perhaps it was the inspiration of the calm soft August evening and the delicate afterglow of the setting sun; perhaps it was the deep heart of man and woman vibrating still as of yore in human sympathy, and stirred to its innermost recesses by the unutterable breath of human emotion. But at any rate there they sat, the beautiful strong man in his shapely chiton, and the dainty fair girl in her long white robe with the dark green embroidered border, looking far into the fathomless depths of one another's eyes, in silence sweeter and more eloquent than many words. It was Olive's tenth-day holiday from her share in the maidens' household duty of the community; and Clarence, by arrangement with his friend Germain, had made exchange from his own decade (which fell on Plato) to this quiet Milton evening, that he might wander through the park and gardens with his chosen love, and speak his full mind to her now without reserve.

"If only the phalanstery will give its consent, Clarence," Olive said at last with a little sigh, releasing her hand from his, and gathering up the folds of her stole from the marble flooring of the seat; "if only the phalanstery will give its consent! but I have my doubts about it. Is it quite right? Have we chosen quite wisely? Will the hierarch and the elder brothers think I am strong enough and fit enough for the duties of the task? It is no light matter, we know, to enter into bonds with one another for the responsibilities of fatherhood and motherhood. I sometimes feel—forgive me, Clarence—but I sometimes feel as if I were allowing my own heart and my own wishes to guide me too exclusively in this solemn question: thinking too much about you and me, about ourselves (which is only an enlarged form of selfishness, after all), and too little about the future good of the community and—and—" blushing a little, for women will be women even in a phalanstery—"and of the precious lives we may be the means of adding to it. You remember, Clarence, what the hierarch said, that we ought to think least and last of our own feelings, first and foremost of the progressive evolution of universal humanity."

"I remember, darling," Clarence answered, leaning over towards her tenderly; "I remember well, and in my own way, so far as a man can (for we men haven't the moral earnestness of you women, I'm afraid, Olive), I try to act up to it. But, dearest, I think your fears are greater than they need be: you must recollect that humanity requires for its higher development tenderness, and truth, and love, and all the softer qualities, as well as strength and manliness; and if you are a trifle less strong than most of our sisters here, you seem to me at least (and I really believe to the hierarch and to the elder brothers too) to make up for it, and more than make up for it, in your sweet and lovable inner nature. The men of the future mustn't all be cast in one unvarying stereotyped mould; we must have a little of all good types combined, in order to make a perfect phalanstery."

Olive sighed again. "I don't know," she said pensively. "I don't feel sure. I hope I am doing right. In my aspirations every evening I have desired light on this matter, and have earnestly hoped that I was not being misled by my own feelings; for, oh, Clarence, I do love you so dearly, so truly, so absorbingly, that I half fear my love may be taking me unwittingly astray. I try to curb it; I try to think of it all as the hierarch tells us we ought to; but in my own heart I sometimes almost fear that I may be lapsing into the idolatrous love of the old days, when people married and were given in marriage, and thought only of the gratification of their own personal emotions and affections, and nothing of the ultimate good of humanity. Oh, Clarence, don't hate me and despise me for it; don't turn upon me and scold me: but I love you, I love you, I love you; oh, I'm afraid I love you almost idolatrously!"

Clarence lifted her small white hand slowly to his lips, with that natural air of chivalrous respect which came so easily to the young men of the phalanstery, and kissed it twice over fervidly with quiet reverence. "Let us go into the music-room, Olive dearest," he said as he rose; "you are too sad to-night. You shall play me that sweet piece of Marian's that you love so much; and that will quiet you, darling, from thinking too earnestly about this serious matter."

II

Next day, when Clarence had finished his daily spell of work in the fruit-garden (he was third under-gardener to the community), he went up to his own study, and wrote out a little notice in due form to be posted at dinner-time on the refectory door: "Clarence and Olive ask leave of the phalanstery to enter with one another into free contract of holy matrimony." His pen trembled a little in his hand as he framed that familiar set form of words (strange that he had read it so often with so little emotion, and wrote it now with so much: we men are so selfish!); but he fixed it boldly with four small brass nails on the regulation notice-board, and waited, not without a certain quiet confidence, for the final result of the communal council.

"Aha!" said the hierarch to himself with a kindly smile, as he passed into the refectory at dinner-time that day, "has it come to that, then? Well, well, I thought as much; I felt sure it would. A good girl, Olive: a true, earnest, lovable girl: and she has chosen wisely, too; for Clarence is the very man to balance her own character as man's and wife's should do. Whether Clarence has done well in selecting her is another matter. For my own part, I had rather hoped she would have joined the celibate sisters, and have taken nurse duty for the sick and the children. It's her natural function in life, the work she's best fitted for; and I should have liked to see her take to it. But after all, the business of the phalanstery is not to decide vicariously for its individual members—not to thwart their natural harmless inclinations and wishes; on the contrary, we ought to allow every man and girl the fullest liberty to follow their own personal taste and judgment in every possible matter. Our power of interference as a community, I've always felt and said, should only extend to the prevention of obviously wrong and immoral acts, such as marriage with a person in ill-health, or of inferior mental power, or with a distinctly bad or insubordinate temper. Things of that sort, of course, are as clearly wicked as idling in work hours or marriage with a first cousin. Olive's health, however, isn't really bad, nothing more than a very slight feebleness of constitution, as constitutions go with us; and Eustace, who has attended her medically from her babyhood (what a dear crowing little thing she used to be in the nursery, to be sure), tells me she's perfectly fitted for the duties of her proposed situation. Ah well, ah well; I've no doubt they'll be perfectly happy; and the wishes of the whole phalanstery will go with them, in any case, that's certain."

Everybody knew that whatever the hierarch said or thought was pretty sure to be approved by the unanimous voice of the entire community. Not that he was at all a dictatorial or dogmatic old man; quite the contrary; but his gentle kindly way had its full weight with the brothers; and his intimate acquaintance, through the exercise of his spiritual functions, with the inmost thoughts and ideas of every individual member, man or woman, made him a safe guide in all difficult or delicate questions, as to what the decision of the council ought to be. So when, on the first Cosmos, the elder brothers assembled to transact phalansteric business, and the hierarch put in Clarence's request with the simple phrase, "In my opinion, there is no reasonable objection," the community at once gave in its adhesion, and formal notice was posted an hour later on, the refectory door, "The phalanstery approves the proposition of Clarence and Olive, and wishes all happiness to them and to humanity from the sacred union they now contemplate." "You see, dearest," Clarence said, kissing her lips for the first time (as unwritten law demanded), now that the seal of the community had been placed upon their choice, "you see, there can't be any harm in our contract, for the elder brothers all approve it."

Olive smiled and sighed from the very bottom of her full heart, and clung to her lover as the ivy clings to a strong supporting oak-tree. "Darling," she murmured in his ear, "if I have you to comfort me, I shall not be afraid, and we will try our best to work together for the advancement and the good of divine humanity."

Four decades later, on a bright Cosmos morning in September, those two stood up beside one another before the altar of humanity, and heard with a thrill the voice of the hierarch uttering that solemn declaration, "In the name of the Past, and of the Present, and of the Future, I hereby admit you, Clarence and Olive, into the holy society of Fathers and Mothers, of the United Avondale Phalanstery, in trust for humanity, whose stewards you are. May you so use and enhance the good gifts you have received from your ancestors that you may hand them on, untarnished and increased, to the bodies and minds of your furthest descendants." And Clarence and Olive answered humbly and reverently, "If grace be given us, we will."

III

Brother Eustace, physiologist to the phalanstery, looked very grave and sad indeed as he passed from the Mothers' Room into the Conversazione in search of the hierarch. "A child is born into the phalanstery," he said gloomily; but his face conveyed at once a far deeper and more pregnant meaning than his mere words could carry to the ear.

The hierarch rose hastily and glanced into his dark keen eyes with an inquiring look. "Not something amiss?" he said eagerly, with an infinite tenderness in his fatherly voice. "Don't tell me that, Eustace. Not ... oh, not a child that the phalanstery must not for its own sake permit to live! Oh, Eustace, not, I hope, idiotic! And I gave my consent too; I gave my consent for pretty gentle little Olive's sake! Heaven grant I was not too much moved by her prettiness and her delicacy, for I love her, Eustace, I love her like a daughter."

"So we all love all the children of the phalanstery Cyriac, we who are elder brothers," said the physiologist gravely, half smiling to himself nevertheless at this quaint expression of old-world feeling on the part even of the very hierarch, whose bounden duty it was to advise and persuade a higher rule of conduct and thought than such antique phraseology implied. "No, not idiotic; not quite so bad as that, Cyriac; not absolutely a hopeless case, but still, very serious and distressing for all that. The dear little baby has its feet turned inward. She'll be a cripple for life, I fear, and no help for it."

Tears rose unchecked into the hierarch's soft grey eyes. "Its feet turned inward," he muttered sadly, half to himself. "Feet turned inward! Oh, how terrible! This will be a frightful blow to Clarence and to Olive. Poor young things: their first-born, too. Oh, Eustace, what an awful thought that, with all the care and precaution we take to keep all causes of misery away from the precincts of the phalanstery, such trials as this must needs come upon us by the blind workings of the unconscious Cosmos! It is terrible, too terrible."

"And yet it isn't all loss," the physiologist answered earnestly. "It isn't all loss, Cyriac, heart-rending as the necessity seems to us. I sometimes think that if we hadn't these occasional distressful objects on which to expend our sympathy and our sorrow, we in our happy little communities might grow too smug, and comfortable, and material, and earthy. But things like this bring tears into our eyes, and we are the better for them in the end, depend upon it, we are the better for them. They try our fortitude, our devotion to principle, our obedience to the highest and the hardest law. Every time some poor little waif like this is born into our midst, we feel the strain of old prephalansteric emotions and fallacies of feeling dragging us steadily and cruelly down. Our first impulse is to pity the poor mother, to pity the poor child, and in our mistaken kindness to let an unhappy life go on indefinitely to its own misery and the preventible distress of all around it. We have to make an effort, a struggle, before the higher and more abstract pity conquers the lower and more concrete one. But in the end we are all the better for it: and each such struggle and each such victory, Cyriac, paves the way for that final and truest morality when we shall do right instinctively and naturally, without any impulse on any side to do wrong in any way at all."

"You speak wisely, Eustace," the hierarch answered with a sad shake of his head, "and I wish I could feel like you. I ought to, but I can't. Your functions make you able to look more dispassionately upon these things than I can. I'm afraid there's a great deal of the old Adam lingering wrongfully in me yet.

And I'm still more afraid there's a great deal of the old Eve lingering even more strongly in all our mothers. It'll be a long time, I doubt me, before they'll ever consent without a struggle to the painless extinction of necessarily unhappy and imperfect lives. A long time: a very long time. Does Clarence know of this yet?"

"Yes, I have told him. His grief is terrible. You had better go and console him as best you can."

"I will, I will. And poor Olive! Poor Olive! It wrings my heart to think of her. Of course she won't be told of it, if you can help, for the probationary four decades?"

"No, not if we can help it: but I don't know how it can ever be kept from her. She will see Clarence, and Clarence will certainly tell her."

The hierarch whistled gently to himself. "It's a sad case," he said ruefully, "a very sad case; and yet I don't see how we can possibly prevent it."

He walked slowly and deliberately into the ante-room where Clarence was seated on a sofa, his head between his hands, rocking himself to and fro in his mute misery, or stopping to groan now and then in a faint feeble inarticulate fashion. Rhoda, one of the elder sisters, held the unconscious baby sleeping in her arms, and the hierarch took it from her like a man accustomed to infants, and looked ruthfully at the poor distorted little feet. Yes, Eustace was evidently quite right. There could be no hope of ever putting those wee twisted ankles back straight and firm into their proper place again like other people's.

He sat down beside Clarence on the sofa, and with a commiserating gesture removed the young man's hands from his pale white face. "My dear, dear friend," he said softly, "what comfort or consolation can we try to give you that is not a cruel mockery? None, none, none. We can only sympathize with you and Olive: and perhaps, after all, the truest sympathy is silence."

Clarence answered nothing for a moment, but buried his face once more in his hands and burst into tears. The men of the phalanstery were less careful to conceal their emotions than we old-time folks in these early centuries. "Oh, dear hierarch," he said, after a long sob, "it is too hard a sacrifice, too hard, too terrible. I don't feel it for the baby's sake: for her 'tis better so: she will be freed from a life of misery and dependence; but for my own sake, and oh, above all, for dear Olive's. It will kill her, hierarch; I feel sure it will kill her!"

The elder brother passed his hand with a troubled gesture across his forehead. "But what else can we do, dear Clarence?" he asked pathetically. "What else can we do? Would you have us bring up the dear child to lead a lingering life of misfortune, to distress the eyes of all around her, to feel herself a useless incumbrance in the midst of so many mutually helpful and serviceable and happy people? How keenly she would realize her own isolation in the joyous busy labouring community of our phalansteries! How terribly she would brood over her own misfortune when surrounded by such a world of hearty, healthy, sound-limbed, useful persons! Would it not be a wicked and a cruel act to bring her up to an old age of unhappiness and imperfection? You have been in Australia, my boy, when we sent you on that plant-hunting expedition, and you have seen cripples with your own eyes, no doubt, which I have never done—thank Heaven!—I who have never gone beyond the limits of the most highly civilized Euramerican countries. You have seen cripples, in those semi-civilized old colonial societies, which have lagged after us so slowly in the path of progress; and would you like your own daughter to grow up to such a life as that, Clarence? would you like her, I ask you, to grow up to such a life as that?"

Clarence clenched his right hand tightly over his left arm, and answered with a groan: "No, hierarch; not even for Olive's sake could I wish for such an act of irrational injustice. You have trained us up to know the good from the evil, and for no personal gratification of our deepest emotions, I hope and trust, shall we ever betray your teaching or depart from your principles. I know what it is: I saw just such a cripple once, at a great town in the heart of Central Australia—a child of eight years old, limping along lamely on her heels by her mother's side: a sickening sight: to think of it even now turns the blood in one's arteries: and I could never wish Olive's baby to live and grow up to be a thing like that. But, oh, I wish to heaven it might have been otherwise: I wish to heaven this trial might have been spared us both. Oh, hierarch, dear hierarch, the sacrifice is one that no good man or woman would wish selfishly to forego; yet for all that, our hearts, our hearts are human still; and though we may reason and may act up to our reasoning, the human feeling in us—relic of the idolatrous days or whatever you like to call it—it will not choose to be so put down and stifled: it will out, hierarch, it will out for all that, in real hot, human tears. Oh, dear, dear kind father and brother, it will kill Olive: I know it will kill her!"

"Olive is a good girl," the hierarch answered slowly. "A good girl, well brought up, and with sound principles. She will not flinch from doing her duty, I know, Clarence: but her emotional nature is a very delicate one, and we have reason indeed to fear the shock to her nervous system. That she will do right bravely, I don't doubt: the only danger is lest the effort to do right should cost her too dear. Whatever can be done to spare her shall be done, Clarence. It is a sad misfortune for the whole phalanstery, such a child being born to us as this: and we all sympathize with you: we sympathize with you more deeply than words can say."

The young man only rocked up and down drearily as before, and murmured to himself, "It will kill her, it will kill her! My Olive, my Olive, I know it will kill her."

IV

They didn't keep the secret of the baby's crippled condition from Olive till the four decades were over, nor anything like it. The moment she saw Clarence, she guessed at once with a woman's instinct that something serious had happened: and she didn't rest till she had found out from him all about it. Rhoda brought her the poor wee mite, carefully wrapped after the phalansteric fashion in a long strip of fine flannel, and Olive unrolled the piece until she came at last upon the small crippled feet, that looked so soft and tender and dainty and waxen in their very deformity. The young mother leant over the child a moment in speechless misery. "Spirit of Humanity," she whispered at length feebly, "oh give me strength to bear this terrible unutterable trial! It will break my heart. But I will try to bear it."

There was something so touching in her attempted resignation that Rhoda, for the first time in her life, felt almost tempted to wish she had been born in the old wicked prephalansteric days, when they would have let the poor baby grow up to womanhood as a matter of course, and bear its own burden through life as best it might. Presently, Olive raised her head again from the crimson silken pillow. "Clarence," she said, in a trembling voice, pressing the sleeping baby hard against her breast, "when will it be? How long? Is there no hope, no chance of respite?"

"Not for a long time yet, dearest Olive," Clarence answered through his tears. "The phalanstery will be very gentle and patient with us, we know: and brother Eustace will do everything that lies in his power, though he's afraid he can give us very little hope indeed. In any case, Olive darling, the community waits for four decades before deciding anything: it waits to see whether there is any chance for physiological or surgical relief: it decides nothing hastily or thoughtlessly: it waits for every possible improvement, hoping against hope till hope itself is hopeless. And then, if at the end of the quartet, as I fear will be the case—for we must face the worst, darling, we must face the worst—if at the end of the quartet it seems clear to brother Eustace, and the three assessor physiologists from the neighbouring phalansteries, that the dear child would be a cripple for life, we're still allowed four decades more to prepare ourselves in: four whole decades more, Olive, to take our leave of the darling baby. You'll have your baby with you for eighty days. And we must wean ourselves from her in that time, darling. We must try to wean ourselves. But oh Olive, oh Rhoda, it's very hard: very, very, very hard."

Olive answered not a word, but lay silently weeping and pressing the baby against her breast, with her large brown eyes fixed vacantly upon the fretted woodwork of the panelled ceiling.

"You mustn't do like that, Olive dear," sister Rhoda said in a half-frightened voice. "You must cry right out, and sob, and not restrain yourself, darling, or else you'll break your heart with silence and repression. Do cry aloud, there's a dear girl: do cry aloud and relieve yourself. A good cry would be the best thing on earth for you. And think, dear, how much happier it will really be for the sweet baby to sink asleep so peacefully than to live a long life of conscious inferiority and felt imperfection! What a blessing it is to think you were born in a phalansteric land, where the dear child will be happily and painlessly rid of its poor little unconscious existence, before it has reached the age when it might begin to know its own incurable and inevitable misfortune. Oh, Olive, what a blessing that is, and how thankful we ought all to be that we live in a world where the sweet pet will be saved so much humiliation, and mortification, and misery!"

At that moment, Olive, looking within into her own wicked rebellious heart, was conscious, with a mingled glow, half shame, half indignation, that so far from appreciating the priceless blessings of her own situation, she would gladly have changed places then and there with any barbaric woman of the old semi-civilized prephalansteric days. We can so little appreciate our own mercies. It was very wrong and anti-cosmic, she knew; very wrong, indeed, and the hierarch would have told her so at once; but in her own woman's soul she felt she would rather be a miserable naked savage in a wattled hut, like those one saw in old books about Africa before the illumination, if only she could keep that one little angel of a crippled baby, than dwell among all the enlightenment, and knowledge, and art, and perfected social arrangements of phalansteric England without her child— her dear, helpless, beautiful baby. How truly the Founder himself had said, "Think you there will be no more tragedies and dramas in the world when we have reformed it, nothing but one dreary dead level of monotonous content? Ay, indeed, there will; for that, fear not; while the heart of man remains, there will be tragedy enough on earth and to spare for a hundred poets to take for their saddest epics."

Olive looked up at Rhoda wistfully. "Sister Rhoda," she said in a timid tone, "it may be very wicked—I feel sure it is—but do you know, I've read somewhere in old stories of the unenlightened days that a mother always loved the most afflicted of her children the best. And I can understand it now, sister Rhoda; I can feel it here," and she put her hand upon her poor still heart. "If only I could keep this one dear crippled baby, I could give up all the world beside—except you, Clarence."

"Oh, hush, darling!" Rhoda cried in an awed voice, stooping down half alarmed to kiss her pale forehead. "You mustn't talk like that, Olive dearest. It's wicked; it's undutiful. I know how hard it is not to repine and to rebel; but you mustn't, Olive, you mustn't. We must each strive to bear our own burdens (with the help of the community), and not to put any of them off upon a poor, helpless, crippled little baby."

"But our natures," Clarence said, wiping his eyes dreamily; "our natures are only half attuned as yet to the necessities of the higher social existence. Of course it's very wrong and very sad, but we can't help feeling it, sister Rhoda, though we try our hardest. Remember, it's not so many generations since our fathers would have reared the child without a thought that they were doing anything wicked—nay, rather, would even have held (so powerful is custom) that it was positively wrong to save it by preventive means from a certain life of predestined misery. Our conscience in this matter isn't yet fully formed. We feel that it's right, of course; oh yes, we know the phalanstery has ordered everything for the best; but we can't help grieving over it; the human heart within us is too unregenerate still to acquiesce without a struggle in the dictates of right and reason."

Olive again said nothing, but fixed her eyes silently upon the grave, earnest portrait of the Founder over the carved oak mantelpiece, and let the hot tears stream their own way over her cold, white, pallid, bloodless cheek without reproof for many minutes. Her heart was too full for either speech or comfort.

V

Eight decades passed away slowly in the Avondale Phalanstery; and day after day seemed more and more terrible to poor, weak, disconsolate Olive. The quiet refinement and delicate surroundings of their placid life seemed to make her poignant misery and long anxious term of waiting only the more intense in its sorrow and its awesomeness. Every day, the younger sisters turned as of old to their allotted round of pleasant housework; every day the elder sisters, who had earned their leisure, brought in their dainty embroidery, or their drawing materials, or their other occupations, and tried to console her, or rather to condole with her, in her great sorrow. She couldn't complain of any unkindness; on the contrary, all the brothers and sisters were sympathy itself; while Clarence, though he tried hard not to be too idolatrous to her (which is wrong and antisocial, of course), was still overflowing with tenderness and consideration for her in their common grief. But all that seemed merely to make things worse. If only somebody would have been cruel to her; if only the hierarch would have scolded her, or the elder sisters have shown any distant coldness, or the other girls have been wanting in sisterly sympathy, she might have got angry or brooded over her wrongs; whereas, now, she could do nothing save cry passively with a vain attempt at resignation. It was nobody's fault; there was nobody to be angry with, there was nothing to blame except the great impersonal laws and circumstances of the Cosmos, which it would be rank impiety and wickedness to question or to gainsay. So she endured in silence, loving only to sit with Clarence's hand in hers, and the dear doomed baby lying peacefully upon the stole in her lap. It was inevitable and there was no use repining; for so profoundly had the phalanstery schooled the minds and natures of those two unhappy young parents (and all their compeers), that, grieve as they might, they never for one moment dreamt of attempting to relax or set aside the fundamental principles of phalansteric society in these matters.

By the kindly rule of the phalanstery, every mother had complete freedom from household duties for two years after the birth of her child; and Clarence, though he would not willingly have given up his own particular work in the grounds and garden, spent all the time he could spare from his short daily task (every one worked five hours every lawful day, and few worked longer, save on special emergencies) by Olive's side. At last, the eight decades passed slowly away, and the fatal day for the removal of little Rosebud arrived. Olive called her Rosebud because, she said, she was a sweet bud that could never be opened into a full-blown rose. All the community felt the solemnity of the painful occasion; and by common consent the day (Darwin, December 20) was held as an intra-phalansteric fast by the whole body of brothers and sisters.

On that terrible morning Olive rose early, and dressed herself carefully in a long white stole with a broad black border of Greek key pattern. But she had not the heart to put any black upon dear little Rosebud; and so she put on her fine flannel wrapper, and decorated it instead with the pretty coloured things that Veronica and Philomela had worked for her, to make her baby as beautiful as possible on this its last day in a world of happiness. The other girls helped her and tried to sustain her, crying all together at the sad event. "She's a sweet little thing," they said to one another as they held her up to see how she looked. "If only it could have been her reception to-day instead of her removal!" But Olive moved through them all with stoical resignation—dry-eyed and parched in the throat, yet saying not a word save for necessary instructions and directions to the nursing sisters. The iron of her creed had entered into her very soul.

After breakfast, brother Eustace and the hierarch came sadly in their official robes into the lesser infirmary. Olive was there already, pale and trembling, with little Rosebud sleeping peacefully in the hollow of her lap. What a picture she looked, the wee dear thing, with the hothouse flowers from the conservatory that Clarence had brought to adorn her, fastened neatly on to her fine flannel robe! The physiologist took out a little phial from his pocket, and began to open a sort of inhaler of white muslin. At the same moment, the grave, kind old hierarch stretched out his hands to take the sleeping baby from its mother's arms. Olive shrank back in terror, and clasped the child softly to her heart. "No, no, let me hold her myself, dear hierarch," she said, without flinching. "Grant me this one last favour. Let me hold her myself." It was contrary to all fixed rules; but neither the hierarch nor any one else there present had the heart to refuse that beseeching voice on so supreme and spirit-rending an occasion.

Brother Eustace poured the chloroform solemnly and quietly on to the muslin inhaler. "By resolution of the phalanstery," he said, in a voice husky with emotion, "I release you, Rosebud, from a life for which you are naturally unfitted. In pity for your hard fate, we save you from the misfortune you have never known, and will never now experience." As he spoke, he held the inhaler to the baby's face, and watched its breathing grow fainter and fainter, till at last, after a few minutes, it faded gradually and entirely away. The little one had slept from life into death, painlessly and happily, even as they looked.

Clarence, tearful but silent, felt the baby's pulse for a moment, and then, with a burst of tears, shook his head bitterly. "It is all over," he cried with a loud cry. "It is all over; and we hope and trust it is better so."

But Olive still said nothing.

The physiologist turned to her with an anxious gaze. Her eyes were open, but they looked blank and staring into vacant space. He took her hand, and it felt limp and powerless. "Great heaven," he cried, in evident alarm, "what is this? Olive, Olive, our dear Olive, why don't you speak?"

Clarence sprang up from the ground, where he had knelt to try the dead baby's pulse, and took her unresisting wrist anxiously in his. "Oh, brother Eustace," he cried passionately, "help us, save us; what's the matter with Olive? she's fainting, she's fainting! I can't feel her heart beat, no, not ever so little."

Brother Eustace let the pale white hand drop listlessly from his grasp upon the pale white stole beneath, and answered slowly and distinctly: "She isn't fainting, Clarence; not fainting, my dear brother. The shock and the fumes of chloroform together have been too much for the action of the heart. She's dead too, Clarence; our dear, dear sister; she's dead too."

Clarence flung his arms wildly round Olive's neck, and listened eagerly with his ear against her bosom to hear her heart beat. But no sound came from the folds of the simple black-bordered stole; no sound from anywhere save the suppressed sobs of the frightened women who huddled closely together in the corner, and gazed horror-stricken upon the two warm fresh corpses.

"She was a brave girl," brother Eustace said at last, wiping his eyes and composing her hands reverently. "Olive was a brave girl, and she died doing her duty, without one murmur against the sad necessity that fate had unhappily placed upon her. No sister on earth could wish to die more nobly than by thus sacrificing her own life and her own weak human affections on the altar of humanity for the sake of her child and of the world at large."

"And yet, I sometimes almost fancy," the hierarch murmured with a violent effort to control his emotions, "when I see a scene like this, that even the unenlightened practices of the old era may not have been quite so bad as we usually think them, for all that. Surely an end such as Olive's is a sad and a terrible end to have forced upon us as the final outcome and natural close of all our modern phalansteric civilization."

"The ways of the Cosmos are wonderful," said brother Eustace solemnly; "and we, who are no more than atoms and mites upon the surface of its meanest satellite, cannot hope so to order all things after our own fashion that all its minutest turns and chances may approve themselves to us as light in our own eyes."

The sisters all made instinctively the reverential genuflexion. "The Cosmos is infinite," they said together, in the fixed formula of their cherished religion. "The Cosmos is infinite, and man is but a parasite upon the face of the least among its satellite members. May we so act as to further all that is best within us, and to fulfil our own small place in the system of the Cosmos with all becoming reverence and humility! In the name of universal Humanity. So be it."

OUR SCIENTIFIC OBSERVATIONS ON A GHOST

"Then nothing would convince you of the existence of ghosts, Harry," I said, "except seeing one."

"Not even seeing one, my dear Jim," said Harry. "Nothing on earth would make me believe in them, unless I were turned into a ghost myself."

So saying, Harry drained his glass of whisky toddy, shook out the last ashes from his pipe, and went off upstairs to bed. I sat for a while over the remnants of my cigar, and ruminated upon the subject of our conversation. For my own part, I was as little inclined to believe in ghosts as anybody; but Harry seemed to go one degree beyond me in scepticism. His argument amounted in brief to this, that a ghost was by definition the spirit of a dead man in a visible form here on earth; but however strange might be the apparition which a ghost-seer thought he had observed, there was no evidence possible or actual to connect such apparition with any dead person whatsoever. It might resemble the deceased in face and figure, but so, said Harry, does a portrait. It might resemble him in voice and manner, but so does an actor or a mimic. It might resemble him in every possible particular, but even then we should only be justified in saying that it formed a close counterpart of the person in question, not that it was his ghost or spirit. In short, Harry maintained, with considerable show of reason, that nobody could ever have any scientific ground for identifying any external object, whether shadowy or material, with a past human existence of any sort. According to him, a man might conceivably see a phantom, but could not possibly know that he saw a ghost.

Harry and I were two Oxford bachelors, studying at the time for our degree in Medicine, and with an ardent love for the scientific side of our future profession. Indeed, we took a greater interest in comparative physiology and anatomy than in physic proper; and at this particular moment we were stopping in a very comfortable farm-house on the coast of Flintshire for our long vacation, with the special object of observing histologically a peculiar sea-side organism, the Thingumbobbum Whatumaycallianum, which is found so plentifully on the shores of North Wales, and which has been identified by Professor Haeckel with the larva of that famous marine ascidian from whom the Professor himself and the remainder of humanity generally are supposed to be undoubtedly descended. We had brought with us a full complement of lancets and scalpels, chemicals and test-tubes, galvanic batteries and thermo-electric piles; and we were splendidly equipped for a thorough-going scientific campaign of the first water. The farm-house in which we lodged had formerly belonged to the county family of the Egertons; and though an Elizabethan manor replaced the ancient defensive building which had been wisely dismantled by Henry VIII., the modern farm-house into which it had finally degenerated still bore the name of Egerton Castle. The whole house had a reputation in the neighbourhood for being haunted by the ghost of one Algernon Egerton, who was beheaded under James II. for his participation, or rather his intention to participate, in Monmouth's rebellion. A wretched portrait of the hapless Protestant hero hung upon the wall of our joint sitting-room, having been left behind when the family moved to their new seat in Cheshire, as being unworthy of a place in the present baronet's splendid apartments. It was a few remarks upon the subject of Algernon's ghost which had introduced the question of ghosts in general; and after Harry had left the room, I sat for a while slowly finishing my cigar, and contemplating the battered features of the deceased gentleman.

As I did so, I was somewhat startled to hear a voice at my side observe in a bland and graceful tone, not unmixed with aristocratic hauteur, "You have been speaking of me, I believe, in fact, I have unavoidably overheard your conversation, and I have decided to assume the visible form and make a few remarks upon what seems to me a very hasty decision on your friend's part."

I turned round at once, and saw, in the easy-chair which Harry had just vacated, a shadowy shape, which grew clearer and clearer the longer I looked at it. It was that of a man of forty, fashionably dressed in the costume of the year 1685 or thereabouts, and bearing a close resemblance to the faded portrait on the wall just opposite. But the striking point about the object was this, that it evidently did not consist of any ordinary material substance, as its outline seemed vague and wavy, like that of a photograph where the sitter has moved; while all the objects behind it, such as the back of the chair and the clock in the corner, showed through the filmy head and body, in the very manner which painters have always adopted in representing a ghost. I saw at once that whatever else the object before might be, it certainly formed a fine specimen of the orthodox and old-fashioned apparition. In dress, appearance, and every other particular, it distinctly answered to what the unscientific mind would unhesitatingly have called the ghost of Algernon Egerton.

Here was a piece of extraordinary luck! In a house with two trained observers, supplied with every instrument of modern experimental research, we had lighted upon an undoubted specimen of the common spectre, which had so long eluded the scientific grasp. I was beside myself with delight. "Really, sir," I said, cheerfully, "it is most kind of you to pay us this visit, and I'm sure my friend will be only too happy to hear your remarks. Of course you will permit me to call him?"

The apparition appeared somewhat surprised at the philosophic manner in which I received his advances; for ghosts are accustomed to find people faint away or scream with terror at their first appearance; but for my own part I regarded him merely in the light of a very interesting phenomenon, which required immediate observation by two independent witnesses. However, he smothered his chagrin, for I believe he was really disappointed at my cool deportment, and answered that he would be very glad to see my friend if I wished it, though he had specially intended this visit for myself alone.

I ran upstairs hastily and found Harry in his dressing-gown, on the point of removing his nether garments. "Harry," I cried breathlessly, "you must come downstairs at once. Algernon Egerton's ghost wants to speak to you."

Harry held up the candle and looked in my face with great deliberation. "Jim, my boy," he said quietly, "you've been having too much whisky."

"Not a bit of it," I answered, angrily. "Come downstairs and see. I swear to you positively that a Thing, the very counterpart of Algernon Egerton's picture, is sitting in your easy-chair downstairs, anxious to convert you to a belief in ghosts."

It took about three minutes to induce Harry to leave his room; but at last, merely to satisfy himself that I was demented, he gave way and accompanied me into the sitting-room. I was half afraid that the spectre would have taken umbrage at my long delay, and gone off in a huff and a blue flame; but when we reached the room, there he was, in propriâ personâ, gazing at his own portrait, or should I rather say his counterpart?—on the wall, with the utmost composure.

"Well, Harry," I said, "what do you call that?"

Harry put up his eyeglass, peered suspiciously at the phantom, and answered in a mollified tone, "It certainly is a most interesting phenomenon. It looks like a case of fluorescence; but you say the object can talk?"

"Decidedly," I answered, "it can talk as well as you or me. Allow me to introduce you to one another, gentlemen:—Mr. Henry Stevens, Mr. Algernon Egerton; for though you didn't mention your name, Mr. Egerton, I presume from what you said that I am right in my conjecture."

"Quite right," replied the phantom, rising as it spoke, and making a low bow to Harry from the waist upward. "I suppose your friend is one of the Lincolnshire Stevenses, sir?"

"Upon my soul," said Harry, "I haven't the faintest conception where my family came from. My grandfather, who made what little money we have got, was a cotton-spinner at Rochdale, but he might have come from heaven knows where. I only know he was a very honest old gentleman, and he remembered me handsomely in his will."

"Indeed, sir," said the apparition coldly. "My family were the Egertons of Egerton Castle, in the county of Flint, Armigeri; whose ancestor, Radulphus de Egerton, is mentioned in Domesday as one of the esquires of Hugh Lupus, Earl Palatine of Chester. Radulphus de Egerton had a son—"

"Whose history," said Harry, anxious to cut short these genealogical details, "I have read in the Annals of Flintshire, which lies in the next room, with the name you give as yours on the fly-leaf. But it seems, sir, you are anxious to converse with me on the subject of ghosts. As that question interests us all at present, much more than family descent, will you kindly begin by telling us whether you yourself lay claim to be a ghost?"

"Undoubtedly I do," replied the phantom.

"The ghost of Algernon Egerton, formerly of Egerton Castle?" I interposed.

"Formerly and now," said the phantom, in correction. "I have long inhabited, and I still habitually inhabit, by night at least, the room in which we are at present seated."

"The deuce you do," said Harry warmly. "This is a most illegal and unconstitutional proceeding. The house belongs to our landlord, Mr. Hay: and my friend here and myself have hired it for the summer, sharing the expenses, and claiming the sole title to the use of the rooms." (Harry omitted to mention that he took the best bedroom himself and put me off with a shabby little closet, while we divided the rent on equal terms.)

"True," said the spectre good-humouredly; "but you can't eject a ghost, you know. You may get a writ of habeas corpus, but the English law doesn't supply you with a writ of habeas animam. The infamous Jeffreys left me that at least. I am sure the enlightened nineteenth century wouldn't seek to deprive me of it."

"Well," said Harry, relenting, "provided you don't interfere with the experiments, or make away with the tea and sugar, I'm sure I have no objection. But if you are anxious to prove to us the existence of ghosts, perhaps you will kindly allow us to make a few simple observations?"

"With all the pleasure in death," answered the apparition courteously. "Such, in fact, is the very object for which I've assumed visibility."

"In that case, Harry," I said, "the correct thing will be to get out some paper, and draw up a running report which we may both attest afterwards. A few simple notes on the chemical and physical properties of a spectre will be an interesting novelty for the Royal Society, and they ought all to be jotted down in black and white at once."

This course having been unanimously determined upon as strictly regular, I laid a large folio of foolscap on the writing-table, and the apparition proceeded to put itself in an attitude for careful inspection.

"The first point to decide," said I, "is obviously the physical properties of our visitor. Mr. Egerton, will you kindly allow us to feel your hand?"

"You may try to feel it if you like," said the phantom quietly, "but I doubt if you will succeed to any brilliant extent." As he spoke, he held out his arm. Harry and I endeavoured successively to grasp it: our fingers slipped through the faintly luminous object as though it were air or shadow. The phantom bowed forward his head; we attempted to touch it, but our hands once more passed unopposed across the whole face and shoulders, without finding any trace whatsoever of mechanical resistance. "Experience the first," said Harry; "the apparition has no tangible material substratum." I seized the pen and jotted down the words as he spoke them. This was really turning out a very full-blown specimen of the ordinary ghost!

"The next question to settle," I said, "is that of gravity.—Harry, give me a hand out here with the weighing-machine.—Mr. Egerton, will you be good enough to step upon this board?"

Mirabile dictu! The board remained steady as ever. Not a tremor of the steelyard betrayed the weight of its shadowy occupant. "Experience the second," cried Harry, in his cool, scientific way: "the apparition has the specific gravity of atmospheric air." I jotted down this note also, and quietly prepared for the next observation.

"Wouldn't it be well," I inquired of Harry, "to try the weight in vacuo? It is possible that, while the specific gravity in air is equal to that of the atmosphere, the specific gravity in vacuo may be zero. The apparition—pray excuse me, Mr. Egerton, if the terms in which I allude to you seem disrespectful, but to call you a ghost would be to prejudge the point at issue—the apparition may have no proper weight of its own at all."

"It would be very inconvenient, though," said Harry, "to put the whole apparition under a bell-glass: in fact, we have none big enough. Besides, suppose we were to find that by exhausting the air we got rid of the object altogether, as is very possible, that would awkwardly interfere with the future prosecution of our researches into its nature and properties."

"Permit me to make a suggestion," interposed the phantom, "if a person whom you choose to relegate to the neuter gender may be allowed to have a voice in so scientific a question. My friend, the ingenious Mr. Boyle, has lately explained to me the construction of his air-pump, which we saw at one of the Friday evenings at the Royal Institution. It seems to me that your object would be attained if I were to put one hand only on the scale under the bell-glass, and permit the air to be exhausted."

"Capital," said Harry: and we got the air-pump in readiness accordingly. The spectre then put his right hand into the scale, and we plumped the bell-glass on top of it. The connecting portion of the arm shone through the severing glass, exactly as though the spectre consisted merely of an immaterial light. In a few minutes the air was exhausted, and the scales remained evenly balanced as before.

"This experiment," said Harry judicially, "slightly modifies the opinion which we formed from the preceding one. The specific gravity evidently amounts in itself to nothing, being as air in air, and as vacuum in vacuo. Jot down the result, Jim, will you?"

I did so faithfully, and then turning to the spectre I observed, "You mentioned a Mr. Boyle, sir, just now. You allude, I suppose, to the father of chemistry?"

"And uncle of the Earl of Cork," replied the apparition, promptly filling up the well-known quotation. "Exactly so. I knew Mr. Boyle slightly during our lifetime, and I have known him intimately ever since he joined the majority."

"May I ask, while my friend makes the necessary preparations for the spectrum analysis and the chemical investigation, whether you are in the habit of associating much with—er—well, with other ghosts?"

"Oh yes, I see a good deal of society."

"Contemporaries of your own, or persons of earlier and later dates?"

"Dates really matter very little to us. We may have Socrates and Bacon chatting in the same group. For my own part, I prefer modern society—I may say, the society of the latest arrivals."

"That's exactly why I asked," said I. "The excessively modern tone of your language and idioms struck me, so to speak, as a sort of anachronism with your Restoration costume—an anachronism which I fancy I have noticed in many printed accounts of gentlemen from your portion of the universe."

"Your observation is quite true," replied the apparition. "We continue always to wear the clothes which were in fashion at the time of our decease; but we pick up from new-comers the latest additions to the English language, and even, I may say, to the slang dictionary. I know many ghosts who talk familiarly of 'awfully jolly hops,' and allude to their progenitors as 'the governor.' Indeed, it is considered quite behind the times to describe a lady as 'vastly pretty,' and poor Mr. Pepys, who still preserves the antiquated idiom of his diary, is looked upon among us as a dreadfully slow old fogey."

"But why, then," said I, "do you wear your old costumes for ever? Why not imitate the latest fashions from Poole's and Worth's, as well as the latest cant phrase from the popular novels?"

"Why, my dear sir," answered the phantom, "we must have something to mark our original period. Besides, most people to whom we appear know something about costume, while very few know anything about changes in idiom,"—that I must say seemed to me, in passing, a powerful argument indeed—"and so we all preserve the dress which we habitually wore during our lifetime."

"Then," said Harry irreverently, looking up from his chemicals, "the society in your part of the country must closely resemble a fancy-dress ball."

"Without the tinsel and vulgarity, we flatter ourselves," answered the phantom.

By this time the preparations were complete, and Harry inquired whether the apparition would object to our putting out the lights in order to obtain definite results with the spectroscope. Our visitor politely replied that he was better accustomed to darkness than to the painful glare of our paraffin candles. "In fact," he added, "only the strong desire which I felt to convince you of our existence as ghosts could have induced me to present myself in so bright a room. Light is very trying to the eyes of spirits, and we generally take our constitutionals between eleven at night and four in the morning, stopping at home entirely during the moonlit half of the month."

"Ah, yes," said Harry, extinguishing the candles; "I've read, of course, that your authorities exactly reverse our own Oxford rules. You are all gated, I believe, from dawn to sunset, instead of from sunset to dawn, and have to run away helter-skelter at the first streaks of daylight, for fear of being too late for admission without a fine of twopence. But you will allow that your usual habit of showing yourselves only in the very darkest places and seasons naturally militates somewhat against the credibility of your existence. If all apparitions would only follow your sensible example by coming out before two scientific people in a well-lighted room, they would stand a much better chance of getting believed: though even in the present case I must allow that I should have felt far more confidence in your positive reality if you'd presented yourself in broad daylight, when Jim and I hadn't punished the whisky quite as fully as we've done this evening."

When the candles were out, our apparition still retained its fluorescent, luminous appearance, and seemed to burn with a faint bluish light of its own. We projected a pencil through the spectroscope, and obtained, for the first time in the history of science, the spectrum of a spectre. The result was a startling one indeed. We had expected to find lines indicating the presence of sulphur or phosphorus: instead of that, we obtained a continuous band of pale luminosity, clearly pointing to the fact that the apparition had no known terrestial element in its composition. Though we felt rather surprised at this discovery, we simply noted it down on our paper, and proceeded to verify it by chemical analysis.

The phantom obligingly allowed us to fill a small phial with the luminous matter, which Harry immediately proceeded to test with all the resources at our disposal. For purposes of comparison I filled a corresponding phial with air from another part of the room, which I subjected to precisely similar tests. At the end of half an hour we had completed our examination—the spectre meanwhile watching us with mingled curiosity and amusement; and we laid our written quantitative results side by side. They agreed to a decimal. The table, being interesting, deserves a place in this memoir. It ran as follows:—

Chemical Analysis of an Apparition.

Atmospheric air 96.45 per cent. Aqueous vapour 23.1 " Carbonic acid 1.08 " Tobacco smoke 0.16 " Volatile alcohol A trace ———- 100.00 "

The alcohol Harry plausibly attributed to the presence of glasses which had contained whisky toddy. The other constituents would have been normally present in the atmosphere of a room where two fellows had been smoking uninterruptedly ever since dinner. This important experiment clearly showed that the apparition had no proper chemical constitution of its own, but consisted entirely of the same materials as the surrounding air.

"Only one thing remains to be done now, Jim," said Harry, glancing significantly at a plain deal table in the corner, with whose uses we were both familiar; "but then the question arises, does this gentleman come within the meaning of the Act? I don't feel certain about it in my own mind, and with the present unsettled state of public opinion on this subject, our first duty is to obey the law."

"Within the meaning of the Act?" I answered; "decidedly not. The words of the forty-second section say distinctly 'any living animal.' Now, Mr. Egerton, according to his own account, is a ghost, and has been dead for some two hundred years or thereabouts: so that we needn't have the slightest scruple on that account."

"Quite so," said Harry, in a tone of relief. "Well then, sir," turning to the apparition, "may I ask you whether you would object to our vivisecting you?"

"Mortuisecting, you mean, Harry," I interposed parenthetically. "Let us keep ourselves strictly within the utmost letter of the law."

"Vivisecting? Mortuisecting?" exclaimed the spectre, with some amusement. "Really, the proposal is so very novel that I hardly know how to answer it. I don't think you will find it a very practicable undertaking: but still, if you like, yes, you may try your hands upon me."

We were both much gratified at this generous readiness to further the cause of science, for which, to say the truth, we had hardly felt prepared. No doubt, we were constantly in the habit of maintaining that vivisection didn't really hurt, and that rabbits or dogs rather enjoyed the process than otherwise; still, we did not quite expect an apparition in human form to accede in this gentlemanly manner to a personal request which after all is rather a startling one. I seized our new friend's hand with warmth and effusion (though my emotion was somewhat checked by finding it slip through my fingers immaterially), and observed in a voice trembling with admiration, "Sir, you display a spirit of self-sacrifice which does honour to your head and heart. Your total freedom from prejudice is perfectly refreshing to the anatomical mind. If all 'subjects' were equally ready to be vivisected—no, I mean mortuisected—oh, well, there," I added (for I began to perceive that my argument didn't hang together, as "subjects" usually accepted mortuisection with the utmost resignation), "perhaps it wouldn't make much difference after all."

Meanwhile Harry had pulled the table into the centre of the room, and arranged the necessary instruments at one end. The bright steel had a most charming and scientific appearance, which added greatly to the general effect. I saw myself already in imagination drawing up an elaborate report for the Royal Society, and delivering a Croonian Oration, with diagrams and sections complete, in illustration of the "Vascular System of a Ghost." But alas, it was not to be. A preliminary difficulty, slight in itself, yet enormous in its preventive effects, unhappily defeated our well-made plans.

"Before you lay yourself on the table," said Harry, gracefully indicating that article of furniture to the spectre with his lancet, "may I ask you to oblige me by removing your clothes? It is usual in all these operations to—ahem—in short, to proceed in puris naturalibus. As you have been so very kind in allowing us to operate upon you, of course you won't object to this minor but indispensable accompaniment."

"Well, really, sir," answered the ghost, "I should have no personal objection whatsoever; but I'm rather afraid it can't be done. To tell you the truth, my clothes are an integral part of myself. Indeed, I consist chiefly of clothes, with only a head and hands protruding at the principal extremities. You must have noticed that all persons of my sort about whom you have read or heard were fully clothed in the fashion of their own day. I fear it would be quite impossible to remove these clothes. For example, how very absurd it would be to see the shadowy outline of a ghostly coat hanging up on a peg behind a door. The bare notion would be sufficient to cast ridicule upon the whole community. No, gentlemen, much as I should like to gratify you, I fear the thing's impossible. And, to let the whole secret out, I'm inclined to think, for my part, that I haven't got any independent body whatsoever."

"But, surely," I interposed, "you must have some internal economy, or else how can you walk and talk? For example, have you a heart?"

"Most certainly, my dear sir, and I humbly trust it is in the right place."

"You misunderstand me," I repeated: "I am speaking literally, not figuratively. Have you a central vascular organ on your left-hand side, with two auricles and ventricles, a mitral and a tricuspid valve, and the usual accompaniment of aorta, pulmonary vein, pulmonary artery, systole and diastole, and so forth?"

"Upon my soul, sir," replied the spectre with an air of bewilderment, "I have never even heard the names of these various objects to which you refer, and so I am quite unable to answer your question. But if you mean to ask whether I have something beating just under my fob (excuse the antiquated word, but as I wear the thing in question I must necessarily use the name), why then, most undoubtedly I have."

"Will you oblige me, sir," said Harry, "by showing me your wrist? It is true I can't feel your pulse, owing to what you must acknowledge as a very unpleasant tenuity in your component tissues: but perhaps I may succeed in seeing it."

The apparition held out its arm. Harry instinctively endeavoured to balance the wrist in his hand, but of course failed in catching it. We were both amused throughout to observe how difficult it remained, after several experiences, to realize the fact that this visible object had no material and tangible background underlying it. Harry put up his eyeglass and gazed steadily at the phantom arm; not a trace of veins or arteries could anywhere be seen. "Upon my word," he muttered, "I believe it's true, and the subject has no internal economy at all. This is really very interesting."

"As it is quite impossible to undress you," I observed, turning to our visitor, "may I venture to make a section through your chest, in order, if practicable, to satisfy myself as to your organs generally?"

"Certainly," replied the good-humoured spectre; "I am quite at your service."

I took my longest lancet from its case and made a very neat cut, right across the sternum, so as to pass directly through all the principal viscera. The effect, I regret to say, was absolutely nugatory. The two halves of the body reunited instantaneously behind the instrument, just as a mass of mercury reunites behind a knife. Evidently there was no chance of getting at the anatomical details, if any existed, underneath that brocaded waistcoat of phantasmagoric satin. We gave up the attempt in despair.

"And now," said the shadowy form, with a smile of conscious triumph, flinging itself easily but noiselessly into a comfortable arm-chair, "I hope you are convinced that ghosts really do exist. I think I have pretty fully demonstrated to you my own purely spiritual and immaterial nature."

"Excuse me," said Harry, seating himself in his turn on the ottoman: "I regret to say that I remain as sceptical as at the beginning. You have merely convinced me that a certain visible shape exists apparently unaccompanied by any tangible properties. With this phenomenon I am already familiar in the case of phosphorescent gaseous effluvia. You also seem to utter audible words without the aid of a proper larynx or other muscular apparatus; but the telephone has taught me that sounds exactly resembling those of the human voice may be produced by a very simple membrane. You have afforded us probably the best opportunity ever given for examining a so-called ghost, and my private conviction at the end of it is that you are very likely an egregious humbug."

I confess I was rather surprised at this energetic conclusion, for my own faith had been rapidly expanding under the strange experiences of that memorable evening. But the visitor himself seemed much hurt and distressed. "Surely," he said, "you won't doubt my word when I tell you plainly that I am the authentic ghost of Algernon Egerton. The word of an Egerton of Egerton Castle was always better than another man's oath, and it is so still, I hope. Besides, my frank and courteous conduct to you both to-night, and the readiness with which I have met all your proposals for scientific examination, certainly entitle me to better treatment at your hands."

"I must beg ten thousand pardons," Harry replied, "for the plain language which I am compelled to use. But let us look at the case in a different point of view. During your occasional visits to the world of living men, you may sometimes have travelled in a railway carriage in your invisible form."

"I have taken a trip now and then (by a night train, of course), just to see what the invention was like."

"Exactly so. Well, now, you must have noticed that a guard insisted from time to time upon waking up the sleepy passengers for no other purpose than to look at their tickets. Such a precaution might be resented, say by an Egerton of Egerton Castle, as an insult to his veracity and his honesty. But, you see, the guard doesn't know an Egerton from a Muggins: and the mere word of a passenger to the effect that he belongs to that distinguished family is in itself of no more value than his personal assertion that his ticket is perfectly en règle."

"I see your analogy, and I must allow its remarkable force."

"Not only so," continued Harry firmly, "but you must remember that in the case I have put, the guard is dealing with known beings of the ordinary human type. Now, when a living person introduces himself to me as Egerton of Egerton Castle, or Sir Roger Tichborne of Alresford, I accept his statement with a certain amount of doubt, proportionate to the natural improbability of the circumstances. But when a gentleman of shadowy appearance and immaterial substance, like yourself, makes a similar assertion, to the effect that he is Algernon Egerton who died two hundred years ago, then I am reluctantly compelled to acknowledge, even at the risk of hurting that gentleman's susceptible feelings, that I can form no proper opinion whatsoever of his probable veracity. Even men, whose habits and constitution I familiarly understand, cannot always be trusted to tell me the truth: and how then can I expect implicitly to believe a being whose very existence contradicts all my previous experiences, and whose properties give the lie to all my scientific conceptions—a being who moves without muscles and speaks without lungs? Look at the possible alternatives, and then you will see that I am guilty of no personal rudeness when I respectfully decline to accept your uncorroborated assertions. You may be Mr. Algernon Egerton, it is true, and your general style of dress and appearance certainly bears out that supposition; but then you may equally well be his Satanic Majesty in person—in which case you can hardly expect me to credit your character for implicit truthfulness. Or again, you may be a mere hallucination of my fancy: I may be suddenly gone mad, or I may be totally drunk, and now that I look at the bottle, Jim, we must certainly allow that we have fully appreciated the excellent qualities of your capital Glenlivat. In short, a number of alternatives exist, any one of which is quite as probable as the supposition of your being a genuine ghost; which supposition I must therefore lay aside as a mere matter for the exercise of a suspended judgment."

I thought Harry had him on the hip, there: and the spectre evidently thought so too; for he rose at once and said rather stiffly, "I fear, sir, you are a confirmed sceptic upon this point, and further argument might only result in one or the other of us losing his temper. Perhaps it would be better for me to withdraw. I have the honour to wish you both a very good evening." He spoke once more with the hauteur and grand mannerism of the old school, besides bowing very low at each of us separately as he wished us good-night.

"Stop a moment," said Harry rather hastily. "I wouldn't for the world be guilty of any inhospitality, and least of all to a gentleman, however indefinite in his outline, who has been so anxious to afford us every chance of settling an interesting question as you have. Won't you take a glass of whisky and water before you go, just to show there's no animosity?"

"I thank you," answered the apparition, in the same chilly tone; "I cannot accept your kind offer. My visit has already extended to a very unusual length, and I have no doubt I shall be blamed as it is by more reticent ghosts for the excessive openness with which I have conversed upon subjects generally kept back from the living world. Once more," with another ceremonious bow, "I have the honour to wish you a pleasant evening."

As he said these words, the fluorescent light brightened for a second, and then faded entirely away. A slightly unpleasant odour also accompanied the departure of our guest. In a moment, spectre and scent alike disappeared; but careful examination with a delicate test exhibited a faint reaction which proved the presence of sulphur in small quantities. The ghost had evidently vanished quite according to established precedent.

We filled our glasses once more, drained them off meditatively, and turned into our bedrooms as the clock was striking four.

Next morning, Harry and I drew up a formal account of the whole circumstance, which we sent to the Royal Society, with a request that they would publish it in their Transactions. To our great surprise, that learned body refused the paper, I may say with contumely. We next applied to the Anthropological Institute, where, strange to tell, we met with a like inexplicable rebuff. Nothing daunted by our double failure, we despatched a copy of our analysis to the Chemical Society; but the only acknowledgment accorded to us was a letter from the secretary, who stated that "such a sorry joke was at once impertinent and undignified." In short, the scientific world utterly refuses to credit our simple and straightforward narrative; so that we are compelled to throw ourselves for justice upon the general reading public at large. As the latter invariably peruse the pages of "BELGRAVIA," I have ventured to appeal to them in the present article, confident that they will redress our wrongs, and accept this valuable contribution to a great scientific question at its proper worth. It may be many years before another chance occurs for watching an undoubted and interesting Apparition under such favourable circumstances for careful observation; and all the above information may be regarded as absolutely correct, down to five places of decimals.

Still, it must be borne in mind that unless an apparition had been scientifically observed as we two independent witnesses observed this one, the grounds for believing in its existence would have been next to none. And even after the clear evidence which we obtained of its immaterial nature, we yet remain entirely in the dark as to its objective reality, and we have not the faintest reason for believing it to have been a genuine unadulterated ghost. At the best we can only say that we saw and heard Something, and that this Something differed very widely from almost any other object we had ever seen and heard before. To leap at the conclusion that the Something was therefore a ghost, would be, I venture humbly to submit, without offence to the Psychical Research Society, a most unscientific and illogical specimen of that peculiar fallacy known as Begging the Question.

RAM DAS OF CAWNPORE

We Germans do not spare trouble where literary or scientific work is on hand: and so when I was appointed by the University of Breslau to the travelling scholarship in the Neo-Sanskritic languages, I made up my mind at once to spend the next five years of my life in India. I knew already a good deal more Hindi and Urdu than most English officials who have spent twenty years in the country; but I was anxious to perfect my knowledge by practice on the spot, and to acquire thorough proficiency in conversation by intercourse with the people themselves. I therefore went out to India at once, and avoiding the great towns, such as Calcutta or Allahabad, which have been largely anglicised by residents and soldiers, I took up my abode in the little village of Bithoor on the Ganges, a few miles from Cawnpore, celebrated as having been the residence of the Nana Sahib, whom you English always describe as "the most ferocious rebel in the Mutiny." Here I spent four years in daily intercourse with the native gentry, whose natural repugnance to foreigners I soon conquered by invariable respect for their feelings and prejudices. At the end of eighteen months I had so won my way to their hearts that the Muhammedans regarded me as scarcely outside the pale of Islam, while the Hindoos usually addressed me by the religious title of Bhai or brother.

Of course, however, the English officials did not look with any favouring eye upon my proceedings, especially as I sometimes felt called upon to remonstrate with them upon their hasty and often ignorant method of dispensing justice. This coolness towards the authorities increased the friendship felt towards me by the native population; and "the European Sahib who is not a Feringhee" became a general adviser of many among the poorer people in their legal difficulties. I merely mention these facts to account for the confidence reposed in me, of which the story I am about to relate is a striking example.

I had a syce or groom who passed by the name of Lal Biro. This man was a tall, reserved, white-haired old Hindoo, a Jat by caste, but with a figure which might have been taken for that of a Brahman. His manner to me was always cold and sometimes sullen; and I found it difficult to place myself on the same terms with him as with my other servants. One dark evening, however, during the cold season, I had driven back from Cawnpore with him late at night in a small open trap, and found him far more chatty and communicative than usual. When we reached the bungalow, we discovered that the lights were out, and the house almost shut up, as the servants had fancied that I meant to sleep at the club. Lal Biro accordingly came in with me, and helped me to get my supper ready. Then at my request he sat down cross-legged near the door and continued to give me some reminiscences of the Mutiny which had been interrupted by our arrival.

"Yes, Sahib," he said quietly, composing himself on a little mat with a respectful inclination of the body; "I am Ram Das of Cawnpore."

I was startled by the confession, for I knew the name of Ram Das as one of the most dangerous petty rebels, on whose head Government had fixed a large price; but I was gratified by the confidence he reposed in me, and I begged him to go on with his story. I write it down now in very nearly the literal English equivalent of his exact words.

"Yes, Sahib, it is a long story truly. I will tell you how it all came about. I was a cultivator on the uplands there by Cawnpore, and I had a nice plot of land in Zameendari near the village there, good land with wheat and millet and a little tobacco. My millet was joar, and I got a rupee for eighteen seers, good money. I was well-to-do in those days. No man in the village but spoke well of Ram Das. I had a wife and three children, and a good mud cottage, and I paid my dues regularly to Mahadeo, oil and grain, most properly. The Brahmans said I was a most pious man, and everybody thought well of me.

"One day Shaikh Ali, a Muhammedan, a landowner from over the river in Oude, whom I knew in the bazaar at Cawnpore, he met me near the bridge resting. He said to me, 'Well, Ram Das, these are strange things coming to pass. They say the sepoys have mutinied at Meerut, and the Feringhees are to be driven into the sea.'

"I said, 'That would not do us Hindoos much good. We should fall under you Musalmans again, and you would have an emperor at Delhi, and he would tax us and trouble us as our fathers tell us the Moguls did before the Feringhees came.'

"Shaikh Ali said to me, 'Are you a good man and true?'

"I answered, 'I pay my dues regularly and do poojah, but I don't know what you, a Musalman, mean by a good man.'

"'Can you keep counsel against the accursed Feringhees?' said he.

"'That is an easy thing to do,' I answered. 'They tax us, and number us, and make our salt dear, and mean to take our daughters away from us, for which purpose they have made a census, to see how many young women there are of twelve years and upwards. Besides, they slaughter cows the same as you do.'

"'Listen to me, Ram Das,' he said, 'and keep your counsel. Do you know that they have tried to make all the sepoys lose caste and become like dogs and Pariahs, by putting cow's grease on the cartridges?'

"'I know it,' I replied, 'because my brother is a sepoy at Allahabad, and he sent me word of it by a son of our neighbour.'

"'Did we Musalmans ever do so?' he asked again.

"'I never heard it,' said I: 'but indeed I am ignorant of all these things, for I am not an old man, and I have only heard imperfectly from my elders. Still, I don't know that you ever tried to make us lose caste.'

"'Well, Ram Das,' said the Shaikh, 'listen to what we propose. The sepoys from Meerut have gone to Delhi and have proclaimed the King as Emperor. But now the Nana of Bithoor has something to say about it. If the Nana were made king, would you fight for him?'

"'Certainly,' said I, 'for he is a Mahratta and a good Hindoo. He should by rights be Peshwa of the Mahrattas, and hold power even over your emperor at Delhi.'

"'That is quite true,' the Shaikh answered. 'The Peshwa was always the right hand and director of the Emperor. If we put the Mogul on the throne once more, the Nana would be his real sovereign, and Hindoos and Musalmans alike would rejoice in the change.'

"'But suppose we fall out among ourselves!'

"'What does that matter in the end?' he answered. 'Let us first drive out the accursed Feringhees, and then, if Allah prosper us, we may divide the land as we like between the two creeds. We are all sons of the soil, Hindoo and Musalman alike, and we can live together in peace. But these hateful Feringhees, they come across the sea, they overrun all India, they tax us all alike, they treat your Sindiah and Holkar as they treat our Nizam and our king of Oude, they take away our slaves, they tax our food, they pollute your sacred rivers, they destroy your castes, and as for us, they take their women to picnic in our mosques, as I have seen myself at Agra. Shall we not first drive them into the sea?'

"'You say well,' I answered, 'and I shall ask more of this matter at Bithoor.'

"That was the first that I heard of it all. Next day, the village was all in commotion. It was said that the Nana had called on all good Hindoos to help him to clear out the Feringhees. I left my hut and my children, and I came to Bithoor here. Then they gave me a rifle, and told me I should march with them to Cawnpore to kill the Feringhees. There were not many of the dogs, and the gods were on our side; and when we had killed them all we should have the whole of India for the Hindoos, with no land-tax or salt-tax, and there should be no more cattle slaughtered nor no more interference with the pilgrims at Hurdwar. It was a grand day that, and the Nana, dressed out in all the Peshwa's jewels, looked like a very king.

"Well, we went to Cawnpore and began to besiege the entrenchments which Wheeler Sahib had thrown up round the cantonment. We had great guns and many men, both sepoys and volunteers.

Inside, the Feringhees had only a few, and not much artillery. We all thought that the gods had given us the Feringhees to slay, and that there would be no more of them left at all.

"For twenty days we continued besieging, and the Feringhees got weaker and weaker. They had no food, and scarcely any water. At last Wheeler Sahib sent to tell the Nana that he would give himself up, if the Nana would spare their lives. The Nana was a merciful man, and he said, 'I might go on and take the entrenchment, and kill you all if I wished; but to save time, because I want to get away and join the others, I will let you off.' So he took all the money in the treasury, and the guns, and promised to provide boats to take them all down to Allahabad.

"I was standing about near one of our guns that day, when Chunder Lal, a Brahman in the Nana's troops, came up to me and said, 'Well, Ram Das, what do you think of this?'

"'I think,' said I, 'that it is a sin and a shame, after we have broken down the hospital, and starved out the Feringhees, to let them go down the river to Allahabad, to strengthen the garrison that pollutes that holy city. For I hear that they do all kinds of wrong there, and insult the Brahmans, and the bathers, and the sacred fig-tree. And if these men go and join them, the garrison will be stronger, and they will be able to hold out longer against the people, which may the gods avert!'

"'So I think too, Ram Das,' said he; 'and for my part, I would try to prevent their going.'

"A little later, we went down to the river, by the Nana's orders. There some men had got boats together, and were putting the Feringhees into them. It was getting dark, and we all went down to guard them. A few of them had got into the boats; the rest were on the bank. I can see it all now: the white men with their proud looks abashed, going meekly into the boats, and the women stepping, all afraid and shrinking from the black faces—shrinking from us as if we were unclean and they would lose caste by touching us. Though they were so frightened, they were proud still. Then three guns went off somewhere in the camp. Chunder Lal was near me, and he said to me, 'That is the signal for us to fire. The Nana ordered me to fire when I heard those guns.' I don't know if it was true: perhaps the Nana ordered it, perhaps Chunder Lal told a lie: but I never could find out the truth about it, for they blew Chunder Lal from the guns at Cawnpore afterwards, and I have never seen the Nana since to ask him. At any rate, I levelled my musket and fired. I hit an officer Sahib, and wounded him, not mortally. In a moment there was a great report, and I looked round, and saw all our men firing. I don't know if they had the word of command, but I think not. I think they all saw me fire, and fired because I did, and because they thought it a shame to let the Feringhees escape; as though the head man of a village should entrap a tiger, a man-eater that had killed many cultivators in their dal-fields, and then should let it go. If a headman ordered the villagers to loose it from the trap, do you think they would obey him? No, and if he loosed it himself, they would take muskets and sticks and weapons of all kinds, and kill the man-eater at once. That is what we did with the Feringhees.

"It was a terrible sight, and I did not like to see it. Some of them leapt into the water and were drowned. Others swam away madly, like wild fowl, and we shot at them as they swam; and then they dived, and when they came up again, we fired at them again, and the water was red with their blood. I hit one man on the shoulder, and broke his arm, but still he swam on with his other arm, till somebody put a bullet through his head, and he sank. I ran into the water, as did many others, and we followed them down until all the swimmers were picked off. Some of the boats crossed the river: but there was a regiment waiting on the Oude shore—some said by accident, others that the Nana had posted it there—and the sepoys hacked them all to pieces as they tried to escape. It was a dreadful sight, and I am an older man now, and do not like to think of it: but I was younger then, and our blood was hot with fighting, and we thought we were going to drive the Feringhees out of the country, and that the gods would be well pleased with our day's work.

"Some boats got away a little way, but they were afterwards sent back. The women and children, some of them badly wounded, we took back into Cawnpore. We put them in the Bibi's house, near the Assembly Rooms. Then in a few days, the others who were sent back from Futteypore arrived, and the Nana said, 'What shall I do with them?' Everybody said, 'Shoot them:' so we took out all the men the same day and shot them at once. The women and children the Nana spared, because he was a humane man; and he sent them to the others in the Bibi's house. There they were well treated; and though they had not punkahs, and tattis, and cow's flesh, as formerly, yet they got better rations than any of the Nana's own soldiers: for the Feringhees, like all you Europeans, Sahib, are very luxurious, and will not live off rice or dal and a little ghee like other people. You have conquered every place in the world, from Ceylon to Cashmere, and so you have got luxurious, and live off wheaten bread, and cow's flesh, and wine, and many such ungodly things. But the rest of the world think it a great thing if they have ghee to their rice.

"After a fortnight the Nana's troops were defeated at Futteypore, and it was said that the Feringhee ladies were sending letters to the army. Then the Nana was very angry. He said, 'I have spared these women's lives, and yet they are sending news to my enemies. I will tell you what I will do: I will put them all to death.' So he gave word to have them shot. I was one of the guards at the Bibi's house, and I got orders to shoot them. Then we all tried to bring them out in front of the house; but they would not come; so we had to go in and put an end to them there with swords and bayonets. Poor things! they shrieked piteously; and I was sorry for them, because they were some of them young and pretty, and it is not the women's fault if the Feringhees come here, for the Feringhee ladies hate India, and will all go away again across the water if they can get a chance. And then there were the children! One poor lady clung to my knees and begged hard for her daughter: but I had to obey orders, so I cut her down. It was very sad. But then, the Feringhee ladies are even prouder than the men, and they hate us Hindoos. They would not care if they killed a thousand of us if their little fingers ached. Look how they make us salaam, and punish us for small faults, and compel us to work punkahs, and to run on foot after their carriages, and insult our gods. Ah, they are a cruel, proud race. They are lower than the lowest Sudra, and yet they will treat a twice-born Brahman like a dog.

"We threw all the bodies into the well at Cawnpore where now they have put up an image of one of their gods—a cold, white god, with two wings—to avenge their death. Then there was great joy in Cawnpore. We had killed the last of the Feringhees, and India should be our own. Soon, we might make the Nana into a real Peshwa, and turn against the Musalmans, and put down all slaughtering of cattle altogether, as the Rani did at Jhansi. We should have no more land-tax to pay, for the Musalmans should pay all the taxes, as is just: but the Hindoos should have their land for nothing, and live upon chupatties and ghee and honey every day. Ah, that was the grandest day that was ever seen in Cawnpore!

"But that was not the end of it. In the mysterious providence of the all-wise gods it was otherwise ordained. A few days before all this, I was standing about in the bazaar, when I met a jemadar. He said to me, 'So the Feringhees are marching from Allahabad!'

"'The Feringhees!' I said: 'why, no, we have killed them all off out of India, thanks be to the gods. At Delhi they are all killed, and at Meerut, and at Cawnpore here, and I believe everywhere but at Allahabad and at Calcutta.'

"'Ram Das,' he answered, 'you are a child; you know nothing. Do you think the Feringhees are so few? They are swarming across the water like locusts across the Ganges. In a few months, they will all come from where they have been helping the Sultan of Roum against the other Christians, and

they will make the whole Doab into a desert, as they made Rohilcund in the days of Hostein Sahib*
Shall I tell you the news from Delhi?'

*Warren Hastings

"'Yes,' I said, 'tell me by all means, for I don't believe the Feringhees will ever again hold rule in India, the land of the all-wise gods.' In those days, Sahib, I was very foolish. I did not know that the Feringhees were in number like the green parrots, and that they could send countless shiploads across the water as easily as we could send a cargo of dal down the river to Benares.

"'Well, then,' he said, 'Delhi has been besieged, and before long it will be taken. And the Feringhees have sent up men from Calcutta who have reached Allahabad, and are now on the march for Cawnpore. When they come, they will take us all, and kill the Nana, and there will be an end of the Hindoos forever. They are going to make us all into Christians by force, baptising us with unclean water, and making Brahmans and Pariahs eat together of cow's flesh, and destroying all caste, and modesty, and religion altogether.'

"'They will do all these things, doubtless,' I replied, 'if they can succeed in catching us: but it is impossible. The Feringhees are but a handful: they could never have ruled us if it were not for the sepoys. They had all the muskets and the ammunition, and they kept them from us. But now that the sepoys have mutinied, the Feringhees are but a few officers and half-a-dozen regiments. And I cannot believe that the gods would allow men like them, who are worse than Musalmans, and have no caste, to conquer us who are the best blood in India, Brahmans, and Jats, and Mahrattas.'

"But the jemadar laughed at me. 'I tell you,' he said, 'this rebellion is all child's play. For I have myself been across the water once, as an officer's servant, and have been to England, and to their great town, London. It is so great that a man can hardly walk across it from end to end in a day; and if you were to put Allahabad or Cawnpore down in its midst, the people would not know that any new thing had come about. They have ships in their rivers as thick as the canes in a sugar-field; and iron roads with cars drawn by steam horses. They have so many men that they could overrun all India as easily as the people of Cawnpore could overrun Bihtoor. And so when I hear their guns outside the town, I will run away to them, and I advise you to do so too.'

"I didn't believe him at the time; but a few days afterwards, I found out that the Feringhees were really marching from Allahabad. And when we killed the ladies, they were almost at the door. They fought like demons, and we know that the demons must all be on their side. Many times we went out to meet them, but in four separate battles they cut our men to pieces like sheep. At last, just after we had got rid of the ladies, they got to Cawnpore.

"Then there was no end of the confusion. The Nana got frightened, and fled away. We blew up the magazine, so that they might not have powder; and the Feringhees came at once into the town. There never were people so savage or angry. The sight of the well and the Bibi's house seemed to drive them wild. They were more like tigers than human beings. Every sepoy whom they caught they shot at once for vengeance, because that is their religion: and many who were not sepoys, and who had not borne arms against them, they shot on false evidence. Every man who had a grudge against another told the Feringhees that their enemy had helped to cut down the ladies; and the Feringhees were so greedy for blood that they believed it all, and shot them down at once. So much blood was never shed in Cawnpore: for one life they took ten. Then we knew it was all true what the jemadar had said, and that they would take the whole Doab back, and put back the land-tax, and the salt-tax; and we thought too that they would make us all into Christians; but that they have not done, for so long as they get their taxes, and have high pay and good bungalows, and cow's flesh and beer, they don't care about, or reverence any religion, not even their own. For we Hindoos respect our fakeers, and even the Musalmans respect their pirs; but the Feringhees think as little of the missionaries as we do ourselves, and care more for dances than for their churches. That is why they have not compelled us to become Christians.

"All the time the Feringhees were in Cawnpore, I lay hid in the jemadar's house. He was a good man, though he had gone over to the Feringhees as soon as they came in sight: and nobody suspected his house, because he was now on their side, and had given them news of all that took place in the town when we killed the officers and the ladies. So I was quite safe there, and got dal and water every day, and was in no danger at all.

"Presently, the Feringhees moved off again, abandoning Cawnpore, because Havelock Sahib, who was the most terrible of their generals, wanted to go on to Lucknow. There the Musalmans of Oude had risen and were besieging the Presidency, with all the soldiers and officers. I would not go to Oude, because I did not care to fight for Musalmans, preferring rather to wait the chance of the Nana coming back; for only a Mahratta could now recover the kingdom for the Hindoos; and the Musalmans are almost as bad as the Feringhees themselves. In a short time, however, the Gwalior men came. They were good men, the Gwalior men: for though Sindiah, their rajah, had commanded them not to fight, they would not desert the other Hindoos, when there were Feringhees to be killed: and they disobeyed Sindiah, and rebelled, and so I joined them gladly. They pitched only fifteen miles from Cawnpore, and there I went out and enlisted with them.

"By-and-by most of the Gwalior men got frightened, and went back again. Then things became very bad. A few of us marched southward, and hid in the jungles that slope down towards the Jumna. We were very frightened, because there are tigers in that jungle: and two Gwalior men were eaten by the tigers. But soon some Feringhees from Etawa heard of our being there, and they came out to stalk us. It was just like shooting nil-ghae. They came on horseback, and closed all round the jungle where we were. Then they crept on into the jungle, and we crept away from them. Every now and then they drove a man into an open space; and then they all shouted like fiends, and shot at him. When they hit him and rolled him over, they laughed, and shouted louder still. I was hidden under some low bushes; and two Feringhees passed close to me, one on each side of the bushes; but they did not see me. Soon after, they started a man who had been a sepoy, and he ran back towards my bushes. I never said a word. Then they all fired at him, and killed him: but one bullet hit me on the arm, and went through the flesh of my arm, and partly splintered the bone. But still I said nothing. All day long I lay moaning to myself very low, and the Feringhees scoured all the jungle, and killed everybody but me, and went away saying to themselves that they had had a good day's sport. For they hunted us just as if we were antelopes.

"I lay for a fortnight, wounded, in the jungle, and had nothing to eat but Mahua berries. I was feverish and wandered in my mind: but at the end of a fortnight I could crawl out, and managed to drag along my wounded arm. Then I went to the nearest village, and gave out that I was a cultivator who had been wounded by the Gwalior men in trying to defend a tuhseelie[*] for the Feringhees. For that, they took great care of me, and sent me on to Cawnpore.

*Village Treasury

"I was not afraid to go back to the town, for my own people would not know me again. In that fortnight I had grown from a young man into the man you see me; only I was older-looking then than I am now, for I have got younger in the Sahib's service. My hair had turned white, and so had my beard, which was longer and more matted than before. My forehead was wrinkled, and my cheeks had fallen away. As soon as I had got to Cawnpore, I went straight to the jemadar's house, to see if he would recognize me; but he did not: for even my voice was hoarser and harsher than of old, through fever and exposure. So I went and told my story to the Feringhee doctor, how I had been wounded in keeping the tuhseelie for his people; and he tended my arm, and made it well again. For though the Feringhees are savage like tigers to their enemies, if you befriend them, they will treat you well. In that they are better than the Musalmans.

"Soon after, I went out to the parade ground, because I heard there was to be a dreadful sight. They were going to blow the rebels they had taken, from the guns. I went out and looked on. Then they took all the men, Brahmans and Chumars alike, and broke caste, and tied them each to a gun. I could not have done it, though I cut down the Feringhee ladies; but they did it, and made a light matter of it. Then they fired the guns, and in a whiff their bodies were all blown away utterly, so that there was nothing left of them. This they did so as utterly to destroy the rebels, leaving neither body nor soul, but annihilating them altogether, which is worse than death. They would have done it to me, if they had caught me. Do you wonder that I hate the Feringhees, Sahib? Why, they did it even to the twice-born Brahmans, let alone a Jat. The gods will avenge it on them.

"Then I went out to look at my plot of land. The Feringhees knew of me from many traitors, some of whom had given up my name to save themselves from being blown away—and no wonder. They had seized my plot, and sold it to another man, a zameendar, a Kayath in Cawnpore, who had made money by supplying them with food—the curse of all the gods upon him! And as for my wife and children, they had gone wandering out, and I have never seen them since. My wife was with child, and she went into Cawnpore, and thence elsewhere, I know not where, and starved to death, I suppose, or died in some other shameful way. But one of my daughters a missionary got, and sent her to Meerut to a school; and there they are teaching her to be a Christian, and to hate her own gods and her own people, and to love the Feringhees who suck the blood of India, and grind down the poor with taxes, and dispossess the Thakurs, who ought, of course, by right to own the land. This much I learned by inquiring at Cawnpore; but how my wife died, or whether they killed her, or what, that I have never been able to learn.

"So that was the end of it all. The Nana was hidden away somewhere up Nepaul way; and the Feringhees had got back Lucknow; and all over the Doab and the Punjab they were established again, and the hopes of the people were all broken. And I had lost my land, and my wife, and my children, and had nothing to live upon or to live for. And we had not driven out the accursed strangers, after all, but on the contrary they made themselves stronger than ever, and sent more soldiers, as the jemadar had prophesied, and put down the Company, who used to be their rajah, and sent up a Maharani instead, who is now Empress of India. And they made new taxes and a new census and all sorts of imposts. But since that time they have been more afraid of us, and are not so insolent to the temples, or the pilgrims, or to the sacred monkeys. And I came to Bithoor, and became a syce, and I have been a syce ever since. That is all I know about the Mutiny, Sahib."

The old man stopped suddenly, having told all his story in a dull, monotonous voice, with little feeling and no dramatic display. I have tried to reproduce it just as he said it. There was no passion, no fierceness, no cruelty in his manner; but simply a deep, settled, uniform tone of hatred to the English. It was the only time I had ever heard the story of the Mutiny from a native point of view, and I give it as I heard it, without mitigating aught either of its horror or its truth.

"And you are not afraid of telling me all this?" I asked.

He shook his head. "The Sahib has a white face," he answered, "but his heart is black."

"And the Nana?" I inquired. "Do you know if he is living still?"

His eyes flashed fire for the first time since he had begun. "Ay," he cried; "he is living. That I know from many trusty friends. And he will come again whenever there is trouble between the Feringhees and the other Christians: and then we shall have no quarrelling among ourselves; but Sindiah, and Holkar, and the Nizam, and the Oude people, and even the Bengalis will rise up together; and we will cut every Feringhee's throat in all India, and the gods will give us the land for ever after.... Good night, Sahib: my salaam to you." And he glided like a serpent from the room.

Grant Allen – A Short Biography

Charles Grant Blairfindie Allen was born on February 24th, 1848 at Alwington, near Kingston, Canada West (now part of Ontario). He was the second son of the Rev. Joseph Antisell Allen, a Protestant minister from Dublin, Ireland and Catharine Ann Grant, the daughter of the fifth Baron of Longueuil.

Grant was educated at home until he was thirteen at which time the family moved, initially to the United States, then France and finally settling in the United Kingdom.

Whilst growing up the family background was obviously religious but Grant developed his own views on life and the world and turned to agnosticism and socialism.

He was educated at King Edward's School in Birmingham and Merton College in Oxford. After graduating, Grant studied in France and also taught at Brighton College. By 1870, still only in his mid-twenties, he became a professor at Queen's College, a black college in Jamaica.

Whilst in Jamaica Grant met and married his first wife Ellen Jerrard in 1873 and they produced a son five years later; Jerrard Grant Allen, who grew up to become a theatrical agent/manager.

In 1876 Grant and his family left Jamaica to return to England with both the talent and ambition to become a writer.

He quickly turned to writing essays, gaining a reputation for his work on science and literary works. An early article, 'Note-Deafness' a description of what is now called amusia, was published in 1878 in the learned journal Mind and was cited approvingly by Oliver Sacks very recently.

From essays in magazines and journals he now turned to books, initially on scientific subjects. These include Physiological Æsthetics 1877 and Flowers and Their Pedigrees 1886.

His first major influence was associationist psychology, as then expounded by Alexander Bain and Herbert Spencer, the latter is often considered the most important individual in the transition from associationist psychology to Darwinian functionalism. In Grant's many articles on flowers and perception in insects, Darwinian arguments now replaced the old Spencerian terms.

On a personal level, a long friendship that started when Grant met Herbert Spencer on his return from Jamaica, turned eventually to one of unease over its long course. Grant was to write a critical and revealing biographical article on Spencer that was published after Spencer was dead.

In the early 1880's Grant began to assist Sir W. W. Hunter in his Gazeteer of India. It is at this time that Grant now turned his full attention away from the factual and towards the world of imagination and fiction.

Between this shift to fiction in 1884 and his death fifteen years later Grant was to write about 30 novels.

Many were adventure novels which were very common in the late Victorian period as writers turned their literary talents to the voracious appetites of the weekly or monthly serial magazines.

Some however were to cause quite a stir. For instance in 1895 Grant took the subject of children born out of wedlock as his subject matter. The result was The Woman Who Did, that suggested, indeed pushed, for its time, certain quite startling views on marriage and related areas. In keeping with his then glowing reputation it became a bestseller despite it being seemingly at odds with society's unease at its provocative subject matter.

Interestingly Grant wrote novels under female pseudonyms. One of these was the short novel The Type-writer Girl, which he wrote under the name Olive Pratt Rayner.

Another work, The Evolution of the Idea of God 1897, propounding a theory of religion on heterodox lines, has the disadvantage of endeavoring to explain everything by one theory. This "ghost theory" was often seen as a derivative of Herbert Spencer's theory. However, at the time, it was well known and brief references to it can be found in a review by Marcel Mauss, Durkheim's nephew, in the articles of William James and in the works of Sigmund Freud. The young G. K. Chesterton wrote on what he considered the flawed premise of the idea, arguing that the idea of God preceded human mythologies, rather than developing from them. Chesterton said of Grant Allen's book on the evolution of the idea of God "it would be much more interesting if God wrote a book on the evolution of the idea of Grant Allen".

From this and other instances, it can be seen that his work was in debate and whether agreed with or not could always ensure a lively discussion.

Grant also helped to pioneer science fiction, with the 1895 novel The British Barbarians. This book, was published at about the same time as H. G. Wells was to publish The Time Machine. The plots are quite different but both describe time travel. A few years later his short story The Thames Valley Catastrophe (published 1901 in The Strand magazine) describes the destruction of London by a massive volcanic eruption. Whilst the premise now may seem outlandish, at the time genuine panic and concern set in as, like his contemporary, Jules Verne, much of great science fiction writing is rooted in a plausibility that is set out very convincingly.

In detective fiction too his works include female detectives, very much an innovation in the young genre and his gentleman rogue, Colonel Clay, is seen as a forerunner to other, perhaps more famous characters, by other later writers.

In 1881 he had settled at Dorking, where he took great delight in botanical walks in the woods and sandy heaths. He never enjoyed particularly good health and so almost every winter he would depart for milder climes, to winter in the south of Europe, usually at Antibes, though occasionally as far as Algiers and Egypt.

In 1892 he bought land almost on the summit of Hind Head, and built himself a charming cottage which he called the Croft. Here he found that it was possible to endure the vagaries of the English winter and in landscape more beautiful and wilder than at Dorking and that his long scientific training could better appreciate.

His growing re-discovery and interest in art in the later part of his life allowed him to blend together literature, art and history in a series of guide books on Paris, Florence, Venice, and the cities of Belgium.

On October 25th 1899 Grant Allen died at his home in Hindhead, Haslemere, Surrey, England. He died just before finishing Hilda Wade. The novel's final episode, which he dictated to his friend, doctor and neighbour Sir Arthur Conan Doyle from his bed appeared under the appropriate title, The Episode of the Dead Man Who Spoke in the Strand Magazine in 1900.

Grant Allen is rarely heard of today, although an occasional short story can be heard on the radio or reprinted among magazine enthusiasts but in his time he did much to entertain the masses and push several genres along a richer journey they are still proceeding on today.

Grant Allen – A Concise Bibliography

Physiological Æsthetics. 1877
The Colour-Sense: Its Origin and Development. 1879
Evolutionist at Large. 1881
Vignettes from Nature. 1881
The Colours of Flowers. 1882
Colin Clout's Calendar. 1883
Flowers and Their Pedigrees. 1883
Philistia. 1884
Strange Stories. Short Stories. 1884
Babylon. A novel in 3 volumes. 1885
For Mamie's Sake. 1886
In All Shades. 1886
The Beckoning Hand & Other Stories. 1887
This Mortal Coil: A Novel. 1888
Force and Energy. 1888
The Devil's Die. 1888
The White Man's Foot. 1888
Falling in Love. 1889
The Tents of Shem. 1889
Wednesday the Tenth. 1890
The Great Taboo. 1890
Dumaresq's Daughter. 1891
What's Bred in the Bone. 1891
The Duchess of Powysland. 1892
The Scallywag. 1893
Michael's Crag. 1893
The Lower Slopes. 1894
Post-Prandial Philosophy. 1894
The British Barbarians. 1895
At Market Value. 1895
The Story of the Plants. 1895
The Desire of the Eyes. 1895
The Woman Who Did. 1895
The Jaws of Death. 1896

A Bride from the Desert. 1896
Under Sealed Orders. 1896
Moorland Idylls. 1896
An African Millionaire. Colonel Clay's novel. 1897
The Evolution of the Idea of God. 1897
Paris. 1897
The Type-writer Girl. (as Olive Pratt Rayner) 1897
Tom, Unlimited. (as Martin Leach Warborough) 1897
Flashlights on Nature. 1898
The Incidental Bishop. 1898
Venice. 1898
The European Tour. 1899
A Splendid Sin. 1899
Miss Cayley's Adventures. 1899
Twelve Tales: With a Headpiece, a Tailpiece, and an Intermezzo. 1899
Hilda Wade (finished by Arthur Conan Doyle). 1900
Linnet. 1900
The Backslider. 1901
Sir Theodore's Guest & Other Stories. 1902
Evolution in Italian Art. 1908
The Hand of God. 1909
The Plants. 1909

Short Stories
The Empress of Andorra. 1878
My New Year Among the Mummies. 1878
Lucretia. 1879
My Circular Tour. 1880
A Ballade of Evolution. 1880
Ram Das of Cawnpore. 1880
The Chinese Play at the Haymarket. 1880
The Senior Proctor's Wooing. 1881
Pausodyne. 1881
Caribbean Twelve Per Cents. 1882
An Episode in High Life. 1882
Mr Chung. 1882
Isadine and I. 1883
The Backsider. 1883
The Reverend John Creedy. 1883
The Foundering of the Fortuna. 1883
The Third Time
The Gold Wulfric
My Uncle's Will. 1884
Carvalho. 1884
The Mysterious Occurence in Piccadilly. 1884
Dr Greatex's Engagement. 1884
Hugh Portledown's Return from Normandy. 1884
The Child of Phalanstery. 1884
The Curate of Churnside. 1884
John Cann's Treasure. 1884

Olga Davidoff's Husband. 1884
The Search Party's Find. 1885
The Two Carnegie's. 1885
Professor Milliter's Dilemma. 1885
In Strict Confidence. 1885
The Beckoning Hand. 1885
The Third Time. 1886
Harry's Inheritance. 1886
The Gold Wulfric. 1886
Mr Pierpoint's Repentance. 1886
Claude Tyack's Ordeal. 1887
Leonard's Recovery. 1887
A Social Difficulty. 1887
Dr Palliser's Patient. 1888
My Christmas Eve at Marzin. 1888
The Sultan's Sister. 1888
His First Crime. 1889
The Mayfield Mystery. 1889
Andre Canivet's Curse. 1890
Old Margaret. 1890
My One Gorilla. 1890
Dick Prothero's Luck. 1890
A Deadly Dilemna. 1891
Jerry Stokes. 1891
Selwyn Utterton's Nemesis. 1891
General Passavant's Will. 1891
The Briefless Barrister. 1891
Melissa's Tour. 1891
Karen – A Canadian Romance. 1891
The Prisoner of Assiout. 1891
The Abbe's Repentance. 1891
Masie Bowman's Fate. 1891
Naomi's Christmas Eves. 1891
That Friend of Sylvia's. 1892
The Conscientious Burglar. 1892
The Minor Poet. 1892
The Governor's Story. 1892
The Pot Boiler. 1892
The Great Ruby. 1892
Ewen Murray's Swim. 1892
Ivan Greet's Masterpiece. 1892
Pallinghurst Barrow. 1892
Langalula. 1893
The Assasin's Knife. 1893
The Artist and the Penny-a-Liner. 1893
A Casual Conversation. 1893
How To Succeed in Literature. 1893
Torrigiano. 1893
A Modern Sibyl: A Florentine Sketch. 1893
Nemesis Wins. 1894
Cecca's Lover. 1894

A Self Respecting Servant. 1894
Passiflora Sanguinea. 1894
An Excellent Match. 1894
Major Kinfaun's Marriage. 1894
Grateful Joe. 1894
An Idyll of the Ice. 1894
Criss Cross Love. 1894
Poor Little Soul. 1894
Amour de Voyage. 1894
The Dynamiter's Sweetheart. 1894
A Triumph of Civilisation. 1894
Dr Wardroper's Lie. 1894
The Miraclous Explorer. 1894
Leon and Leonie. 1895
A Comic Emotion. 1895
Joe's Rascality. 1895
Evelyn Moore's Poet. 1895
Frasine's First Communion. 1895
TheDead Man Speaks. 1895
A Study From the Nude. 1895
Cecca's Choice. 1895
The Desire of the Eyes. 1895
The Making of a Poet. 1895
The Man From Cumbrae. 1895
Fogo Skerries. 1895
The Great Californian Heiress. 1895
Cap'n Tom Woolley. 1895
The Girl at the Fair. 1895
Love's Old Dream. 1895
A Modern Pygmalion. 1895
A Bride From the Desert. 1895
The Practical Test. 1896
A Confidential Communication. 1896
The Great Temperance Preacher. 1896
A Day on the River. 1896
The Episode of the Mexican Seer. 1896
A Midsummer Episode. 1896
The Episode of the Diamond Links. 1896
Omar at Marlow. 1896
A Mere Matter of Standpoint. 1896
Fair Exchange. 1896
The Cowardly Dynamiter. 1896
The Episode of the Old Master. 1896
The Episode of the Tyrolean Castle. 1896
Janet's Nemesis. 1896
Entirely Accidential. 1896
The Episode of the Drawn Game. 1896
Wolverden Tower. 1896
The Episode of the German Professor. 1896
The Episode of the Arrest of the Colonel. 1896
The Episode of the Seldom Gold Mine. 1897

The Camisard's Bride. 1897
The Episode of the Japanned Dispatch Box. 1897
Llanfihangel Skerries. 1897
The Episode of the Game of Poker. 1897
The Episode of the Bertillon Method. 1897
A Lady of Florence. 1897
The Episode of the Old Bailey. 1897
A British Verdict. 1897
A Domestic Tragedy. 1897
A College Charm. 1897
A Freak of Memory. 1897
The Judge's Cross. 1897
The Thames Valley Catastrophe. 1897
The Great Oriental Seer. 1897
The Adventures of the Cantankerous Old Lady. 1898
The Adventure of the Supercilious Attache. 1898
The Pirate of Cliveden Reach. 1898
The Adventure of the Amateur Commission. 1898.
The Adventure of the Impromptu Mountaineer. 1898
Joe's Wife. 1898
The Adventure of the Urbane Old Gentleman. 1898
The Adventure of the Unobtrusive Oasis. 1898
The Adventure of the Pea Green Patrician. 1898
Isenberg's Regiment. 1898
The Adventure of the Magnificent Maharajah. 1898
A Woman's Hand: A Story. 1898
The Adventure of the Cross Eyed QC. 1898
The Christmas Eve Concert. 1898
The Adventure of the Oriental Attendant. 1899
Joseph's Dream. 1899
The Adventure of the Unprofessional Detective. 1899
Hobbling Mary. 1899
The Episode of the Patient Who Disappointed Her Doctor. 1899
The Episode of the Gentleman Who Had Failed For Everything. 1899
The Episode of the Wife Who Did Her Duty. 1899
The Episode of the Man Who Would Not Commit Suicide. 1899
A Regrettable Error. 1899
Peace-At-Any-Price Bill. 1899
The Episode of the Letter with a Basingstoke Post-Mark. 1899
The Episode of the Stone That Looked About It. 1899
His Ways Inscrutable. 1899
The Episode of the European With A Kaffir Heart. 1899
The Episode of the Lady Who Was Very Exclusive. 1899
The Episode of the Guide Who Knew the Country. 1899
Luigi and the Salvationist. 1899.
A Christmas Adventure. 1899.
The Episode of the Officer Who Understood Perfectly. 1900
Meriel Stanley, Poacher. 1900
The Episode of the Dead Man Who Spoke. 1900
A Question of Colour. 1900
Fra Benedett's Medal: A Story. 1900

The Temple of Fate: A Fable. 1900
The Way to Keronan. 1902
Lucy Lockett. 1902
Spencerian. 1904

Articles

1878. Hellas and Civilization, Gentleman's Magazine, Vol. CCXLIII
1878. Nation-making: A Theory of National Characters, Gentleman's Magazine, Vol. CCXLIII
1878. The Origin of Fruits, in Popular Science Monthly Volume 13
1879. Why Do We Eat our Dinner? in Popular Science Monthly Volume 14
1879. A Problem in Human Evolution, in Popular Science Monthly Volume
1879. Pleased with a Feather, in Popular Science Monthly Volume 15
1880. Why Keep India? The Contemporary Review, Vol. XXXVIII
1880. The Growth of Sculpture, The Cornhill Magazine, Vol. XLII
1880. The English Chronicle, Gentleman's Magazine, Vol. CCXLV
1880. The Venerable Bede, Gentleman's Magazine, Vol. CCXLIX
1880. The Dog's Universe, Gentleman's Magazine, Vol. CCXLIX
1880. Evolution and Geological Time, Gentleman's Magazine, Vol. CCXLIX
1880. Geology and History, in Popular Science Monthly Volume 17
1880. Aesthetic Feeling in Birds, in Popular Science Monthly Volume 17
1880. Aesthetic Evolution in Man, in Popular Science Monthly Volume 18
1881. The Story of Wulfgeat, Gentleman's Magazine, Vol. CCLI
1882. An English Shire, Gentleman's Magazine, Vol. CCLII
1882. The Welsh in the West Country, Gentleman's Magazine, Vol. CCLIII
1882. The Colours of Flowers, The Cornhill Magazine, Vol. XLV
1882. An English Weed, The Cornhill Magazine, Vol. XLV
1882. Sir Charles Lyell, in Popular Science Monthly Volume 20
1882. Hyacinth-Bulbs, in Popular Science Monthly Volume 20
1882. Who was Primitive Man? in Popular Science Monthly Volume 22
1883. The Pedigree of Wheat, in Popular Science Monthly Volume 22
1883. From Buttercups to Monk's-Hood, in Popular Science Monthly Volume 23
1883. Honeysuckle, Gentleman's Magazine, Vol. CCLV
1884. The Garden Snail, Gentleman's Magazine, Vol. CCLVI
1884. Our Debt to Insects, Gentleman's Magazine, Vol. CCLVI
1884. Idiosyncrasy, in Popular Science Monthly Volume 24
1884. The Ancestry of Birds, in Popular Science Monthly Volume 24
1884. The Milk in the Cocoa-Nut, in Popular Science Monthly Volume 25
1884. Our Debt to Insects, in Popular Science Monthly Volume 25
1884. Hickory-Nuts and Butternuts, in Popular Science Monthly Volume 25
1884. Queer Flowers, in Popular Science Monthly Volume 26
1885. Food and Feeding, in Popular Science Monthly Volume 26
1885. Concerning Clover, in Popular Science Monthly Volume 28
1886. A Thinking Machine, Gentleman's Magazine, Vol. CCLX
1886. Fish Out of Water, in Popular Science Monthly Volume 28
1886. A Thinking Machine, in Popular Science Monthly Volume 28
1886. Thistles, in Popular Science Monthly Volume 30, November 1886
1887. A Mount Washington Sandwort, in Popular Science Monthly Volume 30
1887. Among the Thousand Islands, in Popular Science Monthly Volume 31
1887. The Progress of Science from 1836 to 1886, in Popular Science Monthly Volume 31
1887. American Cinque-Foils, in Popular Science Monthly Volume 32

1888. Gourds and Bottles, in Popular Science Monthly Volume 33
1888. A Living Mystery, in Popular Science Monthly Volume 33
1888. Evolving the Camel, in Popular Science Monthly Volume 34
1889. From Africa, Gentleman's Magazine, Vol. CCLXVII
1889. Genius and Talent, in Popular Science Monthly Volume 34
1889. Plain Words on the Woman Question, in Popular Science Monthly Volume 36
1890. The Girl of the Future, Universal Review, Vol. VII.
1891. Democracy and Diamonds, The Contemporary Review, Vol. LIX
1892. A Desert Fruit, in Popular Science Monthly Volume 41
1893. Ghost Worship and Tree Worship I, in Popular Science Monthly Volume 42
1893. Ghost Worship and Tree Worship II, in Popular Science Monthly Volume 42
1897. Spencer and Darwin, in Popular Science Monthly Volume 50
1898. The Romance of Race, in Popular Science Monthly Volume 53
1898. The Season of the Year, in Popular Science Monthly Volume 54

Poetry

Grant Allen wrote various poems published in many magazines etc. We have not listed them here
but hope to record some of them in the future.